HUNTED BY THE PAST

A PSY-IV Team Novel

JAMI GRAY

Cover Art: Robin Ludwig Design, Inc.
Publisher: Celtic Moon Press Revised edition, 2018
ISBN: 978-1-948884-02-0 (ebook) ISBN: 978-1-948884-03-7 (print)

First edition, July 2014, MuseItUp Publishing ISBN: 978-1-77127-553-8 (ebook) ISBN: 978-1-77127-798-3 (paperback)

Sign up for free reads from Jami!

Join Jami's newsletter to be the first to hear about new releases, free books, special prices and other nifty events.

Sign up at: https://www.subscribepage.com/jami-gray-books

What Readers Say...

About Arcane Transporter:
"Taking a refreshing approach to fantasy magic, this fast-paced, economical thriller is told from a highly likable perspective." —Red Adept Editing

About PSY-IV Teams:
"This story is an emotional roller coaster, from betrayal, anger, fear, love..." —InD'tale Magazine

About the Kyn Kronicles:
"...a fantastic paranormal action novel is quite possibly the best book I've read this year. I could not put it down, and had to exercise serious self-control to keep from staying up all night to finish it." — The Romance Reviews

About Fate's Vultures:
"...if you like your characters with a bit more bite, with secrets, with hidden agendas, and all those sorts of things, and your worlds are a far more deadlier place, then this is for you." —Archaeolibrarian

Also by Jami Gray

ARCANE WONDERLAND

Last Call

Bitter Spirits

Rune & Tonic

ARCANE TRANSPORTER

Ignition Point (*Prequel Novella*)

Grave Cargo

Risky Goods

Lethal Contents

Collision Course

Blind Spot

Terminal Drift

THE KYN KRONICLES

Shadow's Edge

Shadow's Soul

Shadow's Moon

Shadow's Curse

Shadow's Dream

Shadow's Fall

Tangled in Shadows (*Short Story Collection*)

FATE'S VULTURES

Lying in Ruins

Beg for Mercy

Caught in the Aftermath

Fear the Reaper

PSY-IV TEAMS

Hunted by the Past

Touched by Fate

Marked by Obsession

Fractured by Deceit

Linked by Deception

BOX SETS

PSY-IV Teams Box Set I (Books 1-3)

The Collapse: Fate's Vultures (Books 1-4)

The Kyn Kronicles Box Set (Books 1-6)

Arcane Transporter Box Set I (Books 1-3)

Arcane Transporter Box Set II (Books 4-6)

Dedication

To all those who chose to serve our country and stand tall in the presence of harsh realities, your sacrifices allow me and mine to enjoy our blessings. My deepest thanks and may your way home be lit by the love of those who miss you.

Acknowledgments

As with every book I write, there are a great many people who take the time to respond to my strange questions without calling the authorities. So all my military, firearm experts, and first responders who took the time to help me out, I give you a big thank you, and proclaim any errors solely mine.

Contents

Chapter One

Phoenix in July. People called it Mother Nature's rendition of hell on earth.

They were wrong. Hell existed on the other side of the world, in a much more treacherous desert. If it let you go, you ran, as long and hard and as fast as you could to escape.

But sometimes even running didn't work, I tried. I spent the last six months, jumping from one remote place to another, chasing wildlife with a camera for a paycheck. A safer endeavor than chasing two footed monsters.

Unfortunately, there was one thing I couldn't outrun, family. Or the closest thing to it in my case, Kelsey. Sister by circumstances, not blood, and the only human on the planet I would consider returning to civilization for. Right now, she should be on her own plane with a group of fellow lawyers for some boring-ass conference. Her words, not mine. Instead, she managed to get a message to me, despite me being in the wilds of America's last frontier. Someone was asking questions about me and watching her.

Which meant one disturbing message and eight hours later,

I found myself crammed into the sardine can doubling as a plane. As it rolled to a stop on the tarmac, I moved into the narrow aisle, squishing between a young mother holding a squirming toddler, and a heavy set, cranky businessman as we jockeyed for a place.

Juggling my camera bag while I dug out my cell phone didn't do much to endear me to my fellow passengers either. Since our flight out of Fairbanks, Alaska had been delayed, everyone wanted off, right now. People were pulling out bags and resetting their various electronic devices.

Muted conversations swelled around me while the toddler took advantage of his mother's inattention to flash me a gap-tooth grin. I wiggled my fingers in return. His grin widened, at least until his mom distracted him with a stuffed toy.

Thumbing my phone's screen, I discovered seven missed calls and two voice mails. Nerves tightened.

Numbers scrolled across my incoming call list. The first one held a 619-area code. Coronado, California. It repeated twice. My stomach lurched and old anger snarled. I scrolled past it like all the others I'd received in the last few months, and then found the one I needed. It was listed four times.

Damn it!

My stomach roiled.

I hit the icon to retrieve my voicemails, then tucked the phone between my shoulder and ear. It made pulling my battered backpack from the overhead compartment tricky. Finally getting it free, I settled the strap on my shoulder, only then able to reclaim my phone.

The awkward juggle allowed me to ignore the strange visual dance of adverted glances from my fellow passengers. The burn scars curling under my jaw and dripping like delicate lace down my neck before disappearing under my T-shirt were hard to miss. Hell, even I wasn't used to them yet.

"Cyn? You need to call me as soon as you land." Frantic and breathless, I almost didn't recognize Kelsey's voice. My fingers tightened on my phone. "Look, there's been a change of plans. I'm heading north to hole up and wait for you." Her harsh breathing was audible over the rumblings of the departing passengers as we shuffled to the exit. "Whoever's been watching me, I think they got in my condo. You know that itch you talk about? Yeah, well it's graduated to hives." Her voice became muffled, and then cleared, "…not comfortable sharing over the phone, so just hurry the hell up and get here, okay?"

The next message came from the same area code so I didn't bother listening. I hit speed dial, praying Kelsey would pick up. Her phone rang and went to voicemail. "Kels, it's me. I'm on my way. Call me back." I checked to see when she called. Forty-five minutes ago.

Stuck in the exit shuffle, I hit the oven masquerading as the jetway at a stuttering run. Once there was room, I dodged through the zombie-like crowd of departing passengers, ignoring the muttered complaints trailing in my wake.

Like I gave a shit right now.

Kelsey was an up-and-coming corporate lawyer in a Phoenix law firm and the last person to panic. The underlying fear in her message scared the bejesus out of me because we had both navigated the wonderfully warped world of foster care with guts and bravado. That was until the Ardens took us in as teenagers.

My bags thumped against my shoulders and hips as my booted feet pounded down the seemingly never-ending airport corridors. Exiting through the automated doors, the sucking wall of a hundred-plus degrees of Phoenix summer put a hitch in my step. I hopped on the shuttle for long-term parking.

As it made its way to where I parked my Jeep two and a

half weeks ago, I tried Kelsey's number again. No answer. Next call was to my cabin up north. The stupid machine picked up. "Kels? Are you there?" I waited, trying not to pant like a racehorse. Nothing. Sickening dread tightened my stomach muscles. Third call was her condo in Tempe. Nothing.

The shuttle lurched to a stop at the curb in a cloud of exhaust. I ran, weaving my way through the blistering metal of parked cars under the relentless afternoon sun, my T-shirt sticking to my back like a leech.

Finding my Jeep, I threw my backpack in the back and, with a little more care, set my padded camera bag on the passenger floorboard. Habit had me plugging in my phone before I settled behind the wheel. Not waiting for my poor air conditioner to beat back the searing heat, I started the engine, navigated out of the lot, and hit the freeway.

My fingers danced on the steering wheel with frenetic worry and my left leg bounced like a piston. My body got busy stressing out, while my mind remained startlingly clear. The dichotomy felt all too familiar. Lessons learned during my stint with the U.S. Marine's Intelligence Unit stuck like glue. Logic took center stage, shoving my emotions to the side, and survival became the name of the game.

Kelsey would head north to the cabin we inherited in Sedona from our foster parents. The one I called home when I bothered to stick around. A little haven of security tucked away from the world. It was listed under our foster mother's maiden name and known only to us, which made it a perfect hideout.

A glance at the Jeep's dash confirmed there was enough gas to get me there. If I followed the speed limit, I should hit Sedona in little over two hours. I sent a quick prayer to whatever deities were listening and pressed my foot on the gas. Speed limits be damned.

By the time the exit for Sedona appeared, my raging emotions had crowded out logic, insisting on mentally torturing me with scenarios more in line with those slasher films Kelsey loved so much. It left my stomach and head a mess.

Regardless of Sedona's beauty, the towering, red rock cliff faces weren't doing a thing for my photographer's heart. My jaw ached, and it'd be a miracle if I didn't crack a tooth. With one main road in and out of town, traffic was a meandering crawl.

Fifteen of the longest minutes of my life passed before I turned onto the semi-paved road winding up Oak Creek Canyon. Taking it faster than normal, I bounced along the rough road, trailing a cloud of dust and marking my passage through every turn.

My home came into view as I cleared the last bend. Kelsey's older model Lexus sat to the side of the cabin and the tight bands across my chest began to loosen in relief.

Scattered trees stood guard in the partially cleared front yard. Two old Juniper trees flanked the raised wraparound front porch and the half-moon drive. Various desert shrubs and flowers added a cheerful splash of color to the scene.

The Jeep came to a skidding halt on the loose gravel. Scrambling out, my weak leg threatened to fold under me, the stiff muscles a reminder that six months was not long enough for my body to forget the damage dealt to it.

I grabbed the metal doorframe for support, and heat seared my palm. My breath escaped in a pain-filled hiss as I readjusted my hold and studied the house. The afternoon shadows weren't deep, but unless they were playing tricks on me, my front door stood ajar and my relief at seeing Kelsey's car was short-lived.

Spurred into action, I crossed the front yard, my limp

disappearing as my muscles got with the program. The loud crunch of gravel under my boots made my approach the furthest thing from stealthy. Not that rolling in like a motorized stampede had been any better. Regardless of my rather obvious arrival, I could still take pains to be careful. A glance to the carport confirmed Kelsey's car was empty.

I angled to the side of the door just in case someone was inside watching. Tucking into the space between the front door and the carport, the rough walls of the house rasped against my back. Up close, I couldn't miss the long crack running along the doorframe, or the tread mark from a heavy-soled shoe decorating the paint above the deadbolt.

Someone kicked in my door.

With the reminder that there were times when outwaiting your enemy could prove more vital than any other action you could take, I resisted my urge to charge in. It didn't stop the nightmare images of how much damage a human could inflict on another in a matter of minutes, and when those images wore Kelsey's face, my restraint frayed.

Sour dread coated my tongue and had my instincts jittering like jumping beans on crack. The normal chorus of birds and insects was missing, leaving behind an eerie quiet broken by the occasional light, heated breezes whispering through the trees.

At the window, something, a shadow, or a movement of the curtains, caught my attention, and worry beat the hell out of caution. Channeling my adrenaline rush steadied my nerves and snapped my surroundings into painful clarity.

Kelsey wasn't alone.

One of the many desirable traits for owning property up in the canyon meant my nearest neighbor sat a half-mile out, which translated into the isolation being a bit of a bitch. Normally that wasn't a problem, but right now? Not so much. I reached into my pocket and silently cursed when I found it empty. My phone was sitting in my Jeep. Granted, there wasn't much of a signal out here, but calling in the authorities as possible backup was worth a shot.

Now what?

Taking a quick inventory, I pulled out my keys, careful to keep them from jingling, and wove them between my clenched fingers, creating a primitive set of brass knuckles. My voice of reason muttered it wasn't much, but at five foot five and just under a hundred thirty pounds, even a little bit of damage could give me a needed edge.

I strained my ears, hoping to hear something, anything. Nothing.

Using my empty hand, I pushed the door. It swung open on silent hinges, disgorging a draft of cool air. When no one rushed out, my breath escaped in a little puff of air. Poised at the side of the door, the disquieting sense of foreboding ran under my skin, raising the fine hairs on my arms.

It took a moment for the shadows in the dim interior to resolve into recognizable objects. An old-fashion coat rack, decorated with a couple of flannel jackets, reached from the glass block corner. The wooden bench with cubbies for shoes squatted against the hall wall where one of Kelsey's much-loved abstract paintings hung.

Nothing disturbed the murky shadows. No rasping sounds of heavy breathing broke the humming quiet. No discernible signs of chaos, other than splinters from the door that littered the entryway.

I stepped gingerly over the threshold, every sense on alert. Keeping my attention on the hallway, I pushed the door partially shut behind me. I didn't want to leave it wide open but couldn't risk the noise of closing it completely.

Spotting the oak walking stick tucked in the corner, excitement sparked at a second weapon. I grabbed the smooth wood, and my nerves steadied as it warmed against my palm.

An unnerving stillness lay over the house like a lurking predator, stifling my urge to call out. Facing the hall, I had a choice to make. Go left to the back bedrooms, or right to the open living room and kitchen. Either way, left my back exposed.

Decisions, decisions.

Knowing I could clear two rooms in one shot, I went right. Keeping my spine to the wall, I stopped at the arch into the living room, and snuck a quick glance around the corner.

Nothing but familiar furniture in the living room and an empty kitchen. Spotting Kelsey's sunglasses and keys by the blinking answering machine on the counter reinforced my unease.

With her keys and car here, where the hell was she?

Trying not to panic, I turned and cautiously rushed toward the bedrooms on the other side of the hall. The two bedrooms were split by a bathroom. I cleared the one serving as my office first, and then closed the door behind me.

Creeping past the bathroom, the partially open door to my bedroom beckoned. Nerves and dread tangled together, squeezing my lungs tight and causing a fine tremor in the hand holding the makeshift brass knuckles. The sense of foreboding paralyzed me. Just because I couldn't see the threat, didn't make it any less real.

The AC kicked on and the overly loud snick of the front door being sucked closed had an undignified *eep* escaping. I swiveled toward the noise, my pulse spiking hard, only to leave me lightheaded.

I leaned against the wall, deliberately loosening my grip on the metal keys biting into my palm. A variety of awful images played through my mind, offering a horrific selection of what could lurk in my room. My hand shook, and I used the back of my fist to wipe away the cold sweat beading my forehead.

Pull your shit together, woman.

Taking a deep breath, I shoved my imagination down, stiffened my spine, and forced my feet to move forward. Pressing against the door, it slowly swung open. The blinds were half pulled, and the afternoon sunlight spilled across an open suitcase sitting on my king bed. A discarded shirt lay half hung on a hanger with Kelsey's hobo bag peeking out from under it. In the dresser, one of the drawers was lolling open.

I stepped into the room. "Kels?" I kept my voice low and quiet, as if it would really bring Kelsey out from under the bed or out of the closet. The room remained frustratingly silent.

The uneasiness continued to play havoc on my nerves, while my helpless frustration graduated to a simmering anger.

What in the hell was going on? Where was she? Maybe her stalker had grabbed her? Or had she run out into the woods like the too-stupid-to-live women in the cheesy horror flicks she loved so much?

That last thought left me shaking my head. Kelsey wouldn't run, she'd stand and fight. An unfortunate trait, according to our adoptive parents, we both shared. I needed more information.

I stuffed my keys into my pocket, but kept my walking stick close. It made a great security blanket. I might be the only person in the house, but it didn't stop me from going back and conducting a more thorough search.

After clearing the house once more, I stood in the living room, as worry cracked my interior barriers letting the fear slither through. There were no glaring clues for me to follow. Kelsey was just gone. If wasn't for the fact her cell was on the kitchen counter, I would've called her carrier to trace her GPS. For the first time, the concept of tagging people with GPS chips sounded good.

Another solution rose and for a brief moment I considered calling on old acquaintances in shadowy places for a few favors. I nixed that idea in the bud. If I popped back up on the radar, there would be too many questions to answer. I wasn't that desperate. Yet.

Which left me with what?

I tapped the end of my staff against the floor. Looking around, a nebulous plan began to form. There was one option, and as much as I didn't relish the idea, it was one I could use. With no other solutions on the horizon, the question of whether or not it would work remained beside the point.

I tightened my grip on the staff, and then headed back toward my room. With each step my stomach lurched, and cotton filled my mouth, but this was my best chance at finding Kelsey. I left the staff propped just inside the door and crossed to my bed. My fingers stroked over her shirt as I found the courage to take the next step. Months has passed since the last time I tried this. Knowing what needed to be done and doing it were two very different things.

I slowly sat on the edge of the bed, my fingers crushing the soft material, and the light scent Kelsey wore brushed me. Even that small comfort couldn't counter the sickening apprehension swirling in my stomach, my body rebelling at what was to come. I balled up the material and held it chest high, needing the focus of something she'd touched.

My nerves tightened and a mental voice questioned the sanity of going through with this when it could end up a pointless endeavor. I told it to shut the hell up, I wasn't abandoning Kelsey. It would work, it always did.

And if it went wrong? That stupid voice pushed. *What then?*

I tightened my lips. *So long as it helped me find Kelsey, I'd handle it, dammit.*

Blowing out a breath, I dropped my cloth-covered hands to rest on my thighs and closed my eyes. Dragging in a deep breath, my chest expanded. I held it and then let it go. Kelsey's scent colored my thoughts. My mind raced. Maintaining the pattern of breath, I forced everything out of my head but an awareness of Kelsey.

Slow in. Hold. Push out.

Slow in. Hold. Push out.

The AC hit its prearranged goal and clicked off, the sudden blanket of silence snapping my spine straight and interrupting my breathing. My eyes flashed open, and I waited for my spiking pulse to level off before starting over.

The creepy silence curled around me, and pushing it away took longer than anticipated. Eventually my thoughts cleared and with frustrating slowness the mental path to the secret spot in my mind took shape. The delay wasn't unexpected considering the lack of use and a whole shitload of denial piled on top of it.

Once uncovered, I followed it down beyond memories, both good and bad, until I reached the end. On the never-ending horizon of my mind, a towering wall loomed. For a moment I stood and stared. Buried behind the formidable barrier of my subconscious pulsed a strange energy, the one thing in this world guaranteed to turn me into a blathering idiot.

Bracing myself, I began tearing the wall down. Piece by piece, I demolished the blocks until the entire subconscious structure shuddered and collapsed. I opened my eyes, careful to keep my focus on my lap and my sense of Kelsey foremost in my mind. I braced and looked up, only to flinch.

Yep, definitely missed a few things.

The past replayed like a crazy barrage of scattered, silent-film images, layered in moments of time. The confusing whirlwind scouring gouges in my heart. This house held so many memories of those I loved and each one played out in snatches of stolen time, one memory on top of another, creating a visual pandemonium. Some were faint, while others shoved forward only to be pulled back under, but each one was fragmented. This was what could drive me insane. Almost had at one point.

I struggled to find my mental footing, not easily accomplished thanks to rusty skills, but like riding a bike, I found my balance and zeroed in on what I needed.

A pale and worried Kelsey strode through my bedroom door. Her image wavered, threatening to fade. I narrowed my concentration, determined not to lose her. The visuals steadied, firmed. Her white-blonde hair was pulled back into a ponytail at the base of her neck, her jaw was clenched as she dropped her hobo purse onto the bed, and then dragged her suitcase onto the mattress.

Considering how clear the images were, her emotions had to have been off the charts. My strange ability tended to be a complete mystery, but generally when I played Peeping Tom with the past, it was choppy and hazy. Painful experience taught me the more emotionally connected I was to a person or event, the clearer the picture.

I watched Kelsey unpack. Then the image began to fade as an older one tried to take center stage. My fingers tightened on the shirt in my lap as I struggled to bring Kelsey's image back. It took a few nerve stretching moments, but she reappeared. This time she was getting ready to hang up her shirt, when her head lifted like a hound coming on point and turned to the door.

Old frustrations and resentments tried to tumble forth, but I shoved them back. Wishing for a reliable soundtrack to the images in front of me would get me nowhere. It was hard enough to keep my attention centered on the right memory. Most times I was lucky to get a comprehensive scene. I seemed to be eternally relegated to a watcher position, and not once had I been able to hear anything. That quirk hammered home early on the old axiom of 'you can't change the past'.

As my concentration wavered, the image in front of me

broke up like clouds after a storm. Mental focus pounded into me by the U.S. Marines snapped into place and once more, Kelsey reappeared. This time, she pulled something out of her bag. When her hand reappeared, it was wrapped around a nine mil Sig Sauer P226. A gun which should be tucked inside the gun safe at her condo. In Tempe. Twisting slightly to stay with the scene, I couldn't stop my muttered, "What the hell, Kels?"

Kelsey hated guns, but loved me, hence her agreement to keep a small gun safe at her condo for my occasional visits. Guns were my version of Teddy Bears. I didn't like being without one, so Kelsey eventually gave in and let me keep one or two at her place when I was out of town.

The marines had uncovered a natural shooting skill, one I kept up even after my discharge. I taught Kelsey a few basics, and the lessons had obviously stuck, because she kept the barrel aimed at the floor, and her finger to the side of the trigger. She crept toward the bedroom door, the gun steady in her two-handed grip.

Fully caught in the past, I rose from the bed to follow the image of the gun-toting Kelsey through the bedroom door. Her image disappeared into a swirl of disjointed memories. I stumbled down the hall, desperate to recapture the scene, my pulse racing. Based on Kelsey's actions, someone was about to make an appearance.

Near the front entryway, I hit pay dirt. She stood with her back to the wall, the gun extended in front of her as she sidled closer to the door. Her eyes widened, fear racing across her face, as her grip loosened. Her inattention lasted maybe one or two seconds, but that's all it took for her to lose any advantage. Her fear had to be bone deep to leave such a sharp memory behind.

I needed to get beyond the front door, because too many emotions occurred when people came and went, muddying the residual memories. Sure enough, the ever-changing impressions swirled, and Kelsey's image disappeared. Struggling to find her, I worked my way through the front hall until a flash of pale hair behind something big near the living room caught my attention.

I drew closer. Kelsey faced off against a looming figure. Male, judging by the size. I noted the jeans, drab T-shirt, and heavy-soled boots for later reference as I worked my way around. I needed a face, but when I got in position I frowned in confusion. Like a channel just off center, his head and shoulders were covered by a disturbing blur of static that created a lingering menace.

That was new. Maybe Kelsey's fear was behind this unusual phenomenon?

Then my heart stopped as he moved his hands in a familiar, lightning-quick disarm move until the gun was pointed at Kelsey. My emotions spiked, fracturing my concentration, and the scene wavered. I fought for calm, scared to lose what little control I held. Everything steadied. I sucked in a breath of relief, but it was too soon.

Kelsey's emotions crested like a deadly undercurrent. Frantic, I struggled to gather as much information as I could before it dragged me under. When her shock morphed to anger, it added a desperate edge to her movements. Her self-defense skills were rusty, but she kept him off balance. A quick strike knocked the gun out of his hand and out of the scene. His efficient counterattack revealed he was simply playing with her.

Judging by her rapidly encroaching panic, she knew it too. She began to back away, her lips moving, her fear evident in the white lines around her mouth and her fists clenched at her sides. The only indicator of her underlying fear were her sidelong glances for escape.

Even knowing I could change nothing, instinct had me

stepping closer so I could reach out and drag her to safety. My hand closed on empty air.

She disappeared.

Frustration boiled, and I spun around, frantic to find her again. Wisps of other memories circled, but I shoved through them. Rubbing at the dull ache in my temples, the soft brush of forgotten cloth reminded me I still held her shirt. Bunching it up, I pressed it to my face and dragged her scent into my lungs. Her familiar fragrance wrapped around me and stalled my rising frustration. The minute break gave me a chance to reclaim my focus.

I dropped my hands and looked around. It took precious time to work through the layers of memories, but I found Kelsey on the floor, her attacker's hand wrapped around her throat. Her fingers scrabbled at his tanned wrist, leaving behind bloody gouges. A bright red, hand-shaped mark covered one side of her face, indicating she'd been hit at least once.

My anger joined her panic, increasing the emotional draw exponentially. It seeped through my mental barriers and sent me to a level I rarely experienced. One where the lines blurred between my reality and the past.

Rough hands tightened around my throat, choking off my air. I clawed at the phantom grip, as terror soared, buoying me above Kelsey's emotional waves. The pressure on my throat disappeared, and I sucked in air as I instinctively lunged for the guy still holding Kelsey to the floor. The sharp pain of my shin meeting the edge of an end table not only shattered the scene but brought me back to the present with the brutal reminder I couldn't change a thing. All I could do was stand by and helplessly watch the echoes. Swearing on a harsh sob, I limped around the table trying to recapture the past.

I made it to the counter separating the kitchen and dining room when Kelsey reappeared. This time her attacker had her against his chest, his arm locked against her throat. Bright blood trickled from the side of her mouth and her lips were swollen. Still, she continued to struggle.

He leaned in and said something I couldn't hear.

Her movements stilled, her face whitened, and pure terror turned her eyes a deep blue. Those terrified eyes locked on to mine and I staggered as I heard Kelsey's voice whisper through my mind. "Run, Cyn!"

Then they disappeared.

Chapter Two

Shock held me motionless at actually hearing Kelsey's warning. It meant something, but damned if I knew what. There was no 'normal' for reliving the past, no handy user guide.

What had changed?

The images were gone, but there had to be something more. Something I could use. Even as my head began to pound, I kept my weird other sight open and retraced my steps through the hall, frantically searching for any other signs. Anything I might have missed.

The swirling images coalesced in a confused blur and faded even faster, as if my intensity chased them away. Frustration peaked.

Maybe if I went back to my room and started over?

As I passed the front door, a shadow wavered across the glass-block window. I froze. Someone, a large someone, stood outside the door. My gaze dropped to the doorknob. Unlocked.

Shit!

It began to turn slowly. I had a handful of seconds before it would open. Slamming my mental walls back up sent a ferocious ache behind my eyes, but the need to know what was real and now, and what wasn't, was critical. The door crept open.

Praying the glass column wouldn't give away my presence, I carefully shifted against the wall behind the door. As the door continued to move, it also blocked line of sight. Of course, whoever was behind it, couldn't see me either.

Which meant I had one shot. Wrapping my hand on the knob, I shoved my shoulder and weight into the door, slamming it forward.

A muffled grunt confirmed the presence of a real, live body. Unfortunately, the door encountered a freaking battering ram and bounced back. Since I didn't want to be stuck between the door and the wall, I stumbled out of the tight space and into the hall. My weak leg did not like the twists and turns, but I needed distance from whoever came through my door and my escape routes were limited.

Open living room or the bedrooms?

Remembering my staff propped by my bedroom door, I turned to run. Behind me, the sound of the door being shoved flat against the wall jerked my attention back to the entryway. Cold sweat erupted down my spine.

The man strong-arming my door stood at least six two and he wasn't selling cookies. A black T-shirt outlined broad shoulders and a heavy chest, explaining why my brilliant plan of knocking him back through the doorway was destined for failure.

My mind processed the details, trying to put the pieces together. Brown hair, thick and shaggy, framed dark eyes in a startlingly savage face. Still reeling from using my stupid ability, I couldn't make the picture stick, but a niggling sense of familiarity lingered. But now wasn't the time for polite introductions.

An impressive snarl emerged from inside the neatly

trimmed goatee, "Hello, Cyn." His deep voice raised every hair on my body and sent my pulse into overdrive. It tore through me, unlocking memories better left alone.

Unprepared, bitter anger joined the fear blooming thick and hot, shattering my immobility. I lunged down the hall. My hand was within a hair's breadth of my walking stick when my forward momentum came to an abrupt halt. Fingers bit into my upper right arm, spinning me around. Since my left arm remained free, I used the spin's movement for an awkward elbow strike.

He leaned back. I missed, but he let go of my arm. However, his leg sweep took me by surprise. The asshole knew which leg to target too.

The narrow hallway made it impossible to avoid crashing my shoulder into the wall. A grunt escaped as I hit the ground. Mindless fury vied for a toehold, but I beat it back. He might be bigger, but I fought dirtier. Down on the floor was not my first choice, but daring a quick glance behind me confirmed a few more inches would even the odds. Scrambling back with awkward speed, I dodged the hand set to lock around my ankle. I kicked and gained another inch.

His low, frustrated growl proved the needed impetus for my last desperate bid for my staff. A rough tug on my pant leg dragged me down the hall, and I almost lost my tentative hold on the staff.

Breath pummeled my chest, while claws of panic and resentment dug in deep. Clutching the staff in both hands, I swung down. Not the strongest way to hit, but it might buy me a chance to get back on my feet. If it hit his thick skull, so much the better.

He let go of my jeans and blocked the strike. Admiration for his quick reflexes sparked on some weirdly disconnected level. Unfortunately, he grabbed the other end and I soon found myself in a tug-of-war for the staff.

"Arden! Enough," he barked out.

Old habits are a bitch to break, and his sharp command slapped me into momentary stillness. Narrowing my eyes, I studied my opponent. The hair was longer, the goatee was new, but the mocking anger in his face, that was all too familiar. So was the stinging emotion I refused to recognize, but shoved into a deep, dark corner. "What the hell do you want?"

"Always so polite. Nice to see some things don't change." His sardonic tone grated over my nerves like sandpaper.

"Screw you." I yanked on the staff.

He arched an eyebrow. "Are you offering?"

"Not in this lifetime," I snapped. "Let go, dammit."

He smiled. "Promise not to brain me?"

I kept my mouth shut.

He must have seen something reassuring on my face, because he slowly let go of the staff. Yanking it back, I put as much space as I could between us, only to stop when my spine met the doorjamb. He ran a hand over the back of his neck, and settled against the hall wall, pulling his long legs up until his feet were flat on the floor. The flash of an impressive tattoo peeked from under the T-shirt's sleeve.

My gaze went to his wrists, looking for evidence he was behind Kelsey's attack. If so, all bets were off. They appeared scratch free.

I assured myself it wasn't relief I felt as I studied him. I knew he was dangerous, but the knowledge did little to ease the ache of his presence. Reminders of why this particular man didn't deserve shit from me, and nothing that he said could be trusted, ran through my head.

He stared back with a disconcerting intensity. He had the dark and dangerous look down pat. It wasn't his coloring. His sun-streaked brown hair just brushed his collar, and his skin told of someone who enjoyed the outdoors, but the strong, edgy aura surrounding him made me pause. So did the grim look in his navy-blue eyes, turning them darker than the impending clouds during monsoon season.

I held his gaze and fought the urge to squirm as memories pressed close and heat bloomed in my face.

"Should I pose for a picture?" His voice held a knowing edge that left me grinding my teeth in a mix of embarrassment and frustration.

Unwilling to reveal how deep he was wedged under my skin, I forced my lips into a mockingly sweet smile. "Lieutenant Kayden Shaw." Yeah, there was enough scorn in that one name to get me in serious trouble if I cared or still wore a uniform. Since I no longer did either, it didn't matter. "Ever hear of knocking?"

His broad shoulders rose and fell in a casual shrug. "Since your last visitor left a footprint by the doorknob, I thought knocking would be overrated."

His unexpected quip snuck under my guard and made my lips twitch. I covered my reaction with a delicate snort. "Why are you here?"

Instead of answering, he asked, "Spoken to Tag lately?"

"No." A stone settled in my stomach, and I blinked at the unexpected sting of my former teammate's name. *Answering a question with a question. Nice diversionary tactic. What did good ol' Tag have to do with anything?* "Been a little busy."

Kayden's curse was too soft to catch. "He was going to call you."

"Well if he did, I didn't get a message." I squashed the twinge of guilt at the lie, recalling the second number on my cell that I had deliberately ignored for months. Using the staff I still held, I pushed to my feet and avoided his gaze. "Besides, I just got back into town."

He watched me stand. "Where were you?"

Resentment rose at the implied order underlying his question. Keeping my face pleasantly blank, I met his gaze. "In case

it slipped your mind, Shaw, I no longer answer to the Corps."
Some of my fury slipped through. "Since I'm a private citizen,
why don't you get the hell out of my house." I stepped over his
legs and headed back to the front of the house.

"Cyn."

The seriousness in his tone and the strong fingers wrapped
around my calf stopped me, but I didn't look down.

"You need to listen."

Couldn't miss the order in that one. Alpha males might be fun
on the pages of a book, but in real life they were a pain in my
ass. Based on his current fashion choices, Kayden couldn't
possibly still be in active service, so there was no reason to
follow his orders ever again. What was the worst he could do?
Haul me back before a kangaroo court? *Been there, done that,
didn't even get to keep the T-shirt.*

Yanking my leg free, I headed toward the kitchen. If I was
lucky, he'd leave.

I set the walking stick against the counter and grabbed a
glass. Sticking it under the tap, I let it fill, using the familiar
motions to still the small tremors wracking my body. Unfortunately, the sound of the front door closing never came. I got a
few small sips in before my attempt to calm was interrupted.

"If you won't talk to me, then call Tag." For such a big man,
Kayden moved like a cat.

Persistent little bugger. My fingers tightened on the glass that
was halfway to my lips, then I took one last, deliberate sip
before setting my glass on the counter with studied care. I
turned to the man who once fascinated me beyond reason, and
found him leaning against the entryway, his arms crossed, and
blocking any chance of escape. Obviously, I wasn't leaving
until he got what he wanted.

Mimicking his pose, I drawled, "My cell doesn't get reception out here." Not entirely true, but his attitude left me
obstinate.

"You have a land line." He nodded to the blinking answering machine sitting on the counter.

My priority was Kelsey, not whatever crap was dodging Kayden and Tag, but my fickle curiosity perked up. "Why would you think I'd want to talk to Tag any more than I want to talk to you?"

His wince was hastily veiled, but not before I caught it. That tiny tell ignited a spurt of dark satisfaction from the less charitable part of me that was buried deep. He didn't answer.

Not a shocker. Did he really think the silent male thing worked? Studying his rigid position, icy fingers of suspicion slid along my spine. *Why was he here now? Just when Kelsey had felt someone watching her, asking questions about me?*

Pushing away from the counter's edge, I closed the distance between us. With each step I took, his jaw tightened. When only a few inches remained, I stopped.

It took concentrated effort to set aside my resentment and mistrust, but when I succeeded, I compared the staticky image from my trip into the past against the very real, flesh and blood male in front of me. Kayden stood a couple of inches taller than whoever attacked Kelsey, which put him a good six inches above me. But more telling, his shoulders were broader. It took a great deal of fortitude to study his chiseled face and not be intimidated. He watched me, his gaze carrying the weight of other, shared memories, untouched by hurt and pain. *It didn't matter, couldn't matter.* Holding out my hands palms up, I waited.

"What?" There was a husky note to his voice.

"Let me see your wrists."

Never looking away, he unfolded his arms and held his hands above my palms, so close the heat from his skin curled against mine. Ignoring my clamoring emotions, I checked his wrists once more. Besides a very masculine, heavy watch and old scars, they remained unmarred. I dropped my hands and met his stare head on, refusing to blink first.

He made me nervous on a level it was unsafe to acknowledge. I needed to get some space between us, but that would require touching him. Again. Probably not a good idea.

Since I didn't want to touch him—much—I poked a finger against his chest, ignoring the unexpected zap of awareness. "I don't know how you found me or why, but right now I have other, more important things to do. So, why don't—"

My tirade was interrupted by a phone ringing. Not my cell, but the landline. I shot a look at the phone sitting on the counter to our left, and then narrowed my gaze at Kayden.

He quirked an eyebrow. The phone rang again.

"You going to answer it?" he drawled.

Stepping back, I plucked the receiver off the cradle. "Hello?"

"Cyn?"

What do you know, it was Thomas Anderson Gunderson, AKA Tag. I stared at the man standing across from me. "Yeah."

"Where have you been? And why the hell won't you answer my calls?" Despite his questions, there was a thread of relief in my friend's voice.

Ex-friend, remember? "Why would I?" I answered absently, watching Kayden move to the other side of the counter and take a seat on a bar stool.

In my ear, Tag cursed. "Dammit, Cyn. I don't have time to explain shit now—"

"Why are you calling me?" I cut him off, ice coating every word.

"Why are you in Sedona?" he shot back, his voice hard.

"I'm more concerned with how you got this number, and why everyone seems determined to turn my cabin in to Grand Central Station."

Momentary silence filled the line. "Shaw's there?"

"Got it in one."

"Thank God," Tag muttered. "Be as bitchy as you want, Cyn, but tell me you're okay. You ran away—"

"I didn't run from shit, Tag," I snapped. "I was kicked to the fucking curb as soon as you and everyone else got what you wanted."

"That's not what happened."

My chin lifted, even though he couldn't see it. "Really? Because from where I stood, it sure as hell looked like it."

Silence answered.

Turning away from Kayden's too-avid gaze, I tried to regain control so I could shove both men back out of my life. "I'm fine, but I'm little busy dealing with my own situation."

"What kind of situation?" His voice sounded sincerely concerned.

Closing my eyes, I fought the urge to bang my head against a wall at the single-minded intensity of the male gender. "My sister is AWOL. Now, can we just focus on why you're bothering me, and Kayden has decided to pursue a career in B and E?"

Tag didn't budge from his conversational target. "How long has Kelsey been missing?"

The urgent note underlying his question fanned the flame of my earlier unease. *Was there something bigger at play here?* Worry for Kelsey trumped hurt feelings, so I answered. "Not sure, a couple of hours maybe. Her car is here."

Over the line a string of oaths erupted, and Tag proved no one could swear like a marine. "Son of mangy bitch," he wound down before taking a deep breath. "The cabin's an hour and half outside of Phoenix?" He didn't wait for my confirmation. "I'll meet you up there. Stay with Kayden."

"Tag." I put all signs of my waning patience into his name as my fingers tightened around the phone. It took an amazing amount of willpower not to share my own colorful vocabulary.

"You need to tell me what's going on. Right. Now." The last two words squeezed around clenched teeth.

"It's about Flash." His unexpected answer stabbed deep, drawing blood under my skin. "His killer is out." Brutal memories boiled forth, almost making me miss his, "Stay with Kayden, Cyn."

My world spun as the drone of a dial tone filled my ear. I concentrated on replacing the phone in the cradle. My legs did a great impression of spaghetti noodles and folded under me, until I was sitting on the cool tile drowning in memories.

For six months, I ran as hard, as fast, and as far as I could, but in a matter of minutes I was right back where I started, trapped in a never-ending nightmare. It was enough to make me wonder which fickle fate decided to dump everything on me at once. If I ever got my hands on her, I'd happily beat her to a pulp. *Damn, damn, and triple damn!*

The past surged and broke through my flimsy barriers. Ghostly screams and the stench of burned flesh rose on a choking wave of horror. I dug my fingers deep into my thigh muscles in a desperate attempt to stave it off. It didn't work. Greedy memories sucked me under.

My kitchen disappeared, replaced by a fetid alley behind a dive in Where-the-fuckistan. Sprawled on the ground, my head spun with dizzying sickness and my leg screamed with agony, yet all I could do was watch and listen. Watch the spreading pool of blood and brains seep from Ortega, his sightless eyes staring past me. Listen to the snap and crackle of a raging fire hissing through the night, while the foul smell of burnt flesh wrapped around me. Behind me, someone screamed, his wail high-pitched and full of hopeless agony.

I knew that broken voice.

Even as excruciating pain beat inside my skull, I turned my head. A figure took shape in the midst of the hellish scene and recognition hit. Searing loss, rage, and fear clawed for a way out. My mouth opened and the stench coiled down my throat, blocking the air in my chest. *No, no, no!*

Hands cradled my face, the touch shocking enough to snap through my paralysis, and bring the present into the past. Desperate to escape, I struck out, my hand connecting with flesh. "Don't touch me!"

Pain radiated down my leg and in my head. Harsh breathing filled the air. It took a few seconds to realize the sound was coming from me, and even a few more before the low soothing voice penetrated the layers of the past.

"Come on back, Cyn. You're safe."

I concentrated on the voice, drawing in sharp drafts of air until I relearned to breathe. The strangely hypnotic voice thinned the nightmare, allowing the present seep in. My kitchen re-formed. The press of wooden cabinets against my spine, the cool tile under my ass, the sound of Kayden's soft reassurances that I was safe. I wanted to laugh. I hadn't been safe in a very long time.

Feeling shaky and aching in unseen parts, I drew my knees up and wrapped my arms around them. I dropped my forehead to my knees, holding tight to the comfort of Kayden's voice, but refusing the shelter of his touch. When I could stop imitating a fish on land, I managed one word. "Sorry."

Kayden was silent for a moment, then, "No apology needed."

I wish I felt the same. I kept my eyes closed and my head down as shame and humiliation flooded me. Logically, I knew there was no reason for it, but logic didn't exist in my night-mares. Tag's comment about Flash had flipped a trigger I thought was disabled.

Apparently not.

The air next to me shifted as Kayden settled at my side. "We need to talk about it."

His statement earned a bitter, choked laugh from me. "No, we really don't."

"Time to come back in, Cyn." His voice was unusually gentle. "You can't hide anymore."

Opening my eyes, I turned my head, and kept my cheek on my knees. "Why?" Bitterness left a sour taste behind, but it didn't stop my sarcastic, "Do you need another sacrificial goat?"

Years of hard-won control kept me from shaking apart. I worked hard to hide the damage of what happened in that alley, despite its repercussions. When those I thought had my back, walked away, and left me hanging, I did the best I could. Even under relentless questioning I could see how the incident was being shaped, so I stuck with selective dissociative amnesia. It was the only protection available at the time. If I revealed what really happened, I would have been bounced out of the service for mental instability. Instead, the screen of trauma induced, sporadic memory loss resulted in a Section Eight medical discharge.

Kayden's expression remained impassive. "I read the report you gave to the inquiry board." He watched me carefully. "You want to stick to that story?"

"I don't owe you shit, Shaw," I spat. *Did he really expect me to share anything with him after he, Tag, and the others left me twisting in the wind?* Choking back the accusations, I sneered, "White jackets with buckles and padded rooms are bad for my digestion. Besides, drool is so not my style."

Instead of the expected anger, his lips quirked. I looked away and muttered, "So glad I could amuse."

"You're being hunted." I looked up. His brief show of humor was replaced by a strange seriousness. "I think he already has Kelsey."

My heart stopped.

Chapter Three

"Start talking."

It was a demand, ice cold and filled with protective rage. A rage that barely concealed a noxious mix of fear, worry, and sickening terror. Vicious, graphic images twisted through my mind. If Kelsey was in the hands of the psycho who stalked my nightmares, I knew too well what horrors she could be enduring. It was times like this when I abhorred how much shit lived in my head.

"Ellery escaped custody." Kayden's answer was brutally short.

"Escaped?"

"During transport to Pendleton, five months ago."

"Five months?" Shock wiped out my higher brain functions and left me sounding like a parrot. I pushed unsteadily to my feet. When Kayden rose to help me, I waved him off. Gripping the counter, I kept my back to him and did my best to untangle my gnarled thoughts.

Eleven months ago, I was assigned to a specialized, eight-person team to unravel the who and why behind the theft and possible sale of information on an experimental weaponized virus delivery system. It took us five months to uncover the who and close in. Unfortunately, the cost of bringing in Master Sergeant Reeve Ellery to stand trial for espionage had been high. Too high. Two of my team came home in flag-draped coffins. One of which belonged to my mentor and friend, Flash.

Ugly memories stirred, a bitter reminder of the price I was forced to pay. A price that looked as if I was still paying. The question was, why?

Granted, my testimony, as questionable as it was, helped cement Ellery's conviction, but most of the evidence rested on previously gathered intel. My remaining four team members had been "unavailable". Actual translation—hiding behind bigger uniforms or tucked away on classified missions. Which left me facing Ellery, the inquiry board, and their uncomfortable questions all alone. A situation that still chaffed my ass.

Old hurts didn't matter. Couldn't matter. Finding Kelsey, getting her back, that was all that mattered now. "And you think he has Kelsey? Why?"

"He's trying to draw you out. The best way to do that is through your family." His calm demeanor rankled. "With the Ardens dead, Kelsey is the only family you have left."

"Which is why I don't broadcast our relationship. He couldn't have found her easily." With our foster parents gone, my connection to Kelsey wasn't common knowledge. Our last names were different, we ran in completely different circles, and we kept separate residences that couldn't be linked. Small things I exploited with ruthless efficiency, especially after I came home.

Paranoid and disillusioned, I didn't want the trouble surrounding me to touch her. Unfortunately, there were two people who knew enough about us to change that. Flash and Tag. But Flash was dead. Warning bells clamored. I shook my head. No, Tag wouldn't do that to me.

He had no problem walking away before, a nasty little voice reminded me.

Sure, to save his career, but this? Putting the last of my family in the line of fire? He wouldn't. But others? Others, like the ones behind the highly sterilized report my lawyer handed me after the trial? The one that revealed how little my loyalty to the Corps really meant? Yeah, they would. In a goddamn heartbeat. I kept my back to the disturbingly silent male behind me. "Who are you working for, Kayden?"

"It's classified."

A bitter smile twisted my lips at his expected answer even as old fury reignited. Regardless of his non-regulation appearance, it seemed Kayden still worked for the military. Disappointment curled through me. I turned, leaned back, and let the edge of the sink press against my lower back. Then I folded my arms across my chest. "I was medically discharged, not demoted. Since it's my family we're discussing, don't you think I deserve to know who I'm considering working with?"

"When they're ready," he shot back, artfully sidestepping my actual question as he mirrored me on the other side of my kitchen. "By the way, discharged is better than an honorable separation."

The arrogant assurance behind his clarification pissed me off. "So, I should be grateful to be labeled physically unfit versus mentally unfit? According to who? You? Your superiors?" Roiling emotions morphed into a cold, cutting scorn and I didn't give him a chance to answer. "Nice of you all to keep me in the loop. Oh wait, you didn't, though, did you? You all were on 'assignment' or 'unavailable'." I used my fingers to do air quotes, then glared at him. "Fuck you, Shaw."

He didn't move, his body steady and relaxed, completely unruffled by my tirade. "It was a command decision made for your protection."

"Excuse me if I don't believe you." *God, why did I even*

bother? Was I still hoping for an apology? If so, I was pretty sure I was out of luck. "I don't have time for your games, so I'll ask one more time. Why are you here now, and why is Ellery after me?"

"I'm here to protect you and get your help." His quiet statement hung between us.

"Your protection sucks," I snapped, even as I mulled over the implications of the second part. I would need his help to keep Ellery off my ass. Kayden's and whoever he worked for. I choked down a frustrated scream. Time for a different tact. "Exactly how do you think I can help?"

His gaze remained level as the lines in his face softened with some emotion I couldn't read. "We know what you can do."

Studying his too-knowing gaze, worry flickered. *Again, with the mysterious 'we'.* "Excuse me?"

A grim little smile quirked his lips. "You see things others don't."

His bombshell trapped my breath under the one-ton elephant that parked its ass on my chest. "Uh?" I wheezed. *Witty repartee, that's me.*

"You're not the only one out there with psychic abilities."

Recoiling, I struggled to keep my voice even. "Who said anything about being psychic?"

"Just stop," his warning growl cut my protestations short. "If you want the truth, you have to give it. Otherwise, I can't help and I'm out of here."

Somehow, he knew, and wasn't that a kick in the ass? What now? Admit or deny? My options were limited. One, I could kick his ass out and stumble around trying to find Kelsey on my own. Or, two, I could use him and his resources. Contrary to his opinion, I wasn't stupid. Going after Ellery alone amounted to a suicide mission. Plus, it wouldn't save Kelsey. But if I could use him and Tag? Not to mention the resources they could access that I couldn't touch, then my chances increased dramatically.

I looked away and the sight of Kelsey's discarded sunglasses lying forlornly on the counter made my heart clench. To save her, I would shout the truth from the rooftops and damn the consequences. No matter how much it grated to depend on him, I couldn't risk Kelsey's life for my injured pride.

It wasn't like anyone would believe the truth if Kayden and company decided to share it. Hell, they were quick to dismiss all the irregularities in the initial report. And yes I knew there was a 'they', because there were a bunch of powerful someone else's behind Kayden.

For now, that 'they' would be nothing more than a possible tool to get Kelsey home safe. Afterward, if I played it smart, I could deny everything. My word against theirs. I took a deep breath and dove in, "Fine."

Kayden's lashes lowered, veiling a strange flicker before I could figure out what it meant. "Tell me how your ability works."

Stalling for time, I straightened my shoulders and countered, "I have a better idea. Let's trade."

His reluctant humor came and went. "Question for a question?"

Tempted by the thought of controlling our exchange of information, I nodded. "You level with me and I'll level with you."

Speculative interest colored his voice. "I'll go first."

I shook my head. "Uh-uh. I go first."

He took the couple of steps necessary to crowd into my personal space. Then he leaned in until a mere breath separated us, reminding me of things I didn't want to remember. He was so close, too close. "Trust issues?"

I bared my teeth in a parody of a smile. "Just the ones you

taught me." *Good lord, he was hot.* Literally. A disturbing heat radiated from him and curled around me, dulling the chill edge of nerves. Sucking in a shallow breath, I fought not to reveal how unsteady he made me. "First question, why is he after me now?"

His gaze sharpened, an indicator that my attempt to appear unfazed failed miserably. He drew back, turned, and went to sit on the other side of the counter. As he moved, his T-shirt tightened over the telltale lump in the middle of his back.

Nice to know he hadn't resorted to pulling out his gun while we were wrestling in the hallway. Which reminded me, I needed to find my gun.

"You're hard to pin down."

"Obviously not hard enough, since you and Tag found me just fine." I narrowed my eyes, his answer felt more like an evasion. "And that's not an answer. Why now? Why me?"

He wagged his finger at me. "That's two."

I crossed my arms and stared.

He dropped his hand and drummed his fingers against the Formica. "You're next on his list."

"List?" Not the answer I was expecting. "What list?"

"Nope, it's my turn." Despite his casual tone, his gaze remained serious. "Tell me about your ability."

"That's not a question." It took effort to keep my voice light and unaffected, while every other part of me wanted to bolt. Instead, I headed toward the living room with studied nonchalance, leaving Kayden to follow or not.

The scrape of wooden chair legs over tile preceded his response. "Fine. What is your ability?"

Against my chest bone, my heart beat like a hummingbird on crack. Nerves left my mouth dry, and a light sweat beaded my forehead. Classic signs of an impending panic attack. Less than an hour in his company and whatever progress I made in the last few months went up in a puff of smoke.

Focus on the missing gun, Cyn.

With shaking hands, I pulled the cushions from the sofa. Maybe my gun had fallen between them? No gun, instead my search garnered a total of eighty-three cents, a paper clip, and stale popcorn.

"Answer for an answer, remember?" Kayden's deep voice came from right behind me.

I gave a tiny jump and turned, holding the cushion in front of me like some plush shield.

"Tell me what your gift can do." His quiet demand cornered me, leaving me with nowhere to hide.

Strength drained from my legs, and I sank to the edge of the couch, my fingers plucking at the cushion. "It won't help you."

He crouched in front of me, not touching me. "It won't, or you won't?"

"That's two questions," I muttered, avoiding his gaze.

"Put it on my tab." Then he waited, giving me time to find my waning courage.

Maybe I should've considered my Q&A dare a little more thoroughly as things were about to get FUBAR. Fear slithered low in my belly. My ability was the furthest thing from a gift you could get, and what I shared next could send me to therapy, and therapy and I were not good friends. When I was a kid, everyone's answer to my strange behavior was pills.

Needing distance from both the man and his questions, I pushed to my feet and resettled the cushion. "Sometimes I can see what happened in the past." No exclamations of disbelief sounded from behind me, and when I turned around, he didn't stare at me like I was bat-shit crazy. Strange.

"Post-cog." His answer raised something old and hungry. At my raised eyebrow, he explained, "The official term is retro cognition, the ability to read the past of a person or object."

"Just people, not objects." Granted, sometimes certain

objects could help my focus, but they never automatically triggered my ability. A shudder ran through me at the prospect of how much worse things could be if the objects around me could drag me into the past. Guess I should be grateful for small blessings.

Speaking of objects. I rounded the sofa, determined to find the missing gun. "How do you know this?"

"Is that really the question you want to ask?"

Was it? No, but asking what I wanted meant I was seriously considering working with him again, willing to join the hunt for the monster who turned my world upside down. And how stupid was that? Rubbing the dull ache under my scar and along my jaw, I dropped to my knees to peer beneath the sofa and continue my search. I wasn't hiding. "Maybe."

"You sure?"

Dignity be damned, I leaned down until my cheek pressed flat against the cool floor and scoured the forest of dust bunnies. And there toward the far end, just out of reach lay the gun.

From somewhere above me, Kayden asked, "What are you doing?"

"Looking for a gun."

"You generally keep one under the couch?"

Snorting in this position would result in a never-ending chain reaction of sneezing. "No, smartass." Sitting up, I found him standing over the back of the couch. I nodded toward the far end. "Do me a favor and lift that, would you?" While he got into position, I couldn't help but add, "By the way, your tab o' questions is now at four and counting."

He sank into a squat, gripped the edge of the sofa, and lifted, making it look easy. Guess those muscles were more than ornamentation. "Actually, three," he grunted.

"Uh?" Realizing I was staring instead of getting the gun, I gave myself a mental slap and dropped to the floor. I shifted my shoulder, snagged the black matte grip, and sat up, determined to stick to our conversation.

He set the couch back in place. "Your request to lift the couch? Took my tally back down to three."

Appreciating his willingness to play along, which gave me a chance to get my bearings back, I checked my gun. Ejecting the magazine, I racked the slide, emptying the bullet from the chamber. "Fine, three then."

I counted the bullets in the magazine—fourteen. Kelsey never got a shot off. "So, Ellery took Kelsey to get to me, and now you think playing Peeping Tom with the past will help you catch him?"

He settled beside me on the floor, his shoulder brushing mine as I re-inserted the magazine. He rested his arms on his upraised knees. "I don't think so, I know so."

The surety in his answer scared me, enough that I gave up keeping score on our question-and-answer game. "Why?"

He looked to the weapon I held. "How did you know the gun was under the couch?"

I answered before my mental brakes kicked in. "Kelsey managed to knock it out of his hand during her fight."

His eyes narrowed. "Who was Kelsey fighting?"

Nice slip there, Cyn. Never comfortable about actually talking about my little quirk, I got to my feet.

He caught my wrist, stopping me before I could walk away. When my gaze dropped to his, he asked, "Who did you see, Cyn?"

Twisting against his grip proved useless. Not that I tried very hard. The warmth of his fingers sank past skin and bone and was strangely reassuring. "Just her, I couldn't see his face."

He rolled to his feet with surprising grace. "Is that normal?"

A short, caustic laugh escaped. "Normal? What exactly about being a voyeur to the past is normal?"

He let me go but studied me with an unsettling intensity. "How much do you understand about your gift?"

His careful question scraped over emotions still raw from watching Kelsey's attack. "Not one damn thing, which makes living with it challenging, to say the least."

Difficult wasn't even close to describing how it was to grow up under the watchful eyes of the foster care system, especially knowing you were different. When I was younger, telling the past from the present was a challenge, one that took a while to master. Even then, trying to explain how hard it was not to get lost in the past, made it sound like I lived in some fantasy world.

It took me years to discover how to suppress this stupid 'gift' and find my place in the real world, instead of floundering in the past. By then, understanding the how's and why's didn't matter, as long as I could keep it tamped down, I was good. Only then could I function 'normally'.

"Then let's start from the beginning." A steely undertone of his words rode the edge of an order. "Tell me what triggers your ability."

He wanted answers? Fine. "Emotions. The stronger the emotion, the clearer the picture."

"Does it matter if the emotion is negative or positive?"

I shook my head, but qualified, "Generally negative. The more intense the situation, the closer I am to the subject, the deeper the imprint it leaves behind." I struggled to explain something I never tried to put into words. "It's like developing a photograph. If the emotional intensity of the person involved is the developing solution, then the scene etches itself in more detail on whatever it is that causes this ability."

Now that I was giving him what he wanted, he relaxed. Leaning against the back of the couch, he crossed his arms across his chest and gave a small nod. "That makes sense." His relaxed pose was deceptive because his next question was sharp. "How sensitive are you?"

Confused, I uttered an intelligent, "Huh?"

Studied patience colored his voice. "When you're reliving a scene, how deep do you go into it?"

Understanding dawned. "It depends. Generally, if it's someone I know, I can prepare for it. Surfing the waves is like watching a silent film."

"Silent films?" He frowned. "So, you can't hear anything, just watch?"

I nodded, not ready to admit that might have changed.

"If you're not prepared?"

Revealing any weakness to this man made me uncomfortable, but he wasn't giving me much choice. "Then someone better be around to snap me out of it."

"How?"

My hands curled into fists. "Physical distraction."

"Like what?"

Heat crawled up my face and it took a lot to meet his gaze. "Shaking or slapping works."

His eyebrows rose. "Aren't there other ways that don't involve hurting you?"

My shoulders hunched. "Not that I've found."

"That sucks."

I didn't bother responding because he was right. It did suck.

"I'm not judging," he said.

"Sounded like it." I turned away and went back to the kitchen. With no holster available, I tucked the gun between the waist of my jeans and the small of my back. Not the best place to stash it, but it might stave off the temptation to use it. Besides, if things kept being as weird as they were now, I wanted it with me.

He followed me. "Look, I need whatever information you

can give me. I need to know what you saw. Maybe there was some clue to where Ellery took Kelsey."

"If it was Ellery."

"What do you mean?"

Stopping short, I spun around, and threw up my hands. My sudden move pulled him up short. "What do you want me to tell you, Kayden?" I resettled my hands on my hips. "Kelsey walked into her room, someone broke in, attacked her, and then they both disappeared. I couldn't see his face, but I can tell you he stood close to your size and had military training."

"Show me."

His steely demand snapped my mouth close and made me blink. "Excuse me?"

"Show me what you saw."

Taken aback, I managed, "That's not how it works."

He folded his arms across his chest and stuck out his chin. "Does now."

Chapter Four

"Explain this one more time."

We were back at the couch, me sitting, knees bouncing with nerves. Kayden knelt in front of me and rested his hands on my knees, holding them still. With more patience than I expected, he did just that. "Every person leaves an energy signature behind. I'm a Tracker, which means, most times, I can follow those signatures. Considering your ability, I have an idea that might help us."

"I still don't understand." I studied him. Something wasn't adding up. "If you can track psychic energy signatures, you should be able to read what happened without me."

His big shoulders rose and fell in a casual shrug. "I could, but theory has it that post-cogs like you, can recreate the past by re-energizing the echoes of what happened. If the theory is right, it means while you're reliving the past, the energy signatures should be stronger than if I read whatever is currently left in the room."

"How does having a stronger picture of psychic signatures help us to determine what happened to Kelsey?"

"Think of it like a power boost. If we're lucky, maybe your

silent films will develop a soundtrack." His fingers tightened on my knees. "Sometimes, with a strong enough signature, I can get a glimpse of what someone is planning on doing next. So, if this is Ellery…"

My mouth dropped open. "You can see the future?" I squeaked.

"What?" Startled, he shook his head. "No, I don't see the future, only seers hold that ability." Before I could process that, he continued, "Think about it, Cyn. When you were on a mission, did you plan your next move or stay focused on the task at hand?"

I opened mouth to answer, only to stop and think. A glimmer of understanding rose. "We always went in with a set plan, but things change at the drop of a hat. If you kept running various scenarios in your mind, you could adjust your actions instinctively." I studied the man kneeling in front of me. "You think that if it is Ellery, and that's what he's doing, you might catch an echo of his plans. That's a hell of a lot of maybes."

Kayden's gaze didn't waver. "Probably, but it's better than doing nothing."

That was debatable. "So, a power boost, uh? And we have to touch?"

Under his goatee a small smile appeared. "Pretty much. Physical touch has proven to increase psychic connections. Once I have all three signatures, it's just a matter of separating yours and Kelsey's out so I can focus on the last one. Hopefully, together we'll get a better picture of what happened and confirm who attacked her."

I bit my lip, considering. "You're not seeing what I'm seeing?"

He shook his head.

It still didn't make sense, but he seemed to believe it would work. He had me go back over everything from my earlier trip down memory lane, then he suggested we concentrate on the last scene, explaining he hoped his presence would trigger more details. That explanation made me wonder if I was missing something. I searched his face and the studied calm he gave me. "What aren't you telling me?"

Something too quick to read flashed across his face. "I've never tried this with anyone else, so I'm not sure what will happen."

"Can we hurt each other doing this?"

"I don't know," he said. "But if it helps find Kelsey, does it matter?"

Nope, not one damn bit. I sighed and gingerly laid my hands on top of his. Heat curled through my palms as my pulse picked up speed.

Obviously catching it, he said, "I'll be right here, Cyn."

I appreciated his attempt at comfort, but he couldn't understand. Reliving things left me open and vulnerable. Having him witness what was about to happen was akin to standing in front of him naked.

Unexpectedly, a whole other type of heat rose, and mortification had me closing my eyes in a vain attempt to block out the dangerously good-looking man at my feet. *What the hell was wrong with me?* Yeah, it had been a while, but there were reasons, good reasons not to let this edgy awareness sink its teeth in. Not now, and if I was smart, not ever again.

Shoving the distraction far, far away, I took a deep breath. Then another. The feel of Kayden's hands under mine helped me to center. Within minutes, my hastily rebuilt mental wall resembled a pile of rubble. Nerves trembled. If this worked as he expected, Kayden would see the psychic signatures loud and clear as we cruised through the memories, some of which belonged to me. It was unsettling to consider what he might pick up.

Opening my eyes, I met Kayden's gaze and my vision filled

with flecks of gray sprinkled through the blue depths. For a suspended moment, I swore I could feel him in my mind—strong, bright, determined, rock steady. His presence acted like a magnet on my ability, drawing it close and deepening the connection between us. My stomach bottomed out and my breath stalled at the unusual sensation. I blinked once and the feeling faded, leaving me strangely bereft.

Shaking it off, a flicker of movement around Kayden caught my attention. Bracing, I switched my focus beyond him to the hall. Concentrating on the nebulous image, I rose and lost my grip on Kayden's hands. The world spun, then steadied.

"You okay?" Kayden's question came from behind me, and a warm weight settled on my shoulders, a welcome anchor in the disquieting deluge of images.

I nodded but watched the entryway. With the touch of his hands, the memories around me brightened, becoming more concise than before, and allowed me to zero in on the one I wanted quickly. Seemed his idea about keeping a physical connection had some merit.

Kelsey's attacker stepped into the living room. Then he backed a frightened but determined Kelsey up. She swung out, knocking my gun from his hand. This time, I watched it skitter under the couch. A faint scrape of metal against the hardwood floor followed.

At the slight noise, excitement rose and so did Kelsey's emotions, stronger than before. They curled like waves, dragging me relentlessly closer. I fought to keep my distance. Not an easy feat as her emotional imprint grew in strength. The effort to stay above it, roughened my voice. "Are you getting what you need?"

Kayden's fingers dug in, his voice tight. "Holy shit."

Sounded like a resounding yes to me. I focused on her attacker, but that strange static cloud still covered his face. Part of me hoped with Kayden tagging along this wouldn't happen.

Frustration rose and the images shook, threatening to break apart. I drew in a slow breath and tried to push my careening emotions aside. The images steadied, but the strange occurrence remained behind. "Damn it."

"What's wrong?" Kayden's voice was low.

"Can't see his face." I took a step closer, but he held me back.

"Maybe you should tell me what you're seeing, Cyn," he said.

Puzzled, I looked back to him over my shoulder with a frown. Watching the memories hovering around him proved to be a strange experience. "Can't you follow the signatures?"

"They're a hell of a lot stronger than I'm used to, but all I see are faint pieces of actual images. I just can't make out who's who." His gaze narrowed on the scene in front of us and for a moment I couldn't remember what I wanted to say. Instead of fading into the background, like most people tended to do when I relived a scene, Kayden remained etched with startling clarity. It made it almost painful to look at him. Weird.

Turning back to the scene, Kelsey was once more struggling with the man. "The gun's gone and he's going after Kelsey."

"Can you get a positive ID of his face?"

"No, it's still blocked, but he's toying with her." I pulled against his grip, needing to get closer. I could hear a low buzz, like a radio just off channel. Excitement spiked and I murmured, "There are voices." The urge to get closer tugged at me. I moved forward, forcing Kayden to follow or lose his grip. "I need to get closer."

"Closer to what?"

"Kelsey." The invisible currents of the emotional storm between Kelsey and her attacker buffeted me. Even as a warning chittered away in my brain, an idea of what was needed to get more information formed. Something tightened my chest. "Kayden?"

"Yeah?"

"Remember what I said about using pain to bring me back?"

"What the hell are you thinking?"

"Don't leave a bruise." With no more warning, I dropped down into the maelstrom of Kelsey's residual emotions and left Kayden behind as my anchor.

Like a churning sea, fear rose first, swamping me and then sucking me under. Shoving it away, I worked to clear my mind until I could bob to the surface and ride the storm as the real world disappeared and the memories washed over me.

The annoying low buzz slowly cleared, and words began to echo in hollow bursts. At the same time my perspective shifted. Now I was on the floor facing the entryway, the couch behind me. A large presence loomed over me while the buzz faded in and out, slowly shifting to actual words. A low, evil taunt filled my head, "…want to play…tle girl? Fin…but… rather play…sister."

"Fuck you!" Stuck inside Kelsey's fear and fury, her response came through loud and clear. When he struck her, there was no way to avoid the stinging lash of pain or the faint taste of blood blooming in my mouth.

"Dammit, stop pissing him off, Kels," I muttered. Rattled, I tried focusing on the face above us. The static morphed into a nightmarish blur of ever-shifting waves of black and gray. My stomach lurched at the nauseating motion.

"… one more time…she…?" What I could catch of his voice was pitiless and turned my blood to ice.

Kelsey's terror spiked, pulling me a little deeper into the past. The line between Cyn and Kelsey blurred, then my sense of self disappeared until all that was left was a petrified Kelsey.

Our mouth was dry, but it didn't stop us from sending blood and spit at the cloud of static.

A vicious yank dragged us backward over the floor. Our

hands scrabbled against the grip tangled in our hair. Our nails gouged material and skin, tearing skin as we tried to get our feet under us for leverage. But we were being dragged too fast and our heels skidded across the floor. Then the pressure at the back of our head disappeared.

Before we could scramble away, a large, calloused hand clamped around our throat, cutting off our air and dragging us up to our knees. One hard shove slammed our head against the wall, sending starbursts across our vision as the edges grayed. Then the grip disappeared.

We sucked in air. Desperate, noisy gulps. Our vision began to clear. Somewhere a deep voice tugged at us, leading us away. "C'mon, Cyn, breathe, you're okay."

Kayden. Like a sliver of wood wedged under the skin, the spark of recognition allowed me a chance to pull back from Kelsey just a tiny bit. Enough so I could rise above the shared panic and remember that I couldn't change what had already happened.

Kelsey's fear peaked. The edges of the blocking static began to fade. Still, she struggled against his chokehold, her movements getting more and more sloppy. *Details. I needed details.*

The strange static broke in places. Bits and pieces appeared and disappeared. I tried to catch as much as I could. "Clean shaven, sharp chin, short hair…" I could barely hear myself and had no idea if Kayden was getting any of it, but I had to try. Details came together, merging with those from the night half a world away.

Reeve Ellery.

"…or another…bring her…me…bitch." Ellery leaned in close and loosened his grip. His hand rose and fell once more. Our head snapped back under the blow, but the distance I gained diminished under the impact. The swirling mass re-solidified, obscuring any other details.

I pulled back a little further, trying for more distance from

Kelsey so I could watch the scene. It was harder this time, as if I swam through syrup. When I was able to refocus, I realized I lost part of the scene as I was now kneeling next to Kelsey. Terror had drained everything but the startling red marks of violence from her bloodless face.

The low buzz returned. Worried I'd pulled too far back from the memories, I reached for Kelsey as the strident notes of Rob Zombie's "American Witch" cut through the buzz.

Kelsey's chest stilled, her eyes flickering toward the kitchen counter. My assigned ringtone continued, capturing Ellery's attention. He stiffened and staying in his crouch turned to look toward the front door. He couldn't tell where the noise was coming from.

My only warning was a desperate spike in Kelsey's emotions as she took advantage of his momentary distraction. She pushed to her feet, one hand on her throat, the other reaching for the edge of the wall. She stumbled forward a few feet before a growl sounded and hard hand caught her.

"Naughty...not done...yet."

My pulse stuttered. Kelsey's struggles turned frantic as he dragged her around the corner to the counter. Desperate to do something, anything, I followed them.

"...calling?" He shoved her hard. The counter's edge cut into her stomach, and she shuddered. He used his body to keep her pinned next to the blinking answering machine, her face inches from her sunglasses and her ringing cell phone, where my name spilled across the screen, making it hard to miss.

"Look...already...er running." A cruel hum of satisfaction colored his voice as he picked up her phone, his finger wiped over the touch screen. The tune cut short.

Kelsey's cheeks were streaked with tears that mixed with the blood trickling from her swollen mouth. "What do you want?" Her question was rough and unsteady, but I caught every bit of it.

He put his face next to hers, the muscles in his arm flexing as he pressed down. Her eyes widened, terror blowing her pupils. "Nothing much...we're going...leave Cyn... message..."

He tossed her cell on the counter and yanked her back against his chest. Kelsey's fear crested, and my pulse stuttered under the looming wave. As his arm wrapped around her neck and began to lift her off her feet, she clawed and gouged his skin. Somewhere in the background a phone rang dimly.

The scene paused. For a breathless moment the line between past and present blurred. My heart shattered at the grim acceptance darkening Kelsey's eyes. A sickening knowing rose, one I didn't want to acknowledge.

Ellery jerked her up and back, and her desperate warning to run whispered across my soul. A sharp stinging sensation tore across my cheekbone and the scene began to fracture with an audible snap and slip away. Even as I rose to the present with Kayden's help, unbelievable pain ripped through my mind and heart.

Screaming with fury and fear, I lunged forward to capture the images falling away like a broken windowpane and fell into the yawning pit.

Awareness came back in pieces. First was the sound of my name blending in with the bongo drums pounding in my skull. Then the dull ache radiating from my temple to jaw joined in. When I tried to speak, the razor blades lining my throat changed my words into whimpers. It was almost enough to drive me back into oblivion, but the niggling sensation of impending disaster blocked the tempting escape route. As the discordant symphony of aches and pain began to recede, I realized Kayden was yelling at me.

"Cyn! Dammit, Cyn, answer me."

I forced my eyes open and flinched at the shadow hovering over me.

"Relax, it's me." Kayden pulled back and my surroundings came into hazy focus. "Are you with me?"

I raised a hand to my throat, swallowed, and winced. Instead of answering, I nodded.

"If you can sit up, I'll get you water."

No wonder my floor was so comfortable. I was half sitting in Kayden's lap.

With his help, I managed to prop myself against the wall under the counter while he grabbed a glass of water. I focused on just breathing, doing my best not to trigger the emotional avalanche poised to crash on my head.

A glass appeared on the edge of my vision. My arm shook as I reached out. Kayden kept his hand on the glass, steadying it. "Take it slow," he warned.

I sipped until the razor blades dulled enough to speak. "Did you get anything?" He let me take the glass and I cradle it in my lap.

"It's Ellery's signature." He brushed gentle fingers over my aching cheek, down my throat, and over my scars, some strong emotion darkening his eyes and tightening his jaw. "You're going to have some very interesting bruises."

My hand rose and covered his on my neck. "They're Kelsey's. They'll fade."

His gaze flickered to my cheek. "Not that one." His fingers stilled. "Does this always happen?"

My fingers tightened, then dropped away. I shook my head. "No, just when I go too deep."

He pulled his hand free and cradled the side of my face. "Is she okay?"

"I don't know." My answer was a mere whisper. And a horrible lie.

Hot tears rose and burned a path over my cold cheeks. I pulled away, struggling to get to my feet. Ignoring Kayden's attempts to help, I grabbed the cell phone off the counter. This time, I would force my ability to bend to my demands. For once it would help me.

Sharp, stabbing pains sliced lines across my vision and Kayden's curses turned into background noise. It hurt so much, I wanted to drop to my knees, but the need to prove I hadn't failed my sister kept me upright.

I almost missed the flickering images as they had resumed their amorphous nature. Still, I was able to catch a glimpse of Ellery's back as he headed toward the front door. It was hard to make out what he was doing, but I stumbled behind the rapidly disintegrating visuals. I hit the porch, trying to track his movements. A strange numbness inched over me, and I couldn't feel the phone or my fingers. Something thumped to the ground. Outside in the bright, hot afternoon the image flickered near the carport, then disappeared. Someone kept saying, "No, no, no." It was irritating, and I wished they'd shut up.

My body felt clumsy, and I tripped down the steps to the loose gravel. My fingers began to tingle as if small pins were trying to poke their way out of my skin. The disturbing sensation raced up my arms and wrapped tight bands around my chest. Caught in this strange reality, it took a moment to understand that I was standing in front of Kelsey's car. My hands hovered over the trunk, shaking violently.

Just do it, Cyn. Open the trunk and prove you're just losing your mind.

My hands didn't move.

"Cyn?" Kayden's careful use of my name snapped my paralysis. My fingers fumbled for the release latch. Suddenly, larger hands covered mine, stilling my frantic movements. "We'll do it together, okay?" His voice came from behind me, gentle and soft. His hands steady.

I gave a sharp nod, choking off the sob trapped in my throat. Together we raised the lid. A thin wail broke through the quiet afternoon and my heart shattered.

I'd found Kelsey.

Chapter Five

I sat on the porch in a numb haze. My fingers tracing random patterns over the gun lying in my lap. Behind me, Kayden talked to someone on his cell, his words sliding over me without meaning. He'd been talking for a while.

There were things I needed to do, questions I needed to ask. Yet I didn't move. The emptiness carving deep gouges on my heart and soul, laid new wounds over old scars. Eventually grief would come and dull the ragged edges. Maybe.

I'd been here once before, years ago. The night my foster parents were killed by a drunk driver. Then, I had Kelsey to hold on to as our world tore apart. Now, I wondered if I'd find my way out or just drown in this deafening quiet.

My entire family was gone.

A vehicle barreled into the driveway.

I closed my eyes in a futile wish. Maybe, if I made enough deals with whoever upstairs was listening, I could open my eyes...

The dull thump of a car door slamming shut was followed by the sound of cautiously approaching footsteps.

...and find...

"Cyn?"

Familiar and deep, it wasn't the voice I had been wishing for, and it left searing, unrealistic disappointment in its wake. I opened my eyes.

It took effort to look away from the gun and focus on the person crouched in front of me. Tall and lanky, with dirt-blond hair no comb could tame, Tag stared back, his compassion obvious.

The need to connect to someone familiar overrode past hurts busy huddling behind my grief. I swallowed, and then reached for my voice, "Hey, Hayseed."

His nickname came out dull, but it didn't stop him from reaching out to cover my restless fingers, stilling them against the warm surface of my gun. "Hey, you."

Leave it to Tag not to ask me the totally inane question of how I was doing. It was painfully obvious.

"Kelsey's dead." Saying the words out loud made them real, cracking the barrier holding my emotions back. Tears threatened, but crying was pointless. Kelsey was gone.

My sister had been brutally ripped from my world, leaving behind a wound so raw and bitter, I didn't think I'd ever recover. No matter what I chose to do from here, I would never make up for the fact her death could be laid indirectly at my feet. "Make me understand." Half plea, half accusation.

"I can't." Two words. One lie.

I searched Tag's face. Under his compassion lay a wary watchfulness, a clear sign he expected me to break, as if it was a forgone conclusion. His look morphed my helplessness to fury, and it seared through my veins chasing out the numbness. My fingers curled around my gun, and I yanked my hands out from under his. "Can't or won't?"

He didn't answer, instead he recaptured my hands. His touch sent a small jolt of static electricity zinging along my skin. It almost made me miss his flash of quickly squashed guilt.

Almost.

"You bastard," I hissed, a sickening sense of certainty crashing through me. He knew something, something he didn't want to share. He was going to screw me again. I scrambled to my feet, knocking him away. "My sister is dead! You don't get to shut me out!"

"It's not my decision, you know that." He remained crouched in front of me. Somewhere behind me Kayden must have made a move because Tag signaled him to hold.

"No, I don't." I stood there, shaking with the force of my raging emotions as the past and the present collided, boiling into an incandescent storm.

At one time, he was the big brother I needed, pushy and protective. I believed him without question, trusted him to cover my back for years in some of the biggest hellholes on earth. Until the day I sat in a cold courtroom, alone, answering the unanswerable in a flurry of accusations. Now, when I needed his honesty the most, he wouldn't talk. "What the hell is really going on here, Thomas?" I bit out the question.

Tag slowly straightened to his full six foot four, his face blanking into a familiar stonewall. "It's classified."

"No." I shook my head slowly, never breaking eye contact. "No, you don't get to pull this shit on me again. The two of you are going to level with me."

"Or what?" Kayden's question jerked my head around. He pocketed his cell phone and came closer.

I raised my hand to hold him off. "Or I walk away."

He stopped a few feet from me.

"Ellery is hunting me." Just saying it out loud choked me with fear. "You don't have a goddamn clue where to find him, or you wouldn't have tracked me down."

With one man on the porch and one on the steps, I shifted

my position so I could watch them both. If they were trying to pin me in, it wouldn't work. I tucked my gun into the back of my waistband to combat the temptation it presented. My control wasn't as strong as I'd hoped. "You're here because you have no other choice, and you need me as bait. As of right now, I can't think of a single reason I need you."

Kayden's expression turned stony. "I can think of three, Elizabeth Gaskey, Michael Layton and Nathan Visic."

Each name of my former teammates hit like bullets, tearing through half-healed wounds. The impacts left me speechless and leaning against the low porch railing.

"What the hell, Shaw?" Tag growled behind me.

"As of five minutes ago, the orders have changed. Now that we know for sure it's Ellery on her ass, she needs to know what we're dealing with before she does something stupid."

Kayden's comment burned, but it restored my voice. "What happened to Liza, Mike, and Nate?"

"They're dead." Too much emotion existed in Tag's answer. Way too much. It scared me.

"Dead?" The question escaped on a harsh whisper. "How?"

Instead of answering me, Kayden snapped, "Give her the file. Let her see what Ellery's become."

Grabbing his wrist as he went to step around me, I asked, "File?"

He stopped and looked down at me, "You want to help hunt Kelsey's killer, you need to understand who you're going up against." Something uneasy hovered behind his words. "Maybe it'll make you rethink playing bait."

"I've seen his handiwork, Kayden." The words slipped out as brutal memories hovered close. "Just because no one wanted to listen the first time, doesn't mean it didn't happen. I haven't forgotten what he's capable of."

"He's changed," Tag added. "Killers escalate."

"Read the file, Cyn," Kayden's voice stayed gruff. "Then maybe you'll understand."

Goosebumps pebbled my skin at his ominous tone. "Fine."

For the first time I wondered what I was getting myself into. Fading sunlight glinted off Kelsey's car. *Did I really care?* Ellery needed to pay for what he'd taken from me. Tearing my gaze away from the trunk with its heartbreaking baggage, I could only manage one word. "Thanks."

"Don't thank me, it wasn't my decision." Kayden studied me, then shook his head. "We need to get moving."

"What about Kelsey?" I was proud how steady my voice was.

The stern lines of his face softened for a moment. "She'll be taken care of, I promise." He covered my hand with his and squeezed.

His show of compassion snuck under my guard and pierced deep, but I shored up my defenses. I gave him a jerky nod and pulled away.

Kelsey deserved answers, even if the end result left me buried in truths better left alone.

•◦●◦●◦•

A short time later, I found myself tucked into the passenger seat of my Jeep and an inch-thick file resting like an anchor on my lap while Kayden drove. No one wanted me staying at the cabin. Hell, I wasn't sure I wanted to stay. Not now. Plus, they needed me out of the way while whoever they worked for came in and took care of Kelsey.

Walking away and leaving her there hurt. My chest ached. Tears were a hot pressure behind my eyes, leaking in a slow fall over my cheeks. It felt like I was abandoning her, leaving her with strangers. Not even Tag's reassurance he would stay to watch over her helped. Yet, instead of pushing on the who and why of things, I let him take over.

I leaned my forehead against the warm glass of the window, blind to the passing scenery. As Kayden put distance between us and the cabin, I considered the brown file in my lap.

Watermarks dotted the cover, smearing over a couple of brown rings similar to coffee stains, and one corner was missing. Its rough condition proof it had been around awhile, and wasn't that daunting?

All I had to do was open it and some of my answers would be there for the taking. Unfortunately, I was in no shape to handle them. Not yet. Not when the past crowded so close and bled into the present.

Scrubbing my hands over my face, I wiped away my tears, and tucked my grief in a small, hidden corner. Later, after I got justice for Kelsey, my kind of justice, I'd let it free. Until then, I needed to get my head in the game. Time to embrace the suck and deal with the shitstorm barreling toward me.

Step one, discovering who called the shots on this operation. Sitting back, I cleared my throat and turned to Kayden. "Let's get the most obvious question out of the way. Who are you working for?"

His lips thinned, but his hands remained steady on the wheel. "Why don't you read the file first?"

"No."

"Why not?"

Because I don't want you to see me fall apart. Instead of admitting that, I said, "Tell me who you're working for."

"PSY-IV."

Cipher? "Never heard of it." Which said something, considering how much the military loved their acronyms. No need for a secret code, since everything had some catchy phrase attached.

"Wouldn't have expected you to," Kayden drawled. "It's one of multiple teams under the Specialized Criminal Investigations Division."

At twenty-four, a year into my second enlistment, I had joined MCIA, Marine Criminal Investigations Agency. They were the ones who arranged my last joint assignment. This unit sounded suspiciously similar.

"Specialized, uh?" I tapped my fingers against the file. "So, you're still in. I didn't think the military had relaxed its personal appearance requirements."

"What? You don't like the 'do?" He deftly sidestepped my question as he ran a hand through his shaggy hair.

Actually, the longer look suited him. The wholly inappropriate thought had heat climbing my face. In the marines, whenever a capital crime occurred, MCIA would run the resulting investigations and prosecutions. As long as it involved a marine, they were there to uncover, or in my personal experience, cover up, the truth. Whichever worked best. Considering the file in my lap, it would follow that Kayden's team functioned in the same fashion. That thought made me pause. "So PSY-IV is, what? A joint task force for the MCIA?"

Kayden's brief humor faded. "First, none of the teams officially exist. Second, we investigate paranormal crimes."

It took my brain a few seconds to process his matter of fact answer. "Wait. Are you telling me you're a covert paranormal cop? For the military?"

His jaw tightened at my question.

Okay, even I could hear the disbelief in my voice. *But seriously?*

Six months ago, my initial account of what happened to my team would have had my superiors bouncing my ass into a psych ward so fast no one could've stopped them. Hence the amnesia alibi. Now Kayden was sitting here telling me he worked for them?

The military never admitted to things they couldn't prove. I was proof of that. Granted, you couldn't escape the rumors of crackpot conspiracy theorists on how the military housed deeply buried specialized divisions running from unchecked, black ops groups to genetically mutated soldiers. Yet, everyone knew it was just bullshit. Yes, the military ran numerous, undisclosed operations and highly secretive divisions, but not the woo-woo type that would give *X-Files* a run for its money.

"You really find it that hard to believe?" he asked. "I told you earlier, you aren't the only psychic out there. Extraordinary abilities tend to result in extraordinary crimes."

While I considered my ability more a curse than extraordinary, I could admit to wondering if there were others out there like me. It was just I never thought to find anyone willing to admit it. Still, I had to ask, "You belong to a unit of psychics?"

Not taking his gaze off the road, he nodded.

Stunned, I let his latest bombshell tumble in my mind. When it settled, I muttered, "Wow, that's not encouraging."

Puzzled, Kayden frowned. "What?"

"If an entire police force is needed to keep all us psychics in line, what does that say about our mental states?"

He stroked his goatee, to hide a smile or out of habit, I couldn't tell. "Some abilities lend themselves to serious repercussions. Say a pyrokinetic gets into a heated argument with a friend over a bad hand of cards and sets the room on fire. Everyone gets out alive, but the building is torched. Investigators get involved, claim it's arson and attempted murder. The fire-starter gets sentenced to twenty-five years for basically losing his temper, because for all intents and purposes there's no way the fire wasn't intentional. Is that fair?"

"No." Reluctantly intrigued, I asked, "Did that happen?"

He nodded. "Yeah. We were able to overturn the sentence because of lack of evidence on how the blaze started, but he still spent three years behind bars."

"For losing his temper." I couldn't imagine living under the constant worry of harming those around you simply because you got mad. "That sucks."

He slid me a look. "Justice may be blind as a bat, but it isn't always fair, especially when it can't understand what's really happening." He turned his attention back to the road. "What do you know about CIA's psychic experiments from the fifties and sixties?"

"Back after World War II the CIA got their panties in a bunch when they thought Russia had developed a psychic warfare program. Not wanting to get left in the dust, they started their own programs. Most of which, if I remember correctly, were defunct by the seventies."

He nodded and took over. "The CIA wanted to find ways to create the perfect sleeper soldier, someone they could plant behind enemy lines, then use when the time was right. They collaborated with leading psychologists and scientists, all under the cover of research. They tried it all, drugs, electroshock therapy, hypnosis. You name it they did it."

"At the time there wasn't as much oversight from the government, so boundaries were nonexistent. Because their subjects were either convicted criminals, mental patients, or enemies of the state, no one cared about human rights. When they created MKULTRA, only then, did they turn their attention to U.S. soldiers, turning them into unwitting subjects."

His history lesson rang a few bells. "Didn't a guy named John Marks do an exposé on this?"

"Yeah, wrote a whole book about it. He culled information from unnamed sources and redacted documents. He focused on the CIA drug experiments and how the government tried to cover its ass. What he missed, and what the government kept deep under wraps, was that they had found some individuals who were the real deal."

I grimaced. "And the government, being who they are, aren't going to sit by and let an advantage slip through their fingers."

"Nope," he agreed. "Since you can't force the general public to disclose private information without just cause, the powers-that-be focused on military recruits. One of the personality exams administered to prospective recruits tested for actual psychic ability. From there, it became a matter of tracking those individuals and combining them into cohesive groups. Over time, they managed to create specialized units in each branch."

Something began to scratch at the back of my brain, but, caught up in the conversation, I ignored it. "If you have a unit comprised of untried psychics, something is bound to happen," I said, starting to see where he was headed. "So, there were accidents?"

"Right. With the creation of the teams, the military found a way to explain away the unexplainable."

I watched his profile. "You said they don't officially exist."

He slid a glance to me and dipped his chin. "The government needs distance if the public catches wind of its existence. It's funded by a sub-committee of a sub-committee of a special interest group that works with the Department of Defense."

"Buried under layers for deniability." Years in the military and dusty hells of foreign battlefields rubbed all the shiny off a soldier and revealed the seamier side of politics. "So, who's currently in charge?"

"Charlene Delacourt."

His answer set off my alarm bells. I swallowed hard. "Colonel Delacourt?"

"The one and only."

During my years in service, Delacourt's name had been

uttered with terrifying respect. A powerful female in a male-dominated environment, she was the stuff of legends. Unfortunately, she also served on the inquiry board that raked me over the coals. Unease settled over me, making my voice tight. "Sounds like you're still working for the marines."

"Delacourt has been the official head of the teams for the last four years."

I fell silent, processing the information Kayden had dumped in my lap.

Four years ago, I joined MCIA and was assigned to Captain Eric "Flash" Fowler's team. At the time, I was ecstatic. Not only was Flash a close friend of my adoptive father, but he'd helped me through my first enlistment when I questioned signing the dotted line. He'd shared some of the stories surrounding Delacourt, providing examples of what a determined woman could do in the Corps.

During Ellery's trial, I found out just how determined Delacourt was, and it made one hell of an impression. Sitting in the courtroom, confused by my teammates' mysterious absences, fuzzy from the painkillers still winging their way through my system, I endured question after brutal question, most asked by Delacourt.

Maybe if I hadn't been reeling from the shock of my discoveries, I would've handled it better. But fearing an actual court-martial, or worse, being labeled mentally unstable, I stuck to my amnesia excuse like super glue.

The inquiry board's frustration with my lack of answers at what had happened to Flash was understandable. If I had been on the other side of the equation, I would have had a hard time believing me, too. So, when the case was closed without a deeper probe, I didn't push it.

Flash and Ortega were dead and buried. The rest of my team was reassigned and scattered to the winds. No one was talking to me. A whitewashed report emerged, and I received a medical discharge, the Corp's polite way of saying, "you screwed up, but we don't want people to know". As soon as the doctor cleared me, I ran as fast and as far as I could, knowing for all intents and purposes, my career with the Corps was done.

Hindsight is twenty/twenty. Looking back, it wasn't hard to recognize the transparency of my alibi. Delacourt had to have guessed the truth, especially if she ran a group of covert psychic teams. Not only did I have psychic abilities, but that horrific night, I discovered so did Flash. Pieces clicked together. "Kayden?"

"Hmm?"

"Is Tag psychic?" My pulse raced as I waited for his answer.

He turned toward me. "You need to ask him."

Not a denial. The sting of betrayal zipped through me. Why wouldn't Tag have told me?

Like you told him? A nasty voice perked up.

My stomach dropped as my world shifted. If half of the eight-person joint team had been psychic, chances were good all of us were. Which meant our team had been one of the government's little experimental units. My thoughts stumbled to a halt. *All that effort to hide something everyone seemed to know about?* "The entire team was psychic."

"Yes."

"Were you working for PSY-IV at the time?"

He nodded.

"Just you?" I pushed.

He didn't answer right away. "No."

Kayden's quiet answer left me grasping for mental footing. According to him, PSY-IV monitored psychics, watched them, and recruited them. That meant if they sent Kayden in to join my team, not only was he recruiting, but we were under investigation as well. And if that was the case, it was because Delacourt thought there was a link between Ellery and the team. Considering the horrific outcome of our assignment, she might be right. But Kayden would not have been sent in on his own, not to investigate, and not to recruit. Suspicion bloomed. "Who else?"

"Flash."

Confirmation hurt. Yet, I couldn't let it go just yet. "Not Tag?"

"He was approached but hadn't made a decision at the time to join the team."

Stunned, I stared blindly at the innocuous folder in my lap. My mind struggled with this new information as I tried not to acknowledge my growing sense of disillusionment. Had they considered me the leak? Neither my mentor, nor my best friend, had clued me in, which may be an answer in itself.

I put my life on the line time and time again for the marines, for Flash, for Tag. At eighteen, after the ten-week hell of boot camp, followed by the fifty-four-hour, ten-mile endurance course known as the Crucible, I had forged lifelong bonds that grew with each enlistment. Bonds necessary to survive the ordeal of war.

Learning that those I had trusted most kept things, important things, from me hurt. Their implied rejection sent a long, snaking crack through my heart. "How long had Flash been working for you?" I choked out. *How long had he kept me in the dark? How long had he not trusted me?*

Kayden turned off the highway and navigated his way through the twists and turns of a tucked away neighborhood on the outskirts of Sedona. "It's not my place to answer."

Numb from too many emotional hits, I said, "No, it's not."

He shot me a sharp look as he pulled into a small, dusty parking lot in front of a wooden building. A sign reading JASPER BED AND BREAKFAST hung between two painted posts on the porch. "Cyn?"

"I'm fine." And I would be. I checked out the place. "Why are we here?"

He shut the engine off and opened his door. "Delacourt wanted a secured place to meet."

That information jerked me out of my numb state, but it was the sound of the back hatch lifting that made me scramble out of the Jeep. I rounded the Jeep, file in hand, and watched as he pulled out his bag. "Delacourt's here?" That wasn't panic in my voice, really it wasn't.

Kayden, duffle bag slung over his shoulder, shot me an amused look and handed me my bag. "You wanted answers, right?"

"Not that badly." I grabbed my camera bag from the back.

His grin flashed. "Don't worry, she'll be here in a few hours, so you have time to prepare."

A few days wouldn't be enough, much less a few hours. Instead of admitting that, I followed his wide back as he strode to the far end of the property where a small, wooden cabin with dark windows sat. What was the worst that could happen anyway?

She could shoot you and put you out of your misery, offered a helpful little shit in my head.

I snorted. Yeah, she could, but I doubted it. She'd never let me off that easy.

Chapter Six

Kayden took the cabin's two front steps with ease and punched in a series of numbers into the electronic lock. The lock released with a soft beep, and he pushed the door open. Motioning for me to stay put, he pulled his weapon out, and disappeared into the shadowed interior.

A light came on inside less than a minute later, causing me to blink rapidly. When my sight cleared, Kayden stood in the doorway. "It's clear. Make yourself at home." He stepped back, giving me space to enter.

I checked out the cabin. "Nice."

The layout was simple and straight forward, with the small, but functional kitchen sitting to my left. I set my gun and the file on the round, wooden table standing between the kitchen and the living room. Near the French doors leading to a shadowed patio, an L-shaped couch faced a stone fireplace. "How long are we staying?"

"Just a night." Kayden dropped the car keys on the table and set his duffle beside the couch. "Tag should be here before Delacourt."

The clock on the wall indicated it was only six-thirty. My

body disagreed. I dropped my bag next to his, and then made my way to the couch and collapsed. The cushions cuddled me, and I let my head fall back. I closed my eyes. My headache from earlier was back, this time with friends. For a few precious minutes the ache kept the inside of my head relatively quiet.

From the kitchen the sound of a cupboard being opened, and then closed, was followed by the rattle of ice against a glass. My mini oasis of peace broke when the cushion next to me sank under Kayden's weight.

"Here."

I blinked my eyes open and rolled my head to the side. Lifting it would make my headache worse.

Kayden held out a glass of ice water. Two white tablets lay in his palm. I took the glass but eyed the tablets.

"Aspirin," he said.

Sighing, I picked them up and popped them in my mouth. After washing them down, I mumbled my thanks and closed my eyes. The silence resettled, quiet and surprisingly calm.

The file waited for me on the table, a Pandora's Box of answers for my questions. A selfish part of me didn't want to deal with them right now, not while I was still processing Kelsey's death. And, yeah, all that Kayden shared. For now, I let the information gather in a corner and mutter to itself.

Trying not to think is harder than it sounds. My brain wanted to sprint forward, but the bands of pain throbbing across my cerebral cortex kept the urge in check. The aspirin needed time to work their magic. I did my best to regulate my breathing and relax, muscle by muscle. The concentration it took to do so helped chase away the mental images and voices hovering for attention.

It took time, but eventually I managed. When my shoulders downgraded from seriously stressed to anxious anticipation, I floated in the hazy in-between state of awareness and sleep.

The cushions next to me shifted, not much, just enough to snag my attention. Curiosity had me lifting heavy lids.

Sunlight spilled through the French doors and dusted over Kayden as he sprawled out next to me. The soft light played over his angles and contours. His legs were propped on the square coffee table, his head was cradled against the back of the couch, and his eyes were closed. Even at rest, his face was intriguing.

Drifting in an emotional limbo, my fingers twitched for my camera. He was attractive. Not the drop-dead gorgeousness that had panties dropping when he walked into a room, but something else, something intangible.

Even at our initial meet and greet, he drew me in. Maybe it was the way he held himself, or his ability to adeptly handle anything thrown his way. Whatever it was, it snuck under my normal reserve and created cracks in my emotional blockade. He managed to make a place for himself, and it wasn't until after the trial that I realized how deep he got in. Obviously, I underestimated his impact because that same draw still tugged at me.

Or you're an emotional train wreck, my inner snark remarked.

Whatever.

Now that he wasn't trying to smash me into the floor and tell me six impossible things before breakfast, I could appreciate the view. I let my gaze wander unchecked. The blond highlights twisting through the dark, brown strands didn't come from a bottle, but from actual time spent outside. His nose sported a small bump. Probably broken at some point. It didn't detract, instead complimented, the strong jaw line highlighted by his gold-streaked goatee.

The spark of heat from earlier made a comeback. Instead of squashing it, I let it burn, mentally shrugging my shoulders. At twenty-eight, the flash bang of sexual attraction no longer knocked me for a loop. I could be female enough to enjoy this moment without indulging. We would return to the horrifically gory reality waiting outside the cabin door soon enough. Besides, I didn't want to stop my visual study. Too much waited to take its place.

His black T-shirt failed to hide his defined muscles. It stretched across his broad shoulders to lie against his flat abdomen, before tucking into the waistband of his jeans. Almost every marine I ever met had some level of muscle definition—swimmer sleek or no-neck thick. Kayden managed to hit the sweet spot between lean and mean, and weightlifter.

I carried the tactile memory of mapping the sleek muscles under that broad chest. The tattoo I spotted earlier peeked under one sleeve. Dark tribal lines curled around a solid bicep. That was new. His skin held a burnished hint of sun, the color broken by scattered scars, the white marks telling their own stories. His long-fingered hands rested against his stomach, just above where his leather belt wrapped around a narrow waist. Long legs and scuffed desert combat boots completed the picture. No way anyone could mistake him for anything other than a straight-up warrior.

He shifted against the cushions and my gaze went to his face. He was watching me, the blue of his eyes had lightened to a storm-tossed gray. "I'd tell you take a picture, but you probably would."

I struggled to keep my blush from rising. It was a losing battle. "My camera's still packed."

"I saw some of your pictures in a gallery in San Diego, about a month ago."

I looked away, knowing which photos he was talking about. The same photos which led to my invite to chase the four-footed wildlife in Alaska.

"They were..."

When he trailed off, I finished, "Brutal?"

"Real." His correction brought my gaze back to his. "Some I recognized. You took while you were on tour?"

I gave a short nod.

"But the others?"

"Came after." After my discharge, when being home left me feeling displaced. It hadn't taken long to pack up my camera and head back where my nightmares roamed.

I hid the truth of my trip from Kelsey, telling her it was a proposed photo shoot for a national magazine. I spent seven long weeks retracing my steps over the shifting sands to those places and faces haunting my nightmares and my darkroom. The ravaged villages, shattered families, and hollow-eyed children may have disappeared, but their ghosts still walked the desert landscapes. The soldiers who tried to save them had paid a heavy price, sometimes too heavy. Someone had to bear witness.

"Why?"

"I had to finish what I started." My simplistic answer barely scratched the complex surface. Revisiting the past was one of many steps needed to move forward.

"Did you?"

Around the lump in my throat, I pushed out, "Yeah, for now." There were times when I thought I left the panic, the fear, and the uncertainty of choices I had made behind. Then, when I least expected it, they would sneak up and kick me in the ass.

"So why photography?"

"Safer to shoot a camera than a gun?" My statement switched to a question.

He slowly shook his head without raising it. "No, I've seen your records. You're a natural sharpshooter."

"Didn't discover that until I enlisted, but photography…" I turned away and stared at the ceiling before continuing. "I got my first camera right before I started high school, right after

Kelsey and I moved in with the Ardens." At the mention of my family, grief intruded. I kept my attention on the conversation.

"Your foster parents?"

"My parents," I corrected softly. "Becca and Carl Arden were the only parents I've ever had."

My past rose and it took a second before I could continue. "Carl had a friend, Eric, who would stop by and visit. Every time he came, he had a camera. He would traipse through Oak Canyon, taking picture after picture. I'd sneak out and follow, trying not to be seen." I smiled at the memory of stalking Eric through the high-desert terrain. "After a couple of weeks, he started handing me the camera, giving me pointers. I was hooked."

"Your parents didn't mind you tagging after their friend?"

My grin sharpened at the suspicion in his question. "Eric served under Carl when he first joined the marines. Kept in him one piece, Carl used to say before giving a huff and changing the subject. When I enlisted, Eric said it was his turn to keep Carl's daughter in one piece."

Understanding dawned. "Flash?"

I nodded, grateful to Kayden for reminding me of better times. "Yeah, he was a good soldier, but he was an even better artist with his camera. I learned a lot from him."

"So, you joined the marines because of Carl and Flash?"

I opened my mouth, and then closed it, really thinking about his question. *Had I?*

Yeah, probably.

The Ardens saved me, taking me in when no one else would, and I wanted to repay their belief in me. Before they came into the picture, I learned early on just how fucked the world could be. Seeing the world through my eyes left me on the brink of insanity. In an effort not to get committed, I kept my mouth shut. Most times. Only once had I broken my silence. Although when I did, it eventually led me to Kelsey, then the Ardens, the road there was a massive bitch.

My time in school didn't fare much better, my grades were meh, and friends were non-existent. Through photography, I found a way to watch the world from behind the safety of a lens. The camera allowed me to be part of the crowd and yet still keep my distance. The only time I set the camera down was with Kelsey, Becca, and Carl.

Even with the achingly familiar rapport rising between Kayden and I, old habits die hard. I couldn't share that with Kayden, not now. Too many broken promises stood between us, so instead, I went with a different answer. "Maybe, a little, but honestly, it was because of the GI Bill. With my grades, scholarships weren't an option. Serve four years with the marines and get a free education. At the time, it sounded good." Needing the spotlight off of me, I turned it around. "How about you? How'd you get into the Corps?"

"Did it on a dare."

"Seriously?"

"Yep, had a friend who dared me to join. Shocked us both when we both made it through." At my disbelieving snort, he raised an eyebrow. "What?"

"Never would have pegged you for someone who joined the most intensive military boot camp on a dare."

"Thought you had me figured out, huh?" he drawled. "Sorry to burst your bubble." A totally unrepentant grin appeared. "My mom's a nurse. Retired now. My dad still teaches history at the local college. Grew up pretty standard, small suburb in Southern California. Did the whole outdoor activity circuit; surfing, biking, skating."

"Yeah, I got that part." I had even teased him about it at one point.

He continued, "Senior year in high school, my buddy Zach ended up in the hospital after taking a spill on a motorbike.

When he got out, he had this bug up his ass about taking life by the horns. Somehow, we both ended up at the recruiter's office. Then it was off to San Diego."

"Your parents must have loved that."

He grimaced. "Mom took longer than Dad to accept it. I'm the first military in my family. I think they were hoping I'd outgrow my rebellious phase."

Hearing the love and respect as he talked about his family, reminded me of how much family meant to him. A bittersweet emotion rose, but I pushed it back. There was no reason to be jealous of Kayden, that was how family should be.

For a moment, I could feel Becca's arm around my waist, Carl's arm resting on my shoulders as Kelsey instructed us to *"Smile on three! One…two…three."* as we stood on cracked asphalt under the South Carolina sun after I completed boot camp at Parris Island. Sorrow and anger rose in a rushing wave. I turned away, threw an arm over my eyes, and tried to breathe around the pressure.

"Hey." Next to me, his weight shifted on the sofa, then a warm hand cupped the side of my face. "You with me?" Kayden's question was soft.

I forced myself to nod. When I dropped my arm and opened my eyes, I couldn't get my voice to work.

Kayden's face filled my field of vision. Concern and something else, something much more tempting, watched me.

I wrapped my fingers around his wrist, to hold him still or to pull him off, I wasn't sure. The flare of desire from earlier made a comeback, giving me something else to concentrate on. I tried to suck in some air, but he was too close. His uniquely male scent seeped under my skin, leaving trails of disturbing heat in its wake. Nerve endings sparked, and my pulse began a heavy anticipatory beat. Captured by the rising heat and awareness in his gaze, I couldn't look away.

He leaned forward, and I met him halfway. Our first touch

was tentative, as if we were testing the waters. I had forgotten how warm and firm his lips were. The brush of his goatee was a soft tease against my skin, layering my memories with something new. My fingers on his wrist tightened, my other hand curling into his T-shirt, holding him captive.

He brushed his lips across mine. I followed his tantalizing lead. When he gently nipped my bottom lip, I opened on a gasp. As if he had been waiting for the invite, he dove in. With devastating technique, he turned the questing kiss into a firestorm. His mouth taunted and teased, stoking my desire until it burned away the ragged edges of my grief and seared through every nerve ending.

Memories combined with the present, drawing me deeper, until all the reasons I shouldn't be doing this faded away. Lost in the heat, I answered his every demand. Content to let him lead, I followed every nip, every lick, every stroke until he groaned. The sound spiraled through me, slowing me down.

My hands rose and cupped his face, the contrast between his warm skin and the rasp of his goatee sent shivers cascading through me. I captured his bottom lip in a delicate bite and drew back slightly to watch his eyes darkened and his pupils dilate. I let go, only to soothe the spot with my tongue, before gently tracing the curving outline of his lips. I pulled him closer and sank into his mouth, his taste intoxicating, letting my tongue tease and taunt.

The sound of the electronic door lock being disengaged broke through the sensual spell. "Yo, anyone home?" Tag's voice rang down the short entry hall.

Kayden covered my hands with his, and pulled back slowly, resting his forehead against mine. Our chests rose and fell in tandem. I closed my eyes as he let go and moved away, leaving the couch to meet Tag. I needed to get my hormones back under control. *Dear God, that man could kiss.* My hand shook as I ran it over my tender lips.

Kayden was talking to Tag. "Where's your bag?"

"Back at the car, I wanted to make sure you guys were here first."

"Come on, let's go grab it." Kayden herded Tag back to the door.

Tag threw a look over Kayden's shoulder, his eyes narrowing on me, then he looked back at Kayden. "Everything okay?"

"Yeah. Let's just give Cyn a minute." Kayden didn't let go of Tag's arm as they went back to the front door.

When the door closed behind them, I let out an unsteady breath. What was I thinking? Letting Kayden back in wasn't smart. I needed to be part of what brought Kelsey's killer to justice and to do that I would need to prove my usefulness to their team. If I wanted to work with Tag and Kayden, I couldn't afford to screw things up by messing around with Kayden.

The first time we came together we tiptoed around whatever it was growing between us. Both of us knew damn good and well, a unit functioned properly only as long as its members knew their roles. Initially, I thought he held back because pursuing it would blur those lines and jeopardize the mission. After what he shared in the ride over, I wondered if that was the real reason, or if what I thought had been real was just another tactic to uncover a possible traitor.

Not that it mattered, not anymore.

I was honest enough to admit if this didn't stop now, it wouldn't be long before we ended up in a sweaty tangle of skin and sheets. According to my reawakened hormones, it would be a great short-term solution, but long term? It would take more than I was willing to pay.

Disgust spiraled through me. What the hell was I doing worrying about a non-existent relationship when there were other things I needed to face? My only priority should be stopping Ellery. I might have failed Kelsey in life, but I sure as hell wasn't going to fail her now.

Getting to my feet, I walked to the table where the file sat. I picked it up and headed to the kitchen. Scrounging around, I found a notebook and a couple of pens shoved in a drawer. The door opened, and Kayden came down the hall with Tag on his heels. Materials in hand, I stood in the entryway, watching them.

"We'll throw our stuff in the room on the left, Cyn can have the one on the right," Kayden directed as he grabbed the two duffels by the couch.

"Kayden," I called, stopping him from following Tag. "How much of this has been cleaned?" I held up the file.

"It hasn't."

"Really? You're actually going to share all the information with little ol' me?" *Sarcasm, it was the way of my people.*

Shifting his grip on the duffels, he sighed. "I warned Delacourt that giving you partial information would be the wrong move."

"Why? Because Ellery wants me dead, so I must not be the leak?" Low blow, but it served as a reminder, to both of us, of what brought us to here and now.

"I never thought you were the leak, Cyn."

"Whatever." I looked away, unsettled by his admission. "Do I have to sign something in blood before I open this?" No military or quasi-military outfit would grant full access without some sort of leverage.

Exasperation flashed across his face. "Read the file, then ask Delacourt whatever the hell you want." He turned and disappeared down the hall.

Refusing to acknowledge the flash of shame at provoking him, I headed to the small patio. I needed some privacy. I closed the French doors behind me, knowing the partially open blinds on the glass would let the guys know where I was without feeling like they were looking over my shoulder. Going through this file would be akin to walking through an emotional minefield. No way did I want either one of them witnessing resulting damage.

Two faded wooden Adirondack chairs sat on either side of a small, square table. I dropped into the first one and opened the file. A collection of garish photographs fell across the surface and tumbled into my lap. "Dammit."

I began gathering those that had fallen and setting them next to the others, trying hard not to really look at them yet. It wasn't until I picked up the one that had fallen half under my chair that I reconsidered being out here alone.

I stared at the horrific image as it shook in my hand. The twisted, burned body in glaring color snapped the chains holding back the past. Nausea and horror climbed the back of my throat, choking me. The sun-washed wilderness faded away only to be replaced by that cursed alley half a world away.

Night had fallen quick and hard in the desert. There were no streetlights offering pools of resistance in this two-camel town, only shifting shadows and shades of darkness.

Our eight-person team had split into two smaller teams of four, better to capture our target in a pincer move. My NVGs, night vision goggles, were a godsend, but they impeded peripheral awareness.

The four of us spread out, covering as many angles as we could as we moved in. Sound traveled, so we relied on silent hand gestures and maintained radio silence. Ortega took the lead with Tag on his heels. Behind me, Flash watched our six. Together we made our way into a narrow alley.

Crumbling mud walls stretched around us, blocking out what little moonlight existed. Our best vantage point lay at the ally's end, where the two buildings faced the open area of the small village and provided an optimal line of sight into the supposed meeting place. The other team, led by Kayden, should be making their way from the other side, cutting down the possible escape routes of our tango.

Instead of my camera, my hands were wrapped around my M162A. The camera would come out once we were in place. Uneasy, I kept my attention on the shifting shadows. Something felt off. We all knew it, but not one of us could pinpoint it. Unfortunately, until we could tag it and bag it, we were under orders.

We were almost to the end of the alley when death stepped forward and turned a simple operation into a nightmare.

Ortega went down first. The sharp crack of a sniper rifle echoed as his body crumpled to the ground. Shouted questions and the short, staccato pops of rifle fire came through the radios. Both teams were under attack.

Time warped, and shock froze me in place. Between one blink and the next, the heavy shadows resolved into black-clad assailants. The night erupted into harsh breathing, curses, and the heavy sound of flesh and bone meeting.

Chaos reigned.

I caught a brief glimpse of Tag struggling with two unknowns. Behind me, the sounds of fighting rose, merging with the clamor ringing in my ears. Then I was too busy trying to stay alive to notice anything else. I managed to block the first strike with my M162A, but the fucker I faced was stronger than I expected. Faster, too. Unnaturally so.

My rifle went flying as the brunt of the hit sent searing pain through my hand and wrist. My head rocked to the side with the next hit, and the din in my ear disappeared as my radio flew into the night. My world narrowed to a flurry of fists, kicks, and dodges. He matched every move I made, and it didn't take long to recognize his military training.

Covered in black material from head to toe, only his eyes were visible. Not that it did me any good. Darkness made it difficult to determine color. Taller, heavier, those things I could identify, but nothing else. His hits became progressively harder, striking vulner-

able parts of my body. They fell with such precision and accuracy, it wasn't long before he dropped my ass with a well-aimed kick to my thigh. The bone snapped under the blow and my vision whitened. I barely registered the next few strategically placed blows. Pain soared past any threshold I'd previously held and became all encompassing. When my head hit the ground, I lost track of time.

Sight winked in and out. The unrelenting bitch of pain turned my leg into a useless weight, and my ribs were their own vicious weapon, keeping my breaths shallow. My vision wavered, but not enough to miss Ortega's sightless eyes or the spreading pool of blood glistening like an oil slick around his head.

Frantic, I forced my hands under my chest and shoved. My right wrist crumpled, and fire lanced across my chest as I landed on damaged ribs. Searing agony triggered a choked scream. Panting, I forced myself to dig deep and keep going. Gravel bit into my damaged hands, but I managed to drag my body closer to Ortega.

"Ortega?" My voice shook, so did the crippled hand I pressed to his neck.

Nothing.

Cracks of gunfire punctuated the night. I lifted my head, hoping to locate the rest of the team. My vision wavered and twisted, but somebody lay at the head of the alley, motionless. My heart clenched.

Tag.

I couldn't tell if he was breathing or not. It didn't look good. Fear overrode my damaged body, and I dug my hands into the hard-packed dirt, prepared to drag myself toward him. Behind me a hoarse scream ripped through the night.

"God, no!"

I knew that voice. It raked against my panic and pain like razor blades. Petrified, but unable to stop, I rolled over, half-propped by Ortega to watch the horror unfolding behind me.

Part way down the alley, two men had someone pinned against the wall. My vision wavered, and then cleared. Flash was still being held in place while a third man moved to stand in front of him. Flickering light came from somewhere, illuminating the terror etching cruel lines across Flash's face.

The third man, dressed in black, with wide shoulders, removed his gloves, revealing pale skin that seemed to glow against the night. Flash continued to struggle against the other two. My mind tried to grasp the fact that a thin line of blue-white flames outlined Flash's arms without seeming to burn him.

"Go ahead and fight, Captain, I don't mind." The perverse enjoyment in the voice chilled my soul. He raised his bare hands to cup Flash's face, breaking the line of the blue-white flames.

There was no way to see what changed, but those horrific flames surged, turning solid white, then changing bit by bit to yellow. Yet neither Flash nor his assailant burned. Not yet. Those flames weren't normal. What was he using? Why couldn't I see his weapon?

I shoved my questions away, knowing if I didn't do something now, they would kill my friend, my mentor, in front of me. I searched Ortega's body for a weapon and came up empty as my heart raced. With no gun readily available, I reached down my damaged leg and found my knife. With my vision swimming, my hand broken, and terror screaming through my veins, throwing it wasn't smart, but I was out of options. I aimed for the one holding Flash's face. I must have made some noise because the man closest to me looked up.

Then my knife did the impossible. It stopped in mid-air as if running into an invisible barrier and dropped to the ground.

My mind stumbled.

A dark chuckle cut through the night.

The flames went from yellow to a hellish, reddish orange and Flash began to scream.

The sound. Dear God, as if he was being ripped apart from the inside out. The flames cast Flash's face in an unearthly nimbus of fire. His screams increased, driving me forward.

Harsh sobs wracked my body. Then the smell drifted toward me. I began to gag as the sickening odor of burning flesh replaced the dust-dried air. Horror engulfed me even as Flash became the wick in a *grisly pyre, the fire painting macabre shadows on the surrounding mud walls.*

The two holding him stepped away, but the third still held his face, his hands untouched by the flames.

I blinked away the darkness edging my vision and fought to stay conscious. "Flash! No! Stop! Please!" It didn't matter how much I begged, the nightmare continued.

When the only screams left were the ones in my head, the third man turned and walked toward me, slow, deliberate. As he got closer, his body blocked out what was left of Flash. He crouched in front of me and a flickering light to my left caught my gaze. I stared at his right hand as it dripped blue-tinged flames.

"Your turn." He reached out to touch my face.

I jerked backward, but my battered body was slow to respond.

His hand moved closer until a mere breath separated our skin. It wasn't enough. He traced a torturous line from my cheek and down my neck, to my shoulder. The heat from his burning hand left melted skin and material in his wake.

My screams pierced the night, then nothing.

Chapter Seven

The sound of the door opening behind me brought me back into the present. Too busy hiding my nightmare, I didn't turn.

"Cyn? You good?"

At Tag's question, I managed a jerky nod.

He stepped out onto the small porch and closed the door behind him. His shadow blocked the light of the afternoon as a glass of water appeared in front of my face.

Setting the photo face down on the table, I took his offering.

He crossed in front of me to the other chair. He sat down without a word, setting a second glass on the table. A brittle silence settled between us. Finally, he broke it. "Are you going to ignore me?"

"Will it work?" My question was short, because I was still shaking from my trip down memory lane and the jumble of emotions crashing in its wake.

"Nope." He slumped down, stretching his legs out in front of him. He folded his hands on his stomach and frowned, concern clear on his face. "You're looking a little pale."

My fingers tightened around the sweating glass. "What do you want, Tag?"

"I know you're pissed."

I met his gaze and said nothing.

He sighed, then his chin rose, a clear indication he was about to get stubborn. "I'm not going away until you talk to me."

"Why?"

Puzzled, he asked, "Why what?"

"Why now?"

His lips thinned and his gaze hardened. "Harder for you to ignore me when I'm in your face. Since you refuse to take my calls, you've left me no other option. So, we're going to clear the air once and for all."

I opened my mouth, but the words died before they could escape. I closed my mouth and then rubbed a hand over my face. He was right, it was time to talk. Even Kelsey had pushed for me to reach out before I left on my last job. My heart clenched. I breathed through the ache, as I examined the part of me that didn't want to have this conversation, so much so it was smothering the urge to rail at him for keeping things from me. That reluctance pulled me up short.

Why couldn't I get the words out? The questions were simple. *What psychic ability do you have, Tag? Why didn't you tell me? Why'd you leave me?*

They were trapped in silence. What held them back? What could he say that I hadn't considered in the last six months? Would finding out his ability change things for me?

I hadn't shared my lovely little quirk in all the years we had known each other, so why should I expect him to share? Digging deeper under my superficial excuses and protective anger, I found an ugly truth.

I was scared and jealous.

Jealous that Tag and Flash were chosen to be part of something without me. Even though I hid my ability for years in an effort to be 'normal', there was no doubt Tag's answers now would redefine my idea of normal. But even more intimidating, I was scared. Scared he would blame me for things I knew were my fault. Scared he wouldn't blame me. If we aired everything, would I recognize my oldest friend after everything was said and done? With Kelsey gone, my relationship with Tag was my last, steady anchor. I didn't want to find out how much of it was an illusion. If he wasn't who I thought he was, I was in trouble.

Suck it up, Cyn. Running never did a damn thing for you. My little pep talk couldn't calm the fissures of insecurity spreading through me like a spider web. Taking a deep breath, I decided to wade in. "Fine, what is it you can do?"

"I'm a touch empath."

I blinked a few times, processing. That little spark of electricity when he touched me at the cabin. It was such a typical occurrence around him, I hadn't given it a second thought. Now, though… "You're a human lie detector?" An underlying accusation wove through my question.

His easygoing expression disappeared behind a blank mask and his negligent slouch straightened. "Yeah." No excuses.

"Would you have ever told me?"

"Why? So, you could wonder if I read you every time I touched you?"

"Do you?"

"Do I what?" he growled.

"Crawl around my head each time you touch me?" As soon as the question hit the air, I wanted to call it back. It was a childish taunt, one brought to life by hurt feelings, but like any taunt it found its mark.

He covered his flinch pretty quick before anger had him leaning across the small table and grabbing my chin, holding me captive so I couldn't look away. "I don't crawl around anything, Arden, ever."

Behind his bitter words was a glimpse of a familiar fear. Instead of jerking away, which is what he probably expected me to do, I curled my fingers around his wrist to hold him in place. "Fine, then tell me how it works." My voice was surprisingly level.

The pressure of his fingers against my chin relaxed, and then disappeared. He twisted his wrist until I let go, then leaned back. "I read emotions. Touch makes the reception clearer."

What would it be like to know exactly what someone thought of you? Considering how hard he was hiding his reactions right now, my guess is it would royally suck. "Does that mean it's constantly on, or is there an off switch?"

"I've figured a few ways to keep the noise down." He played with the glass in front of him. "My control has increased since I joined PSY-IV."

The mention of his current employer spiked my infantile jealousy. "Lucky you."

His restless movements stilled, and then he looked up and frowned. "After Flash's death it didn't take much to put two and two together. I had been approached by Delacourt, and then those bastards targeted Flash. Considering how he died..." he shook his head. "Besides, your gut feelings turned out too freakin' right too many times. Add in the fact at logic indicated at least two of us had abilities, it didn't take long to figure out you were in our unit for a reason." He leaned forward, and his eyes reflected the same hurt swirling in my chest. "You never said a word. What was I supposed to think?"

The raw emotion in his question pulled the rug out from under my tumultuous emotions, leaving me exposed. The past crowded too close, and I had to cough a couple of times to clear the lump in my throat. "You left me." My unexpected accusation squeezed out, shocking us both. "You blamed me." Now that the words were free, I couldn't stop them. "After Flash's death, everyone disappeared. I get Liza, Nate, and Mike, maybe even Kayden. But you?" My voice cracked.

Stunned comprehension dawned and he reached out in a recognizable attempt to comfort. The minute he touched the back of my hand the little zing reappeared. "Jesus, Cyn, I never blamed you for the attack." He cocked his head. "But you blame yourself, it's why you won't talk to me."

I flinched. Hoping to block his too perceptive ability, I pulled my hand out from under his. "You all left me in the dark."

"I was in the hospital for two months. As for the others..." He shook his head, his gaze narrowing. "Nope, that excuse isn't going to work this time. You're going to tell me what you think you could have done to change what happened."

I tightened my lips, refusing to look at him.

"Tell me what you think you could have done differently with a punctured lung, third degree burns, broken ribs, shattered femur, a broken wrist, and broken fingers? Oh wait, let's not forget the concussion." By the time he was done listing my injuries his voice had deepened into a growl. "What could you have done, Cyn?"

"I shouldn't have thrown the damn knife!"

We sat there, my words ringing between us.

Confusion twisted his face. "What are you talking about?"

"Ellery had Flash pinned to the wall, but the flames, they weren't burning him. They changed colors, but it wasn't until I threw the knife that it all changed. Until then, Flash was okay." I rubbed a hand over my aching chest. "He was okay."

"No, he wasn't." Kayden's voice came from behind me, causing me to start in my chair. He went to lean against the railing, facing Tag and me. "Flash was a pyrokinetic. What you saw was Ellery's ability in action."

Kayden's revelation confirmed my burgeoning suspicions. "Ellery's psychic?"

Kayden nodded. "He's what we call a Syphon. Someone who absorbs other psychic abilities. What you saw that night? The flames changing colors? Did they go from bluish white to yellow to orange?"

Stunned, all I could do was nod.

"Ellery was syphoning Flash's ability. It didn't matter what you did, Cyn, Flash couldn't fight indefinitely." He looked at the file on the table. "When you read the file, you'll realize Ellery's getting more and more creative at how he steals abilities."

My gut clenched. *This* was the monster hunting me? "Why didn't anyone tell me?"

"Hello? Hospital for two months, remember?" Tag said. "When I got out, you wouldn't talk to me."

Looking between both men, I knew it all had to come out. If I didn't lance this wound, there would be no working together to stop Ellery. To let things go and move on, I needed answers. "No one would tell me where you all were, or what had happened. I woke up in Landstuhl and the higher-ups wanted answers. I couldn't tell them what happened. It didn't even make sense to me. Ellery wasn't talking to anyone, not even his lawyer."

I rubbed my hands down my thighs. "All I knew was Flash and Ortega were dead, you and the others were out of touch. I didn't even know the information on the delivery system was still missing until the actual trial. I tried to reach out, but when no one answered I knew what was coming. Someone had to answer for the op going sideways, and I was the only one standing before the panel. It wasn't like I had options."

"You wouldn't have been answering alone if I could've been there," Tag offered.

Maybe, maybe not, but not wanting to ruffle the tenuous

truce, I blew out a harsh breath. "I still don't know how they got Ellery into custody."

"Liza warned us something was off," Kayden said. "It took time to clear out the two snipers nests. By then, all hell was breaking loose on your end." His gaze flickered to my scars. "When we hit your position, Ellery was so focused on you, he didn't get a chance to get away. We took out his partners and took him into custody. After turning him over, we were sent back out to retrieve the missing information."

"You never found it." I could tell.

He shook his head.

"I didn't leave you, Cyn. You left me." Tag's quiet comment wasn't quite an accusation, but it still felt like one.

"You left the team," Kayden added. "When we got back, you were already gone. Tag said you weren't answering your calls. We figured you wanted nothing to do with us, so we steered clear."

"What a mess." Lowering my head, I acknowledge the truth in what they said. For the first time in six months, the resentful anger and hurt I lived with began to recede. My choices were clear. Either I continued to blame Tag and Kayden for a shitty situation, or I accepted my culpability and moved on.

Run, or stand and fight?

I was tired of running. Kelsey deserved justice, so did Liza, Mike, and Nate. It was time to face the nightmares and fight back.

At Tag and Kayden's urging, I moved back inside to the larger, kitchen table where there was more space to spread out the gory details contained in the file. During my years in the service, I witnessed things I wish I hadn't, the images forever branded on my cerebral cortex. Those images took turns starring in some of my more inventive nightmares. During those nights, sleep was a stranger, but whiskey was my best friend. After wading through the most recent reports, the photos only added to my certainty that human cruelty knew no bounds. The more deviant the imagination, the more brutal the outcome.

Working past the initial repulsive horror, I started comparing the coroner's reports against the crime scene photos. As I laid out the phots in sequential order, the angles of the shots allowed me to follow the evidentiary collection of the crime scene techs. When I hit the last report, complete with photos, I sucked in a breath.

Captain Eric "Flash" Fowler.

My stomach cramped, but I carefully set the items in place. Hard didn't begin to cover how it felt to see the familiar face spread across on the marred wooden surface. Absently, I rubbed the itchy sensation running along the scar lines on my neck. As difficult as it was, I spent a few minutes letting the chaotic mix of anger, grief, rage, and pain storm rage before clearing my head to focus.

Counting Kelsey, we were looking at eight confirmed victims and one missing person. Flash had been killed first. Then there were the two guards during Ellery's escape mid-transport, before he focused on the joint team.

Sergeant Major Michael Layton was killed just over two months ago. Layton was Flash's friend. I remember Flash mentioning they had a fishing trip planned once our last mission was in the box. Then, closing in on five weeks ago, Staff Sergeant Nathan Visic was found. Three weeks later, the bodies of First Sergeant Elizabeth Gaskey and Senior Chief Petty Officer Jeff Gomez, were discovered.

"What was Liza doing with Navy?" I asked.

"Dating," Tag answered.

"Really? Wow, could've sworn hell would have frozen over before that happened." Elizabeth had completed basic with me and Tag before joining a different team. Since women tended to disappear the higher you moved in the marines, we stayed in sporadic touch until we reconnected on our last assignment.

"Yeah, things were going really well, she was happy."

Now she was dead, and, from what the pictures showed, it hadn't come easy. After the guards, the crime scenes turn progressively more vicious and brutal, a sure sign Ellery was relishing the pain and agony of his victims. At least until Kelsey. As sickening as his actions were, at least he'd made it quick for her.

Staring at the mutilations listed on each report, I wasn't sure I could have held it together if he had taken his time with her like he had with the rest. My hand shook as I pulled my notebook closer and began to make notes.

Based on locations, it seemed Ellery had been making the rounds of the west coast. When Jeff hadn't reported back to base in San Diego after weekend leave, one of his buddies went to the Marina to check his boat. He found the savaged remains of Liza and Jeff instead. According to the coroner's report, Liza's eyes had been gouged out with a small blade. She then endured another day or two of torture before succumbing to her injuries. Jeff was just as bad. His body was a patchwork of third degree burns and various cuts.

Nate was found early in the morning, nailed to the side of a building in a seedier section of Coronado. Death arrived in a slit throat, but his body was riddled with various sharp objects, presumably pulled from a nearby trash bin. Pipes, nails, pens, glass—whatever could double as knife.

When Michael's abandoned fishing boat was found stalled in the middle of San Francisco Bay, the Coast Guard called out a search. It took four days to recover his body. Even though the aquatic life used him as a buffet, it was determined his fingers had been removed prior to death. Additional burns and cuts were identified, leading to the conclusion that he, too, was tortured before death claimed him.

Finished with the reports, I reviewed my notes. Nothing much jumped out at me. Very little was found by way of trace evidence, which probably explained why, until he'd hooked up with me, Kayden hadn't been certain it really was Ellery. As for me, I didn't have any doubts. Every death in this file made it very clear Ellery was out for payback.

The guys had left me alone. Kayden keeping a low conversation with Tag as they sprawled on the couch. Whatever they were talking about didn't slow Tag's fingers as they flew over the laptop balanced on his legs. Needing more details than what was in the file, I cleared my throat to get their attention. Their conversation stopped and they both looked at me. "What were their abilities?"

Kayden answered first. "Liza was a pre-cog." Catching my puzzlement, he clarified, "She was able to see possible future events. Mike healed by touch."

"Nathan?"

"He could move small objects."

"Telekinetic." Nice to be able to name one psychic ability. Propping my arm on the table, I rested my chin in my hand, trying to wrap my head around a world where fortunetellers and healers were your next-door neighbors. "And Jeff?"

This time it was Tag who answered. "He didn't have an ability."

"He was collateral damage," Kayden added, a grimness settling over his face.

My stomach sank. "Like Kelsey, then, an opportunity kill. Somebody to use to get what he wants."

Trying to understand Ellery's mind would require more information than what I currently had access to, so I really hoped Delacourt came prepared with some answers. In the meantime, I studied the impromptu timeline in front of me. Ellery escaped five months ago but killed Mike only a couple months back. "Why did Ellery wait so long?" I wondered aloud.

Kayden heard and asked, "For what?"

"To go after Mike." I got up and started pacing between the table and the couch, doing my best to burn off some of my restlessness. On the couch, Tag continued working on his laptop, but Kayden shifted to watch me. I rubbed the back of my neck as I moved. "What was Ellery doing for three months?"

"Retrieving the missing information?" Kayden suggested.

It almost felt right. "Three months to pull it out from wherever he hid it? That seems a bit long."

"Maybe, but remember, the investigators are pretty sure one of the guards managed to shoot him, so if he was injured, he'd have to hole up."

"Okay, but if he was injured, wouldn't he go after Mike first, then retrieve the information? If Ellery sucks up psychic abilities and Mike was a healer, wouldn't Ellery be inclined to fix himself before moving on?"

"If Ellery was injured, there's no way in hell he'd risk taking on Mike." Tag didn't bother looking up from his laptop. "Hand to hand, Mike could take almost anyone down."

Shit, Tag was right. Besides fishing, Mike enjoyed moonlighting in bouts of mixed martial arts. Nixing that line of logic, I forged ahead. "Fine, let's say it took Ellery a month to get his hands on the information. What's his next move?"

"Selling it." Kayden leaned back, tucked his hands behind his head and narrowed his gaze at the ceiling. "Chances are his initial buyers pulled out after things went tits up. We all know there's no shortage of interested parties for experimental viral weapons, so it wouldn't take much to set up new ones."

True. "How long would that take?"

Tag lifted his head, his attention zeroing in on me as I

paced. "Considering you have to get word out to attract the right kind of attention—"

"More like wrong kind of attention," I corrected.

He grinned. "And you can't rely on standard phone calls and emails, it could easily take a month or so to set up communications with middlemen or with the buyers directly." He shared a look with Kayden. "With what Ellery was offering, the need to stay under the radar would be vital to staying alive."

I stopped and looked between the two men. "What am I missing?"

Kayden grimaced and Tag ducked his head, fingers resuming their dance over the keyboard.

Kayden finally spoke up. "Ask Delacourt."

My hands went to my hips, and I narrowed my gaze. "How much information is she holding?"

"Enough." Kayden shot a look at the clock. "She'll be here soon, so you can pester her to your heart's content then." He sat up and stretched. "In the meantime, I'm hungry. Let's order dinner."

Not the most subtle of conversation changers, but since I wasn't sure my stomach could handle anything, I let them argue the merits of pizza versus hamburgers without chiming in. I went back to the table and my notebook, determined to get my questions ready.

Delacourt would be here soon, and when she showed up, I wanted answers.

Chapter Eight

Sometime later, a sharp knock on the door jerked my head up and brought Tag and Kayden's conversation to a halt. I shot a startled glance at the clock. Nine o'clock.

While I was still processing the interruption, Tag set his laptop on the coffee table, and then moved down the hall, gun down by his side. Kayden took up residence in the kitchen, just out of sight of the front door. A taut silence filled the cabin.

A second knock sounded, followed by a curt, "Gunderson, open up."

As Tag undid the locks on the door, I scrambled to my feet. In the kitchen, Kayden tucked his gun into the waistband of his faded jeans and moved into the hall.

"Sir." Respect colored Tag's voice. I caught his movement through the kitchen opening as he stood aside letting our visitor step inside.

"Your dinner, I presume?" The rustle of paper bags preceded the aroma of grilled beef and French Fries.

Six months wasn't long enough to squash my automatic response to the sound of Colonel Delacourt's voice. By the time she entered the room, I was at parade rest with my face carefully blank.

At five foot seven, Delacourt had an inch on me, but her mere presence still made me feel small. Silver streaked her short cap of dark hair and there were more lines around her slightly tilted eyes. Somewhere along the line, Delacourt's family boasted some Asian flare. In uniform or out, she breathed command. Ever since we first met on a dusty soccer field doubling as a temporary base, she intimidated me. However, thanks to the circumstances surrounding our last meeting, intimidation was no longer my primary emotional response.

"Arden." The rough slide of her voice remained unchanged. "Nice to see you."

Polite, I had to be polite. "Wish I could say the same, sir." Okay, I'd settle for civil. "Considering the situation." I winced at my lame attempt to temper my attitude.

Her lips twitched, and her unexpected sign of humor threw me for a loop. "Here." She handed a large paper bag to Tag. "Don't let me keep you from your dinner." With her hands free, she shrugged a leather satchel from her shoulder.

Kayden tucked the photos and papers into a hasty pile, making room for Tag to set out our food. With the file somewhat back together, I went to set it aside, only to stop when Delacourt held out her hand. "Do you mind?"

I handed it over. She commandeered the plush chair next to the couch. Its position allowing her to watch the three of us as we settled down to eat.

Before I could take a bite, the manners Becca spent years drumming into my head came to the fore. "Sir, would you like to join us? I won't be able to eat all of this. You're welcome to half of it."

"No, thank you, I ate earlier." She stopped straightening the papers in the file and looked up. Her lips twitched. "I'm no longer your commanding officer, Arden, I think we can dispense with the 'sir'."

"Yes, sir," I mumbled, then proceeded to take a bite of my cheeseburger. My concern about not being able to eat proved unfounded when my stomach woke up with a low grumble.

For a few minutes the quiet of the cabin filled with the rustle of paper and hamburger wrappers, broken by the occasional, "Could you pass me that?"

"I suppose you have questions for me?" Delacourt's voice burrowed past my preoccupation with my cheeseburger.

I swallowed my latest bite. "A few." Wiping my face with tissue paper masquerading as a napkin, I pushed the other half of my dinner away, and then pulled over my list of questions.

Delacourt's husky laugh brought my head up. "Nice to see some things never change." She motioned to the notebook. "Your lists were infamous."

Seriously? I shot Tag a look and sure enough, the man was grinning like a fool. I squirmed. "What? If I don't write it down, I might forget what I wanted to ask."

Ketchup covered French Fry halfway to his mouth, he said, "And that would be a tragedy."

"Bite me." I turned my attention back to Delacourt and braced. My questions would serve as a test of sorts, a way to see how much information I could get out of her before she shut me down. "Okay, I need to go over a couple of things to make sure I have this straight." Taking her nod as confirmation, I continued, "You identify potential psychics by a collection of personality tests given during recruitment?"

"Not me," she corrected, pulling me up short.

I blinked. "Not you, what?"

"I don't give the tests. As a matter of fact, the names of confirmed psychics are shared on a need-to-know basis with specific commanding officers based on unit placements. The tests are given to all recruits and is proctored by a joint committee."

No surprise there, everyone would want a piece of the psychic pie. "Let me guess, the joint committee is made up of representatives from each military branch?"

She inclined her head. "Plus, a couple of other interested parties."

I squashed the urge to follow the rabbit hole and held kept my questions on track. "So, the names of the psychic units are not common knowledge?"

"No."

"What about who works in your unit?"

Her fingers began a slow rhythm on the chair arm. "That decision falls to me and my leadership team."

"And the names of those working for you?" I pressed.

"Need to know basis."

Even the clear reluctance in her voice couldn't get me to back down now. As she pointed out earlier, I no longer answered to a commanding officer. "If that's the case, it means someone close to you had to leak the names connected with our last mission, correct?"

Her head jerked as if I had physically slapped her. Her eyes narrowed. "Excuse me?"

"You ran the joint team, correct? Which means Ellery either had the best luck in the world, or someone in the know gave him a heads up we were coming. That would lead me to believe someone close to you was compromised."

Her hazel eyes flashed and the lines around her mouth whitened. "Or Ellery was given the information by someone with a much bigger agenda."

My thoughts stumbled over that unexpected piece of information. "Wait, what?"

"Do you think the U.S. Military is the only one who's thought of utilizing psychics?" She arched a brow. "Six years ago, Ellery's name came up for consideration for PSY-IV. He didn't make the cut." She uncrossed and re-crossed her legs, her unusually restless movement revealing her discomfort. "However, that doesn't mean he wasn't approached by another interested party. One whose goals don't align with ours."

"A psychic version of 'Come to the dark side'?" It made sense, in a twisted sort of way.

Tag choked on a bite as he tried to smother a laugh.

Even Delacourt's lips twitched. Barely. "Instead of cookies, they offer money and power."

"For a price."

"For a price," she agreed.

Implications, scary and too numerous to count, swirled around that bit of information. Dragging my brain back on track, I decided to pursue a different avenue. "Why didn't he make the cut?"

Something grim wiped away her brief show of humor, leaving it shadowed. "His ability was deemed too unreliable to be an asset to the unit."

"Why?" How did one determine a psychic ability 'unreliable'? Since mine appeared to have a mind of its own for the most part, it was easy to assume most abilities would be considered 'unreliable'.

"Judging psychic ability isn't easy, and no matter how much we want to try and explain it, it's not a science, not yet," she explained. "When Ellery's ability came to light under evaluation, it registered on the lower end. Unfortunately, we learned the hard way that his particular talent grows and evolves with use."

She templed her fingers under her chin. "Abilities can vary equally in strength and inherent weaknesses. Some will exact a steeper cost than others." Her glance slid over Tag and Kayden who were quietly listening to our conversation. "For example, a strong touch empath can lose his sense of self in another's emotions. That fear will keep them from physically touching another person."

Tag shifted in his chair, but I kept my attention on Delacourt.

"A seer," she continued, "may fall so deep into the maze of possible futures, her mind will fracture. Whereas someone who is a pre-cog will see only an individual's immediate future based on their most recent choices, so the chances of a mental break are much, much lower. Healing empaths will take on grievous wounds, and the price they'll pay is sacrificing a percentage of their life expectancy. Yet, the flip side of that deal is that they can't heal themselves. The ability to create fire can literally burn a pyrotechnic from the inside out if the wielder loses control."

My stomach roiled at the picture painted by her words. "And for Ellery?"

"Schizophrenia." This time it was Kayden who answered, his voice hard. "There's a reason his designation is Syphon. When he drains his victims, he not only absorbs their ability, but takes in bits and pieces of what makes them *them*. As he collects abilities, the lines between his personality and those of his victims start to blur until there are so many voices in his head, he can no longer hear his own."

My cheeseburger threatened to make a comeback. Worried the slightest movement might encourage it, I held still. It took serious concentration to breathe through the nauseating paralysis as the reality of the dangers I faced set in. "Was Ellery using Mike's ability to try and heal himself?"

"It's a possibility," Delacourt said. "But if he did, it didn't help."

"It made it worse," Kayden supplied.

The concept that I was being hunted by a schizophrenic sociopath had poisonous fear seeping under my skin, burrowing through bone and sinew, only to sink its fangs deep.

You've survived worse, my survival instinct whispered.

Barely.

Obviously unhappy with my lack luster response and eager to prove his point, the stubborn little bastard started a twisted game of *This Is Your Life*, complete with a series of disturbing and painful vignettes inhabiting my past.

First to emerge, a pale, dark-haired child sitting on neatly painted porch steps, clutching a paper bag filled with clothes, while a woman huddled behind a screen door and screamed at the police. *"Get her out of here, she's not natural."*

Next was the endless tour of foster homes and therapists, where no one could reach the strange little girl trapped in her silent world.

Then when I met Kelsey, who turned out to be a godsend. She got through where all the adults failed. We became inseparable. Together, we navigated the trials and tribulations of inattentive and, sometimes, too attentive, foster families until the Ardens had stepped up.

The years skipped forward until desert vistas and chaos dominated the scenes, culminating in the nightmare of Flash's death. His screams blended with Kelsey's fresh cries still echoing in my mind.

Fine, dammit, yes, I had survived worse. But here I was, arguing with the voices in my head.

A touch on my arm interrupted my interior dialog. Kayden. Uncomfortable, I jerked my arm away. He opened his mouth to say something, but frustrated and anxious, I flattened my palms against the table and shoved to my feet. The legs of the chair scraped over the tiles with a harsh screech. Delacourt and Tag watched, their faces carefully blank. "I need a minute," I muttered, not making eye contact.

I pulled open the French doors and stepped on to the night-shrouded patio. Gripping the wooden railing, I concentrated on the bite of the rough wood against my palms and sucked in the desert air. The scent of damp earth from the nearby creek was overlaid with the spice of desert wildflowers. The combination helped corral my memories, pushing them back in the box where they belonged. I heard someone approach but didn't turn around.

Delacourt came up beside me, close, but with enough space between us to keep me from feeling crowded. "Becca always loved Sedona. I used to tease her that she loved it more than Carl."

The implications of her comment took a moment to register. "You knew them?"

"Met Carl when I first joined the Corps. Years later, before you and Kelsey joined them, he introduced me to Becca. She was one of the few females who didn't find me strange for pursuing a military command. She called me courageous." Her soft laugh drifted into the night. "I told her it took more courage to marry a marine than to be one. She just laughed."

"She would," I murmured, lifting my face to the night sky. "They loved each other so much. Kels and I were grateful they went together. We weren't sure one would survive without the other."

"They wouldn't have left either of you girls, if they had a choice."

Her unexpected offer of comfort tightened my throat. I dropped my head. "Thanks." The word squeezed past the lump lodging in my throat. My brain continued to chew over things and bit-by-bit, pieces clicking into place. With as close as she had been to Carl and Becca, she had to have known about me. I broke the quiet between us. "You knew, didn't you? Even before the test."

"Yes."

I tried not to flinch. I spent years doing my best to hide what I could do from my adoptive parents, worried they would leave me like all those before them. It took time to realize Kelsey and I were safe with the Ardens. Once I began to believe that I brutally shoved my ability down, refusing to see what it could offer, more afraid it would ruin everything. For the six years I lived under the Ardens' roof, wallowing in the precious peace I found. It never occurred to me that my parents had seen right through it. "How long?"

"Your question needs to be more specific if you want to understand the answer you seek."

Her Zen-like rebuke set my teeth on edge. "Fine, at what point did Carl tell you about me?"

"Your senior year in high school." Delacourt turned until her back rested against the porch rail and set her elbows on the edge. "Once Carl and Becca realized you were going to go to the marines, they worried, so they reached out to Flash and me. Carl had pulled some strings and managed to get ahold of your juvenile records. What he found raised some serious concerns."

A sickening blow of betrayal weakened my knees, until the railing was the only thing holding me up. Those records had been sealed for a reason. Suspicion lifted its ugly head. *Had it all been a lie? The smiles, the acceptance, the love? Was it real?*

A bead of cold sweat ran down the side of my face, using the lace-like scar patterns as its path. If I let go of the railing to wipe it away, I'd end up on the ground, so I held tight.

"Arden, stop!" Her sharp command acted like a slap, knocking me out of the dark spiral. "They loved you. You and Kelsey both. Don't you ever doubt it, girl."

I had no idea how she managed to see through my emotional mess, but I grabbed onto her reassurance like a drowning child. They loved me, I knew they had. With every word and every action, they proved they saw me as someone worth loving, repeatedly. Throwing it all away now because my world was in the midst of remaking itself, was a piss poor way to honor that.

Forcing my fingers to uncurl, I turned and mimicked her position. "I know." The words were shaky. "I know they did, sir." This time they were stronger. "What did Carl find out?"

"It wasn't what, it was who he talked to; Officer Payton and Audrey Peltier."

The names seared through my brain, triggering lightning flashes of memories. The young, picture-perfect couple who picked the quiet, green-eyed, dark-haired girl with the mysterious past. Older and cynical, it was easy to recognize Audrey Peltier's belief she would find her way through my emotional walls and uncover the daughter she always wanted. Instead, she lost her husband, her dream family, and ended up in psychiatric ward on suicide watch. I refused to say anything until I heard exactly what Delacourt knew. I met her gaze, raised my chin, and kept my mouth shut.

Her small, sad smile came and went. "Hell of a thing for a child to discover."

Forcing my shoulders to move in a negligent shrug, I shared a hard-earned truth. "Monsters come in all shapes and sizes."

"True." She stared into the cabin where Kayden and Tag still sat at the table, probably in an attempt to give us some semblance of privacy. "Carl spoke to Payton. Seems he remembers the incident quite clearly. It took Carl awhile to get him to share his version."

I grimaced. "It didn't match up with the official record."

Her attention didn't stray from the cabin's interior. "No, it didn't." She didn't wait for a response. "According to him, he accompanied a caseworker out to the home of a hysterical young woman claiming the child they were considering adopting was a demon. He and the caseworker arrived at the house to find a six-year-old girl, sitting on the front porch, clutching a paper bag. The scared-looking woman locked behind the screen door held a crucifix."

Etched into my brain with painful clarity, I didn't need Delacourt's recital of events to remember that day. When the caseworker's nondescript sedan had pulled into the driveway, closely followed by a black and white patrol car, all I had felt was relief. A short-lived relief, it turned out, because as I headed down the porch steps, Mr. Peltier pulled in behind them. I remember the choking fear and panic that cemented my feet to the porch steps. The flimsy shield of the paper bag with all my things clutched to my chest. My mind screaming at me to run, but my small body refusing to obey.

Through the sucking morass of memory, Delacourt's rough voice continued, "It seems the woman had called her husband, who rushed home to be with her. A great deal of confusion and yelling ensued, so Payton took the child to his car. He told Carl when he opened the door, the little girl had whispered something. Since he couldn't hear her, he crouched down and asked her to repeat what she said. She looked at him with spookiest eyes he'd ever seen, and said—"

"He got mad and hit Sara." I repeated those long-ago words. "When she didn't get up, he buried her in the garden." I finished in a low tone.

The world went quiet. For a moment, I was six and terror's cruel hands were wrapped around my chest. But six was a damn long time ago, no matter how close it felt. I cleared my throat and shared the rest of the story. "A few years before, Peltier had kidnapped a local girl, Sara Colton, when his wife was out of town. He lost his temper when she struggled, and he killed her before hiding her in the garden. The case was all over the news."

Delacourt turned to me, the shadows failing to hide her sharp gaze. "Payton worked that case. There was no connection between Peltier and the Coltons, no link. Without your help, Peltier would have gotten away with it."

Old, familiar bitterness broke through. "Audrey Peltier probably wishes he had."

Her mouth opened, but after a moment, it closed. We both knew there was no response for that little gem.

I rubbed my face and when I dropped my hands, I said, "The only way the authorities could make the whole situation understandable was to claim I had seen something, or that Peltier had attacked me and let something slip." My smile was all teeth. "Because everyone knows there's no other explanation."

"Carl believed Payton." Delacourt paused. "Carl believed in you."

Her statement hung in the air. The hastily erected walls holding my grief back crumbled under the unwavering conviction in her voice. Ignorant of the verbal sucker punch she had just delivered, Delacourt shook her head at my silence and stepped back into the cabin, leaving me alone.

I turned my back to the lighted interior and faced the darkness. Overwhelming waves of heartache and guilt rose, swallowing everything in their path. I clenched my teeth, trapping harsh sobs in my chest. Gut wrenching pain hollowed out my stomach, and I wrapped my arms around my waist, hunching over. Gasping with silent sobs, I acknowledged I had failed the last of my family, the only people who had seen me as someone worth saving.

I had been unable to keep them safe.

I had been out of the country when the drunk driver had slammed Carl and Becca's car off the road. And Kelsey... oh god!

My legs went loose, and I slid to the deck. The image of Kelsey's grim acceptance of her impending death would haunt me forever. Useless, scalding tears fell.

For years, it seemed no matter where I turned, monsters waited and took everything. For a while, I allowed the Ardens to convince me safety lay with your family. Memories swirled and gathered—Carl's quiet strength, Becca's unconditional love, Kelsey's laughter—together they gave me a protective light to hold back the dark. Now that the three most precious things in my world were gone, and the darkness pressed closer than ever, eager to suck me down. Under my sorrow, a furious determination emerged.

This time I wouldn't fail my family, or their memories. It was time to make the monsters pay.

Chapter Nine

With my emotional breakdown clumsily packed away, I headed back inside to resume wading through the available information on Ellery. Tag and Delacourt were at the table, and Kayden was coming back from the kitchen, two cups of coffee in hand. He held one up and raised an eyebrow in silent question. Grateful, I took his offering, and then settled into an empty chair. The man truly was psychic. I took a sip, indulging in the bitter bite of caffeine. "Tell me what you have so far on Ellery."

Paperwork from the file was arranged in some kind of order. Probably by Tag, since he was adding another layer to a pile as he spoke. "Master Sergeant Reeve Ellery, age thirty-three, born in Richmond, Virginia to a nice, middle-income family. Life was good for little Reeve until his dad got laid off, made friends with Chivas Regal, and lost his wife to an old friend. The wife and now ex-friend disappeared, leaving Reeve with Daddy and Mr. Chivas."

Kayden, leaning against the pass-through counter, picked up the retelling. "Joined the Corps straight out of high school.

Went overseas, moved up the ranks, ran a series of successful missions, until he went MIA when his team was ambushed."

Delacourt pushed the laptop over to me. "Ellery's personality profile."

Setting my coffee on the table, I dragged it closer, quickly perusing the report. "Nice," I murmured. "Organized, self-interested, callous, able to blend in, lacks accountability. Yet no bumps on his record."

"Traits of a sociopath."

Blinking at Kayden's grim statement, I corrected, "Psychopath. He may have started out as a sociopath, but with his tendency toward collateral damage and the assumption his personality is fracturing under each assumed ability, he's more of a psychopath now."

Despite the topic, a quick grin flashed over Tag's face. "That psychology class is coming in handy."

I gave him the answer his comment demanded. I flipped him off.

"Psycho or sociopath," Kayden said. "It doesn't matter what label you give him, what matters is stopping him."

Ellery was like any killer, he had to start somewhere. There was only one person here who would know what tipped him over edge and started him on this path. I turned to Delacourt. "What happened on his last mission?"

"The details are still classified, but," she held up a hand when I opened my mouth to argue, "his last operation went sideways. According to the official after-action report, their initial target, a small band of rebels, turned out to be a bigger force than anticipated. All but four of the men made it back. After repeated failed recovery efforts, command declared the four missing men, including Ellery, killed in action." Her impassive expression hid her thoughts. "That was nine months before your team was attacked."

"Our team had been working the case for four months." I

worked through the timeline. "So he was missing for five months before the investigation started?"

She gave me a short nod.

"Which meant there was no reason to link a dead man to the theft and possible sale of classified information." I looked to Tag. "Do you have copies of our initial assessments?"

He did his mojo with the scattered piles and handed me a set of reports. Kayden came and read over my shoulder.

I worried my bottom lip with my teeth as I reviewed the documented information. Our leads on that last assignment had been slim, our interviews fruitless. Yet something had to connect Ellery to our investigation. I just couldn't see it. "What am I missing?"

"Not what," Delacourt corrected and handed me another piece of paper. "Who."

I took it and examined the list of names. One of them rang a bell. "Ramirez."

Going back to the initial reports, I found what I was looking for, an interview done with one Tito Ramirez, Private. The attached picture brought back my initial impressions. Ramirez was a twitchy little Hispanic guy who served as a clerk at the base depot. At the time, his disciplinary record with its minor infractions pinged on my radar, but nothing had panned out.

I looked at Delacourt and something in her expression had me asking, "What's his connection to Ellery?"

"Shortly after his interview, Ramirez came under investigation by the MCID. Some prescription painkillers went missing from an incoming delivery. Nothing could be proven, but he was discharged under a cloud of suspicion."

I set the report aside. "Which means he was already gone when Ellery went to trial."

Behind me, Kayden stilled, then reached around me, and snatched the report. "This Ramirez?"

"Yeah."

"I saw him," he murmured, studying the image carefully.

"When?"

"At the cabin."

Startled, my brain came to a full stop. "My cabin?"

He nodded.

"No way was he in my house," I argued. "He wasn't in any of the scenes, Kayden. I know what I saw and trust me, he wasn't anywhere around." Only after the words left my mouth did his earlier words about catching glimpses of Ellery's thoughts resurface. "Wait, you mean it worked?"

He nodded. "Yeah, this face," he tapped the photo, "was there for just a moment, and then gone."

"*It* worked?" Delacourt snapped, setting tension alight. "What exactly did you do, Shaw?"

Uh-oh. Looking between Kayden's chagrined expression and Delacourt's cold command face, I leaned out of the line of fire. Even Tag pushed back from the table a bit. Smart man.

Kayden's jaw tightened, but his self-preservation switch must be malfunctioning because he didn't back down under the Colonel's stare. "In an attempt to retrieve more accurate information regarding Kelsey's attack, I piggybacked on Cyn's ability to boost the energy signatures." He paused before adding, "Sir."

Her eyebrows disappeared under her neat hair. "You attempted to combine psychic abilities unmonitored?"

Why was it, when she asked it that way, it sounded like a really bad idea?

Disapproval colored her face, but Kayden held his ground remarkably well, considering. "It worked." His answer emerged a little tight and defensive.

"And you considered the possible repercussions worth the risk of disregarding one of the few rules you agreed to when you signed up for this team?"

Oh shit! Something more serious was at play here, and I

started to worry for Kayden. Hell, I started to worry for me. Maybe I should have asked him a few more questions, but it was a little hard to ask the right ones, if you don't know what you're doing in the first place.

He held her gaze without flinching. "I did, yes."

Breaking their silent staring contest wasn't something I really wanted to do, but I waded in bravely. "What kind of repercussions are we talking about here?"

For a few heartbeats, Delacourt continued to watch Kayden. Then she turned all that disconcerting regard to me. "When two sympathetic abilities, such as a Tracker and a Watcher—"

"Watcher?"

"Someone who views the past or present, but can't actively change it," Tag, the ever helpful, clarified.

Delacourt nodded. "When similar talents combine their energies, strange changes take place."

"Define strange," I prompted.

"When discussing psychic abilities, it depends on the individuals involved. Combining two talents has three outcomes." She began to tick them off with her fingers. "One, one ability will cancel out the other. Two, one ability will become dominant, or three, the two will combine into something unique to the pairing."

"There's a fourth," Kayden added.

For a moment, something peeked from behind her controlled expression, but I didn't know her well enough to understand it. She turned back to him. "Yes, there is, but it comes only if you merge two talents continually over an extended period of time. Unless there's something neither of you shared, I think we can consider that off the table."

What the hell were they talking about?

Before I could ask, Delacourt continued, "What were your results?"

When Kayden played statue, I answered. "All it did was amp things up." Her attention swung back to me, so I fumbled along. "For both of us."

Since Kayden didn't refute my statement, I kept going. "The first time, before Kayden came crashing in, I couldn't hear a thing." I managed the small white lie as memories rose to replay in vivid detail. "The images...memories,"—the same memories making it so hard to get through this now— "they had no soundtrack until he joined in." Hidden by the edge of the table, my hands curled into fists. *Suck it up, Cyn.* "Plus, I couldn't make out Ellery's face either, thanks to some strange staticky mask. When we combined our talents, the mask cleared enough to confirm Ellery's identity."

"The energy signatures were stronger," Kayden finally spoke. "I think that's why I caught a glimpse of Ramirez's face."

"And you don't think that could be attributed to the situation you two were viewing?" Delacourt asked. "According to our phone conversation, Shaw, Arden watched her sister being killed. You don't think that might have more bearing on the intensity of what you two saw than combining your talents?"

The stark words triggered a sucker punch of grief. While I did my best to relearn how to breathe, Kayden put a warm hand on my shoulder in an unexpected show of support, before answering Delacourt. "What happened didn't change. The first time through, Cyn had no audio, and her visual was limited. When we linked up, not only did she get more information, but so did I."

Still stinging from the colonel's unintentional hit, I didn't mask the cutting edge in my voice. "Which means between the two of us, we got a positive ID, a soundtrack, and a possible lead. So, yeah, I'd have to agree with Kayden, it was worth it."

She studied both of us, and whatever thoughts spun in her

head were indecipherable to us mere mortals. Finally, she said, "Perhaps repeat performances should be avoided."

It came across as an order, not a question. I didn't dare look at Kayden as he had no choice but to answer to her. As for me? My teeth snapped together before some very unwise words fell out of my mouth. She was no longer my commanding officer, but I needed her resources, so silence was my best option. There was no way I could agree to not use something that might come in handy down the road. Especially without knowing what facing Ellery would entail. What I did know was that I wouldn't hesitate to use whatever I could to make him pay.

Tag redirected her attention before either Kayden, or I were forced to respond. "Sir, Ramirez's last known is in Phoenix. You want me to check it out?"

Delacourt continued to eye Kayden and I, before she turned to Tag and gave a small head shake. "No, I need you in Vegas to check out the last known addie on our missing person." She rose, stretched, and then turned away. "You can work with Risia."

Despite the strain in the air, it was almost comical how fast Tag's easy-going expression morphed into one of male horror at Delacourt's last order. It was the kind of fear you saw when a man was faced with a crying, or raging, woman. "Risia?" He ran a hand over the back of his neck. "No offense, sir, but it's probably better if you send Kayden."

Slowly, Delacourt turned back to him, and pinned him in place with a implacable stare. "That was not a suggestion, Gunderson."

"Yes, sir." He bit out. He turned back to the table and began to gather up the various stacks. A muscle twitched in his jaw.

Just based on his reaction, I vowed somehow, someway to meet this Risia. I stood and helped him collect the papers. Handing him a pile, I held on until he looked at me. "What's wrong, Tag? Did you finally meet a woman wise to the ways of your charm?"

If fire had been his ability, I'd have been a little charcoal brisket. "Not funny, Cyn," he hissed, snatching the pile out of my hands. "The woman's a pain in my ass."

Patting his arm, I snickered. "There's an ointment for that."

He growled.

Teasing Tag carried a comforting familiarity and loosened something tight and painful inside me. "This Risia, is she part of your team?"

"She's a seer." Kayden took an empty glass from the table to the kitchen. "Scary accurate, too, but she's zealous about her privacy."

"Hopefully she'll be able to work with Tag on locating Megan Rouser," Delacourt chimed in, as she paced the living room, most likely tired of sitting around. The colonel was never one for sitting still.

Running through my recently ingested information, I placed the name. "Lance Corporal Rouser left on leave two weeks ago, right? So why is she listed as a possible victim of Ellery's?"

She came to a stop near the French doors and kept her back to us. "Rouser took vacation. That vacation was up a week ago. She's been my administrative assistant for the past two years and is not one to disappear on a whim."

"Is she psychic?"

Considering who she worked for, Delacourt's answer was unexpected. "No."

She didn't turn around, but if her spine straightened anymore, it would shatter. "But she does have access to information Ellery would find very useful. I'd like to make sure she's not in his hands."

"Understandable." I handed Tag one last pile to tuck away.

Delacourt turned back around. "Shaw, Arden, you two check out Ramirez's last known."

"Roger that." I grabbed the report on Ramirez and tucked it in with my notes. "We may come up empty."

She retrieved her satchel, took some papers Tag offered her, and tucked them inside. "Find him, track his friends, and run his ass down. Ellery needs an into the less desirable connections, and based on Ramirez's history, he has those."

She looked at both of us. "Let's make sure Ellery hasn't reached out lately." She settled her bag on her shoulder. "Watch your asses tomorrow. I don't have time to play nice with the locals if you get stuck in a ten by two cell. Clear?"

"Sir," Kayden acknowledged, and I dipped my chin.

"I want verbal reports at sixteen hundred tomorrow." She included Tag in her orders. "In the meantime, I suggest you all get some rest." Then she looked at me. "Arden, walk me out." Without waiting for an answer, she spun on her heel and headed down the short hall.

Shooting Tag and Kayden a worried look and getting shrugs in return, I double-timed it after her.

Even at eleven at night, the heat still hung around, refusing to give up its hold. This far north though, it was bearable. Lights shone from behind various cabin windows and the faint sounds of music drifted on the air. We made our way to the parking lot and toward a standard black SUV parked right next to my Jeep. The SUV's locks popped and Delacourt dumped her bag on the back seat. Closing the door with a muted thump, she turned and leaned against the SUV, crossed her arms, and studied me.

Not fidgeting was difficult, but I managed. Between the

night and the dim light, it was hard to read her expression, so I waited for her to speak first.

"Flash wanted me to approach you about joining PSY-IV before that last mission," she said. "I refused."

Nerves tightened at her unexpected statement, the impending conversation not the one I envisioned. Uncertain where she was going with this, and unsure I wanted to follow along, I kept my emotions under lock and key. "I'm sure you had your reasons."

"Maybe," she agreed quietly. The night settled between us, and she finally asked, "Do you think rank overrides humanity?"

It was a strange, unexpected question considering who was asking. *What the hell did she want from me?* "Excuse me?"

"If you're going to work for me, we need to clear the air. The last thing this operation needs is for the past to come back and bite us in the ass." She leveled her gaze on me. "You blame me."

Folding my arms, I kept my mouth shut, because there was no way to answer that without lying.

"You blame me," she repeated, softer now. "And you have a right to, but, Cyn, I blame you, too."

Even though it wasn't a surprise, hearing her confirm it, hurt.

She kept talking, leaving me with no choice but to stand there and listen. "I came up through the ranks with Flash, with Eric. He was…" she paused, turned her head to the side for a moment, then raised it back up defiantly. "He was a good man, a great friend, and when he was killed, I was very angry and very hurt."

The amount of throttled emotion behind her simple statement created a huge understatement. Uncomfortable knowledge blossomed, altering my perception of Delacourt. Tonight, I wasn't talking to the intimidating Colonel, I was facing someone who loved Flash, loved him on a level I didn't even want to think about. Under the old resentments rose a new layer of sympathy, and I let her talk. If I interrupted her, I wasn't sure she'd be able to continue, and something told me she needed this.

"Pressure and questions were coming from different directions, and my ability to handle it effectively was compromised." That inner core of strength I admired so much, came to her rescue. Her spine straightened and the slight hunch to her shoulders disappeared. "When you joined, I watched you. Initially for Carl, then because Flash took you under his wing, but then I recognized certain characteristics, ones I knew first-hand. You are a remarkable soldier, Arden. You're quick, you think outside the box, and you're an asset to any team."

Stunned by her unexpected compliments, I dropped my gaze and waited for the other shoe to fall.

"But..."

And here it was.

"Your loyalty can become problematic."

Yep, not taking that one silently. "Explain that to me, because I'm not sure how loyalty can be problematic."

"Let me ask you a question."

I gave her a short nod.

"What comes first? You, your team, or your orders?"

The question was too easy. "The team."

"Why?"

"For a mission to be successful, the team must complete it. Sometimes orders can't take into account what happens in the field."

"Ask me the same question," she prompted.

"Um, what comes first, sir? Team, mission, or you?"

"The mission." Her answer fell between us with merciless finality. "Do you know why?"

I shook my head.

"In any given operation, there are numerous factors that come into play. Most of which, command will not share with their teams. There are reasons soldiers are given information on a need-to-know basis. I knew there was a leak somewhere, either on the joint team, or from someone close at hand. This meant I couldn't tell the team all they were facing, just what was deemed necessary to trap Ellery. I couldn't warn any of you of what might be used against you." Furious emotion turned her voice husky. "I couldn't protect Eric, but I knew you would."

And there it was, the real reason she went after me the way she did at the trial. "I tried," I choked out.

She took a step toward me, and I backed away. She stopped. "I know that now, but then, then I needed someone to blame."

My bitter laugh cut through the night. "Because God forbid you look in the damn mirror, right?"

She took the hit.

I spun around, giving her my back, fighting to pull my shit together. "Sorry," I ground out.

That had been grossly unfair. Delacourt had been stuck between a rock and a hard place, but it still fucking hurt, because she couldn't blame me any more than I did. Even Kayden's reassurance that there was nothing I could do, could erase months of guilt.

"I can apologize until hell freezes over." Her voice was level, quiet. "But it won't change anything. All I ask is that you remember that under the uniform is a flesh and blood woman."

Hot pressure made my eyes sting and my throat closed. I forced air through my lungs until the tightness in my chest loosened and the pressure faded. Finally, I turned around and gave her what I could. "We're all flesh and blood under the uniforms, sir."

"That we are," she said, watching me for a moment. She blew out a quiet breath. "Let me take care of Kelsey while you work with Shaw."

"Why?" Her explanation carried enough truth for me to understand, but it hadn't calmed all my suspicions.

"You have enough to deal with right now. Let me take this on, so you can focus. I don't want to lose anyone else to Ellery."

"Thank you."

She inclined her head and began to turn away.

"Charlene," her name came out quiet. "I won't change. Even if I'm under your command, my team comes first."

A flash of white gave away her smile. "I'm counting on it, Cyn." She rounded the hood of the SUV and opened the driver's side door. Standing on the running board, she looked at me over the roof. "When this is over, when you have justice for Kelsey, we'll talk about your future."

Meeting her gaze, I thought about her unspoken offer. Agreeing to talk was easy to promise, but she might not like my answer. I gave a slow nod.

She returned it, and then disappeared into the SUV. The engine rumbled through the night, and the lights came on, blinding me.

I watched her reverse out of the parking lot and kept my gaze on the disappearing red taillights. Alone in the dark, the urge to walk away from her, Kayden and Tag, and their expectations beckoned. Too many memories, too many emotions kept knocking me off kilter. I wanted to scream, crawl into a hole, rail at a perverse universe that stole my sister, my best friend, and my parents. But I made a promise to make the monsters pay, so for now, as long as it got me what I wanted, I'd play by the rules.

And what I wanted most right now was Ellery's blood. As for afterward? Well, I'd just have to wait and see.

I took my time heading back to the cabin. Slipping inside, I found Kayden sprawled on the couch, Tag once again in the chair. The low drone of a sportscaster's voice played in the background. Locking the door behind me, I made my way down the short hall. I stepped into the dining room and they both looked up.

"You good?" Tag asked.

"Yeah, just tired." It wasn't a lie. Exhaustion curled around me. "I'm going to crash."

Wishing the guys a quiet good night, I headed to the second bedroom. As I prepared for bed, the images in my head made me yearn for a stiff shot, or five, of whiskey. I tried a warm shower, flipped through a battered paperback, and tried some meditative breathing.

Nothing worked.

In the end, I grabbed my pillow and slipped back into the now deserted living room. Curled up into the corner of the couch, I turned the TV down low and let the late-night chatter chase away my nightmares.

Chapter Ten

Downtown Phoenix was a sharp edge mixture of glass and steel, with pockets of dark, fetid poverty. Sometimes the bright sunlight would briefly illuminate the invisible homeless before the shadows swallowed them up again. The corporate drones moved along, completely oblivious as their wireless worlds consumed them. Sadly, the scene was a familiar one.

Different city, same picture.

Kayden wove his way through the maze of one-way streets, guiding us deeper into the graffiti-enhanced neighborhood. Checking out our unsettling surroundings, apprehension curled along my skin. Eyes hidden behind dark lenses, Kayden frowned. "Nice neighborhood."

"Guess drug dealing doesn't pay as good as it used to." Despite my flippant answer, I wondered how anyone survived in this urban jungle. Neighborhoods like this ate people for breakfast, lunch, and dinner.

Slowing down for a shot-up stop sign, he gave me a quick once-over. "You carrying?"

I propped my left foot against the dash and tugged my

jeans up, just enough to flash the modified ankle holster fitted to my boot, my nine-millimeter tucked inside. "Making you bench-press the couch wasn't for kicks."

His lips quirked, and I dropped my leg.

His voice was droll, "Tell me you have a conceal and carry permit."

It wasn't like Arizona required a C&C, but… "We promised Delacourt we wouldn't call for bail." I kept scanning the economically ravaged collection of homes. "However, I'm not feeling particularly optimistic right now. We're going to stick out like sore thumbs."

He didn't answer.

I continued watching the streets. We passed a dark-haired little girl and boy playing in a dusty, barren front yard and a frustrating sorrow seeped through me.

I must have made some kind of noise because Kayden asked, "What's wrong?"

I turned away from the depressing view. "Nothing."

"Didn't sound like nothing." He waited a beat. "Spill."

Chewing my lower lip, I tried to put what it felt like seeing those kids playing in the dirt, knowing if anyone would get it, he would. We both stood witness to the same things during our time overseas. "Those kids, they remind me of the ones in the villages over there. Trying to play in a world where danger can come from around the corner. It's just hard to see here. There, it was…" I trailed off, knowing 'normal' shouldn't fit.

"Unfortunately, it's normal here, too."

And that's what bothered me. Even though I avoided the news on general principle, it was hard to miss the rise of sense-less violence stateside. Shortly after I came home, I spent the night at Kelsey's place in Tempe. After indulging in chocolate and wine, we had a very late-night conversation about perspectives. She started in on me because I, in her words, 'interrogated' the security guy at her condo complex. When I explained I was simply ensuring he was doing his job, she shot back that her chances of being hit crossing the street to her office were higher than someone breaking into her condo and hurting her. "Kels called me paranoid," I muttered.

One of his dark brows rose above the rim of his sunglasses. "I hate to break it to you, Cyn, but I think that's a hazard of our job."

"Paranoid photographers are generally called paparazzi."

"You're not just a photographer, you're a soldier."

I frowned at him. "I'm a civilian."

A full-fledged smile broke out. "Once a marine…"

"Always a marine." My lips quirked. "Yeah, yeah, I know. Leave me my thin illusions."

Pulling into a dead-end street, Kayden slowed to a stop in front of a low-slung building. "This it?"

Checking the address against the one on my phone, I said, "Yep."

At one time, it could have served as a small motel, but it now masqueraded as apartments. There was a disassembled car perched on cinder blocks in the weed choked front yard. Window treatments were predominantly cardboard and cheap vinyl blinds. Plastic milk crates offered seating on the cracked walkways. I stood on the weed choked sidewalk, my skin prickling in awareness.

We were being watched.

Time to channel my inner punk and don the armor of attitude. Straightening my spine, I waited for Kayden to round the car's hood, then followed him across the desolate front yard to one of the doors on the end. With my sunglasses firmly in place, I tried to spot our watchers.

A rapid spat of Spanish fought with canned laughter, while the dull thumps of someone's stereo competed for equal airspace. Behind closed doors, a baby cried, and a fairly impressive argument ensued in a brutal mix of Spanish and

English. All we needed to make this complete was some pit bull bursting around the corner, fangs dripping saliva.

Instead, we made it to the door where a dirty, white number eight hung crookedly, without incident. Kayden knocked. The itch at the back of my neck grew, but I refused to give into the temptation and look around. We waited while our summons went unanswered.

"Now what?" I muttered.

Kayden shot me a look. "Why don't you stand over here?"

"Uh?"

"Get over here." He snagged my arm and placed me between him and the other doors. Then, he pulled a couple of small metal pieces from his pocket and bent over the lock.

Crossing my arms over my chest, I couldn't help myself. "Really, Your Honor, it wasn't what it looked like. We just forgot our key."

Kayden ignored my commentary as he applied the picks. After what seemed liked forever, he shoved his little tools into a pocket, and then grasped the handle. With a quick twist of his wrist the door opened. With Kayden on one side, and me on the other, we let the door swing wide.

"Tito?" Kayden waited for an answer. When none came, he stepped into the silent interior.

I stuck close, shoving my sunglasses up. It took a few moments for my eyes to adjust to the dimness inside. Long enough for the smell to hit me. Sickening sweet, the nauseating stink of weed couldn't be missed. Wrinkling my nose, I did my best to breathe through my mouth. Unfortunately, that just made me cough.

"You good?" Kayden asked.

"Trying to avoid a contact high."

"Good luck." He closed the door behind us, shutting us in the hazy gloom.

I mourned the loss of fresh air but understood we didn't want to encourage the neighbors to visit.

The apartment layout was simple. Living room in front, kitchen in back, and a short hall with possible bedrooms on the left. A battered, sheet-covered sofa slumped under the window to my right, a broken-down recliner, complete with an ashtray resting on the arm, huddled in the corner. A coffee table squatted in front of both, cluttered with various electronics including a TV sitting squarely in the middle, the screen sporting a lovely starburst pattern.

"Guess someone wasn't happy with the outcome of the game," I quipped.

Kayden led the way down a threadbare hall.

I peeked around his back into a truly odoriferous bathroom that the CDC wouldn't even attempt to enter without protection. "There's no way anything human could stay here."

"Maybe it's the maid's week off." He continued to the next doorway.

"Week? Try century," I groused. "Anything?"

He shook his head, and I stepped around him to the next closed door. Twisting the knob, I gingerly pushed it open, only to revise my opinion. "Okay, there's one thing that grows just fine here."

He came up behind me and we stood there, surveying a very expensive grow room. Looked like Tito enjoyed horticulture.

The window was blacked out with a thin layer of plywood. Grow lights lined neat rows of dark green, spiky-leafed plants of varying heights. There were timers on each row. Probably for the automatic watering system. A homemade ventilation system was rigged against the far wall. Close to the door, a table contained a couple of scales, plus a small pile of empty baggies.

Kayden let out a low whistle. "Do-it-yourself dealer?"

A small laugh escaped. "Chances are, he's got himself a grower's card and he's supplying his patients." I used air quotes on the last word.

"Patients?"

Turning out of the doorway, I patted him on the arm. "Welcome to Arizona, where marijuana can cure your ills."

"Stupid to leave this unguarded," he murmured behind me.

"Mmm," I answered noncommittally. "Tito doesn't strike me as a corporate shark."

The last room was Tito's bedroom. A queen mattress lay on the floor, taking up most of the floor space. Something from his time in the Corps must have stuck because the bed was covered in a light blanket, the corners folded with military precision. A small lamp and dirty ashtray sat on the floor next to it. There was a pile of clothes in the corner.

Walking over to the closet, I slid the door open.

T-shirts hung in a neat row above a shelf holding folded, faded jeans and some sweats. The most interesting items in the closet rested on the floor. A small collection of semi-automatic weapons was lined up against the back wall.

Tito's private armory was worth more than what grew in the other room. There was an AK-47, an AR-15, an M16, and more surprising, a DPMS .308 Mark 12. That pretty piece alone cost close to eighteen hundred dollars. In the corner on a shelf, a box of nine-millimeter ammo meant we might be missing a gun. Or two. Guess Tito had his home security covered.

In the back corner of the closet, where the light had a difficult time reaching, a dress uniform hung, and below it sat a battered footlocker.

Together, Kayden and I dragged it out into the open. Once again, he brought out his set of picks and went to work. Much quicker this time, the lock popped open. Flipping the lid revealed folded BDUs, worn boots, a battered helmet, and various duty accessories. Kayden carefully moved them aside, uncovering a couple of battered notebooks. He pulled them out, flipping through them.

"Anything?" I asked, feeling antsy about going through Ramirez's locker, even knowing why it was necessary.

"Looks like a journal, could be useful." He set it on the floor and rummaged a bit more. He came back with a small, blue spiral notebook wrapped in a couple of rubber bands. He handed it to me, so he could continue his search.

I pulled off one of the rubber bands, and it was so brittle, it broke. There were loose pieces of paper tucked in the notebook, so I tried to go through it without dropping anything. A few pages in, I let out a low curse.

Kayden looked up. "What?"

"There are names in here."

Cautious excitement lit his face. "And?"

Holding the little notebook in both hands, I turned it around, so he could see it. Arabic characters filled the page, interspersing the occasional bits of English. "Some of the names aren't English, Kayden."

He rose and took it from me. "True, but some of them ring a bell."

"Guess we have proof that Tito's definitely the go-to guy for slimy connections." My uneasiness about snooping through Ramirez's things disappeared under a slow growing fury that a marine would betray his country in such a way.

Kayden handed the notebook back. I re-wrapped it with the surviving rubber band, then set it aside with the others. He closed the locker and motioned for me to help him push it back into place. "We need to find him."

Kneeling on the floor, I pushed as he pulled. "Guess we stake this place out?"

He didn't get a chance to answer. The unmistakable sound

of the front door slamming open shot me to my feet as I drew my gun, all of it happening in one smooth motion.

For a big man, Kayden moved quick, much faster than me. By the time I hit the hall, he was already at the end, bearing down on a wiry, strung-out Hispanic male. A male that bore no resemblance to Tito's photo.

By the time twitchy boy realized there was a threat, it was too late. Kayden dodged his initial clumsy punch, returning it with a wicked quick blow that doubled him over. Then Kayden wrapped his other hand around the back of twitchy boy's neck and spun him deeper into the apartment.

Without taking my eyes off the two men, I kept my Sig tucked against my thigh, and slid around Kayden to nudge the door shut with my foot.

Kayden shoved the guy onto the couch.

"What the fuck, man?" The question emerged as a croak, as twitchy boy fought to suck air into his abused diaphragm. His eyes darted wildly between Kayden and me as he cringed back into the cushions. "Take whatever you want, but I ain't got shit right now. Swear to God!"

"Not looking to score, asshole," Kayden growled, his face dark with evil intent. It was a look that would scare me shitless if I didn't know any better. As it was, twitchy boy trembled like a leaf. Kayden leaned in. "You Tito?"

The kid's head did a jerky shake in the negative. "Carlos," he squeaked.

"Where's Tito?"

Confusion clouded Carlos's sallow face. "Tito?"

"Don't play stupid with me." Kayden crowded in until mere inches separated them, enunciating each word. "Where is Tito?"

"I...I don't know, man. He asked me to watch his shit." Carlos' eyes darted between Kayden and me. When he spotted my gun, he couldn't hide his flinch. "Look, I don't know where he is, okay?"

Ignoring his plaintive whine, I asked, "When did you see him last?"

"*No sé.*" Kayden straightened, and then shifted his weight causing Carlos to recoil. His hands jerked up to protect his face. "Swear to Jesus, I don't know, man!" he bleated. "Maybe, like a week ago? Maybe two? He came over one night, asked me to check on his…" one hand flopped around.

"Medicinal crop?" I supplied.

Another jerky nod. "Yeah, that shit. Haven't heard from him since."

I shared a look with Kayden. That sounded like Tito had rabbited. I turned back to Carlos, "Anyone else been looking for him?"

A crafty shadow flitted across his face.

Kayden increased his menace factor as he towered over the twitchy man. "Don't fucking think about lying."

Watching Carlos pale was a lesson in how white olive skin could get, and it was close to snow level. "Some scary mother fucker and a young guy."

I dug my cell out of my front pocket one-handed, and pulled up Reeve Ellery's image that I downloaded the night before. I tapped Kayden's shoulder and handed him the phone.

He shoved it under Carlos's bloodless face. "One of them look like this?"

A jerky nod of confirmation. "The scary mofo."

Great, we had a definitive link between Tito and Ellery. Although I wasn't sure what good it would do now. If that wasn't enough, we had additional, unknown players poking around in this mess.

Without taking his attention from Carlos, Kayden handed back my phone. "When did the scary one stop by?"

"A couple of days after he split."

Something heavy hit the front door behind me, rattling it in its frame. "*Yo, Carlos, que pasa?*"

I stepped to the side and adjusted my stance. "Tell him you're fine," I hissed. Explaining a gunfight in downtown Phoenix with some lowlife drug dealer would not go over well with Delacourt.

"*Nada mucho, así estoy bien.*" Carlos's voice emerged somewhat steady with a hint of impatience.

We all stared at the closed door. On the other side, a muted conversation in Spanish ensued, before heavy footsteps moved away. I shared a look with Kayden. We needed to get the hell out of here before our luck ran out.

"What did the scary mother fucker want?" Kayden's low question snapped Carlos's attention back around.

"Same as you, where Tito was."

"What did you tell him?" he pressed.

"Same thing I told the other dude and now you, nothing, man, swear. He didn't leave a forwarding, didn't say shit to me about nothin'." Carlos' hands curled into white-knuckle fists in his lap, and a little bit of spine emerged. "What the hell is going on, man? Why's everyone after him?"

I ignored his question in favor of one of my own. "Where would he go if he had to hide?"

He started to shake his head, but Kayden cut him off. "Think! If things were going to go south, where would he go? Family? Friends? Someone he'd run to for help, maybe?"

Carlos's narrow face scrunched up as he tried to get his remaining brain cells to function. "There was this dude he served with, he mentioned him a couple of times."

"Name?"

He quailed before Kayden. "Boomer, Bomber, something like that, I'm not sure." Something clicked in the reefer-induced haze, and he said, "San Diego. He lived in San Diego."

*Son of a…*I choked back the words. A six-hour road trip to hunt down someone named Boomer or Bomber? Yeah, sounded like a wonderful trip.

Kayden straightened and stepped back.

Carlos took advantage of his reprieve and dragged in a noisy breath. When Kayden turned away and walked toward me, Carlos blurted, "You're not goin' hurt me, are ya?"

Neither one of us bothered to answer. I caught the familiar hand signal from Kayden and switched places with him. Gun drawn, he stepped behind the door as I headed back to retrieve the notebooks in the bedroom.

When I returned, Carlos was watching us carefully. "You ain't stealing the weed, tell me you ain't taking that shit. He'll kill me if that shit goes missing."

Giving the kid my coldest look, I warned, "You might want to consider house sitting for someone else for a while, Carlos."

His head bobbed up and down nervously.

Stepping to the other side of the door, I covered Kayden as he cautiously pulled open the door. I scanned for a possible welcoming committee but found the sunlit ragged yard empty. I motioned to Kayden, and he slipped out, sunglasses in place.

I left mine on my head as the few seconds to slide them down could be costly. Instead, I narrowed my eyes against the glare and followed. Behind us, Carlos wasted no time slamming the door shut.

As we made our way back to the car, my spine crawled. Only when Kayden was settled behind the wheel and the engine running, did I pop the passenger door and slide inside. In minutes we left Carlos and his curious friends behind.

I set the notebooks on the floorboard and then put my Sig back in the ankle holster. "San Diego?"

Kayden shrugged.

I wiped the sweat trickling down the side of my face and sat back. Between the heat and tension, I was a bit lightheaded.

The car's AC valiantly fought to replace the oven-like air in the car. To help it along, I powered the window down.

Kayden wove his way out of the neighborhood. "At least we can give Delacourt a name to run, while we go through those notebooks."

Since he was busy driving, I made the call to Delacourt. It was frustratingly short as there was little information to share. She promised to call back with whatever she could find about Tito's friend in San Diego. After hanging up, I propped my arm on the edge of the window and glanced in our rearview mirror as we pulled out on to Twenty-Fourth Street. "Delacourt said she'd send someone to help us with the notebooks, but identifying Boomer, Bomber, whoever, is going to be like finding a needle in a haystack."

Unruffled, he asked, "You have a better suggestion?"

I drummed my fingers on the edge of the door. "Let's swing by Kelsey's place."

He gave me a look I couldn't read. "You think she may have left something for you there?"

"Maybe." A puff of cooler air escaped the AC, indicating it made progress, so I powered my window back up.

For a moment Kayden remained quiet. "And if it's being watched, so much the better?"

I shrugged, staring steadfastly out the window. "Bait, remember? Maybe Ellery will make this easy on us."

"Address?"

Grateful he wasn't arguing, I gave it to him. Part of me knew it was a shot in the dark, but it didn't matter, couldn't matter. If dangling myself out there was what it took to snag the attention of a psychopath, so be it.

Chapter Eleven

As we walked up to the glass doors of Sixth Street Condos, Kayden tilted his head back to take in the two towers that rose above Mill Avenue in the heart of Tempe. "Nice."

He opened the lobby door and held it for me. Cool air reached out and twined around us, as I crossed the tiled floor.

The man at the security desk was short, stocky, and in his forties. When he recognized me, he called out, "Hey, Cyn, I didn't know you were in town. I think Kelsey's out on a company trip."

Hearing her name put a hitch in my step, but I managed what I hoped was a smile and not a grimace. "Hey, Terrance." Reluctant to get drawn into his normal friendly banter, I kept moving and led Kayden to the elevator. I called back, "Just need to pick up something from my last visit."

When Kelsey first moved in, I put Terrance through an impromptu interview. After which, he decided we were his personal responsibility. Part of the reason I didn't worry about Kelsey living in this fairly new high rise could be traced back to him. As the head of Sixth Street's security, he took his duties seriously. During what Kelsey dubbed as my infamous interrogation, Terrance and I bonded over our shared paranoia on personal safety and swapped stories of our time in the military. Something Kelsey delighted in teasing us both about, claiming we were two peas in a pod.

I hurried into the elevator, haunted by the remembered sounds of Kelsey's laughter. It twisted the small bit of normalcy into something disquieting. Once inside, I leaned against the back wall and crossed my arms over my chest, blindly staring at the floor. I set my jaw and struggled to push my reawakened grief back as the doors slid closed.

"Which floor?"

I lifted my head at Kayden's question and cleared my throat. "Seven."

He hit the button, then met my gaze in the reflective surface of the elevator door. "You okay with this?" Quiet concern threaded his voice.

"Yeah…" I trailed off, bit my lower lip, and then shook my head. "No, it's just I'm not sure how to tell Terrance about Kelsey."

Kayden moved to lean against the wall next to me, our shoulders brushing. "You don't need to do it right now, Cyn." He paused. "If it'd help, I can talk to him later."

His unexpected offer brought pressure to the back of my eyes. Blinking it away, I resisted the urge to rest my head against him for just a moment. It would be easy to use his presence as a comforting crutch against the keen sense of Kelsey's absence. Guilt nipped at me for even considering it, still I was grateful he was here. Even more so because I wouldn't have to face her empty apartment alone.

A soft ding announced our arrival. I stepped out of the elevator and headed down the hall.

Kayden's hand wrapped around my upper arm just below the sleeve of my T-shirt and brought me up short. His thumb absently brushed a small line of heat against my skin. "Let me go first."

I tugged my arm free. "I don't think anyone's lying in wait."

He raised an eyebrow and waited.

I didn't care who went first, but it was obvious his protective instincts were kicking in, so I heaved a put-upon sigh, and stepped back. "Fine, then."

He drew his gun from the small of his back and moved in front of me.

I bent over to retrieve mine, and when I straightened, I offered, "It's seven twenty-four."

He led the way and I followed, digging my keys out of my pocket. As we approached the door, he turned until he was walking backward. I tossed him the keys and he snatched them out of the air. He turned around and crossed to the far side of the door before unlocking it and letting it swing wide. He paused, did a quick peek, and then moved inside. When he didn't return, I stepped inside and closed the door. Standing in the dim entryway, I waited for his all clear.

The condo was close to fifteen hundred square feet with three bedrooms and three bathrooms. Kayden cleared the bath just off the entryway, then continued down the hall. The third bedroom, located to his left before the open-concept kitchen and living room, served as an office.

I noted the small pile of unopened mail tucked next to the bowl of colored glass on the long, narrow entry table to my left. I'd have to go through it later and see if anything worthwhile was in there.

Kayden cleared the office and came back. From where we stood, we had an unimpeded view of the kitchen and living room. I motioned to the doorway to the right of the heavily curtained patio doors. Kelsey's room. He gave a short nod and headed over.

The condo was a corner unit, so glass walls ran from Kelsey's room, through the living room, and into the second bedroom nestled behind the kitchen and office. Despite the massive number of windows, the interior remained cool. The privacy curtains kept both the lookie-loos and the sun at bay.

As Kayden cleared Kelsey's room, I headed toward the second one, where I normally crashed. The pocket door was partially open. The AC shifted the living room curtains in front of me, offering teasing glimpses of the primary patio overlooking the fifth-floor outdoor pool. Taking a deep breath, I sidled closer, using my Sig to nudge the pocket door wider. When nothing moved inside, I headed in.

It had been weeks since my last visit. Because the room doubled as Kelsey's guest room, it wasn't used often. At first glance, nothing looked out of place.

There was the dresser, the bed, a couple of bookshelves, and framed pictures scattered across the surfaces, a couple of which were tipped over. One section of the blackout curtains was pulled back, allowing the afternoon sunlight to paint a bright path across the bed and over the throw rug lying on the tile floor. The sliding glass door led to a second balcony patio, and from where I stood, it appeared empty of threats. It took less than a minute to clear the bathroom and walk-in closet where a gun safe squatted.

I came back into the bedroom, sank to the edge of the bed, and set my gun beside me on the comforter. Being here hurt, but it also didn't. It was a strange, disorienting feeling. Hearing the scrape of a shoe against tile, I looked over to find Kayden standing in the doorway, his gun gone.

"It's clear. Nothing seems out of place." He came over and settled next to me. "This is a hell of an apartment."

"Yeah, Kelsey loves…loved," I corrected myself, "this place. The views are unbeatable."

I stared out to the partially exposed balcony, remembering

Kelsey's excitement when she stood there, the first time she showed it to me. "Tempe Beach Park is just below us, and in front is Hayden Park. Being the tallest building in Tempe has its perks."

All of that was useless information to the man next to me, but the words served as a flimsy barrier against the memories crowding close. Maybe coming here wasn't such a good idea. I fell quiet, unable to say anything more.

"Seems like you two were polar opposites," Kayden said, offering me another distancing layer. "This is all granite, stainless steel, and clean lines."

Intrigued by his astute observation and in no rush to end this small moment out of time, I stretched my legs out, crossing them at the ankles, as I leaned into my hands braced on the bed. A casual position when I felt anything but. "She tried to talk me into moving down here with her, but I was more comfortable at the cabin. Something that endlessly frustrated Kelsey, because she was bound and determined to make sure I had some social interaction. To achieve that goal, she would drag me down here whenever she could."

"Considering its location, it must cost a pretty penny."

I shrugged. "More than I'd be comfortable paying, but on her budget, it worked. When she sat down to explain why it would be beneficial to consider moving in with her, she had a list of pros ready to go. After I finally convinced her, I wasn't budging from the cabin, she threw her hands up and decreed that I would stay with her before and after my out-of-town trips, so she'd know I was still alive."

I winced, and then continued in a softer voice, "It's not that far from the airport and close to her offices. Besides she works —" I stopped, then corrected myself, "worked long hours. There's a restaurant downstairs, along with a slew of others along Mill. A necessity since she preferred eating out than in.

Then there's the fact that the security here is better than normal."

"Thanks to Terrance," he said.

My grief lifted a little. "Yeah."

Quiet settled between us as I stared out the window.

Being here brought so many good memories of Kelsey closer, made the aching pain a little easier to bear. Yet, it wouldn't take much, just one wayward thought, to go down the wrong path where all the sorrow waited to suck me under. The only thing keeping me from taking that wrong turn, was my involvement in this case. Despite the inherent danger involved, I was grateful to Delacourt for including me. Work might not be the solution, but it sure as hell helped.

First up, I needed to check out Kelsey's room for myself. Not that Kayden didn't know what he was doing, but he wouldn't know what to look for. Hell, maybe I wouldn't either, but there was a slim chance I'd get lucky and recognize something out of place when I saw it.

I pushed to my feet and reached for my gun. The comforting weight of the weapon served as a reminder. Kelsey brought my Sig to the cabin. I thought about the gun safe in the walk-in closet on the other side of the attached bathroom. Most times when I headed out of town, I left behind my more valuable pieces. I needed to ensure this was the only piece missing. I left the gun on the bed with Kayden. "I'll be right back."

"That's a great view." There was something dark and lazy in his voice.

I looked back to find he wasn't looking at the balcony as he half-reclined on my bed. Unexpected, slumberous heat woke with a languid stretch at the picture he presented. Grateful for his distraction, intentional or not, I murmured, "Isn't it though?"

His low chuckle followed as I walked through the bathroom and flipped the closet light on. My gaze went to the five-foot, solid steel behemoth serving as a gun safe taking up space under a nearby shelf. No scratches marred the surface, nothing to indicate a forced entry. Not that I expected anything since Kelsey had the combination and a copy of the key to unlock it.

I got the thick door open, and my heart stopped. There was no reason to search Kelsey's room. Sitting dead center, on the side-shelf where the case holding my McMillian TAC-308 sniper rifle rested, and in front of the boxes of extra ammunition, perched a single sniper round.

Dread leached the strength from my legs and left a sour taste in my mouth. Sinking to a crouch, I used the safe to keep from collapsing. My hand shook as I reached out to gently picked up the round. Instead of the expected smooth surface, my fingertips rasped against something etched into the metal. I brought it close and found a simple *K* carved into the casing. A rushing sound filled my ears. Realization slammed home, morphing fear into a cold determination.

The bastard had been here.

Curling my hand around Ellery's unmistakable taunt, I rose, closed the safe, and reset the locks. For a moment I stood there, reaching for the necessary detachment to analyze what I knew so far.

Ellery managed to violate both of my havens. He took what I most loved and left behind a very clear message to prove there was nowhere he couldn't reach. Was he playing with me? Wanting me to suffer and feel hunted? If so, he succeeded. But was there more to this than revenge?

He hunted the other team members one by one, torturing each before sucking down their abilities. Only three of us remained, Tag, Kayden, and I. Ellery killed Kelsey because she was my Achilles' heel, but I had two more weak points left, my partner and my best friend. If Ellery got to either of them, it would be the final straw for me. At least Tag was in Vegas and out of Ellery's immediate reach.

Rolling the round through my fingers, another question arose. When had he left this? Before or after he went to the cabin? Was it a taunt or a threat? If the *K* was for Kelsey, it meant he left it as he chased her north, leaving it as a way to ensure his message was received. If it was for Kayden, then we were in deep shit, because it indicated Ellery knew what we were doing before we did.

With a sinking feeling, I stared at the carefully etched *K*. Had we been chasing ghosts this whole time? If so, chances were high we were missing something. How many steps ahead of us was he? But there was a way to answer one of my questions.

"You okay in there?" Kayden's question startled me. I looked up to find him standing in the bathroom doorway. My fingers tightened on the casing, catching his attention. His face darkened. "What is that?"

Instead of answering, I let it roll into my palm, and held it out, so he could see. The overhead lights caught on the dull gleam of Ellery's message.

"Where was it?"

"In the gun safe."

His fingers whitened on the edge of the doorframe. Instead of his expected explosion, he turned and left.

Slipping the bullet into my pocket, I followed, stopping only to retrieve my Sig from the bed.

Kayden stood in the middle of the living room, clenching, and then unclenching his hands. There was a cloud of tension surrounding him, one that simmered on the edge of a storm.

I kept my voice soft, "Kayden?"

His head rose and his eyes were bright with fury. His jaw was clenched so tight the bone pressed against his skin and flexed under his goatee. "We need to talk to Terrance and get the security footage. I want to know how he got in."

"We don't need to review the security cameras," I said. "We can do one better."

His lips thinned. "Actual footage will give us more details."

I was shaking my head before he finished. "No, you're not thinking."

His brow lowered, and he opened his mouth to argue.

I held up my hand, hoping to cut short whatever diatribe trembled on the tip of his tongue. "The security tapes can only show you the halls, they can't show you what he did inside." My stomach pitched at the reminder of Ellery's violation, but I did my best not to show it. I didn't need it to be the spark that set Kayden off. "Let's use what tools we have."

"What tools—" Comprehension hit him, and he briefly considered it, then he grimaced. "You heard Delacourt. There's no way to determine what will happen if we continue to combine our abilities. I'm not sure it's smart to keep playing with the unknown."

"I don't think combining our talents twice is going to spawn something new and unique." It felt strange to be the one urging him to push the rules, especially after his lack of hesitation the first time around. *What changed?*

He looked away. "You don't know that."

What the hell? "Fine, then let me do it on my own."

That brought his head up.

I met his glare with my own, refusing to back down. This was too important. Whether he agreed to come along for the ride or not, it was going to happen. I needed to know if Ellery's taunt was for the man standing in front of me or had been left behind with Kelsey. The answer was crucial in proving or disproving my burgeoning suspicions. Trying to meet him halfway, I offered, "Look, we can pull the tapes afterward, and use them to confirm whatever I find."

"Pulling the tapes won't set you on your ass," he growled.

He could not possibly be worried about me. "And he may not even be on them, so we could just waste a shitload of time trying to convince Terrance to let us watch them," I snapped back, stepping into his personal space. "You have two choices, watch, or join in. Either way, stop arguing with me and say, 'Yes, Cyn'."

Something undefined flared in his face. "Fine, dammit."

"Good." I let my lips curve with a mocking edge. "So nice to have your permission."

Whatever emotion he battled changed and left behind the more easily identifiable expression of male frustration. He grabbed my upper arms and dragged me close. "You're going to drive me crazy." Then, before I could react, he pressed a punishing kiss against my lips, then pulled away.

Unsure how to handle his quick kiss, I managed a feeble, "I think that's my line."

He studied me, his frustration bleeding away. "You really don't get it do you?"

"Get what?"

"Do you know what it does to watch you go under?" He didn't wait for an answer. "I watched bruises pop out on your neck as you struggled to breathe, and all I could do was sit there and pray. There's not one damn thing I can do if something goes wrong when you're under. You're asking me to sit and watch you get hurt."

A little piece of me melted under his surprising revelation, tempering my normal reaction to such a comment. "I'm asking you to trust me to know my limits."

He cradled my chin, his thumb brushing back and forth. "Trusting you isn't hard. Letting you do it alone is."

He let me go and I missed his touch. Maybe what started all those months ago wasn't as far out of reach as I thought. The notion had no sooner cleared the gate than I shoved it back.

Wrong time, wrong place.

"So don't," I said. "Let's do what we did before. It puts you right there. If I go too deep, I can use you as my way back."

He grimaced. "Did I happen to mention slapping you when you're out of it just feels wrong?"

"If it'll make you feel better, I promise to slap you back."

My attempt to lessen his worry worked, and he chuckled. "Promise?"

I grinned. "Promise."

Chapter Twelve

After a short discussion, we headed into the second bedroom. Since Ellery had passed through it to get to the gun safe, it was our best starting point. Once again, I found myself sitting on the edge of a bed with Kayden crouched in front of me.

"Deja-vu," I muttered under my breath.

Kayden flashed a grin before taking my hands in his. A tremor ran through me and my stomach clenched so tight it hurt. As confident as I was about suggesting this to him, overcoming years' worth of suppression wasn't easy. Not even with knowing how critical the reasons were.

Kayden watched me. "Ready?"

Blowing out a breath, I nodded, and then closed my eyes. This time, my ability met me halfway, as if it was eager to be used. No trip to the brick wall necessary. Stunned at the strength of it, I worried that Kayden might actually have something to worry about.

"Steady."

The sound of his voice settled me. The same bright connection we shared earlier snapped into place with a suddenness that left me off balance. It made me squirm to realize I was literally sharing my headspace with him. Here's hoping his reception was as cloudy as mine because I knew he was there, but that was about it.

My eyes fluttered open and there was no time to brace before the memories sucked me under. At first, they colored the room like a multi-layered tapestry of vignettes, bits and pieces of Kelsey making her home, of guests visiting. Nothing involving me, thank God, because I had no idea how to handle seeing myself. It wasn't something I ever had to worry about, but with Kayden tagging along, anything was possible.

Relief hit when the sound of Kelsey's faint laughter arrowed under still raw wounds. *At least the soundtrack still worked.* I looked around and spotted Kelsey's white-blonde hair strobing like a camera flash. Half-remembered conversations swirled around me, tumbling into a wash of background noise, that let an occasional phrase through.

"Come on, admit it…love this place…can't be attacked by secret ninja warriors."

"…large Kung Pao chicken with crab rolls…"

"Damn deadlines…"

"…go out on Friday?"

Kelsey's life was a sea of memories that circled the edge of my vision. Their emotional strength created a dynamic tide that rose and fell in a mesmerizing cycle. Most were poignant reminders of a time when my heart was whole and tempted me to turn down paths best left untraveled. It was so tempting to stay in the past where the pain of loss was nothing more than a horrific nightmare.

Something warm and solid squeezed my hands, a physical reminder I could only ever be a visitor. Dropping my gaze to the floor, the neutral-colored tile replaced the dizzying scene and allowed me to reign my emotions back. I took a deep breath and reinforced my mental walls. After another inhale, followed by a slow exhale, I raised my head.

No longer a swirling mass, The memories were no longer a swirling mess. Instead, they were calm, which gave me a chance to identify individual moments. I began to pick through them, looking for Ellery. At first, I wasn't sure it would work. Then, something flickered into existence near in the bedroom's doorway. Like a slowly developing photo, the image came together in stages.

A big body covered in jeans and T-shirt, dark hair took shape. The clothes matched what Ellery wore when he killed Kelsey, but the facial features and limbs were still blurry. It made me think it was same day. Now I needed to pin down the time.

Focused on my task, I rose and pulled against the restraints on my hands. I needed to be closer. The pressure on my hands disappeared and the image shivered and thinned. I concentrated harder on the slowly disintegrating image.

"Hold up, Cyn."

I jumped, completely forgetting about Kayden. "I'm going to lose him." Heat crowded at my back, then a weight settled on my shoulders and his fingers tightened. Ellery's image snapped back online, growing sharper and sharper. "Got him."

The swirling remnants of the past faded into the background until Ellery commandeered center stage. It took an effort of will to keep him in focus, as if capturing smoke. He moved into the room, looked around, and brought a container up to his mouth. As he drank, he meandered through the room, like a guest instead of the psychotic home invader he was. Watching him was disturbing on multiple levels.

Was that orange juice? What the hell?

That small distraction was all it took for my hold on the past to slip. Ellery's image stuttered and then disappeared under other memories. The undulating tapestry shimmered as if brushed by a strong wind. When it resettled, Kelsey's figure rushed past and into the bathroom.

Stunned by the sudden switch, it took a few precious moments to realize my scene change was involuntary. Which meant Kelsey's emotions had outranked Ellery's. Not a surprise as psychopaths had the emotional range of a snake, cold, deadly, and practical. Either I followed Kelsey, or I courted a raging headache by fighting free of her powerful emotions to follow Ellery. When she reappeared with my gun in hand, my decision was made moot. Her determination and panic became an emotional leash, tugging me forward, even as she tucked the Sig into her hobo bag on her shoulder and swept past me.

"Kels," I choked out. Desperate to follow, I turned and stumbled into the living room, losing my physical connection to Kayden. My heart clenched so hard, it was an actual pain. I watched her grab a suitcase and head for the hall.

"Kels, wait!" Even knowing how fruitless it was, I darted forward trying to stop what would happen next. At the same time, my shin hit the low coffee table, and something tangled around my wrist, yanking me back.

"Dammit." I hopped on one foot while simultaneously rubbing my stinging leg and trying to keep Kelsey in sight. The unrelenting hold on my wrist tightened, piercing my haze. Then a solid band curled around my waist and spun me around, away from Kelsey.

Steel blue seared past the chaotic brew of the past and I stilled. "Cyn, can you hear me?" Kayden's voice sounded as if it was coming from a deep well. The ruthless determination in his eyes held my attention and I managed a choppy nod. Warmth cupped my face. "You need to refocus. Can you do that?"

Another slow nod, then I forced my eyes closed. Not only did it remove the temptation to chase after Kelsey's memory, but without the distraction, I could crawl into my own mind and reinforce the shaky walls holding the lure of the past back.

What the hell was wrong with me?

Never before had the role of observer been so hard to hold on to. It was as if the memories had grown a will of their own and were determined to find the smallest chinks in my mental barriers. It shattered my protections and left me buried in the amorphous world of what was, and that difference could be lethal. *Think, Cyn, what had changed?*

"Cyn?"

I opened my eyes and focused on the flesh and blood man in front of me, my anchor to the present. Kayden. Snatches of Delacourt's earlier warnings whispered around the edges of my mind. *What if his ability didn't just enhance mine, but pushed me deeper under, blurring the lines between the past and reality?* I took a quick step back to put distance between us, and that strange connection we shared diminished.

He reached out, but his hands fell back when I flinched. His concern shifted to confusion, and then went blank. "What's going on?"

"You're taking me in too deep."

The skin around his eyes tightened in a micro-flinch, one he probably wasn't aware of, but standing this close I couldn't miss it. Remorse rose, but overwhelmed by multiple mental tasks, I couldn't soften the verbal blow. "Don't touch me unless I ask, okay?"

He dropped his chin in silent acknowledgement.

When I got out of this, I needed to apologize, or at least explain. Standing still, I kept my back to the image of Kelsey leaving for the last time and concentrated on the door to the bedroom.

The memories swirled and tangled with each other like some strange wave. Their definitive edges blurred, proving my theory about Kayden's touch correct. I walked slowly forward, doing my best to visually sort through the images. Ellery's cold, masculine presence flickered for a fraction of a second, long enough to snag my attention. I stopped in the bedroom's doorway and used it as touch point.

It wasn't easy. This room was Kelsey's private domain, and her presence dominated his. Which meant trying to capture his image was akin to trying to hold the curl of an incoming wave with bare hands. It was a vicious cycle. Ellery would pop up, only for another, more powerful memory to surge forth and swallow him under. As that memory faded, he'd reemerge and do it all again. With each successive failure, the ache in my head expanded.

Something warm and wet touched my top lip. I wiped it away instinctively. The smear of red on my hand caught my attention and held it.

"Dammit, Cyn."

It was my only warning, then two things happened at once. Kayden's hand wrapped around my wrist, and the band of pain around my temples lessened its hold. Then Ellery's elusive trail became terrifyingly real.

Kelsey's killer stood on the other side of the bed, facing me. A cold, inhuman smile creasing his face. "Sloppy to leave her unprotected, Cyn."

The crystal-clear reception of his voice sent a horrific shockwave through me and shoved Kayden's questions to the background. Then Kayden's touch pulled back. When the image in front of me shivered like a soap bubble about to burst, I instinctively snatched his hand and dug my nails in, holding him tight.

Ellery's image re-solidified. He continued to stare at the doorway as if he could see me.

Logically, I knew he was using my ability against me, a psychological move meant to unnerve his opponent. Unfortunately, it was working.

He took his sweet time moving around the room, the other memories becoming mere wisps that licked along the edges of my awareness. My full attention was held by Ellery.

He picked up a picture of Kels and me from the dresser, and then rubbed the pad of his thumb across the glass. He set it down, then dragged his fingertips along the shelves. He paused to pull out a book, flipping through the pages before replacing it, his actions unnervingly casual.

I wanted to leap across the room and make him stop, his defiling touch leaving a visible smear of evil behind, like a smudge.

He came to a second picture. This one was of Carl and Becca flanked Kelsey and me in my dress blues at graduation. For a moment he stared at it, his face darkening. "What a picture-perfect family."

He turned to where I stood and smashed the frame face first against the shelf.

I winced at the sudden violent action, but the sound of breaking glass never arrived.

His lips curved and a dark, satisfied light entered his eyes.

Pleasure, he was getting such pleasure from this. On a detached level a little voice chittered a warning, *"He knows what you can do."*

A sharp pain radiated along my jaw, and I forced my teeth to unclench, sucking in deep breaths, hoping to regain control.

Ellery kept moving, yanking open drawers, and rifling through them with cold amusement. He pulled out one of Kelsey's chemise tops, crumpled it in his hands and buried his face in it.

Cracks spread through my control like spider webs.

"Mmm…" He lifted his head, and his mouth moved, but I couldn't hear the words. I coughed away the urge to vomit at the lascivious smile on his face. Again, his mouth moved, and this time there were only pieces audible. "…time to play… save her?" He dropped the delicate garment. "Ready?"

He stalked forward so quickly, I stumbled back and flinched when I ran into something solid. *Kayden.* Ellery's image continued forward, and I closed my eyes, burrowing into Kayden as if to escape a physical blow from a ghost.

Instead, an icy chill enveloped me, and my muscles clenched. The sudden tightening acted like a full-body charley horse, and I whimpered. Just as quickly, the sensation disappeared, taking the pain with it, and leaving me to lean limply against Kayden.

"What the hell?" Kayden's growl came through loud and clear. "You all right?"

My mouth was dry, making it impossible to form coherent words so I nodded.

"Ellery's signature just lit up like the Fourth of July, then snapped out." Under my ear Kayden's voice rumbled. He turned both of us away from the bedroom and led us to the living room. He stopped at the sofa, and gently untangled my grip from his shirt. "Sit."

His command was accompanied by a small push. My legs folded, and I collapsed. He crouched in front of me, running his hands up and down my arms in attempt to smooth out the goose bumps. My hindbrain was still quivering from the malice in Ellery's taunts, so I kept my attention on the man at my feet.

He watched me carefully. "What happened?"

"Not…not done yet." Hearing the fear in my voice woke a familiar burn of anger. *Suck it up, Cyn!* Ellery wasn't here. He couldn't hurt me unless I let him. Instead of allowing his verbal attacks to unnerve me, I needed to think, because if I wanted to win, I needed to outsmart him. "I can't tell if he was here before or after." I had been so caught up in the scenes, I hadn't noted the details. "I need to see how he got the bullet into my safe."

I began to get up only to be stopped by Kayden's grip on my shoulders. "Hold up. You need to tell me what he said in there."

"Nothing," I muttered.

His eyes darkened to a navy blue and narrowed. "Try again, Arden." Edgy command lined his voice. "Whatever he said in there dropped your skin tone two shades past death, so tell me."

"He's playing games," I snapped back. "He's provoking me, and it threw me, okay? That's all."

Kayden didn't say a thing, he simply regarded me with a piercing gaze.

Unsettled by his silence, I blurted, "It's a psychological game. One I should've been prepared for based on the info in his file, but I wasn't. It won't happen again." I grabbed his hands and squeezed. "Now, can we *please* go find out how the hell he got in my gun safe?"

"First, let's get you cleaned up." He rose to his feet to tower over me.

I scrambled up, confused, and my head took a sickening spin. "Cleaned up?"

He caught me as I swayed, then he gently took my wrist, and brought my hand up until I could see the blood smeared on it. "You had a nosebleed."

I looked from the rust-colored smear to his face.

Grim determination stared back. "That's not a good sign. Bleeding of any kind with most psychics implies pressure on the brain. It stopped when I touched you." I opened my mouth to protest, but he cut me off. "No. If you want to do this, you'll have to deal with me touching you, because I won't stand by and watch you hemorrhage to death."

Unused to having someone be concerned about me, his

gruff concern burrowed his spot a little deeper in my heart. It felt…nice. "Okay," I said.

When a straight line proved challenging, he took over and guided me to the kitchen. At the sink, I washed my hand, then snagged a paper towel. Wetting it, I went to clean my face only to have Kayden take it from me and grasp my chin. With a gentle touch, he tilted my face back and cleaned it.

Flustered by the strange intimacy, I gripped the counter, so I wouldn't touch him. Unfortunately, my mouth had no such reservations. "I like it when you touch me."

His movements stilled, and his gaze sharpened.

Mortification stained my cheeks. *For fuck's sake, I sounded like some dippy thirteen-year-old with a crush.* I scrambled to explain. "But I think us touching when we do this takes me too deep, too fast."

He resumed his careful ministrations. "So, no touching when you go under."

I shook my head. "I need you to touch me."

His hand stilled, and he quirked an eyebrow at me.

Realizing how that sounded, I winced. "So, I can hear, Kayden. Sharing a physical connection with you gives me a soundtrack."

"And stops the bleeding," he added.

Unable to read the small smile hovering on his lips, I stood mute.

One last brush of the wet towel and he let me go. He tossed it in the trash. "What did he say when you grabbed me?"

Guilt overrode my discomfort. "That I was sloppy to leave Kelsey unprotected."

As we faced each other, Kayden leaned his hip against the island and folded his arms across his chest. "That means he was here before he went to Sedona."

I went to nod, but stopped, unsure. I shrugged. "I don't know."

"Any way to tell when these images are happening?"

I bit my lower lip, thinking. Kelsey's images overpowered Ellery's because her emotional signature was stronger. The timing of the two memories—Kelsey getting ready to leave with my gun and Ellery in the room—were too close together to tell which came first. But there was one thing we could use. "His wrists."

"What?" Kayden asked.

"I need to get a good look at his wrists. If they're scratched, it's after he killed Kelsey. If they're clear, it's before."

Kayden's brows rose. "You want to go back to the bedroom and do this again?"

I shook my head. "No, this time we watch him put the bullet in the safe." Another thought hit. "Plus, if I can't see his wrists, maybe I'll be able to see if the gun was in the safe when he left his calling card."

He considered me for a moment, then he held out his hand. "Ready?"

Swallowing hard, I nodded and placed my hand in his, letting him lead me into the bedroom.

Chapter Thirteen

There was enough room in the walk-in closet to accommodate both Kayden and me, but I chose to perch on the counter just outside. It gave me an unobstructed view of the safe so I could watch every move Ellery made. While I sure as hell didn't want his memory touching me again, because the unsettling feeling it left behind was enough to give me the willies for a year. However, retracing his movements would not only cement each violation of my private life but fuel the additional impetus to run his ass to the ground.

Although Kelsey's death launched me from justice to revenge, the need to stop Ellery was fast becoming an obsession. An obsession that bypassed the personal line any investigator worth their salt knew better than to cross. Which was also why I couldn't currently take Delacourt up on her offer to work for her.

In this case, I didn't want, or need, anyone's rules and regulations to hold me back, because when I got my hands on Ellery, there wouldn't be much left of him to turn over to the appropriate authorities. As dangerous as is was to go down that path, I couldn't see any way that leaving him alive ended well. First, though, I had to catch him, starting with the question that itched under my skin.

How had Ellery gotten into my safe?

"You ready?" Kayden's question cut through my thoughts. He stood next to me, arms folded, and leaning against the counter. He was careful to maintain space between us, the one I requested so I wouldn't fall into the past and sink like a stone.

Ready to dive back into the slimy horror that was Ellery? Umm, no, not really.

My fingers curled around the rough edge of the cool granite, instead of grabbing ahold of Kayden like a security blanket. "Yeah, let's get this show on the road."

This time, when I gave my ability a nudge, the slide happened between one blink and the next. One second everything around me was normal, and in the next, it all took on a hazy, confusing edge. My heart rate skyrocketed. Without Kayden's touch, the speed of the switch shouldn't be this easy. Half-formed fears circled like birds of prey.

What if I couldn't shut it off? Or worse, what if it stayed on all the time? How would I tell what was real and what wasn't?

I shook my head and dislodged the worrisome questions. There was no time for this shit right now.

Kayden caught my unease. "What's wrong?"

I swallowed my anxiety, determined to see this through. "Nothing, just adjusting."

I forced my mind back under control and turned my attention to the entrance between the bedroom and the bathroom, waiting for Ellery to darken the doorway. Undecipherable memories encroached like a dense fog, swirling to fill the small space. I tried to pick out details, but there was nothing there. A frustrated noise escaped, and I reached for Kayden's hand.

When his fingers tightened on mine, the blurred images separated into identifiable layers, which made it easier to pick out individual moments. There was one tinted by a dull, sickly yellow that didn't belong. Concentrating on it, I watched Ellery appear in the bathroom's entryway looking so smug, I wanted to deck him. An unintentional growl of fury escaped.

"Steady." Kayden's calm voice reigned me in.

Ellery's echo filled the normally spacious bathroom, the miasma of evil that followed filling every corner. He rifled through the medicine cabinet on the far end with casual deliberation. Then he pulled out drawers and rummaged through the lower cabinets of the double-sink vanity. He found the vanilla-scented body lotion I left behind and popped the top. He brought it to his nose, closed his eyes, and took a deep whiff. His low groan was disturbing, but what sprang to life just below his belt left black spots swimming in my vision.

I wasn't some naive virgin, but the erection pressing against Ellery's jeans had a nauseating mix of fear and revulsion clawing at my throat. Helpless feminine fury ignited. *Fucking perverted psycho bastard*!

"Breathe."

Holding tight to Kayden, I fought my way free from the anger ignited by Ellery's perverse pleasure. With my emotions under lock and key, Ellery's reactions rose to take their place, his twisted desires upping the creepy factor to the nth degree. It was unsettling to have his emotions drown out mine. Whether it was due to the depth of his depravity, or to the connection I shared with Kayden, the intensity of the wrongness left me rattled.

Warmth stroked over my shoulder, down my arm, and brushed over my wrist, Kayden's touch a physical anchor against Ellery's pull. "Whatever he's doing, it can't touch you."

Hearing the thread of anger in his voice made me realize how hard must it be for him not to be able to see exactly what was happening. Yet I knew that if Kayden witnessed Ellery debauching my body lotion, it would not end well. As for me, I was definitely getting another scent.

"I'm okay." My voice shook, undermining my words. I held tight to Kayden's wrist and straightened my spine. "I'm okay." This time it came out more convincingly.

Ellery sauntered past and I flinched back, even knowing he couldn't touch me. "He's moved to the closet."

Kayden's grip tightened on mine.

I watched happenings in the closet. Ellery had his back to me, but from where I sat I could glimpse his profile. It was enough to tell he was studying the gun safe. He reached into his pocket and pulled out the bullet, then he slowly dropped into a crouch. His mouth moved, and the resulting buzz of sound indicated he was talking to himself. His head cocked as he examined the safe's dual lock that required both an electronic combination and a key.

Kayden shifted, his arm brushing mine, and the image sharpened. Ellery's lips twisted into a cruel smile, and then I heard him, clear as a bell. "Cautious girl, aren't you?"

Whatever he said next faded into that annoying buzz. He adjusted his crouch, and half turned to face the bathroom. I leaned a little harder into Kayden. The present faded and Ellery snapped in focus as if I had found the correct setting on a lens.

Ellery held his palm up, the bullet sitting squarely in the center. "I know what you can do, Cyn."

His words sounded right next to my ear, and I couldn't stop from darting a quick look over my shoulder. Past and present collided, the mirror behind me nothing but a gray haze. When I turned back, Kayden's normally bright image was a smudged, dull glow. Panic rose, but I jerked my attention back to Ellery.

"You, on the other hand." His other hand rested on the safe, deep, raw scratches marring his wrist. My mind stuttered and I almost missed his next words. "You don't have a clue as to what I can do."

He stared in my direction, a disconcerting knowledge adding an unholy light to his gaze. My heart raced, and my breath escaped in short gasps. I could barely feel my hold on Kayden, but I still gripped tight, praying it was enough to keep me safe from the evil in front of me.

Ellery's eyes darkened, the blackness swallowing his pupils. It was terrifying to watch. The air around him shimmered like a heat wave. For the briefest moment, my hold on the past bent and quivered, and my grip on Kayden slipped under the paralyzing fear. Ellery's image morphed into a twisted nightmare, hinting at the evil within. The demonic visual twisted the world sideways, and when it realigned, the bullet in Ellery's hand was gone.

Frozen under the primal fear flooding my mind, I couldn't look away. Ellery blinked, and the color slowly returned to his eyes. He canted his head side to side as if cracking his neck. The movement unlocked the terror holding me in place. I sucked in great gulps of air as I blinked away the lingering images.

His mouth moved, but the words got lost in the past. His head jerked, his gaze darting past me, as if he heard something. A few seconds later his lips tightened, and his brow furrowed. He muttered something I couldn't catch. Abruptly, he slammed the heel of his palms against his temples in two short strikes, then shook his head.

At his weird behavior, tiny spider feet raced along my spine. He was acting weird. Weird enough to wonder if his mental deterioration was happening faster than we assumed.

He raised his head, and a carefully composed smile was firmly in place. He got to his feet and brushed his now empty hands against his jeans. The move flashing the damning scratches that decorated his wrists. Scratches Kelsey left behind when she tried to pry his hands from around her neck.

Violent fury cascaded through me, all sharp edges and

bright intent. Forgetting the very real flesh and blood man standing next to me, I launched myself at the monster taunting me from the past.

Strong arms wrapped around me and held me back. Ellery's image broke and scattered like ashes on the wind.

⁕

I lay on the bed and listened to Kayden pace in the living room as he spoke on the phone with Delacourt. He was retelling what I shared about the weird heat mirage that manifested around Ellery just before his telekinetic drop of the bullet into the gun safe, and his even weirder behavior at the end. I could only hear Kayden's side of the conversation, but it was enough to follow along.

"Yes, sir, she's certain he didn't jimmy the lock in any way." A pause. "No, but we know Nate's ability could have."

For the first time I considered the ramifications of Ellery using the full spectrum of the abilities he stole. If we listed just the ones we knew about—telekinesis, healing, fire, predicting the future—outwitting him would be difficult.

And if he got his hands on my ability?

Dear God, that wouldn't be good. My ability was a spy's wet dream—walk into any building, peek into the past, gather pass codes, see documented information, find out who met with whom, listen in on conversations—all of that and more. Who would consider security being breached *after* something was set in motion? For a moment, the bedroom walls crowded in, and the world took a sickening dive. A small whimper escaped.

Needing air, I got up and on shaky legs crossed to the sliding glass door. I opened the curtains wide and let the warm afternoon sun wash over me. Even this late in the afternoon, the July temperatures guaranteed hundred plus degrees. Right now, I needed that heat to chase away the unnatural chill settling into my bones.

I slid the door open and stepped out on the balcony. I tugged over one of the chairs tucked in the corner and settled in, propping my boots on the railing's edge. I slouched farther down in the chair and rested my head against the chair's back. The heat started to seep through muscles and sinew, until bit by bit, I began to warm. I closed my eyes against the stabbing sunlight. Not that it did much to alleviate the now familiar throb of an impending headache, another legacy of my jaunts into the past, but it helped. Microscopically, but still.

I sat there, trying not to think. I realized, after hearing the condo's AC kick in, that I had left the door open. I'd get up in a minute and close it so the electric bill wouldn't require ritual sacrifice. I just needed a minute. Maybe two. The faint sounds of people and traffic drifted from the street below to add an interesting counterbalance. I drifted, searching for a calm that hovered just out of reach.

Vibrant, ruby grooves carved into masculine wrists.

Kelsey gasping in much-needed air, her face, bruised and pale.

Her fingers gouging into tan-skinned wrists, struggling to pry them from her neck.

The frantic acceptance of her impending death, changing to accusation.

My eyes flashed open, and the sunlight left me blind, my vision white and hazy. Guilt and pain tore through me, jerking me upright, and my boots landed with a loud thump on the deck. I hunched over, drawing my legs up until my heels hooked the edge of my seat. I dropped my head to my knees, and wrapped my arms around my shins, holding myself together so I wouldn't shatter into unrecognizable pieces. I squeezed my eyes shut, gasping against the suffocating, hot air.

God, it hurt. So much so, I wanted to scream. But I couldn't.

Screaming wouldn't solve anything. It wouldn't bring Kelsey back. It wouldn't chase Ellery back into hell where he belonged. It wouldn't make anything right. Instead, I was left with no choice but to suck it up and play Ellery's sick game.

Time slipped by as I sat there, lost in the unlit spaces of my soul. There were lines I'd told myself I'd never cross, but in this particular moment, when grief and rage combined into an unforgiving storm, I would have crossed every single one in exchange for Ellery's destruction. Options I would never consider played through my mind, tempting me a little deeper into the darkness. It would be so easy to let go and give in to the driving need of revenge. There were things I learned, vicious, cold things, from my time in the military.

"Cyn?"

The sound of my name was accompanied by a stroking caress along my spine. It stopped the unconscious rocking motion I adopted and kept me from tumbling headlong into the moral abyss yawning at my feet. I blinked my eyes open, only then noticing the tears weighing down my lashes.

Kayden knelt next to me, his face etched with concern, and his eyes watchful. He waited until I focused on him. "Don't."

"Don't what?" My question was hoarse.

"Don't go down that road, you'll get lost."

I held his gaze, unable to answer, not caring how eerily well he read me. Part of me didn't care anymore. There was too much rage, too much guilt, too much pain; all of it coalescing into a pit that threatened to swallow me whole.

He reached out and brushed away the lingering tears. "You take that road, and you'll lose Kelsey forever." He curved his palm against my cheek. "You'll lose yourself, and then he'll have won. The price is too steep."

There was no judgment in his voice or his expression. Instead, a hint of some hard-won knowledge resonated through his words like a bell, the echoes of it spreading out and chasing back the whispers of vengeance luring me toward the edge.

"I'm not sure I care anymore," I whispered, meeting his gaze without flinching.

"You care, or you wouldn't still be here." He continued to watch me, giving me nowhere to hide.

At any other time, I would dodge the intense eye contact, but now, I feared the loss of it would send me careening into hell.

As if he knew, he asked, "If Kelsey were alive, and you acted on any of those ideas running around in your head to get her back, would she understand?"

His question made me pause and think beyond my immediate pain and chaos. Would she have understood?

Yes.

Would she have approved?

No, because Kelsey's moral compass had always been steadier than mine. Her lines weren't drawn in the dirt but etched into steel. The difference between us made some of our late-night conversations difficult. Yet, there were times when the nightmares wouldn't leave me alone, and she was the one who would sit and listen. When I battled my way through decisions made in my time overseas, she would be the one to ask the tough questions. Those discussions gave me something solid to hold onto until the sun rose.

So now, when the darkness seemed all encompassing, I needed to borrow Kelsey's compass, just for a little bit, just until I could justify the faith of the man sitting in front of me. The decision drew me back from the crumbling edge and firmed the ground under my feet. I turned into his touch and covered his hand with mine. I pressed my lips against his palm. "Thank you."

In that quiet moment of understanding, the nebulous

connection between us strengthened, and for the first time since all this horror started, I didn't feel so alone.

He rocked forward and placed a chaste kiss on my forehead, then rose to his feet, not letting go of my hand.

In an attempt to re-establish some normalcy, I asked, "What did Delacourt say?" I set my feet to the deck and started to rise from my chair.

He let my hand go. "There's been some chatter about a pending sale." He stepped back, turned, and headed to the sliding glass door.

I opened my mouth to reply but a blurry form popped up inches from Kayden and cut my response short. Whoever it was pulled back the curtains on sliding glass door, their attention on the second tower of condos across the way. The image made my skin crawl and the hair on the back of my neck stood at attention. Having the past take part in my present shocked the hell out of me.

I must have made some noise because Kayden paused halfway through the sliding glass door and started to turn toward me.

My body was moving before everything clicked into place. A red dot appeared at the base of Kayden's neck as instincts outpaced thought. I sprang toward him, sending my chair tumbling to the side. I executed a clumsy tackle, hitting him just below his waist. My weight slammed into him, leaving him no time to react as we hit the ground. His pained "umpff" stopped my heart, but the echoing crack had me shoving him deeper into the condo.

For the first time I cursed the floor to ceiling glass windows. The expanse of glass offered zero protection from the sniper. My spine did its best to crawl out of my flesh as I covered Kayden's unmoving body. I cursed as I shoved the close to two hundred pounds of dead weight across tile. Not an easy feat when you were attempting a low profile on the seventh floor of a high-rise. Yet with adrenaline's help, I got us both into the bathroom, where the only opening left was the small, high window in the wall above.

I counted the seconds waiting for a second crack. It didn't come. With each passing second, the chance of a second shot dissipated. When I reached thirty, I felt confident enough to push off of Kayden. The abused muscles in my thigh throbbed as I sat back on my heels next to his prone body and ran my shaking hands over him. My fingers tangled in his hair, tracing over his skull searching for an entry wound.

Nothing met my touch.

Relief began to peek out. Then just above his ear, warm wetness coated my fingers. I pulled back bloody fingers and the world stilled.

Chapter Fourteen

"No, no, no," I whispered. "Kayden, dammit!"

Cracks appeared on my heart, running deeper than expected. I didn't dare turn on the light to get a closer look. I gingerly traced the wound, muttering the entire time. Only when I realized it was a furrow, not a hole, did I stop.

A graze.

I dropped my hands and sat back on my heels. Somehow, some way, we'd gotten lucky. "Thank you, God."

After sending the heartfelt prayer up, I fumbled in the under-sink cabinet until I found a washcloth. Rising just enough to turn on the tap, I got the cloth wet, and then dropped back down to press it against his wound. I kept one hand on his back, finding comfort in the rise and fall of his breathing.

Eventually a low groan signaled his return to consciousness. He tried to push up. "What the hell?"

"Stop, Kayden, take it easy."

Unsurprisingly, he didn't listen. Instead, he shrugged off my hands and gingerly turned over until his head rested in my lap.

I repositioned the washcloth, noting his bleeding had slowed, a good sign. I brushed aside his hair and uncovered an obvious bump high on the left side of his forehead. I winced at the angry red it currently sported. "That's going to leave a mark."

He lifted his hand and carefully probed the area. "Dammit, Cyn next time tackle me where there's padding."

"I figured your chances with the tile were a hell of a lot better than with a bullet."

"Bullet?"

Instead of answering, I asked, "What do you remember?"

He relaxed into my lap. Tiny lines taking up residence on his brow and bracketing his eyes as he went back over recent events. "We were getting ready to talk about Delacourt's call. I was heading back in because it was a furnace outside, then you made a little squeaky sound." Before I could argue that I didn't squeak, he continued, "You were dead white, staring just past my shoulder, then nothing." He blinked and refocused on me. "What did you see that I didn't?"

I bit my lower lip and avoided his piercing gaze, staring determinedly at the washcloth as I repositioned it yet again. His hand came up and caught my wrist, holding me still. He didn't say anything. He didn't have to.

I took a breath and gave in. "Someone was standing next to you, but inside, holding back the curtain. His attention was focused on the second tower." How to explain some-thing instinctual? "Something just..." I trailed off, unable to finish.

"Do we need to be concerned the past is showing up without an invite?"

I pulled on my wrist, just enough to get him to let go. How could he be so calm when my hands were still shaking? "No, maybe it was a fluke." Maybe. "The thing was, there was a laser sight on you."

Kayden folded his hands on his stomach, his attention never wavering. "Sloppy. So, a message then?"

Laser sights left a telltale red dot on a target, which meant a shooter generally used it only when they wanted to keep someone 'polite' without imparting actual physical damage.

"Maybe." I thought of how long we were exposed on the balcony prior to the shot, and corrected, "Yeah, definitely a message."

He settled deeper into my lap, unaware of how much of a temptation he presented. "From Ellery?"

My fingers tingled with the urge to sink into Kayden's thick mix of blond and brown hair. *Damn man should model for some shampoo commercial.* I looked away and considered my answer. There was nothing distinctive about the figure. Hell, I couldn't even tell if it was male or female. Yet part of me didn't think it was Ellery. "I don't think it was him."

"Why not?"

"The clothes weren't the same, and I think whoever it was, was shorter."

"We have another player?" Tension invaded the man lying in my lap.

I looked down and realized my fingers were buried in his hair, absently stroking him. I went to pull my fingers free. "It looks that way."

He stopped me. "Don't, it helps with the headache."

Heat rose in my face, but as soon as he let me go, I restarted the soothing motion. Silence descended between us, and those steel blue eyes searched my face. I had no idea what he was looking for, but I refused to look away. Looking away meant I felt guilty, and I didn't. Not much, anyway. I kept stroking his hair and bit-by-bit he relaxed. Between the soothing motion and his reassuring presence, my thoughts calmed. "Ellery left the bullet after killing Kelsey."

"What makes you so sure?"

"There were fresh scratches on his wrists." My fingers stilled for a moment, then resumed. "Marks Kelsey left behind."

I waited for the inevitable question of who I thought the *K* was meant for. Instead, he proved how much I really didn't understand the male species.

"That only proves it wasn't Ellery behind the scope. If he's serious about taking me out of the equation, he'd never let you spot the sight, nor would he miss."

His nonchalant comment threw me off guard and I stopped mid-stroke. I gave his hair a gentle tug. "Don't, Kayden."

He blinked up at me.

"Don't minimize the threat. Just because it wasn't Ellery's finger on the trigger, doesn't mean he's done playing with us. He's like a cat with a mouse, bat it around enough, it'll never see the end coming." I hesitated, worried that what I said next would seem overly paranoid. "What if he considers us both bait and prey?"

He frowned. "How do you figure?"

"If we aren't the only ones trying to track him down, he could use us to lure them out, or they could us to bring him out. Either way, we're screwed."

He winced, probably from my grip on his hair more than explanation. "If that's the case, we either sit here and wait to get played, or we turn the tables. To do that we need to figure out who else has joined the game and why. Knowing that would give us enough to lure Ellery out of hiding." He tugged my hand out of his hair, then held it against his chest. "I don't know about you, but I'm not fond of being hunted."

No, being hunted wasn't my idea of a good time, either. "You don't think I'm reaching?"

"About Ellery?"

I nodded.

"No, because it makes sense." He let me go and started to sit up. His breath hissed out at the careful movement. "The stolen information is still missing, Ellery's in the wind and looking for payback." Finally upright, he leaned against the wall at our backs. "If his former bosses know anything about him, all they need to do, is sit back and wait for him to surface."

I bent my legs until I could rest my arms on my knees. "It wouldn't take much to connect the dots, not with the bloody trail he's leaving." Smears of rust decorated my fingers.

Kayden went to nod but stopped. "Right, that information is worth a lot of money. Ellery won't hold on to it long. Eventually, he's going to set up a sale. Which, according to Delacourt, may be happening sooner than we think." When I looked at him, he grimaced. "Her source confirmed there were rumors the information will be up for auction in the next couple of days."

"How reliable is this source?" It was a legit question since regular monitoring of unsavory activities rarely panned out.

"Very. The source has been deep undercover for the last two years."

Holy shit, that poor soul. Twenty-four months of living and breathing in the darkest underbellies would leave a hell of a mark. "That doesn't give us much time."

"Nope, but a local name came up. She wants us to check it out." He began the laborious process of getting to his feet.

I watched him, prepared to catch him if he went down. "Want a hand there, hotshot?" He grunted, and taking that as an affirmative, I got up and added my support to his efforts. Getting him vertical didn't take long, but when we were done, pain pinched his face. "Or maybe some aspirin?"

"Couldn't hurt." He leaned against the counter, head bowed.

I grabbed the white tablets from the medicine cabinet, filled the small glass on the counter, and handed him both. "Stay here till I secure the bedroom."

I managed a grand total of three steps before he reached out and stopped me. He opened his mouth, most likely to spout something silly, but I held my hand up, palm out. "Don't, it'll take me a few minutes, and you're in no shape, so just stay here."

He let me go.

Smart man.

Five minutes later, the condo was once again hidden behind heavy curtains and Kayden was sprawled out on the sofa.

In the kitchen, I dumped the OJ down the sink and tossed the container in the recycle bin. "Who are we checking out this time?"

"Joaquin Hobbes, CEO of NSpirit."

I turned on the faucet and rinsed the sink. "NSpirit? Sounds familiar."

"A synthetic biology company headquartered in Chicago. They hold a few contracts with the Department of Defense."

I turned the water off, and then leaned my hip against the counter. "And Hobbes just happens to be in Phoenix?"

"Not only does NSpirit have a building here in the Valley, but it seems Hobbes keeps a summer home just north of Scottsdale, and he's in residence."

"Hmmm." Coincidence be damned, it couldn't be that easy.

Giving myself time to think, I grabbed a glass, filled it with water, and then walked over to collapse in the plush chair next to the couch. Stretching out my legs, I slid down until the toes of my boots almost touched the coffee table leg, and the back of my head rested against the chair's pillow top. I took a sip of my water, then cradled the glass against my stomach. "And Delacourt wants us to go to his home?"

"Nope, she put a team on his house. We get to go to dinner."

"Dinner?"

"Hobbes has a dinner meet on his agenda at The Dragon."

And a GPS stuck up his ass. It shouldn't surprise me that Delacourt had such a detailed agenda for Hobbes. No government group, acknowledged or not, existed without at least one very scary, very good hacker. Everyone lived their life in the electronic world, and for those who could navigate it, those lives were open books. "Who's he meeting?"

"A woman. Not his wife." Kayden sounded weary.

I turned my head and studied him. His arm was thrown over his eyes, his lips were a tight line framed by his neat goatee, and his skin was still pale. "You sure you're up for this?"

"Not like I have much choice."

Too true. Delacourt might not be my commanding officer, but Kayden still had to ask how high when she said, 'jump'. "At least the food will be good."

His lips twitched, but he didn't move from his supine position. "We're not going in, Cyn."

"Fine," I grumbled. "I guess we better grab some drive-thru."

We both fell silent. The cushy chair felt good, so I sank a little deeper and let my eyes drift close. Under my hand, the glass sweated.

Kayden broke the quiet. "We can't stay here."

I didn't bother to open my eyes. "I know."

Kelsey's condo was compromised. First by Ellery, then by whoever followed him. Not that I planned on staying long anyway. My duffle and Tito's journals were locked in the back of my Jeep. The decision to come here was a Hail Mary move that worked out way too well. Plus, there was a part of me that needed to come back, needed to see Kelsey one more time, needed to see her without fear and resignation in her eyes. A solid lump of sorrow settled in my chest.

"It'll get easier."

I blinked my eyes open and turned to him with a frown. "What? Are you reading my mind now?"

"Nope." He lifted the arm over his eyes and captured my gaze. "Your energy. The stronger the emotion, the clearer it comes through. Makes it hard to miss."

I wasn't sure I wanted him knowing how I felt, so I threw up every mental block I could.

He gave me a faint grin. "And you just locked it all down."

Wow, definitely disconcerting. "Have you been able to read me that well from the get-go?"

His grin disappeared. "No, most of the time, the energy signatures resemble faint bands of color. The more we work together, the brighter yours become."

I sat up and the last little pieces of ice rattled against my glass. I set it on the coffee table. "Delacourt was right to worry."

Even lying down, he managed to shrug. "I'd rather not go looking for trouble. We have enough things to stress about, without adding in something we can't change. Besides, Ellery's signature is getting clearer too. I just wish I could get a glimpse at where he's going."

That reminded me of a question that had been spinning around in my head. "You called Liza a pre-cog and Risia a seer. What's the difference?"

He took my change of subject in stride. "It depends on an individual's psychic strength, but pre-cogs see one future, and can determine what will happen in the next hour or so, but the further out they go, the less accurate their predications become. Seers see various futures, but those futures are fluid. Why?"

"I've been trying to figure out how Ellery stays ahead of

everyone. I thought maybe it had to do with the ability he stole from Liza."

"Maybe, but she was a mid-range psychic, which put her accuracy at about forty percent." He sat up slowly, his color a bit closer to normal. "I'd be more concerned if Ellery got his hands on Risia."

"How come?"

"Risia's accuracy is closer to seventy percent."

I gave a low whistle. "Guess she's not mid-range, then."

He shook his head. "She compared being a seer to looking at wall full of screens. If each screen started with the same action and the same players, it wouldn't be long before each screen showed different scenarios. All it takes is one person to make one unexpected decision and everything changes. Seers have to have an anchor that holds them to the present, or they'll get lost watching those screens. She called it a Cassandra Spiral."

The implications of his words sent a shiver of dread down my spine. It sounded eerily similar to slipping too deep into the tides of the past. "That doesn't sound good."

He grimaced. "Yeah, not something I'd wish on anyone."

I sat back with a loud sigh, and tapped my fingers absently on the chair's armrest. Sorting through everything we had on Ellery to this point, I thought it through out loud. "Okay, we know Ellery's got the stolen information and he's getting ready to sell it, probably to Hobbes. What does it get him?"

"The big two, money and power," Kayden offered.

I nodded. "And payback. By selling this information, he not only keeps it out of the government's hands, but also from whoever hired him to steal it in the first place."

"He's playing a dangerous game."

"He doesn't think so."

"You reading minds now?"

I shook my head and got to my feet, needing to move as I

kept sifting through the bits and pieces. "Basic profiling. Ellery is a psychopath, so he believes he's in control and thrives on manipulation. Therefore, he'll make sure he holds the power, using it to force everyone else to move where he wants them. Money, power, manipulation," I ticked off each trait. "Then there's his need for payback. When we stopped the initial sale from going through, we stole his control, so now he's stealing it back."

"By killing each of us and taking our abilities." Kayden sat on the edge of the couch and watched me. "But each time he does, his personality fractures."

"Maybe, maybe not."

His eyes narrowed. "What do you mean?"

I stopped in front of him, the coffee table between us. "If he felt remorse, or shame for killing, then yeah, he'd start to crack, but he's a psychopath, Kayden. Guilt? Shame? Those don't exist for him. The only one that matters to Ellery is Ellery. We screwed with his plans. Whoever hired him, left him hanging in the wind, now he's going to make us all pay. That scares me, because he has no boundaries, nothing to stop how far he'll go. What if he's using this possible sale to lure everyone out into the open so he can take us all out in one big blow?"

"That's awfully arrogant."

"Right." I moved to the couch and perched next to him. "What happens when you believe you've got it all under control?"

Grim acknowledgement colored Kayden's face. "You begin to make mistakes."

"Right." Cautious excitement bloomed as I spotted a possible chink in Ellery's intimidating armor. "If you know who's coming after you, and you have access to Liza's ability, you're arrogant. You begin to believe your own press. To get ahead of him, we have to change our role in the game."

"And how do we do that?" There was a world of reservations in Kayden's question.

I took a deep breath. "We need to check out the other tower."

There was a beat of silence. "Wait," he said. "You want to go over to where the shooter was positioned and do a walk through?"

Not understanding his disbelief, I frowned. "I'm not looking for physical evidence. There's no way anything traceable was left behind. I just want to figure out who was behind the scope."

He pushed to his feet with a muffled oath. He took a couple of steps away, and then returned to lean over me, his hands braced on the back of the sofa, trapping me without touching me.

At his unexpected move, I lifted my chin and met his glare head on. "What?"

"Are you a glutton for punishment?" he growled.

I lifted my hands and set them on the chest looming in front of me. My fingers curled into the heat under my palms. But it didn't stop me from pushing him back or growling with frustration. "No," I scrambled to my feet, forcing him to straighten. It put only a few inches between us, leaving me with nowhere to go. I fisted my hands and set my jaw, trying to ignore how close we were. "You said it yourself, you don't like being hunted. Why not try getting something from the site and see if we can't get the upper hand for once?"

"You keep pushing yourself into the past and you're going to do irreparable damage."

"You don't know that."

His gaze darkened. "Nosebleeds aren't good, Cyn. Add in the fact you're now seeing the past without looking for it, I'd say there are reasons to be concerned."

"Getting shot is pretty irreparable, too," I whispered.

This close to him, I couldn't miss the pale undertones of his normally tanned skin. Behind his shaggy hair, the knot on his forehead was now an angry-looking, reddish-purple, and rusty streaks marred the gold and brown strands. All of it was a stark reminder of the terror that tore through me as he lay unconscious. As much as I wanted him to stay out of the line of fire, it was pointless to ask. He wasn't the kind to stay behind, any more than I was. My fingers moved without permission, gently brushing along his jaw. "I'm tired of playing catch-up, Kayden. If we don't get ahead of him…"

"I know." Frustration and worry lined his face. He captured my hand, squeezed, and then let go. He stepped back, finally letting me move. "A quick peek, nothing more, understand?"

"Roger that."

Chapter Fifteen

There were only two ways to get between the condo tower, the main lobby, or the fifth-floor gym. Since I wasn't up to facing Terrance, I opted for the gym. We stepped out of the elevator onto the fifth floor and my phone rang. Following Kayden as we headed down the hall, I checked the incoming number and answered. "Tag, did you make it?"

"Yeah, for all the good it did me." A myriad of rings and dings played background music to Tag's voice. "She's not here."

I reached out and grabbed Kayden's arm, bringing us both to a stop. My recent optimism at using Risia's ability started to dim. "What do you mean, she's not there?"

"Her apartment is empty, and it looks like she packed in a hurry." Serious disgruntlement colored Tag's words. "I'm going to run down some of her friends and see if I can't find out where she rabbited."

A niggling sense of unease rose, but considering I had no idea if it was legit or just part and parcel of my current circumstances, there wasn't much I could do. "Be careful, Hayseed."

"I will. I'll call you as soon as I get more information."

We said our good-byes, and then I tucked my phone away.

Kayden read my worry. "Don't borrow trouble," he warned. "He'll be fine."

"Yeah, I know."

We continued down the hall, heading toward second tower's elevator. A sign was posted above the call buttons. I nudged Kayden, drawing his attention to it. The sign indicated that the eleventh through fifteenth floors were under construction, and inaccessible by elevator without a special pass.

We exchanged raised eyebrows. He gave me a slow nod and I hit ten. We rode up in silence. Once we disembarked, I took lead, heading toward the door at the far end. I pushed it open and stepped into the stairwell. I held the door open while Kayden slipped by. As soon the door closed, locking us in the stairwell, the temperature rose by a good fifteen degrees.

I snuck a glance at Kayden, his coloring was better but still a little wan. "Ready?"

"After you."

We made our way up the stifling stairs, my boots echoing hollowly in the cement confines. "You have your B and E kit?" I threw over my shoulder, wondering if maybe I should've asked sooner.

I took his grunt for a yes. We stopped at the top of the stairs before the door marked with the big 11. A surreptitious glance up showed no blinking red light in the security camera perched in the corner. "Strange."

He wiped a thin layer of sweat from his forehead. "What?"

"The security camera's down."

He looked up, then turned to me. "That can't be good."

Or maybe we caught a break. "Guess we're starting on this floor."

With lock picks in hand, he made short work of the heavy door. It opened into a plastic-draped hallway. There were no murmurs of voices, no pounds, clicks, or motorized sounds to indicate any workmen remained on site. Still, we stayed as quiet as possible, drifting down the corridor. Based on the trajectory of the shot, we could narrow our search to the condos sitting above the pool.

Unhung doors rested against unpainted walls, while sheets of heavy plastic draped doorways. White dust layered the cement floors and various construction detritus. Not wanting to leave visible footprints, we picked our path carefully. Halfway down the hall on the left side, I found the first possible position for our sniper. I pulled the plastic aside, and slipped inside, Kayden on my heels.

Bare wood frames outlined future interior walls and allowed an unimpeded view of the windows overlooking the pool area. Even knowing our shooter wouldn't have lingered, Kayden and I cleared the space before moving to the windows. Then we started our search from opposing ends.

I studied the dust covered floor for any indication our shooter had been there. No marks. Nothing. I met Kayden at the wall of windows. Together, we ran fingers over the edges, looking for openings, cracks, anything a shooter could use. Nothing. I met Kayden's gaze and shook my head. We moved out and on to the next unfinished condo.

On the third condo we hit pay dirt. An arid breeze swirled drywall powder into mini dust devils that twisted their way through half-built walls and wound over the paint-flecked concrete. At the wall of windows, a missing pane of glass left a gap on the far-right side.

I moved closer, and found the first imprint, a smudged print of a boot toe. Mimicking the angle of the mark, I lined up an imaginary shot. Sure enough, Kelsey's second-bedroom balcony came into line.

Behind me, Kayden's low voice said, "I've got signs of a shell casing."

Half turning, I found him crouched down on his heels,

arms on his knees. I joined him and studied the imprint. "Looks as if the shooter tried to brush it away." Looking around, I said, "Guess this is the place."

He raised his head and caught me with those disturbing navy eyes. "For the record, I'm not keen on you doing this."

My lips quirked, and not with humor. "Noted."

I had my own reservations, but not enough to outweigh the possible benefits. My gut said the shooter was after Ellery, not us. Which made me wonder why he would reveal himself by taking such a risky shot? All he had to do was stay quiet, follow along, and wait. Something had changed, and I wanted to know what it was. If that meant another trip down memory lane, so be it.

Kayden rose and dusted his hands on his jeans.

I followed suit, checking the sparse space for somewhere out of sight of the windows and the plastic-shrouded doorway. No need to advertise our presence. A half-finished interior wall lined by a row of 2x4's, blocked the door's line of sight. "Let's move over here."

He scrutinized the unfinished wall. "Better than nothing, I guess."

I stepped around him and led the way. We stood facing each other with maybe a foot between us.

Kayden folded his arms over his chest. "Touch or no touch?"

"Let's go touch free, maybe we can get what we need with just a surface look."

He backed up so he could lean against the wall. "I want you in front of me."

I looked pointedly at the small space between us. "I am in front of you."

He reached out and tugged me until I stood between his feet. Every breath I took was colored with his unique blend of man and spice. His gaze was hard. "If you start to bleed, I'm bringing you out."

"Fine." The tension in my shoulders loosened. Somewhere in my brain, I equated his presence with protection. Maybe it should bother me to rely on him this much, but Kelsey's death had crumbled my normally stable foundation. Right now, I needed him, needed to feel as if I weren't completely alone. When this was over, and he moved on to the next assignment, his absence would be the equivalent of ripping off the scab from an unhealed wound.

It would suck.

My gaze dropped to the floor as I pushed my brooding thoughts aside and cleared my mind. Once again, the slide into my psychic headspace was akin to stepping from one room to another. Unease tripped along my nerve endings.

"What?"

Caught off guard by his question, I jerked my gaze up. "What, what?"

"You're worried about something."

Stupid aura colors. "Stop reading me."

Kayden's image held a painful clarity, one that put him in stark relief against the room's hazy, watercolor consistency that was associated with the past. The blue of his eyes shifted into a mesmerizing variety of blue, taking on unexpected depth. The strange occurrence was not limited to his eyes. His hair was no longer a combination of blonds, browns, and blacks, but a stunning collection of amber, onyx, and gold. Even his body appeared more etched, for lack of a better word. As compelling as the strange clarity was, the tie between us that was my anchor to the present, remained steady and strong. Even without touching. "Weird."

He crooked an eyebrow at me. "Going to get pissed if I ask what's weird?"

"I'll tell you later." *Maybe.*

I turned around and scanned the half-finished space in front of me and waited. Vague impressions of various men with tools and hard hats moved in overlapping scenes. With no real strong emotions, the past wavered in front of me like a desert mirage. There was no way to tell time, but when a burly, heavy-set man popped out of nowhere to lay a 2x4 against the wall, I jerked back instinctively.

"Cyn?"

"I'm okay, just wasn't expecting to get brained by a 2x4."

"See anything interesting?"

I shook my head. "Not yet. I'm getting pieces of the construction crews." I narrowed my eyes as if that would somehow help me filter through the past. The images became less hectic, and more and more vague. "I think they're packing up for the day."

The images faded away, leaving a ghostly imprint of the empty condo. It reminded me of dealing with a double lens. I f I could find just the right aperture, I could line the two images up until I had a 3-D representation of the real thing. I tried and failed. Repeatedly. Disappointment crept in. Maybe it wasn't this condo.

A breeze reached through the gap in the glass and ruffled the plastic hanging in the doorframe. The material's movement almost obscured the emerging figure, but thankfully I caught it. Battered baseball cap, T-shirt, jeans, and backpack. It gained definition as it moved toward the window but remained slightly out of focus. A fierce smile stretched my face. "Got him."

"Male?"

"Sorry, can't tell, the image isn't clear enough."

The figure, smaller and thinner than Ellery, stood by the open pane, gazing out. The image knelt and shrugged the backpack off to the floor. Piece by piece the rifle emerged and quickly took shape.

"He's using a concealable, precision tactical rifle." If the situation wasn't what it was, I'd be green for one of those customizable bad boys.

Unfortunately, there wasn't enough emotional echoes to get a clearer picture. I wasn't surprised because the sniper's movements spoke of experience and practice. They swung the rifle onto the tripod and adjusted the sight. Focused on the shooter's movements, I sucked in a breath. "The shooter's female."

"You recognize her?"

"No, her wrists, they're narrow. Still can't see her face, stupid baseball hat."

"Any identifying logos?"

"She's gone for the standard black motif."

The sniper set her eye to the sight and waited. The image started to fray and dissipate. Then she gave a tiny jerk, and for a moment the memory held itself together. "She's taking a phone call." *Really? What kind of sniper took a phone call?*

"Can you hear anything?"

I shook my head. "I almost lost her before her phone rang."

"Let's see if this will help." It was my only warning before he curled his hands around my waist.

That fast the scene in front of me graduated from rabbit ears to high definition. "Holy crap." I tried to hang on while the world reset around me.

"They just entered the condo." The sound of our shooter's voice came through without any interference.

"Definitely female. She's reporting to someone." Not wanting to miss any of the conversation, I covered Kayden's hands, ensuring we wouldn't get separated.

"No, haven't seen him." A pause. *"Yes, sir, they had some note-books."* Another pause. *"Understood."*

Our little assassin clicked her phone shut, tucked it away, and reset her eye to the scope.

"Um, did you happen to notice a tail at Ramirez's?"

His fingers tightened. "No, why?"

"She just told someone we pulled notebooks out of his place." She must be a chameleon for neither one of us to spot her. "And we were right, they're waiting for us to lead them to Ellery."

"Do you recognize her?" he pushed.

"Maybe?" Something about her set off little, warning bells. "I think, maybe, I've seen her somewhere before."

"Whe—," An imperious demand trilled. He lifted one hand from my waist and the image shivered, lost a bit of definition, but held. "Time to go, Cyn," he said. "Hobbes just left his office, and we need to get into place, so we can switch out with Bishop."

"I don't think she'll give us anything more." In truth, the image lost it vibrancy, probably because there wasn't much happening.

"Can you fast forward it to make sure?"

"Yeah, give me a moment."

With the extra boost from his touch, I arrowed through the unfocused layers, navigating the memories with an unusual ease. A flash caught my attention and, concentrating, I brought it up front and center. Sure enough, the moment she pulled the trigger, her emotional signature spiked. Other than a soft curse at her miss, she made quick work of breaking down the rifle, retrieving the casing, and getting the hell out of Dodge.

"I got nothing." I stepped away and broke our connection. My surroundings dimmed and resettled. A low-level headache kicking in. "Did you pick up anything?"

"A faint energy signature, but not one I recognize." He tugged me close. "Headache?"

"Yeah," I mumbled.

"Close your eyes and give me a moment."

Following his directions, I rested my forehead against his chest. His clever fingers began a gentle pattern over my temples, around my head, and down my neck. It didn't take long for the tension to melt away under his ministrations. A low groan of relief escaped, and my body curled into his, craving more. "That feels good."

That was a huge understatement. His touch melted muscle, heated skin, and left a languorous craving for more behind. I took what he offered, and reveled in the unexpected experience, floating in the quiet moment out of time. His touch finally slowed. His fingers cupping my neck with a gentle squeeze. I tilted my head back and raised a bemused gaze.

He cradled my head in his hand, holding me in place. Steel blue deepened to a dark navy with his undisguised desire. The look stole my breath and woke something I wasn't sure I was ready for. His breath curled with mine, and my hands were locked around his waist, holding him close, my fingers tracing the indent of his spine.

The temptation was too much.

He dipped his head and captured my mouth with a stunning gentleness. He nibbled softly along my lips until they parted on a sigh. He took the invite for what it was, and our tongues met in a tender tangle.

I ran my short nails over his cloth-covered back, and then traced a path on either side of his spine until I reached his shoulders. Trying to get closer, I rose on tiptoe, the hard evidence of his arousal pressed against me.

Someone groaned.

His hands moved to cradle my face, and the sensation of his calloused palms against my skin ignited a cascade of fireworks. His kiss shifted from gentle to wicked as he stopped teasing us both and took control.

The change acted like dry wood with a spark, and I went up like an inferno. *Easy, it would be so easy to stay here and let the storm take me. Take him.* The promise behind his touch tempted, teased, and burrowed right past my normal self-preservation.

The shock of how fast and deep he managed to get in, had me pulling back, gasping for breath.

Above me, a completely satisfied, and very male look settled on his face. He brushed his thumb over my damp lower lip. "Better?"

My tongue flicked out, swiping over it and a deep color rose under his cheekbones. "You're a dangerous man, Shaw." My voice was husky with unfulfilled wants.

"So are you," his equally rough answer made me smile.

Needing a little payback for the gnawing hunger he woke, I leaned in and pressed against him, feeling him jerk in response. Pushing up on my toes, I nipped his chin, then set him free. "Definitely better than aspirin."

Turning away, I managed one step before a sharp swat on my ass had me spinning around.

"Tease." His wicked grin spiked my pulse.

I laughed. For a moment, despite the fact we were hunting and being hunted, it felt right, free.

We ended up back in my Jeep. This time I drove. We made a quick stop at Kelsey's place one last time to pick up extra ammunition for our nines, and my rifle. I hoped not to need it but felt better having it close. Me and my metal teddy bears. On top of that, I wasn't sure when I'd be back to Kelsey's condo.

Now we were on our way to meet up with the mysterious Bishop. Kayden had his phone out, his fingers flying as we did the stop-and-go dance through rush hour traffic.

"Who's Bishop?"

He didn't even look up. "Part of my team."

I checked my mirrors, and made a lane change from crawling to meandering. "Your team?"

My tone brought his head up and he scowled. "Who else did you think Delacourt would call in for support?"

I kept my attention on the traffic and managed an awkward shrug. "Considering all I know about this unit is that Delacourt runs it, it's filled with psychics—three of whom are you, Tag, and a fortune teller called Risia—I don't have clue. Hence, the question. It's not like there's been time to get the skinny on everything."

And wow, guess I was more bothered about not knowing who I was working with than I realized. Maybe it was time to correct that little detail as I was stuck in a car with nothing more pressing than making sure my front fender didn't kiss someone's bumper.

When Kayden started talking it was clear he was thinking along the same lines. "There are three teams ranging from eight to ten apiece. Each one answers to its team leader. The team leaders answer to Delacourt."

"Do you know who she answers to?"

"Ultimately the POTUS."

I rolled my eyes. "Thanks, smartass, I think I could figure that much out. I meant before him."

"I know you did, but that's not something I can answer right now."

And why did that sting? Our meandering lane became a parking lot, so I looked at him.

He shook his head. "You know better. Until you're brought on officially, you get what you see."

My fingers tapped on the steering wheel as I turned my attention back to the road, the rush of resentment fading under logic. "Yeah, but it was worth a shot." Traffic began to move. "I'm going to assume you're a team leader, and Tag's on your team since you both showed up together. Where does Risia fit in?"

"She's an official, government-sanctioned consultant for PSY-IV."

"A contractor?"

"Her ability makes her worth a pretty penny," Kayden said. "She's got a very impressive client list."

"And there's no conflict of interest there?" The more I found out about Risia, the more curious I became. Maybe when this was over, I'd get a chance to satisfy that curiosity.

"Not that I'm aware of." He paused. "Did Delacourt offer you a job?"

I thought about our conversation in the parking lot in Sedona, and my humor disappeared. I wasn't sure I wanted what Delacourt offered, so I said, "No."

He angled his body, and I felt the weight of his gaze. "Liar."

His accusation lit a flare of temper, but I ignored it. "At this time, we've agreed to help each other until Ellery is stopped. That's it."

"Sorry, don't believe you. You were under consideration before the joint mission, so I'm finding it hard to believe she wouldn't make you the offer now."

I wasn't prepared for the rush of bitterness that sharpened my voice. "Why? Because you all came back and said, 'oops, sorry Cyn,' so now I should be happy drinking the damn psychic Kool-Aid?"

He sighed. "Shit happens. You're going to have to forgive and forget. Tag and I explained what happened. We can't change the past."

No shit, Sherlock. His dismissive attitude rubbed me the wrong way. Of the two of us, did he think I didn't know that? In the last, brutal forty-eight hours the past had come back and bitch-slapped my life into a giant mess. My harsh laugh slashed through air. "Did you forget who you're talking to, Kayden? I get it. Really, I do, but there's a huge difference between forgiving and forgetting. I trusted once and look how well that worked out. Excuse me for being a bit cautious."

Our exit came up and I bullied my way over to it.

"So, you're going to cut off your nose to spite your face?" He pinched the bridge of his nose as if seeking control. When he let go and spoke, his voice was hard. "Look at me and tell me that working with me and using your ability to stop Ellery doesn't do it for you on some level. I dare you."

I kept my mouth shut, refusing to answer.

Disgust laced his voice. "Jesus, Cyn, what happened to the woman I fell for? The one who'd race into hell with a glass of ice water?"

Fell for? What game was he playing? "She got burned," I spit out, furious tears blurring my vision before I blinked them away.

"Pull over." His command was ice cold.

"We don't have time."

"Make it. Pull. Over."

Jerking the wheel, I took a sharp turn into a corner gas station and slammed the Jeep into park. I unbuckled my seat belt, and twisted around until I was face to face with him. "What?"

He leaned in, until our faces were inches apart and all I could see was him. "You are not Ellery's only victim, so stopping acting like it. I'm sorry, so very, fucking sorry, he killed Kelsey. But right now, if we want to make sure he doesn't kill someone else's Kelsey, or Flash or Liza, or Nate or Mike, you need to move past what happened in Pakistan. It sucked. No one will argue that. Was it fair? Not in any way, shape, or form. But was it fair of you to run away and hide?"

"I didn't run away," I ground out between clenched teeth.

"Yes, you did," he snapped back. "You hid. For six months, Cyn. You wouldn't answer my calls. Wouldn't answer Tag's. You shut us out. Shut me out. Why?"

The yawning pit of volatile emotions I successfully avoided since recognizing who was kicking in the door at my cabin, opened between us. Ingrained insecurities blended with new doubts, while paralyzing guilt wrapped around suffocating fear. Thanks to the events from the last two days, old emotions piled on new, crumbling the shaky ground beneath my feet. I floundered for a foothold in the emotional wreckage. My voice emerged as a harsh whisper, "Because..." My throat closed, choking off my voice. *Was I really going to tell him?*

"Because, why?" His voice was careful, quiet.

I shook my head, unable to give the shameful words form, because if I did, it would make them inescapably real. I stared into his face, seeing just how much my actions had hurt him, and the real answer could no longer be tucked away, hidden behind other excuses. The damning words fell between us. "Because why would you want me? You deserve someone better, not me, not this mess."

He reared back as if I had slapped him and ran an unsteady hand through his hair. "You really believe that?"

For a moment I couldn't breathe, scared of his impending rejection, my heart aching, but I nodded. Once.

Instead of pushing away, he gathered me close, and wrapped me in a solid heat, holding on tight. "God, Cyn, you're such a beautiful, mixed-up idiot."

The gruff exasperation in his voice warmed the numb edges of my heart. It was also the final straw. All the chaos of the last six months and the pain of the last two days collided, blowing apart the fragile illusion of control, and left me exposed.

I wound my arms around his neck, buried my face in his chest, and settled into his embrace, needing this unexpected connection, needing him. His soft murmur flowed over me, offering what comfort he could. As the emotional storm raged,

I clung to him, using him as an anchor, knowing he wouldn't let me go. Not this time.

Chapter Sixteen

When the storm finally passed, I sniffled and listened to the steady beat of Kayden's heart, relishing our tenuous connection. Even twisted at an awkward angle with the center console poking in all the wrong places, I didn't want to move. For the first time in what seemed like forever, my mind was blessedly numb, leaving me in a quiet oasis.

"Better?" His chest vibrated under my ear.

I nodded, not sure I could get anything out of my sore throat. The brush of his lips feathered across my forehead and trailed softly down until he reached the corner of my mouth. My breath stuttered at the exquisite touch and the heavy weight from the last couple of days felt lighter.

A wailing siren served as an unfortunate reminder of our surroundings, and a cop blew through the intersection answering unseen summons. Reality intruded, bringing the muted sounds of passing traffic. As much as I preferred to remain in his arms and forget what awaited us, it wasn't to be. We had things to do and people to meet.

Reluctantly, I pulled back, wiped a hand over my wet face, and caught sight of the time. I groaned. "We need to get going.

We're going to be late." I settled back behind the wheel, and threw the Jeep in gear.

Kayden shifted in his seat and winced. "How far out are we?"

"About ten minutes, if we're lucky." When a break in traffic emerged, I pulled out and got us back in the flow.

"I'll let Bishop know."

Kayden typed out a text as a comfortable quiet filled the space between us. Despite my emotional breakdown, the rough edges of my headache had smoothed out. Who knew a crying jag would result in more than a red nose and stuffy sinuses?

It was closer to fifteen minutes when we pulled in, five of which was spent navigating the tiny streets to the out-of-the-way parking lot near The Dragon. A man in dark sunglasses waited for us, leaning against a dust-covered SUV. Tall, broad, and muscles, he oozed menace, enough that if I was alone, I wouldn't step foot out of my Jeep. He walked toward us.

"Please tell me that's Bishop." If he wasn't, I was getting the hell out of dodge.

"Don't shut off the engine yet," Kayden advised as the walking threat got closer.

My hands tightened on the steering wheel as the back-passenger door opened, then Bishop was taking up space behind me. He pulled the door closed and pushed his sunglasses up. The dark frames barely made a dent in the wild explosion of reddish-brown curls.

A coffee-dark gaze swept over me in a quick once-over before moving to Kayden. Those dark eyes narrowed, and a thundercloud settled over the strong face. "What the hell happened to you, Shaw?"

I undid my seat belt, then turned until my back rested against the door. The new position allowed me to watch both men.

"Long story," Kayden brushed his question aside. "Where are we at?"

Bishop shifted his weight and dug into his pocket. "The Colonel called in the rest of the team, but the only ones who've made it in so far are me and Wolf. The others should be here tomorrow. Wolf's got eyes on Hobbes's house." His hand came back with two small ear buds. "Here."

I took the small device and tucked it in my ear. "You really think Ellery's going to try and contact him tonight?"

"Highly doubt it, but Delacourt's worried about the extra shadows," Kayden said.

Bishop sighed. "Nice of Ellery to bring friends to the party."

Kayden tucked his own earpiece in and arched an eyebrow at Bishop. "Are you really surprised?"

"Nah," Bishop answered. "Until we can figure out who the other player is, the Colonel wants eyes on Hobbes at all times. Hobbes and his sidepiece will probably drag out dinner for a couple of hours before heading out. Who's getting dinner tonight?"

"Kayden." My answer overrode Kayden's and brought forth a glare. I matched it with a sweet smile. "You have better people skills, besides…" I tilted my head to indicate the dark bag half hidden on the floorboards behind his seat. "Have camera, will people watch. Trust me, a woman with a camera won't be out of place."

"Fine," he growled, then he turned to the man watching our exchange with a small grin. "Where are you headed?"

Bishop's answer was simple. "Going to report into the Colonel, then hook up with Wolf."

"There better be coffee nearby." I copied Kayden's action and clicked on the earpiece. A soft click indicated an active line, and it was followed by Kayden's "check". Mine followed, then Bishop's.

"Wolf, status check." While Kayden checked in, I motioned to Bishop to hand me the camera bag. I pulled out my Nikon D3, attached one of my shorter lenses, and then dropped the strap over my neck.

"All quiet, no movement." A rough, smoker's voice filled my ear. "Heard you had some excitement on your end, Ghost."

Kayden flicked a look to Bishop, who just grinned. "I'm fine."

Unable to help myself, I snorted and continued my equipment check, propping my leg on the console to retighten my Sig's ankle holster. Kayden's color might be better, but the angry looking knot on his head wasn't. Knowing how pigheaded Kayden could be, I had no doubt he was ignoring a hell of a headache.

"Sounds as if someone doesn't agree," Wolf said. "That you, Bishop?"

The big man in my backseat gave a small smile. "Not me. That would be Ghost's sidekick."

I folded my arms, and then joined the conversation. "He dodged a bullet and ran face first into a floor. It left a mark."

A hoarse bark sounded in my ear. "Yeah, floors tend to do that."

"I'm fine." Kayden untucked his T-shirt to hide his gun. "Enough chitchat, time to gear up. Wolf, Bishop's heading your way. Arden and I will keep eyes on Hobbes and watch for shadows. We'll regroup in a couple of hours. Until then, stay on your toes."

"Roger, that." Wolf's response floated over the line. "Watch your six."

"Roger." Kayden turned to Bishop and me. "Let's go."

This wasn't a crime-riddled neighborhood, but the idea of leaving my Jeep in an open, partially deserted parking lot did not leave me with the warm fuzzies. "Hang on, there are a couple of things I need Bishop to keep, just in case."

I got out and circled around to the lift gate. Ramirez's note-books were in my duffle bag in the cargo area. I dug through my duffle, then gathered up my rifle case. Turning around, I handed Bishop the most precious thing first. "Do not let anything happen to her."

He took the rifle case from me with care and let out a low whistle of appreciation. "Nice piece."

"Yes, she is, and I don't need her tempting possible car jack-ers." I held out the three notebooks. "Best keep these as well."

He tucked them under his arm. "What are they?"

This time it was Kayden's turn to answer. "Found them in Ramirez's locker. If you and Wolf get bored and find your-selves in need of reading material, there might be something useful in there, we haven't had a chance to find out."

Bishop's brows rose. "Interesting. I'll see what we can do."

Now that my Jeep was temptation free, I locked it up. Behind me the men exchanged a quick good-bye. I turned and found myself enveloped in a quick, rib-bending hug. "Be careful you two." With that last warning, Bishop headed out, leaving Kayden and I alone.

Kayden dropped his sunglasses in place. "Ready?"

"Let's rock 'n' roll." No sunglasses for me, not with my camera in hand. It was time to go people watch.

⸻ •◦◆◦• ⸻

It was closing in on eight at night and the sun was sinking below the horizon. Streetlights joined the illumination spilling from storefronts to hold back the coming summer evening. Crouched by a planter on the opposite side of the street where the restaurant sat, I adjusted the aperture on my lens. I raised the camera and framed the small knot of people milling outside The Dragon. Laughter and conversation were inter-spersed with the faint bass lines bleeding from the club a few doors down. Colors and lights swirled together in a frenetic palette of energy, painting the busy street.

"They're starting to get a line outside," I murmured as my Nikon quietly clicked its little heart out.

"If Hobbes doesn't hurry the hell up, Ghost is going to end up with a new girlfriend," Wolf drawled.

Wasn't that the truth?

During the last couple of hours everyone on the line had a ringside seat to the byplay between Kayden and The Dragon's bartender, Teresa. Kayden's warm laugh rang in my ear and my teeth lost another layer of enamel. Although my internal, green-eyed monster painted a very unflattering picture of the woman, I couldn't really blame her for trying. Kayden made a lasting impression. More than his looks, it was the way he moved, so sure of himself and conscious of his surroundings. And when he focused that attention on you? It was a very provocative lure to all things female.

Even you?

The question snuck under my irritation, and poked at something I didn't want to face. Not yet. I reached up and snagged my half-empty second cup of coffee from the edge of the planter. I took a sip, grateful for whoever figured out how to turn beans into ambrosia. My earlier headache had finally called it quits, but now my thigh muscle had chimed in with a complaint about my position. Trying to ease the persistent ache, I straightened and rubbed the heel of my hand in short, deep circles, trying to loosen the tension.

"He always gets the tough jobs." Bishop's comment was dry. "It's not like you or I could go in and blend with that crowd."

His comment made my mind whirl as I tried to picture Wolf. All that came together was another Bishop.

Wolf chuckled. "Maybe we should have Arden go in and switch with him."

"Please," I scoffed, eyeing the creased slacks, collared shirts, heels, and saran wrap masquerading as dresses, that replaced the earlier crowds of shorts and T-shirts. I used my cup to hide my lips and continued to scan the sidewalks. "They'd never let me in. Besides, I don't think Teresa would be as forgiving of my appearance as she was of Shaw's."

"She wanted to kiss his boo-boo," Wolf said.

She wanted to kiss a hell of lot more than his boo-boo.

Male chuckles filled my ear, and I realized my last comment had actually slipped out. *Dammit.* "Found anything interesting in those notebooks, Bishop?" Not the most subtle of topic changes, but whatever worked.

"A few names rang some bells," he said, his earlier humor gone. "A couple of dates were familiar. I sent them over to Delacourt. We're going to have to get these to her soon, so her people can dig a little deeper."

"Anything that would make someone nervous?" Kayden joined the conversation.

Guess Teresa had a cocktail to shake.

There was a distinct pause from Bishop. "Maybe, but until I hear back from Delacourt, I don't want to say anything."

My stomach tightened at the almost imperceptible note in Bishop's answer. Unable to stand still, I picked up my cup and began to stroll down the sidewalk. It wasn't hard to dodge the laughing, beautiful people too caught up in their phones, to pay attention to me. I crossed at the light, only to pull up short as three young men streaked by on skateboards, leaving exclamations and a few curses in their wake. I raised my camera and snapped a shot, catching one in mid-flight as he flipped his board in front of a four-pack modeling the latest in Abercrombie and Finch. The skater's total disregard of their disapproval made me smile.

"Head's up!" The warning came from behind me.

I jumped out of the way of a fourth skateboarder as he blew

past me. Somehow, he managed not to run anyone else down as he raced after his friends. I checked behind me for any stragglers, and my foot stuttered in mid-step as an unexpected face caught my eye. Wary excitement rose as I moved closer, aiming for the planter ahead. Reaching my target, I set my coffee down on the cement edge, and then fiddled with my camera.

One of the benefits to using a digital camera was not needing to put your eye to finder to get your shot. With my head down as if I was adjusting the camera's settings, I angled the lens to the line of storefronts behind me and pressed my finger on the shutter. A near-silent, rapid-fire series of images flickered across the screen. Praying one of the shots had what I needed, I brought the camera up, and aimed at the little coffee shop-bookstore combo sitting across from The Dragon. Then, I quickly scanned through the shots I'd taken. On the fourth shot, I found it.

Lounging in an alcove in front of a darkened store was a male wearing a baseball cap, baggy shorts, and a T-shirt. The sixth frame was the money shot. He turned to look over the street and I caught his profile. Even with the addition of a scruffy, five o'clock shadow, I recognized the narrow features of Private First Class Tito Ramirez. Not wanting to spook him, I held my position, kept the camera aimed at the bookstore, and maintained my charade. "I've got company."

"Who?" Kayden's question snapped over the line.

"Ramirez."

Kayden's oath was soft, but audible. "Did he recognize you?"

"Nope, he's huddled in a doorway, watching, but I think he's waiting on Hobbes."

Bishop chimed in. "Anyone else with him?"

"No, from what I can tell he's flying solo."

"Don't lose him," Kayden ordered.

I rolled my eyes. As if I'd let our only link to Ellery out of my sight. "I'm going to cross to the other side of the street. It'll give me a better vantage point."

Suiting words to action, I tossed my coffee in a nearby garbage can, and then jogged through the slow-moving traffic to the other side of the street. Hidden in shadows was a small break between two buildings, just enough so I could slip inside the concealing dimness. I made sure my flash was off, and then raised the camera, the auto focus zeroing in on Ramirez.

He was slouched against the doorjamb, with a lit cigarette dangling between his fingers. He brought it to his mouth, the dull orange brightening as he took another drag.

"Doesn't he know smoking kills?" I muttered.

"I think that's the least of his worries," Wolf answered.

"Hobbes and his date just ordered dessert." Impatience thrummed through Kayden's voice.

"Stay with them," I said. "I got Ramirez."

"And if Hobbes takes off?" he growled.

"There's an extra key for the Jeep tucked under the driver's front wheel well."

"What are you going to do if Ramirez has his own set of wheels?"

"I'll improvise," I snapped. "He's getting antsy. He just pulled out his phone. I'm betting he'll move before Hobbes does."

We couldn't afford to lose him, which meant I needed to get rid of my camera, so I could stay on his ass. As much as it allowed me to blend, for this I needed to be invisible, and wearing a three-thousand-dollar necklace wasn't going to work. If I had worn my pocket-crazy cargo pants this morning, instead of jeans, I could tuck the camera away and call it good. Since that wasn't an option, and the Jeep was in a parking lot a block over, I needed somewhere else to stash my camera. Somewhere close so I wouldn't lose Ramirez.

Ramirez took another drag on his cancer stick as he texted with one hand. I was running out of time.

Light from the nearby bookstore beckoned. I dashed out of the shadows and ducked into the bookstore. There was a coffee shop just inside. A man stood behind the counter, and light glinted off his wire-frame glasses as he tracked my entrance. He shot me a warm smile. "Back for more coffee, young lady?"

Returning it, I noted his hand-printed name on tag tacked to his shirt. "Hey, Dave, can you do me a favor? There's something I want to check out and I don't want to lose or damage this." I pulled my camera off my neck, wrapped the strap around it, and handed it over. "Could you hold this for me? I'll be back for it."

"Sure." He took it and tucked it on a low shelf behind him. "We close at ten, I can hold it 'til then."

"Thanks." I scribbled my cell number on a scrap of paper, then added Kayden's name and number, just in case. "If I don't make it back, I'll send my friend to pick it up."

"Sounds good."

After giving him a quick wave, I was back out on the street. Thankfully, Ramirez hadn't moved while I made my drop-off. In fact, he was still focused on his phone.

"What the hell are you doing, Arden?" Kayden's voice was a low hiss in my ear.

"Getting ready to follow my target. If you can, pick up my camera on the way to the Jeep, will you? Dave seems nice enough and all, but that camera cost me a pretty penny, I'd like it back."

"Then why the hell did you give it to him?"

I dodged a young mom, her stroller, and her over-excited dog. "Because I'm going to stick to Ramirez's ass when he moves."

"We are not splitting up."

"If he moves, I move." A litany of oaths came back, but I

ignored the angry man in my ear, and worked my way up the street, closing in on Ramirez's position. "Something's up, because he's way too focused on his phone."

Sure enough, my target took another drag, then dropped the cigarette and crushed it beneath his foot. He checked his phone once again and then slid it back into a pocket, before stepping into the current of bodies crowding the sidewalk and headed away from The Dragon.

"He's on the move." My pulse sped up. "Maybe Ellery's calling him off of Hobbes?"

"If he's working with Ellery." There was a hard edge to Kayden's voice, but at least he stopped cursing.

"Only one way to find out." My stomach churned with a noxious mix of anticipation and terror.

"Keep the line open and watch your six, dammit," Kayden bit out.

"Roger."

"Arden, be careful." That was Bishop. "Shaw, I'm sending Wolf out to pick up Hobbes from you."

Which meant I wouldn't be on my own for long, but something in his voice triggered my internal warning system. It hit me I hadn't asked what abilities Bishop and Wolf possessed. "What do you know that I don't?"

Bishop didn't pretend not to understand. "Nothing for sure, but I've got a bad feeling."

I choked back a nervous laugh. "Normally I'd ask if you were psychic but guess that's a bit redundant."

A soft chuckle accompanied Bishop's, "That's not my gift, but my gut's talking."

And that was better than any psychic gift. Anytime a soldier's gut started talking, you needed to pay close attention. More times than not, that was the only warning you got before things went from sugar to shit.

Chapter Seventeen

Ramirez led me out of the well-lit, populated areas and into the dark streets that hid more than graffiti. We were only a couple of streets away from The Dragon, but here, the urban renewal was slow to encroach. Inky eyes of dark storefronts watched our game of cat and mouse, their entryways offering minor concealment. Sprinkled in between were the occasional boarded-up, abandoned shops.

Following him became a test of nerves. He was definitely jumpy, every little noise and flash of movement had him looking over his shoulder. Between his twitchy behavior and Bishop's warning, some of Ramirez's paranoia transferred to me. My spine itched, but no matter how many times I checked my back trail, it stayed clear.

Shadowing someone on a quiet city street was far from easy. Headlights from passing traffic played havoc with my eyesight. Bass-heavy, tricked out cars kept drawing Ramirez's attention and interfering with my ability to stay off his radar. I had to skirt the occasional cardboard home and watch where I stepped so I wouldn't injure myself. By the time Ramirez ducked under a flimsy excuse for a fence, sweat coated my spine, and not just from the heat. Although it was now well after nine at night the temperature still hovered in the nineties.

When he disappeared into the weed-choked lot, I picked up my pace and crossed the street. I stood on the cracked sidewalk and studied the narrow area between the buildings. A tall, looming shadow filled the space. Streetlights couldn't hold the darkness at bay, but I could make out the boards haphazardly covering what were once windows. Large signs ringed the lower half of the two-story structure and proclaimed penalties for trespassing. Someone even added a few lines of spiked wire and metal rods.

It wasn't much of a deterrent. Ramirez was already inside. It took me a few, but I finally managed to bypass the half-ass security. When one of those barbs left a painful scratch along my shoulder, I muffled my soft curse and poked at the tear in my shirt.

Kayden's voice filled my ear. "Where are you?"

I worked my way around the side of the building, my progress accompanied by the overly loud insect choir. "Between First and Central on Monroe. Ramirez just disappeared inside an abandoned building."

"Hobbes just paid his check, I'll meet up with you."

"No." I spotted a gaping hole in the far back corner. "Delacourt's orders were to stay on him, so stay. I'm fine."

There was a pause and when Kayden spoke, he didn't sound happy. "And if that changes?"

"It changes," I shot back.

"Shaw," Wolf broke in. "I'm twenty minutes out."

"Fine," Kayden snarled. "Cyn, you keep your ass in one piece until I get there."

"Don't forget my camera," I reminded him.

His grumbled suggestion made me grin. I stood outside the ragged opening and wished for a flashlight. Much easier to handle with my gun than my phone. I pulled my Sig free and warned the team, "Going quiet."

It took some serious contortions to make it around the rough edges of the opening without losing more of my shirt. But once inside, the heat was stifling and sweat popped out on my forehead. I held still, both hands wrapped around my Sig, waiting for my vision to adjust to the shrouded interior. When the sweat threatened to run into my eyes, I used my shoulder to wipe it away.

I entered from the rear of the building. There was a bit of diffused light that squeezed between the gaping boards and a series of holes that peppered the back wall. Unidentifiable piles were scattered across the floor. Walls divvied the space into something closer to a maze. It left dozens of places for anything or anyone to hide. A thin layer of grit layered the concrete floors underfoot, making it difficult to keep my steps silent. Large panels hung like drunken Legos from the ceiling, just waiting to fall on the unwary.

Sound reached my ears. I held my breath, straining to listen. The indistinct murmur resolved into voices. Did Ramirez have company or was he talking to someone on the phone?

Someone walked across the second-story floor, and dust trickled from the ceiling. I did a slow scan of the interior looking for stairs. They had to be here somewhere. Just when I was about to give up, I found them crouched in the far corner.

I kept my back to the wall and drifted forward. Shifting shadows added a creepy vibe to the gaping doorways and piles dotting the open floor. The tang of smoke found its way up my nose. Using an outstretched hand, I brushed my fingers along the rough surface of the wall. When I brought my hand up, I could make out the smudge of black now staining my fingers.

Great. Nothing like creeping around in a burned-out building.

My arms ached from holding my gun at the ready. To stave off the muscle fatigue, I lowered my gun and kept my finger on the side of the trigger. I stuck close to the walls, not trusting the rest of the structure. Whoever was upstairs walked across the floor again, and more dust rained down. Was Ramirez pacing? Or were there two people up there?

With no easy answers in sight, it was time to brave the unknown. I needed another way to the second floor. One that wouldn't dump me in front of Ramirez and his possible company. It took nerve-wracking patience to work my way through the lower level, but my persistence paid off. Near the front was a small, second, narrow flight of stairs.

Sending a quick prayer that they would hold my weight, I crept up. A handful of steps from the top, the board underfoot gave a loud protest. I dropped into a crouch, and kept my gun aimed at the dark opening. The murmur of voice stopped, replaced by a tense, waiting quiet.

I focused on breathing through the rush of adrenaline, because if someone came this way, I was screwed. I had no idea what waited at the top. Footsteps moved away from where I huddled, heading back toward the other set of stairs. It sounded like just one person. Shadows filled the narrow stairwell, turning it into an inky abyss. My damaged thigh protested at my prolonged position, but I didn't dare move and giveaway my presence.

Above me, a shoe scraped over the floor, but I still couldn't tell if Ramirez was alone or not. A faint rush of air and a shift in the shadows was my only warning that the door above me opening. I held my breath as my limited options ran through my brain in rapid succession. Either I took a chance and rushed whoever waited. Or I held my position and let whoever was at the top come to me. The one small blessing was that the door's position meant if someone was there, they had to move into the stairwell to see me. Of course, I wouldn't see them until they did that.

Right now, it was a waiting game, and I didn't want to be the one to make the first move. Seconds ticked by and the sense of someone waiting and watching, floated down. I pressed into the shadows, barely daring to breathe, and sank into the familiar anticipatory quiet, prepared to react to whatever or whoever came down the stairs.

Finally, the door clicked shut. I let out the breath I'd been holding. *Great, that entry was compromised.* I moved on to my next option, hauling ass back downstairs so I could follow Ramirez out, or, if I got really lucky, catching a glimpse of who he was meeting.

Caution dictated stealth over speed, which made retracing my path down the stairs longer than I liked. Once back on the bottom floor, I crept through the shadows, every sense on alert. The silence created a high-pitched ringing in my ears, and shifting shadows twisted broken furniture into possible attackers. Even the taint of old ash on the air tasted bitter. A chill rode my skin, and my mouth was dry, but at least my hands stayed steady on my gun.

The nocturnal chorus of insects had fallen silent, and the night took on a heavy awareness. Unlike the front stairs, the ones at the back were nothing more than a skeletal incline of metal bones, the space underneath a hollow hole of shadows. It also made the perfect spot to hide and wait.

Almost as soon as I was settled in the dark space, someone moved out on to the steps above me, their weight triggering a low, quiet groan of protest from the unstable structure. A halo of bobbing light seeped down and I curled tighter against the wall, praying the shadows would keep me hidden. I shifted my gaze so the light wouldn't screw with my vision, and followed the illuminating edge as it came down. *Was it Ramirez or someone else?*

The figure crept down the last couple of steps, their back against the wall, and their phone, doubling as their flashlight, was in one outstretched hand. From my concealed position, I watched bare, male legs, then shorts, carefully take each step. When the bite of nicotine followed, I knew it was Ramirez.

He took the last step and stood on the floor, his back to me. He didn't stay still long. When he moved out into the open space, I could see he wasn't armed. I craned my neck, trying to see beyond the shadows and up the stairs to determine if anyone else lay in wait.

The ear cringing sound of something heavy scraping across the rough floor snapped my attention back to Ramirez. His soft oath followed before he continued his slow search of the building.

I didn't want to lose him, but he was getting further and further away. When he stepped out of visual range, I crept out of my hidey-hole, and stalked him, gun at the ready. I tried to keep my back covered just in case someone else decided to join us. My skulking skills were kicking ass until I tried to skirt around what I thought was a solid wall but turned out to be a propped-up piece of deteriorating drywall. My hip caught the edge, sending it crashing to the floor in a cloud of noise and dust.

Ramirez spun, blinding me with his phone. Hissing, I threw up an arm, blinking to clear my vision as I dodged away from the heavy footfalls charging my way. I stumbled back as the debris on the floor became a crippling minefield. And not just for me. Ramirez's fingers clawed across my shoulder, only to miss as he tripped over something. He recovered quickly and I managed to get an arm up to block an incoming punch but missed the next one that sheared across my ribs. I spun out of reach and made the mistake of putting too much weight on my weak leg. It crumpled under me. "Shit!"

Slamming into the floor hurt like hell, but it allowed me to evade his punch, which, had it landed, would have nailed my jaw, knocking me out of commission. Unfortunately, during the scramble, I lost my grip on my gun and it disappeared into the darkness. In my ear, Kayden was yelling at me, but I was a little too busy to answer.

Get up, get up.

My internal chant became a roar. On the floor was not safe, especially not when Ramirez decided to practice his soccer skills. I caught a bone-bruising kick on my other hip. Gritting my teeth, I slammed my boot into the inside of his bracing leg, and then rolled to push to my feet. My strike didn't take him out, but it gave me time to regain my feet.

He stumbled back with a pained bellow. "Fucking bitch." Then he charged.

Shit, this was going to hurt. The thought barely registered before he hit, his shoulder ramming into my stomach and sending it toward my throat. My breath exploded in an audible whoosh, but I hadn't trained in hand-to-hand combat for giggles. My knee met his chin, followed by my elbow drilling into his spine.

His arms loosened, and he performed a strange twist attempting to avoid the competing impacts. I slashed out with a clumsy left hook, desperate to get out his reach. It was enough to upset his balance, and he let me go. I stumbled back, and forced my weak leg to hold, frantically scanning for my gun. I came up empty. The black matte disappeared into the heavy shadows. Ramirez straightened, gearing to come back at me.

Kayden shouted in my ear.

I set my feet and hissed, "Not now, Shaw."

Ramirez and I faced off. Blood trickled down his chin, a line of snaking black in the muted moonlight. Guess he bit his tongue. My smile was nowhere near nice.

His gaze didn't waver as he sent a mouthful of spit and blood to the floor. "Who the fuck are you?"

The cheesy line of 'your worst nightmare' flashed through my mind, but I wisely kept silent. Sometimes being a smart-ass was not the best way to handle things. See, I could be mature.

He inched forward. "What do you want?"

I retreated, trying to figure out how to take him down. "Just looking for a mutual friend."

"We don't have any." He stepped forward and swung out, relying on his superior reach.

I dodged, taking the hit along my forearm as I blocked. The strength of his strike vibrated in my bones, but I still looped my arm over his, and caught his wrist. I shifted my grip, using his momentum to pull him into my kick. As I spun away, determined to go for another elbow strike, he recovered sent a brutal punch into my lower side.

We stumbled apart. A familiar, metallic click echoed behind me, freezing me in place.

"She's looking for Ellery." The masculine voice slithered down my spine. It was a graveyard voice, cold, empty, utterly merciless.

This wasn't good. My muscles twitched with the instinctive itch to turn and face the threat.

"Don't."

I stilled, my chest rising and falling as I sucked air. In my ear, I could hear Kayden. "Report, dammit."

Behind me, the chilling voice snapped to Ramirez, "Check her."

Ramirez stepped in front of me, the murky light unable to hide the sly satisfaction crawling across his face. He crouched at my feet and found the knife I had no chance to use, stuck in my right boot, and then he found my empty holster. His hands left slime in their wake as he dragged them up my legs in a deliberately crude search.

My skin crawled, but I kept my face blank. He rose and shoved a rough hand between my legs. My reaction had nothing to do with reason and everything with rage. I slammed my cupped hands over his ears and yanked my knee up, introducing his balls to his throat. His choked scream was music to my ears. He stumbled back, one hand over an ear and one cupping his questionable jewels.

An arm wrapped around my throat, drawing me up on my toes and bending my spine back. I dug nails into the skin-covered steel holding me up. Only when the feel of cool metal kissed my temple did I stop struggling.

"Get up, dumbass." The growl vibrated under the base of my skull.

"Fuckin' bitch." Ramirez straightened painfully. "You'll pay for that."

The arm at my throat blocked my response and my air. Little black dots started a mad dance at the edge of my vision. Just when I thought I'd lose consciousness, the arm loosened, dropping me to my feet.

Unfortunately, he found a new grip, in my hair. There were reasons, good ones, on why some women soldiers cut their hair. This would be one. I wrapped my hands around his wrist, trying to keep him from pulling my hair out by the roots. He yanked me to my knees, and I hit the ground hard enough to bruise my kneecaps. The gun never wavered. It was too close to try to get away, but I could be patient.

Above me, Iceman told Ramirez, "You deserved it. Now get over here and get the earpiece."

Shit, shit, shit. How the hell had he seen it? Thankfully, Kayden was no longer yelling at me. That was the only good thing about this whole screwed-up situation. Ramirez came close, careful to keep his vulnerable parts out of reach. Not like I could do much with the cruel grip in my hair that kept my neck painfully extended. Then there was the gun that was too close to attempt anything but breathing.

Ramirez yanked out the earpiece, taking a few strands of hair with it. He dropped it and proceeded to crush it beneath his foot. With my head angled like it was I couldn't miss Ramirez's glare aimed at the asshole holding me. "How long before her backup shows?"

"We've got time, they're tied up with Hobbes," Iceman answered.

How the hell did he know that? And time for what? Nerves edged out adrenaline, and the dull ache setting up shop in my head took a turn for the worse when Iceman used his grip to yank me to my feet.

Swearing, my hands flailed against that unrelenting hold, trying to lessen the pressure. Once on my feet, I decided being bald would be better than whatever they had planned. I swung back, twisting to bring up a knee, aiming for his thigh, even as pain became a white smear across my vision and what felt like half of my hair remained behind.

The pressure on my skull disappeared, only to be replaced by a sharp knife of agony over my kidney as Ramirez landed two sharp blows on my back. The hit sent me stumbling forward where I took another blow from Iceman across my face. The combination sent me to my knees, then my hands. Skin tore, the sting buried under the wash of pain from my skull and face. I lost track of both men, too focused on trying not to black out.

When things finally came back into blurry focus my arm was wrenched between my shoulder blades. Every twitch sent a razor-sharp spasm through me. Incomprehensible words rumbled around me as my brain decided to check out. A shove against my back, forced me into a stumbling shuffle. Just as my vision started to clear, Iceman slammed me into something solid, the edge cutting into the back of my knees. My legs folded, and my ass met a hard surface.

He released his hold and pins and needles exploded along every inch of my arm. A groan escaped without permission. Both arms were yanked back and the soft shush of a zip tie preceded the bite of plastic into my wrists. It was nothing compared to the ache blooming in my head like some vicious flower. Fingers dug into my chin, jerking my head up.

"Ow, dammit!"

"At least you're awake." Dark, empty eyes stared into mine.

The dim light made it hard to see, but he didn't look familiar. There was nothing distinctive about his face, it was the kind that could blend with the general population. His short, cropped hair clung close to his scalp, but I couldn't make out the color. All I could see was the chilling emptiness in his dark eyes, eyes rife with cruel amusement.

I licked my lips and tasted the bite of iron from a cut. "What do you want?"

His mouth ticked up. "Same as you. Ellery."

"Sorry, not going to be much help with that."

His smile curdled my blood. "Don't worry, Arden, you will be."

Before trepidation could gain a foothold, I was hit by something solid, and everything turned black.

Chapter Eighteen

The bleat of a car horn and the squeal of rapidly applied brakes dragged me to consciousness. Just as fast as I opened my eyes, I closed them. Extraordinary pain seared everything away, leaving me blind and nauseous. An unknown fear held me in place as I sat slumped on the ground, as my pulse thudded with a dull beat. It hurt to think.

What happened?

The air was heavy, hard to breath, and the heat oppressive. Sweat plastered my T-shirt to my spine and a rivulet trickled between my breasts. The rancid odor of things gone bad competed with dust and baked stone. Everything part of me throbbed with aches and pains. A hollow crack broke through the white noise crowding my pounding skull and echoed around me.

Where the hell was I?

My fingers flexed against the rough, pitted ground, different from the solid surface at my back. For a sickening moment, I was back in some godforsaken village with an unpronounceable name in Pakistan. The illusion was shattered by the shrill song of a siren peeled another layer from my eardrums, allowing the rush of passing traffic to rise to the surface. Awareness seeped in with a careful cautiousness, as if I was one wrong move away from shattering.

Phoenix. I was in Phoenix.

The reminder served to push the foreign desert of my nightmares back where it belonged, thousands of miles away. I pried my eyes open, and tried to muffle the whimper as the light ratcheted the mind-numbing ache in my head higher. Involuntary tears trailed down my chin. I raised a heavy arm to wipe the annoying weakness away, and missed, only then realizing my muscle control was iffy. The second attempt was more successful. Using the same hand to shield my burning eyes, I blinked until my vision slowly returned. When I thought it was safe, I lowered my hands and was met with a cement block fence decorated in urban art made up of intricate curls of white, black, and brown.

Turning my head with care, I took in my surroundings. The grey metal of the garbage dumpster next to me magnified the heat, but it also worked as a great crutch as I struggled to my feet. I leaned against the uncomfortably warm surface and waited for my body and gravity to stop arguing. The sun's unrelenting rays wreaked havoc on my eyes, so I let them close and took a moment to catalogue my aches and pains, an endeavor that became difficult when they melded into one big, throbbing mass.

My stomach was tender, my ribs ached, my left leg trembled, and my face felt like one huge bruise. My head pulsed in time with my heart, and my abused brain protested any movement. The rhythmic pressure of my body's complaints fragmented my thoughts before they could fully form, yet there was an inescapable underlying sense of urgency. Until the waves of pain receded, I wouldn't be able to figure out what was triggering it.

"Miss? Are you all right?"

The cautious question was uttered in a male voice, and my heart kicked into overdrive. I slitted my eyes open just enough to make out a human shaped blob hovering near an open door.

"Miss? Do I need to call someone?" The voice sounded closer.

"No." The one word tore across my vocal cords. I winced, coughed, and tried again. "No, thanks." I didn't dare straighten and lose my metal crutch because my spinning head left my balance shot to hell.

The blob moved closer. It was carrying something. The armful of flattened cardboard came into focus, as did the wary, skeptical expression filling a weathered face. The man wore faded jeans, and a green, collared shirt that stretched over a barrel chest. "You don't look so good, you sure?"

If I looked anything like how I felt, I must have looked like death warmed over. I forced a weak smile and scrambled for a plausible answer. "Long Friday night, just heading home. What time is it?"

The guy frowned, and something in his expression made my stomach pitch. "It's just after three on Sunday."

"Sunday?" Shock and fear crawled through me. *Sunday? What the hell happened to Saturday?* My mind shied away from the unforgiving canvas of empty memory and slid into a black hole of nothing.

I must have whimpered because the guy looked alarmed and took a half step forward. "You sure you're okay, lady?"

"Um, yeah, sorry. Just have a hell of a headache."

"Mmm hmm." He heaved the cardboard he carried into the nearby bin. "You shouldn't drive in your condition."

Yeah, what condition would that be? Clamping down on the urge to release a hysterical giggle, I managed a short nod. "I'll catch a cab." I surreptitiously checked my pockets and found a couple of twenties, my key ring, and driver's license. No phone. "Um, can I borrow a phone?"

I stumbled after him into a small print shop. Under the gimlet eye of the Good Samaritan, who's name tag said Todd, I called a cab to pick me. Thankfully, the phone was near a pile of business cards. The shop's address put me in the middle of downtown Phoenix, miles from Kelsey's condo. After being assured the driver would be there in fifteen minutes, I hung up the phone and asked Todd, who was pretending to do important things while keeping me in sight, "Do you have a bathroom I could use?"

Heeding his directions, I shuffled down the back hall, and slipped inside the bathroom, locking the door behind me. I leaned against the door as tremors raced through me and let out a hitching breath. Safe from curious eyes, I gathered my waning courage and turned to the mirror above the sink.

My dark hair was a tangled mess. My skin was stretched tight over my cheekbones, the shade beyond pale, and closer to gray. It made the soft, purpling bruise that spanned my cheekbone and up to my temple stand out in stark relief. I lifted trembling fingers to brush along the mark where I'd been hit, trying to remember how it got there. Dark circles bagged under my eyes and my lower lip was swollen on one side. I touched it, only to wince when a small sting flared. The green of my eyes, normally tinged with gold, held a haunted, dark jade that made me uncomfortable.

My gaze dropped to the rust-colored ring curled around my wrists. I turned on the faucet, waiting until the water ran warm, and then ignoring the emotions threatening to choke me, I washed away the blood, and dirt on my skin. Once that was done, I gathered my hair and pulled it back, my gaze rising back to the mirror. My breath stalled under a sickening sense of horror. Along my neck the white lines of my scar stood out in stark relief, the pattern broken by raw-looking scratches and a bluish chain of what looked like fingerprints.

The roughness of my voice now made sense. Someone had choked me. Repeatedly.

The tiny room closed in. I curled my hands around the cool porcelain sink and dropped my head. "Hold it together, Cyn. You're okay." My whispered reassurance was a weak defense against the swamping wave of fear and dread. "Kayden, I was with Kayden and…" Another deep voice echoed in my head. "Bishop. We were watching Ramirez. At the Dragon." Saying it out loud helped. The images came together and pushed back the swirling madness eating at the edges of my mind. "I followed him, then…"

Then, what?

Flashes of a burned-out shell of a building, the remembered weight of my gun in my hand, the bright blinding flash, a garbled jumble of words, then…nothing. Nausea churned and I dry heaved over the sink. I fumbled to turn on the water, cupped it in my hands, and drank. When my guts settled, I refocused on the raw lines of my wrists. *Restraints?*

A sob escaped. Panic rose. Questions and fears circled. Deep in the recesses of my battered mind cracks widened and sent tremors through my spirit. "Suck it up." My whisper was a harsh lash. Falling apart right now wouldn't do shit except have Todd calling the cops, who'd ask questions I couldn't answer. Which is also why I wouldn't be calling Kayden or Delacourt. Not yet. Not until I could figure out what the hell had happened to me. To do that, I needed someplace safe, someplace familiar.

Kelsey's condo.

I splashed water on my face, and let it drip off my chin. I lifted my gaze to the mirror. *I will not break.* The haunting edge of fear mocked me.

I stepped out of the cab and handed over the last of my cash. Even as I hustled to the lobby doors, the unsettling sense of being watched tripped over my nerves. For once my timing didn't suck because the security station was thankfully empty. Probably a shift change or something. *Thank you, God.*

I hunched my shoulders and angled away from the watching cameras. Tension rose as I waited for the elevator. When it dinged and slid open, I quickly stepped inside. In minutes, I was outside Kelsey's door, my keys rattling against the lock as my internal shaking from earlier returned with a vengeance. Shoving through, my panicked sobs chased me inside. Fingers fumbled and engaged the locks before I dropped my keys on the long entryway table.

The itch between my shoulder blades disappeared, only to be replaced by bone-rattling shudders. The relief of being safe cooled the sweat from earlier to a grimy film. I braced my hands on the entry table and stared at the bowl of colored stones. They started to blur, and it took me a moment to realize why. Warm tears ran down my cold face. Horrified, I tried to wipe the stupid, useless tears away, but they kept falling.

Stupid.

Useless.

The words echoed inside my head, their ripples setting off a chain reaction. Unconnected images and emotions exploded in my mind's eye like a camera's flash.

A face. Terror.

A voice. Fury.

Blood. Pain.

Laughter.

Dull walls decorated with water stains. Fear.

Shame. Resignation.

Hollowness. Nausea.

They all converged into a cyclonic storm that blasted through the hastily erected wall I used to make it home. I clasped my spinning head in my hands and dragged my fingers through my hair. The sharp tugs on the matted snarls pulled me out of the destructive spiral waiting to suck me down.

Come on, Cyn. Hold it together.

Forcing my feet to move, I headed to the kitchen. I needed something to drink. My mouth was dry, my stomach pitching. By rote, I grabbed a glass, and then stood there.

Water wasn't going to cut it.

I opened the cupboard above the stove. A bottle of whiskey with a few inches left stared back. Jameson in hand, I considered the glass I held, then the bottle. *Screw it.*

I left the glass on the counter and brought the bottle to my mouth. The whiskey burned its way down my throat and eventually chased away the chill. Finally, my teeth stopped rattling against the glass edge. I lowered the bottle and held it in both hands and sucked in deep breaths. I swiped the back of my hand over my sore lips and took another drink. I needed a shower. Then, maybe I could deal with...I let the thought trail off, too scared to follow it through.

Shower, first. Then assess the damage.

Unwilling to give up my alcoholic teddy bear, I took it with me to the guest room. The curtains were still drawn, keeping the sunlight out. I moved across the floor to the bathroom. I didn't bother with the light switch. Still holding the bottle, I turned the shower as hot as it could go with one hand. For a moment I considered setting the whiskey on the counter, but my fingers wouldn't loosen.

Stripping one-handed was not graceful or quick. I got my T-shirt off and more signs that things had gotten real fucking ugly at some point were revealed. Bruises in various shades of green, blue, and purple decorated my ribs and stomach. Some wound around to my back. Most were clustered in mid-body and the tight band around my chest loosened a notch.

I took another drink and shucked my pants. An ugly bruise covered my left thigh, a visible explanation for my re-emerging limp. The only other damage was my skinned knees. Finally naked, I kicked my grungy clothes into the corner, and went to take one last fortifying drink, but came up empty. I set the now empty bottle on the counter's edge and stepped into the steamy enclosure. Between the heat and the alcohol, my head was encased in fluffiness. I tried to enjoy it, but the moment you *try* to become numb, you stop.

I stood there as hot water sluiced over me, my back to the spray, arms braced on the wall in front of me, and my head hanging down. At my feet swirled a murky combination of water, blood, and dirt. Stings made themselves known as the hot water hit the numerous scrapes. I groaned softly as tense muscles slowly uncurled. I tilted my head back, letting the water wash over my hair and face. Now there was no way to tell what was water and what was tears.

The urge to get clean began to crowd out all the rest of my physical complaints. I grabbed my soap and washed every possible inch. Then it was rinse and repeat, then repeated again. Finally, my legs folded, and I slowly slid down the smooth tile wall, until I was a huddled ball of misery. With nothing left to distract me, the deluge of fragmented images, the babel of half understood voices, and the shitstorm of emotional upheaval crowded in and set up shop. Exhausted beyond measure, I couldn't fight back, so all that was left was to endure.

As the storm raged around me, time passed without meaning, but like any other storm, it finally waned. Deep inside my psyche, I was hunkered behind the strongest mental wall I could manage. The taunting whispers began to taper off, and the images stopped striking like wind-tossed missiles. Quiet replaced the mental noise. Either I was in the eye of the storm, or it had finally, blessedly passed.

Not wanting to chance reawakening it, I kept my mental barriers up, and started to poke at what I could remember. The blank spots hurt, so I didn't push too hard. Not yet. I ranged further back, where the pain wasn't, until I finally found the last thing I could remember that didn't make me want to pass out.

Ramirez's snarling face. Kayden's voice yelling in my ear.

A violent shiver snapped my mind back to the present where cold water washed over me. I swiped my eyes clear and uncurled from my huddle. It took teeth-gritting effort to get up, turn off the shower, and wrap my trembling body in a towel. My limbs were numb with cold, but I didn't waste time getting dressed. Instead, I snagged a throw from my chair, and wrapped it around me. Then I crawled into bed, pulled the comfort to my shoulders, and curled against the headboard.

Only then did I begin to work my way through the maze of my mind. But no matter how I came at it, a big, black pit of nothingness swirled where the last twenty-four plus hours should have been. I had memories of Kayden watching Hobbes, me tailing Ramirez, Wolf and Bishop heading to Hobbes's home, and then dark streets, A NO TRESPASSING sign, a broken building filled with shadows, then finally, a sense of panicked desperation.

And that's where I kept stalling.

What happened in that building? Based upon the physical evidence, I knew I had been beaten.

Raped? I paused as the word echoed in my head, and tightened my hold on my blanket, allowing my subconscious to weigh in.

No, not physically.

Something warm dripped on my lip and I wiped it away with a blanket-covered hand. The crimson smear held my attention. My stomach clenched. Kayden said nosebleeds equaled psychic overload. I reached for a tissue and held it to my nose. As far as I knew, I hadn't used my ability.

So, a psychic rape, then? Maybe, but with the gaping hole in my memory there was no way to tell what ability had been in play or who wielded it. I knew Ramirez had been there, but had he been alone? Something told me no, not alone. Okay, so had Ellery joined him? Dread rose as my mind offered twisted ideas as to what it would mean if Ellery had been present. I shoved them away, refusing to get lost down that nightmarish path, and kept pushing.

If it had been Ellery, why dump me in that alley? Hell, why let me leave alive?

Letting me go made no sense, it didn't follow his established pattern. I sucked in a deep breath as fear clawed at me but kept trying to scratch away the shadows hiding the past. I finally gave up when my efforts resulted in a head full of white noise, another blinding headache, and a pile of bloody tissues. Indecipherable whispers crawled inside my skull, dragging pain in their wake. Tears leaked from the corners of my eyes. Something had happened, something bad, but I couldn't see it. That wasn't normal and it scared me. Hard as it was to admit, perhaps it was time to call Kayden in. This wasn't something I could do on my own. I didn't have enough information on how psychic abilities worked, or how to get past the block in my head. I needed what he knew, but... Old doubts resurfaced.

If I went to him, who would I find? The PSY-IV operative? Or the man who was making his own private niche in my heart? Who did I want to face?

As unfair as it was, part of me was angry with Kayden's absence. Where had he been while I was busy being someone's punching bag? Why wasn't he here now? Even if he was out searching for me, someone should've been watching Kelsey's place. The silence of the condo swallowed me, burying me under the weight of loneliness. Whatever future I once envisioned was a distant memory. My family was gone. Whatever remnants of Kelsey's presence that still haunted this home, where she invested so much of her heart, were fading. The team, that was once my secondary family, had been hunted until only three of us remained.

I was so tired of going at it alone. What had it gotten me?

Thanks to past hurts, I cowered here, unable, or, if I was being brutally honest with myself, unwilling to reach out for help. Help I knew Kayden would willingly offer, regardless of the mission. One of Kelsey's last pieces of advice whispered through my mind.

"Someday you're going to have to take a chance and just jump. If you're lucky, someone will be there to catch you."

"And if I hit the ground to shatter in a big, bloody mess?" Old anger and resentments twisted my question.

"Chances are, you'll only have yourself to blame." A brutal response, given in love. *"You walked away, Cyn. You shut him out and hid behind your anger and guilt. If you stay there too long, he'll leave for good. Then where will you be?"*

The same damn place I was right now.

Alone.

Chapter Nineteen

T he sound of the deadbolt clicking open echoed through the silence like a gunshot. I scrambled in a tangle of blankets and limbs, falling in a graceless lump on the floor. Ignoring the renewed complaints from my abused body, I crouched behind the bed and considered my options. I was naked with no gun, no knife, nothing usable in reach. My best bet was the safe in the closet. I made it three steps before the sound of my name froze me in place.

"Cyn?"

Kayden. Relief turned my legs watery. I opened my mouth to call out, but only a soft sob escaped. Mortified, I slapped my hands over the offending orifice.

"Cyn?" This time his voice was sharper, his frustration evident.

"Kayden?" His name was a whisper, but it also had me grabbing my discarded blanket and wrapping it around me toga style. I stumbled to the doorway, sticking to the heavier pools of shadow. "Here, I'm here." My voice was shaky, but he heard me and reached out to turn on the kitchen lights. "No, don't." It came out sharp. Maybe too sharp.

His hand hung in mid-motion, before he slowly dropped it. "Are you okay?"

Instead of answering with a lie, I asked, "How did you get in?"

He held up a key. "Got a copy from Terrance." He moved closer. "Where have you been?"

"That's the million-dollar question." I forced my legs to carry me over to the couch and away from him. I curled into the corner, tucking the blanket around me, and watched him make his way closer.

He sank to his heels in front of me. Exhaustion had left its mark on him, yet those steel-colored eyes darkened as he studied me. He reached out, stopping when I flinched. "Cyn?"

That one word held so many unasked questions, but it was the mix of relief and worry that got to me. I drew in a shaky breath and jumped off Kelsey's hypothetical cliff. "I woke up in an alley in downtown Phoenix. The last thing I remember is following Ramirez into a building on Friday night. Everything in between is an empty hole."

Fury flared across his face, and his jaw tightened, but the fingers he brushed over my bruised cheek were butterfly light. "I got to the building about fifteen minutes after we lost audio contact. It was empty." He dropped his hand to cover my fists in my lap, the warmth of his touch seeping through my chilled skin. "I found your ear bud smashed into pieces, some drops of blood, nothing else." His gaze roamed over my face, his eyes narrowing when they dropped to my neck. "I'm turning on a light."

Before I could protest, he rose in a rush of movement, reached for the lamp on the end table, and snapped it on. I ducked my head and blinked rapidly against the glare, as I huddled on the couch. Hands cradled my face, gentle but inexorably tilting it up. He tucked my hair back behind my shoulders, leaving my neck bare. Uncomfortable with having my scars on display, much less the obvious signs of violence, I stared over his shoulder at the painting on the far wall.

"What else did they do?" Despite his careful touch, a cold, frightening fury wound through his voice.

"I took some hits to my ribs and stomach, and a kick to the thigh. The marks at my wrists indicate restraints of some kind."

His hands left my face and brought up my hands, cradling them carefully. A few tense seconds passed before he said, "From the parallel cuts, I'd guess zip ties, and based on the depth of the wounds, it looks like you struggled."

Something soft brushed against the sore areas on my right wrist. Startled, I looked down. His head was bent over my wrists. He pressed another whisper-soft kiss to the left one, before placing both back in my lap. His head lifted and he caught my gaze. The naked upheaval of emotion in his eyes blew through me, leaving me stunned at the depth of it. "We need to take you to a hospital. Make sure you're okay." His voice cracked, revealing his unspoken fear.

I used my free hand to trace one deep bracket on the side of his mouth. "No hospital, Kayden."

The line deepened. "Dammit, Cyn—"

"No hospital." My voice came out strong, sure. "It's only bruises, I promise."

He studied me for a long moment before muttering, "Hell with a dixie cup." He got up and then sat on the couch beside me. I stayed still while he studied me. "Bruises only?"

I took a deep breath and gave him a nod. "They'll heal; nothing's broken, just achy."

"But?"

When he picked up on what I wasn't saying, I winced and tucked my feet under his thighs, finding comfort in the small touch. "Someone's been messing with my head."

"Ramirez isn't psychic."

"I don't think he wasn't alone."

"Ellery?"

I shrugged. "I'm not sure, maybe. Every time I poke at things, I hit a blank wall." A shiver rushed over me, stealing what little warmth I found. When he didn't ask anything else, I looked up.

He arched an eyebrow and opened his arms. "Come here."

No second invitation was necessary. I scrambled into his lap, blanket and all, and burrowed close. His arms wrapped around me, reassuring in their strength. His heart beat under my ear, strong and steady, chasing away the chill of the unknown. I tucked my forehead under his chin, buried my nose against his throat, and dragged his scent into my lungs. I shared my biggest fear in a whisper. "I don't know what they did, Kayden."

His arms tightened, and a kiss was pressed against the top of my head. "We'll figure it out, baby."

Quiet settled between us and I closed my eyes. Bit by bit, my muscles relaxed, releasing their death grip on the tension twined around every limb. Slipping into the half-sleep state, I lost track of time. A vibration under my hip brought me back. I shifted off of Kayden's lap so he could pull out his phone.

"Shaw." He rubbed a hand over his forehead. "Yeah, she's here." A pause. "Not sure. Why?"

Whatever was being said did not make him happy. He focused on me. "Send me the address and we'll meet you there." He ended his call, but his attention didn't waver. "We need to go."

"Go where?"

"Wolf found something." His earlier emotions disappeared behind a familiar mask.

"Give me a minute." It took me a few awkward moments to get to my feet. Stiff and sore, I shuffled to the bedroom. I dropped the throw to the floor and rummaged through the drawers. I found underthings, an old t-shirt, and a pair of jeans. I got my underwear and oversized T-shirt on before calling out, "Kayden, do you have my duffel somewhere?"

"It's in your Jeep." His answer came from the doorway.

Spinning around with the jeans clutched to my chest, I snapped, "You need to wear a bell or something."

A faint grin broke across his somber face. "I'll take you back to the safe house after we meet with Wolf." The grin disappeared, replaced by something grim.

Disconcerted by the change, I asked, "What?"

Instead of answering, he covered the distance between us in no time and pushed the dangling jeans out of the way. His arm snaked around my waist and tugged me off balance.

"Dammit, Kayden." I clutched at his shoulders as my balance tilted. The oversize T-shirt rode up to reveal the lace edge of my green underwear. "What are you doing?"

The heat of his palm settled just above the huge bruise on my thigh. "You said nothing was broken."

"It's not." I tried to bat his hands away, with no success. "Now, would you let me go so I can get dressed?"

Instead of acquiescing, he grasped the edge of the T-shirt and lifted it. He traced the marks and I flinched away from his careful touch as goosebumps erupted over my skin. His low, mean curses colored the air. He caged me against the dresser and used one hand to hold the T-shirt up while the other carefully checked my ribs and stomach. Since fighting him would just make things worse, I gritted my teeth and held still for his inspection. When he hit particularly tricky, tender spots, I couldn't stop my flinches or small gasps. He finally stopped and let the material drop back down.

"Happy now?" I asked. "Can I get—"

His kiss cut the rest of my snarly question off. He was

careful of my abused lip, but his gentleness was at odds with the edgy heat, desperate fury, creating something infinitely more delicate and tempting. When he drew back, his eyes were glittering, and his fingers flexed on my hips. "No, I'm far from fucking happy right now, Cynthia Arden."

"Cyn." The automatic correction came out on a raspy breath, but my hands cupped his face as I rose on tiptoe and kissed one of the deep lines bracketing his mouth. "I'm okay."

He blew out a hard breath and rested his forehead against mine. "I'll wait for you out front."

His fingers at my hips tightened, then released. He stepped back and left me to get dressed.

❖

Half an hour later, Kayden parked my Jeep in the parking lot of a small, two-story strip mall that was a few miles away from the alley I woke up in. Most of the storefronts were dark, but there was a Chinese restaurant at the end still open for business. No surprise as it was close to eight on a Sunday night. Since I expected Kayden to take me to the burned-out shell where my weekend needed in a black hole, an uneasy apprehension crept over me. I wanted to ignore it and trust the man next to me, but I had questions that needed answers. I waited until we were both standing on the cracked sidewalk before asking, "Why are we here?"

"Wolf found something he thinks we need to see."

Puzzled by his non-answer, I followed him as he strode through an archway and into a small inner courtyard. When he turned to take the stairs, I said, "Slow down, speedy."

He pulled up short, with one foot on the stairs, and turned to watch me limp toward him. "Sorry, forgot. Can you do this?"

I eyed the stairs and grimaced. "As long as I don't have to run them, yeah."

"You go first, I'll follow."

I grabbed the railing and began my trek up. By the time I hit the top, sweat that had nothing to do with the outside temperature, slid down my spine. I stopped and took a few seconds to level my breathing and rest my muscles.

Kayden watched patiently. "You good?"

I nodded. He moved past me and kept his pace slow as he led the way. He stopped in front of the door near the end and knocked. Not much light filtered back here, but we were standing close enough for me to make out the lettering on the dark window. "ALTERED STATES?"

Before Kayden could answer, the door swung open, and a body filled the space. "Shaw."

"Wolf."

The body shifted aside.

Heeding the little push against the base of my spine, I stepped inside with Kayden on my heels. Behind us, Wolf shut the door and a bittersweet smell surrounded us. Light from a back room spilled over the glass display counter stretched along the far side, illuminating the jars and trays lining the cases. I peered closer and realized the shelves held a varied selection of baked goods and candies. If not for the lingering smell, one could be forgiven for thinking it was a bakery. "A very special bakery," I muttered under my breath. I turned back to the two men and folded my arms over my chest. "Why are we at a marijuana dispensary?"

"What's more interesting, is what's in the back." Rough and raspy, Wolf's voice matched his tough exterior. He was tall and built like a linebacker. His height topped Kayden's by a couple of inches, and he was bald. Surprisingly, he did the look well, enough to catch quite a few feminine eyes.

"What's in the back?"

"Better if I show you." He turned and walked into the back room.

Kayden followed. I brought up the rear, my field of vision dominated by two very broad sets of shoulders. Kayden's abrupt stop caused me to backpedal so I wouldn't run into him. I caught myself against the doorjamb. "A little warning next time."

He didn't answer or turn around.

I tugged at his arm. "Hey, move so I can see." Sometimes it sucked to work with tall people. Kayden's body was stiff under my hand, and his reaction tripped my internal warning system. "Kayden, move." This time my command made it through.

He shifted to the side and gave me room to slip past him. I didn't get far. As soon as I stepped in front of him, his hands locked on my waist and held me still. It took a minute for the pieces to come together and make sense. A set of shelves rested haphazardly against the far wall, shattered glass blanketing the floor below, and dried herbs were mixed among the jagged pieces. An overturned chair sat among a Rorschach painting of rust. Those rusty marks splattered across the white walls and a set of framed Jimmy Hendrix posters in a very distinctive pattern.

And just beyond the upturned chair was a crumpled body. A very dead body. The room lurched and only Kayden's grip on my waist kept me upright. Ramirez stared unseeing from the floor where a crimson halo spilled around him, a neat hole marring his forehead. A familiar, black nine-millimeter lay like an inkblot near his feet.

I stared at the gun in disbelief and rising horror. *How had my Sig ended up here?* The last time... Pain seared behind my eyes and brought back the whispers with a vengeance. I grit my teeth, determined to get an answer, a memory, anything that could explain how my gun ended up next to the dead body of our best lead to Ellery. My denial was harsh and angry. "It wasn't me."

"It's your gun." Wolf's eerie sea glass-colored eyes were hard and it was clear he was asking a question, but making a statement.

I wasn't a fool. I snapped my mouth shut and glared.

His calm expression didn't waver. "What happened?"

"Wolf, back off." The growl came from behind me.

That got a reaction. Wolf frowned at Kayden. "You know how this goes, Shaw. Delacourt's going to want answers. Her gun, her phone." He held out my phone in one glove covered hand, the screen shattered. "It doesn't look good."

"The last time I saw Ramirez he was alive." And he was blocks away in a burned-out building. "I think he had a partner."

"Who?"

"I don't know." I bit out as my insides started to quake. I twisted in Kayden's arms, searching his face, needing someone to believe me, because with the gaping hole in my memory, even I wasn't sure of what had happened. "It wasn't me."

As close as I was, I couldn't miss the flash of doubt before he doused it. It hurt. Like being swiped with a sharp blade, the initial sting burned, but what would come later would be worse. The whispers in my head swarmed closer, bursts of taunting laughter driving ice picks into my brain. Flinching, I stepped back, putting distance between myself and the two men watching me.

Spurred by desperation, I reached into the past for answers, only to come up against the heavy emptiness in my head. Fear and frustration drove me on, and I pushed harder. Pain exploded, and blood dripped from my nose.

"Stop." Kayden reached out, but I stumbled back, not wanting him to touch me. Unfortunately, the room was too small to escape, and he grabbed me, dragging me close. His hand wound through my hair and tugged my head back. "I know what you're doing. Knock it the hell off, dammit." He lifted his gaze. "Get me some Kleenex."

It was sloppy on my part to forget his ability to read my energy, but it didn't matter. I continued to circle the abyss, searching for the slightest clue to what happened. I was distantly aware of Wolf rustling around somewhere behind us, then a wad of white tissues appeared over my shoulder.

Kayden grabbed them, shoving all but one into my hand. Holding one against my nose, he stared into my eyes. "Stop it right now, Cyn."

Unable to ignore his command, I backed away from the abyss. The taunting laughter and whispers faded as I backed off. Slowly, I uncurled my nails from his wrist as I held his glare. I wouldn't apologize and there was no way I was apologizing. Only one person was going to save my ass now, and it clearly wasn't him.

"What the hell?" Wolf's quiet question drew Kayden's attention.

"What?"

Wolf's answer was strangely reassuring. "Someone played around in her head."

Kayden frowned. "You're sure."

"Yeah," Wolf said, "but Ramirez wasn't psychic."

"There was someone else with him," I mumbled the reminder. Someone who could've been Ellery, but I didn't think so. To mess with someone's mind you had to be telepathic. *Ellery wasn't a telepath, was he?*

"No, he's not."

Terror spiked my pulse when Wolf answered my unspoken question. It was bad enough having Kayden read my emotions, but Wolf? Wolf was...he was just like...the yawning blankness rose, a mindless fear taking over in a vicious wave. I jerked out of Kayden's hold and bolted for the door, the drive to escape all-encompassing. *I couldn't do this again.*

Hands caught me, dragging me backward. Panicked and drowning in an unnamed terror, I kicked and clawed, desperate to escape. Voices swirled around me, harsh curses, mocking laughter, and evil whispers all rolled together into a mind-shredding howl. They seeped inside my skull, leaving me no place to hide. No way to keep them out.

My spine slammed against unforgiving warmth and steel bands caught my wrists, yanking my arms against my chest. Something trapped my legs, forcing me to bend forward. Left with no other option, I drove my head backward. Another muffled curse came, and then an unrelenting pressure to the back of my knees made me drop.

"Stop, baby, please stop. You're going to hurt yourself. You're safe. I promise, you're safe." The words penetrated my horrified haze.

Terror pulled back enough to realize I was bent double, unable to move or breathe. Gasping sobs filled the room. Me. They were coming from me. I choked them down. Behind me Kayden's voice continued to whisper reassurances, his presence a bulwark against the other noise in my head. As fast as it hit, the fear receded, leaving me too tired, too drained to take advantage when he shifted his weight and loosened his hold on my wrists. We were on the floor, me in his lap, cradled against his chest. I buried my face against him, listening to the harsh edge of my breath. He rubbed small circles along my spine, and his lips pressed against the top of my head.

"I need to take her to the safe house." Kayden's voice rumbled under my ear.

"We can't leave this for the cops to find. The minute they get in here and poke around they'll issue an APB on her. With the meet tomorrow, we're running against the clock."

Wolf was right. My gun, my phone, and chances were, my

prints were all over that chair and God knew what else. Some-how, I didn't think offering the cops a psychic bogey man would help my case, nor would a second claim of amnesia work, no matter how true it was this time around. Besides, if Ellery was meeting with Hobbes tomorrow, we needed to dig out what was in my head.

And if that didn't work?

I ignored that voice and gathered my shredded courage. "I need to remember what happened." Silence descended and under my hands, I felt Kayden's sudden stillness. I shoved against his chest until he dropped his arms, then I used his shoulder for balance and got to my feet. "If you take me back to the building, I can retrace my steps."

Kayden's face darkened. "No."

His instant refusal set my back up, but I struggled for calm because one of us had to be rational. "Without Ramirez we don't have a lot of options. Just because I can't remember it, doesn't mean I won't be able to pick up who was with Ramirez, and follow him."

Kayden rose. "No, you're not in any shape to handle this."

"I'm fine."

"You are so far from fine, you wouldn't recognize it if it came up and slapped you," Kayden snapped, as he ran a hand through his hair. "Christ, Cyn. Did you miss what just happened?"

"I'm fine," I repeated through gritted teeth. "Do you have a better option?"

"I'll figure one out."

"Really?" My hands went to my hips. "How?" I flung one hand toward Ramirez's body without looking at it. "We're kind of at a dead end."

"Children," Wolf chided. "Can we get back on track?" He waited for us to give him our attention. "What do you mean 'pick up who was with Ramirez'?"

I turned to Kayden. "You didn't tell him?"

He shook his head. "Need to know basis."

"I think this qualifies," Wolf grumbled.

Yeah, I had to agree. "I'm a retro-cog." *Wow look at that, the world didn't end.*

"It might work." Wolf folded his arms and leaned against the door jam. "But Shaw's right, it could do more damage, considering…" He pointedly looked at the bloodied tissues on the floor.

Feeling ganged-up on, I snapped, "Give me another option."

"You're going to the safe house," Kayden cut in. "Call in a cleanup crew, Wolf. Give Delacourt the basics but hold off on the gun and phone until we figure how what the hell is going on."

And if we couldn't?

"Then you're seriously screwed."

Instead of reigniting my earlier freak-out, this time Wolf's dry observation had me lifting my head to glare at him. "Get out of my head." Then I did what I should've done the first time, I put up as many mental barriers as I could to keep him out.

His lips curved, not a complete smile, but the bare beginnings of one. "Better, but you're going to need to be faster than that."

"Not if I can keep them up permanently."

"Good luck with that." His eerie eyes filled will cool calculation. "You know what, Shaw, I think I have an idea. I'll get this taken care of, then meet you at the safe house. Maybe we'll get lucky."

Why his comment raised every hair on my body, I didn't know, but there was one way to find out. "What are you thinking?"

"It might be better to uncover what they buried in your

head." He straightened and pulled out his phone, half turning away as he dialed.

"Hold up a damn minute." I caught Wolf's arm. "How exactly are you planning on doing that?" Uneasiness pricked at me, leaving a vile taste behind.

He looked down at me. "We go back in and find out who planted what."

Chapter Twenty

For a moment Wolf's words didn't register. Then comprehension hit. I let go of his arm as if burned and backed away from both men. "No, no way!"

Understanding gleamed in Wolf's eyes, but his expression was inscrutable. "You wanted another option."

"One that doesn't turn my head into an amusement ride would be nice." The insidious spread of Paranoia crushed everything logical in its path. Whether it was mine, or a by-product of whoever had dabbled in my gray matter, it didn't matter. The whirlwind of doubts and fears picked up speed, the random pieces gathering strength to cut across everything touching this case.

Wolf was a telepath. If he thought he could get in my mind and figure out what was done, it meant another telepath was behind my memory loss. That made giving Wolf unfettered access to my mind problematic. I might trust Kayden and Tag at my back, but even Delacourt admitted there was a possible leak in her team. *What if Wolf was that leak?*

Kayden trusted him.

Great, but it wasn't Kayden's head Wolf wanted to poke at, was it?

The persistent little voice just hummed.

Fine, maybe Wolf wasn't the leak, and that was still a big maybe. Yet the fear of what else he could to me while in my head was enough to fuel a truckload of suspicion. Besides, how much did I really know about this team and their abilities? "Besides reading minds, what else can you do?"

Despite my rising concerns, my question came out surprisingly calm, but whatever warmth lingered in Wolf's gaze disappeared, leaving the hard-ass soldier behind. "A strong telepath can plant subliminal orders, tie it to a trigger, and then turn that person loose, knowing they'll do exactly what they were told without ever knowing they were being used."

A sickening sense of violation filled me. *And he wanted me to let him in my head?* What if he left his own commands behind? Or worse, someone else's? My experience with Delacourt was a dual edge sword. Not only had she made it clear she had no qualm using whatever tools available to achieve her desired outcome, but our earlier conversation made it crystal clear she still held me responsible for Flash's death.

Fact: I was in Ellery's crosshairs.

Fact: Delacourt could use me to get rid of Ellery without damaging her precious team of psychics.

If I allowed Wolf in, it wouldn't take much to set me up.

Again.

My mind twisted to the side, and a sharp, stabbing pain seared across my consciousness. The chaos in my head grew louder, drowning out my ability to think. Suddenly Kayden's familiar psychic energy slipped between my mind and the sickening jumble, providing a solid barrier. With his help and some newly awoken instinct, I was able to use the strength he offered to work past the overwhelming trepidation. In that brief moment of clarity, realization hit, and a slowly growing horror replaced the disorienting chaos. "The whispers, that's the message, isn't it?"

Something flickered in Wolf's eyes, but he dipped his head in acknowledgement.

"Whispers?" Kayden's question was sharp but, his arm around my waist stayed firm and kept me grounded.

I ignored my brain's warning to not reveal weakness to these two men and forced the explanation out. "They're like a constant white noise in the background. It feels like I'm fragmenting into two different people." And that scared the holy hell out of me. "My brain tells me one thing, but…" I pressed my fist against my chest.

"Your instincts are telling you differently," Wolf's voice was soft, careful.

I gave a jerky nod. "If I can't trust myself, then I'm more than just a liability, I'm going to get someone killed while I'm trying to decide which truth to believe." Neither man answered, because it was hard to argue with the truth. Desperation and determination goaded me into a decision. I met Wolf's gaze and held it. "Find out what that bastard did to me."

Wolf's eyes searched mine. Whatever he was looking for he found because he looked to the man behind me. "Take her to the house. I'll meet up as soon as I'm finished here."

"We'll see you there." Kayden unwrapped his arm and took my hand. I curled my fingers with his as we headed out.

"Cyn?" Wolf called.

I stopped and turned back.

"Be very certain you want to do this."

I stalled at his ominous warning. "You'll answer my questions before you start?"

He gave me a solemn nod.

"Okay," I tightened my hold on Kayden's hand. "We'll be waiting."

The safe house turned out to be a 1970s ranch-style home that sat on a couple of acres of what was considered horse property in the east valley. As unimposing as the exterior appeared, the interior contained all the amenities of a business hotel—comfortable, but bland and uniform. Kayden came out of a back bedroom where he'd taken my duffle bag and gave me a critical once over. "Why don't you go lay down until Wolf gets here?"

Now that I had committed to hosting a psychic free-for-all inside my head, I was having second thoughts. And third. And fourth. Sleep was out of the question. I rubbed my arms, even though I wasn't cold. "I'd rather just wait until Wolf gets here."

"Fine." He walked into the kitchen, leaving me in the living room to pace the beige carpet. The sounds of cupboards opening and closing emerged from the kitchen. They were soon followed by the dull clunk of a pan hitting a stovetop.

Curious, I went to the kitchen's entryway. "What are you doing?"

He didn't turn from the stove. "What does it look like?"

"Cooking?"

This time, he did turn, just to give me a mock salute. "Give the woman a prize." He returned to his prep.

I leaned against the edge of the wall. "Why?"

His voice rose over the whir of the can opener. "When did you eat last?"

I opened my mouth, only to close it when I couldn't really remember.

He dumped the contents into the pan and glanced up from the stove. "Yeah, that's what I thought. We have thirty minutes to burn, might as well eat something. Hope you like chili."

"Chili works."

I watched him cook and realized this was the first patch of

peace we had since he barged into my cabin. There was no one shooting at us, no one chasing us, it was just me and him. The craziness would start all over once Wolf arrived. I wasn't sure I would get a better chance to actually talk to him, because Kelsey had been right. My ignoring him for months had been the coward's way of dealing with things.

Life, especially considering the last few days, was too damn short. Before Flash's death, Kayden and I had danced around the possibilities. Maybe it was time to find out if he would really be there before I hit the ground. Better yet, would he *want* to be there? Was I just reaching for something to fill the hole of Kelsey's death? Then there was the real question haunting me. If Ellery hadn't been hunting me, would he have ever come back for me?

"Out with it, Cyn."

Startled out of my thoughts, I looked up. "Out with what?"

"Whatever it is that has you looking for the nearest escape." He pulled out two bowls and started dishing up. "I like chasing as much as the next man, but really, I'm not in the mood right now." He handed me a bowl.

I took it and went to the table. "You don't chase."

"I chased you."

"That's not how I remember it." I pulled a chair out from the table, sat, and then waited for him to join me.

He didn't say anything until he was settled across from me. He opened his mouth to say something, but grimaced and shook his head. He picked up a spoon a stirred his chili.

When he stayed quiet, I prompted, "What?"

"I don't want to argue with you." He took a bite.

I recognized my urge to do just that as the self-defense mechanism it was and struggled past it. I took a breath, or two, while I stirred my chili. I didn't dare take a bite because my stomach was too tied in knots to choke anything down. During the last few days, he had been the one to re-open doors to our shared past that I considered sealed shut. This time he wasn't shutting me out, he was just refusing to be the one to hold it open. I couldn't blame him, not after all the times I refused to step up. Gathering my courage, I kept my head down, focusing on my food as if it, not his answer, was the most important thing in the world. "If Ellery hadn't come after me, would you have tried calling me again?"

"Once he was gone, yeah." He paused, but before I could react to the shimmer of joy his response brought, he asked an even tougher question of me. "If I had, would you have answered?"

Thanks to the conversation with Kelsey before I headed up north, my answer was all too obvious. "Yeah. I'd have answered, eventually." I took a deep breath and lifted my head, determined to go for broke. "Are we going somewhere, Kayden?"

His poker face was firmly in place, but the intensity of his gaze made me squirm in my seat. "That depends."

My fingers tightened on my spoon. "On what?" What would he ask of me? Would it be something I could give? Relationships and me, we didn't get along too well. As much as I wanted him, part of me worried I'd screw it all up before it even got off the ground, if I hadn't already.

"Are you going to run the first chance you get?"

I cringed inwardly at his valid question. "I'm still here, aren't I?"

His hand on the table curled into a fist. "For now."

Words weren't going to cut it this time. What was that old saying? *Actions speak louder than words?* I rose from chair, my heart racing, as a strange quivering weakness ran through my legs.

He watched me, tense and waiting.

If he was waiting for me to bolt, he was doomed to disappointment. Second chances rarely came along. I wasn't missing this one. Step by step, I closed the distance between us, refusing to look away. He pushed back his chair, angling it away from the table. I stopped only when I stood between his legs.

I reached out to run my fingers through the sunlit amber of his hair, my hand visibly shaking. That incredible heat, the one I would always associate with him, curled around me. I let my fingers drift down the side of his face, thrilling at the soft rasp against my touch. I cupped his chin, and he let me tilt his head up. I bent down, ignoring the protest from my bruised ribs. This moment was too important. I brushed my lips over his, offering him one of the few remaining unscarred pieces of my heart. Once. Twice. I pulled back, not far, just enough to whisper, "I'm done running."

Fierce satisfaction filled his steel blue eyes turning them navy. His undisguised desire stole my breath and arrowed deep into my heart, anchoring itself and changing me in some undefinable way. "About damn time."

Then there was nothing left to do but hold on, as he pulled me down into his lap. Cradled in his arms, I curled my hands around his jaw and deepened the kiss. Restless, yearning, I coaxed and teased, leading him where I wanted to go. I parted my lips, offering him access. My blood heated as he took full advantage of my invitation.

He was so gentle, so careful, one hand cupping the back of my head, holding me in place while he subtly took control. Our tongues dueled in a seductive combat of advance and retreat. His taste was addicting, leaving me yearning for more. I slid my palm against his chest, pressing it against his heart so I could feel the rapid pulse. Mine picked up the beat and followed suit.

I curled closer, threading my hand into his hair until my fingers could clenched the thick strands. I used my grip to keep him where I wanted him. Not that he tried to escape.

When the need to breathe became imperative, my head fell back, and I sucked in cool air with a fleeting thought it might combat the rising heat between us.

Kayden groaned. Then he took advantage of my exposed neck, and left a stinging trail of small, heated bites along my skin. My body trembled as desire roared through me, wiping out any remaining pieces of sanity. He took his time, tracing the lacework of scars that covered my neck and shoulder with his mouth. Small kisses, as if soothing any lingering ache.

Never comfortable with being touched there, tension began to override my desire. His name emerged on a breathless protest. "Kayden."

"Shhh…" he whispered, dropping another gentle kiss to my neck. "Just let me kiss it better."

Bit by bit, he continued his gentle ministrations. He followed the bruises ringing my neck, then switched to the delicate lacework of scars. Finally, he found that sweet spot between my neck and shoulder. A vicious shiver ratcheted my desire higher until my mind hazed and my body ached. "Kayden, please."

He raised his head and took my mouth with a fierceness that left me breathless. My breasts felt heavy, aching for his touch. I moved restlessly, unable to tear my mouth away from his. I squirmed in his lap, feeling the press of hard male flesh against my hip. The sensation of him triggered my own melting response. His hands began to roam, sliding under my T-shirt, drawing it higher. He skimmed the marks of violence and left melting warmth behind, even as his mouth continued to torment me.

I groaned as cool air hit my overheated skin, arching deeper into his destructive touch. Unwilling to be a passive participant, I twisted around until we were a tangle of limbs and frantic movements. When his T-shirt finally disappeared, we both paused for a breathless moment.

Somehow, in our maneuverings, I managed to straddle him, my legs lying on either side of his hips, and my aching center pressed against his hardness, our jeans the last remaining barrier. My breath came in pants. My hands were splayed across the mouth-watering expanse of exposed skin where various scars decorated his muscles creating a historic map of a warrior. Instead of derailing my desire, I had the strangest urge to kiss each mark. Mesmerized, I couldn't look away as my fingers moved restlessly, petting his chest.

"God, Cyn," he groaned, his hands tightening on my waist. "We have to stop."

I tore my gaze away from the temptation of his chest and met his gaze. It took two tries to get my question out. "Why?"

"You're hurt."

"I'm fine." To prove my point, my hips undulated, riding his erection, and causing us to groan in unison.

His hands trailed up my spine, setting off small explosions along over-stimulated nerve endings. Then he tangled one hand in my hair and dragged me closer for a fierce kiss. When he drew back, his voice was rough. "Be good. Wolf's going to be here soon. We'll pick this up later."

My body didn't really give a damn about Wolf, it wanted the man under me. I closed my eyes to eliminate the distraction he presented and clawed my way free of the drugging need burning through me. The sensation of his fingers gently massaging against the back of my neck helped. A little. "Promise?"

He pressed his forehead to mine and my eyes opened. He was so close I couldn't miss the banked fires and leashed want staring back at me. "Promise."

He sealed his vow with a gentle kiss.

Chapter Twenty-One

It turned out Kayden's decision to call a halt to our make-out session was spot on. Once we got untangled and presentable, we reheated our chili. Just as we finished our dinner, the crunch of gravel under rubber announced Wolf's arrival.

Not only did my earlier trepidation return, but it brought along the annoying whispers. As Kayden greeted Wolf, I gathered the dishes and took them to kitchen. I needed a moment to get a handle on my paranoia. I stretched out the dish washing as long as possible and managed to squander ten minutes. I was tucking the hand towel over the stove's handle, when Kayden said, "You ready?"

I gave a small jump, then turned to face him. My heart was in my throat and all I could manage was a shrug. Obviously noting my discomfort, he came over and pulled me into a hug. I huddled against him and curled my hands in his T-shirt. "The stupid whispers are back."

His arms tightened. "Wolf will help."

Maybe. Maybe not. My faith wasn't as strong as his. Yet, it wasn't like I had much of a choice here. I couldn't continue to go after Ellery when at any second, I could turn on those who were helping, especially Kayden. That fear, more than anything, drove me to straighten my spine and square my shoulders. "Let's get this over with."

We walked into the living room together. Wolf was sprawled in a chair that looked ridiculously overburdened with him in it. He watched us settle on the couch, me taking standard position in the corner. "If you have questions, ask them now, because once we start, I can't stop."

That didn't sound good. "Tell me what you're going to do."

"Let me ask you something first," he said. "When you go back to the past, how does it work?"

"It's like watching numerous film clips, all at the same time. Some are in sharp focus, some are faded, some flicker in and out, some skip through things or loop, repeating over and over. The ones with stronger emotions come in clearer than ordinary, everyday ones."

"Are you able to watch yourself in the past?"

My eyes narrowed because that sounded more like undisguised curiosity. "Never tried it." I thought over what happened earlier and corrected, "Until we were standing over Tito's body, but it didn't work. Don't know if that's because I can't remember anything or what."

If I was hoping to shock Wolf, I failed. His expression didn't change as he drummed his fingers on his knee. "Hopefully, we'll be able to figure out if your ability is damaged or your memories are just blocked. I'm betting on blocked so you can't identify who was with Tito." He cocked his head and asked another question. "How do you identify which past you want to see?"

I nibbled on my lower lip, completely forgetting the swollen edge. I winced and stopped. "I focus on a specific person or event."

"Are you living it with them, or just watching?"

I thought of Kelsey, and endured the resulting ached that was becoming all too familiar. "Until recently, just watching. The closer emotionally I am to someone, the more details I get."

Interest lit in Wolf's eerie eyes. "What changed?"

I couldn't stop my glance to Kayden. He covered my hand that rested on my thigh and wove out fingers together. "We figured out I help boost her reception and strengthen the emotional impact."

Wolf looked between us, whatever he was considering well hidden. "How did you know to combine abilities?" His attention was aimed at Kayden.

"I didn't." Kayden's fingers tightened on mine as the two men stared at each other for a long moment.

Then Wolf shook his head. "Son of bitch, Shaw, you took a hell of a risk."

Color rose under Kayden's skin. "It was mine to take."

"And hers," Wolf snapped.

"Time out!" I cut in before the two could really get going. "Focus, guys. Delacourt's already read us the riot act, so let's move on." Wolf turned to me, anger glittering in his eyes. Undaunted, I lifted my chin. "Look, Kayden told me straight out he wasn't sure it would work or what the consequences could be, but at the time, I didn't care."

Wolf held my gaze for another moment or so before coming to some internal conclusion he didn't bother to share. "How connected are you two now?"

Confused, I repeated, "Connected?"

He snorted and rose to pace in front of us. "Connected, as in how much of your psychic energy is tied to his?"

"I don't know," I offered hesitantly. "I can tell when he's there with me psychically. He comes across as a warm light." Saying it out loud made me squirm.

Wolf rubbed a hand over his bald head and turned to Kayden. "How deep did you two go?"

Next to me, Kayden stiffened. "She needed an anchor so she wouldn't get stuck in the past. I almost lost her twice."

"Once," I corrected, thinking of Ellery's presence in Kelsey's condo.

"Twice," he repeated, looking at me. "At the cabin in Sedona you stopped breathing."

I blinked. That was news to me.

He turned back to Wolf. "We can't connect telepathically, but reading her emotions is becoming easier. What more do you need to know?"

Wait, there was a chance we could talk telepathically? Wow, I wasn't sure how I felt about that.

Wolf stopped his pacing and turned to face us. "Here's the thing, Cyn, when I go in, I want Kayden in there as well."

"And we're all going to fit?" The inane question squeaked out before I could stop it. Waving away whatever he planned on saying, I hurried to say, "Forget I asked. Why?"

"Because I think his presence keeps the suggestions from sinking too deep. Plus, when I go in, you're going to have to use what you know, and the past is going to seem very real to you. If you've trusted him to be your anchor before, that relationship will help you to keep the past in the past."

A chill ran over me. There were some things in my head I didn't want to relive. "How real?"

Wolf's gaze softened. "Unfortunately, pretty damn real." He came over and crouched in front of me. "Honestly, I'll be as gentle as possible, but I don't think untangling whatever was left behind is going to be easy."

I stared into his face as Delacourt's words from days ago slipped into my mind. *"Every psychic pays a price for his ability."* I didn't really know Wolf, but the idea of putting him at risk didn't sit well with me. No matter that my brain kept chattering that to trust him was all wrong and too dangerous. Those instincts I trusted for years hummed this was our only chance at getting to Ellery before he got to us. Still, I had to ask. "What does it do to you?"

His lips turned up, not quite a smile, but not quite a grimace either. "Nothing I won't be able to handle."

Right, I forgot, you should never ask a male if he can handle it, he'll never say no. Pulling my hand free from Kayden, I wiped my palms along my thighs. "Okay, let's get this done. The quicker you get in, poke around, and find out what happened, the faster we can get back on track."

Wolf didn't stand up. Instead, he stayed in place, a very serious expression on his face. "No matter what happens, or what you think is happening, you have to trust Kayden. If you do nothing else, you need to do this one thing. Deal?"

The ominous warning behind his words reverberated through me. I looked over and met Kayden's gaze. What stared back made me realize it wasn't trusting him I had problems with. It was trusting me.

I'm done running.

Time to prove it. I turned back to Wolf, I said, "Deal."

"Good." He went back to his chair.

For the first time, I reached out deliberately and sought his unique energy. It didn't take long to find it and draw it close. I dropped behind layers of mental barriers, dragging him with me, and stopped just before one final wall. We didn't have the time needed to get him behind that particular wall, but once this whole situation was done, we could work on it. For now, we'd work around it. I held both of us in place and the whispering chaos pulled back as if uncertain of what was happening.

Tension I hadn't been aware of, lifted, and back at the safe house, I sat a little straighter. Something lightened in Kayden's face and that warmth wrapped closer, holding me close.

Kayden laid an arm over the back of the couch, and I settled against him.

Wolf retook his chair. "First thing first, we need to get into a meditative state."

I held his gaze and tried to mimic his breathing, but the whispers picked up, gaining strength as if sensing the rising threat. Dread and tension grew, along with the need to move, to check we were really alone. Involuntary twitches shook my body, the physical and mental interruptions not allowing me to find that meditative state Wolf required.

Every time I closed my eyes, they snapped back open. I blew out a hard breath and rubbed my forehead. I forced my eyes closed one more time, determined to succeed, but the choking fear and frantic whispers raced back, stronger than ever. Something or someone was here. Waiting. Watching. My lids flew up and I was huffing like I'd just run a marathon.

"What's wrong?" Kayden asked.

"I can't..." I trailed off, uncertain how to finish the sentence. We were the only three people in the room. I knew this, so what the hell was going on?

Kayden dropped his arm, shifted, then tugged on my shoulder, encouraging me to lay down with my head in his lap. "Lie down. Maybe that will help."

Gingerly, I stretched out, and rested my head on his thigh. He slowly stroked his fingers through my hair. For a few minutes, I laid there, concentrating on the sensation of his touch. Stroke by stroke, my weird tension dissipated, and my eyes finally closed. This time, the suffocating feelings and voices were nowhere to be found. Grateful for the silence, I was finally able to relax enough to slip into that hazy in-between state. I floated along, aware on some level that my breathing was now synced with Kayden's. Wherever I was it wasn't dark, but it wasn't full light, and I couldn't make out much beyond the warm, surrounding light. The strange peacefulness was broken by the sound of my name.

"Can you hear me, Cyn?" Deep, rough, it belonged to Wolf.

"Yeah."

"Shaw?"

"I'm here." Kayden's voice was so close it shook some of the hazy, floaty feeling away.

After a minute, Wolf said, "This isn't working. Cyn, I need you to picture some place for us to meet."

"Me? Isn't this your thing?"

His laugh sounded a little rusty as if it hadn't been used in a while. "Sweetie, we're in your head, and until you have a clearer idea of your surroundings, we're all going to be floating around in a fog. Picture your favorite spot."

Favorite spot?

The fog shifted and realigned itself. Wind-shaped trees twisted above a small creek that meandered through a narrow, red canyon. Large, flat rocks offered sitting spots that jutted out into the creek. As the details became clearer, I recognized it for a well-hidden spot I discovered a couple years back near my cabin in Sedona. The quiet gurgle of water over rocks and the slight song of wind winding through the leaves brought a wistful smile to my face. My last visit had been with Kelsey. We spent the day hiking and had rested here before heading home. The faint sounds of her familiar laughter drifted to me.

A low whistle of appreciation brought my attention back. In front of me, Wolf gazed around as he sat on one of the rocks that was a bit higher than mine. "Nice."

"This place is gorgeous." Kayden's voice vibrated along my spine, and I realized I was sitting in front of him, his legs on either side of me, my back to his chest. One of his arms was casually wrapped around my waist.

The intimacy of his hold brought heat to my face. I cleared my throat. "Thanks. What do I do next?"

Wolf turned away from the surroundings. "Now comes the fun part. We need to work our way backward through your memories. Chances are good we'll hit some blocks, but we'll poke around and see how far we can get."

He rose to his feet, only to hop down to the rock Kayden and I shared. He offered his hand. "Ready?"

I took it and scrambled up until I was standing between the two men. "We aren't staying here?"

Wolf shook his head. "Your mind is trying to make sense of what we're doing, so it's giving us a physical representation of our actions."

Physical representation? Puzzled, I studied our surroundings, thinking it through. To uncover the memories, we would have to travel backward. Where the trees backed up to the cliffs a hiking trail appeared. I pointed it out. "Guess we're hiking."

"Looks like it," Wolf said.

"Right, then." I took the lead, Kayden falling in behind me, and Wolf bringing up the rear. "What am I looking for?"

"You'll know it when you see it," Kayden answered.

I shot him a look over my shoulder. "That's helpful."

He just grinned.

The trail seemed fairly straight forward, as it took us farther from the gurgling sounds of the small creek and deeper into the canyon. An easy silence fell between the three of us, broken only by the sound of rocks shifting underfoot, wind teasing through the trees, and birds calling back and forth. I set a brisk pace and soon found myself falling into a familiar meditative state.

Hiking was one of life's simplest pleasures. Discovering new trails and hidden pockets where technology didn't touch brought me a sense of peace I couldn't find in my normal, everyday life. As much as I enjoyed being on my own, I had even more fun once I convinced Kelsey to tag along. It was always amusing to watch the city-girl Kelsey fade away, to be replaced by the younger, more carefree version I grew up with. We spent hours exploring the areas around our cabin.

Now her feminine laughter curled on the breeze, faint and hauntingly familiar, causing a wistful ache in my heart. I tucked away the treasured memories, only then realizing the light had faded and the shadows had deepened. Ahead, the trail began to cant upward, but I could see where it ended in front of a sprawling, heavy growth of trees. I stopped and considered what lay before us. Kayden and Wolf drew up on either side of me.

Kayden spoke first. "What's up?"

I waved a hand at the old-growth forest stretched in front of us. "That shouldn't be there, and our path is gone."

"It's your mind, Cyn," Wolf said. "If we need a path, make one."

"With what?" The woods left me uneasy, and short of grabbing an ax and making like a woodcutter, getting through that kind of growth would be difficult. A weight settled in my hands, and I looked down, stunned to find a hefty ax. "You have to be kidding me."

Wolf's cough sounded suspiciously close to a laugh. "Got anything a little less work intensive?"

Shooting him a dirty look, I went back to studying the woods. The ax disappeared. Something didn't feel right about this. The canyon oasis, that was all me. But these woods? They didn't look familiar. I was a desert rat. Give me rock canyons, stunning vistas, straight and skinny pines, bushy piñons, and thick junipers and I was happy. These trees were different. Way different. It looked like how I imagined Hansel and Gretel's woods would appear, old, creepy, and scary as hell.

"I don't think this is me, guys." It sounded stupid, but as Wolf pointed out, we were in my head.

Wolf's humor drained away. "Try changing it."

"And I would do that by, what? Snapping my fingers?"

Suiting words to actions, I did just that, only to stare in amazement as the creepy, fairy-tale woods fuzzed out, rippled, and began to re-form. My mouth fell open when the scene in front of us resettled into tall, red, rocky spires dotted with junipers and desert scrub bushes, their edges touched by a setting sun. Now the trail angled down into the valley that lay at the foot of Sedona's red rocks. "Hot damn," I whispered.

"Just like that." Wolf stepped past me on the trail.

"Come on." Kayden nudged me. "Pick up your jaw and let's go, Voodoo Queen."

I took one more sweeping look at what I had created, and then, grinning like a mad woman, I followed Wolf's broad back. We made quick work getting down, although the loose gravel played hell on our ankles. Halfway down, my desire for my walking stick that was stuck back at my cabin, bore fruit. One moment my hand was empty, and I was about to land on my ass, the next I was gripping warm oak. I managed to stay upright and noticed the guys ended up with their own versions as well.

The longer we went without any visible threats, the more my earlier unease faded. At some point, I traded places with Wolf, and once more took the lead. Caught in the normalcy of things, I was woefully unprepared when the trap was sprung.

Solid ground was underfoot one minute, the next I was tumbling through dust-choked darkness. I landed in a painful heap, the impact leaving me unable to focus on anything other than sucking in much needed air. Dust, dirt, and a cascade of rocks rained over me. I covered my face with my arms as I coughed and hacked. When the stinging bites of falling rocks and dirt stopped, a stifling silence snuck in.

I lowered my arms cautiously, and when nothing else fell, rolled over to push up to my hands and knees. With my head down, I spat out the dust coating my mouth until moisture replaced the gritty texture. I wiped my mouth and looked around. Dirt walls stared back.

I used the one in front of me for balance and got to my feet. In the dim light settling dust flickered. I tilted my head back and used a hand to protect my eyes as I looked up, way up. The light was coming from a circle that seemed impossibly high. No way could I have fallen from that height and survived.

"Kayden? Wolf?" Their names ended in a series of coughs.

Silence greeted me.

Where the hell were they? They had been right there. "Guys, where are you?"

Echoes of my question answered.

Looking around, I searched for something to help me get out of here. Nothing.

The narrow dirt walls stretched up out of reach. The space I was in was maybe five or six feet across and it disappeared into a maw of darkness. I shuffled forward and tripped over something hard. I crouched and used my hand to brush away the dirt until warm metal met my touch. A few more swipes revealed an M162A. See that weapon my earlier confidence seeped away. I took a careful look around. Crumbling mud walls stretched off in either direction, and as my personal hell reassembled around me, horrified realization set in. The light above dimmed, and I lifted my head. My heart sped up as something slid over the opening, cutting out the remaining light and my one visible escape route. I jumped to my feet and screamed, "Don't! What are you doing? Kayden! Wolf!"

With an ominous scrape, the opening disappeared, and so did my light. Frozen in the darkness, I tried not to hyperventilate. My body shook with the competing urges to bolt and stand still at the same time.

Okay, I needed to think. This wasn't real. It was in my head, literally. So there had to be a way out, it was just a matter of finding it.

As my mind came online, my breathing slowed, and my body settled. I reached out and my fingers brushed the wall. I flattened my palm against it, concentrating on the rough combination of rock and dirt against my skin. It gave my skittering mind an anchor.

Theoretically, if I could convert an entire forest into a desert panorama, then it shouldn't be that hard to get out of this godforsaken alley of my nightmares.

Silly though it was since it was already dark, I closed my eyes and rebuilt the red rock spires and rolling desert vistas in my mind. Confident in the image, I lifted my lids. Darkness stared back. My heart dropped. "Shit!"

What had Wolf said? If it belonged to me, I could change it. So, if it didn't change, it meant this wasn't my creation. Which meant… "Son of a bitch, you bastard," I muttered, wishing I knew who the hell had been with Tito in that building.

An unexpected chuckle bounced around me, and I spun in a tight circle. "Where are you?" My question hissed out as I tried to see through the murky darkness.

"What are you doing, Cyn?"

The whisper at my back rattled me so badly, I jerked forward in a frantic attempt to get away. Instead, I almost knocked myself silly against the mud wall. I turned, keeping the wall at my back, and tentatively reached out in the emptiness in front of me. My hand passed through air, hitting nothing.

Fear tripped over me, but I reminded myself the alley had been big enough for three, so the other wall was just out of reach. Keeping one hand on the wall, I stretched the other out as far as I could. Nothing. Okay, so whoever belonged to the voice wasn't really here.

Think. If I couldn't change my surroundings, maybe I could change my available tools?

First, light.

I pushed back my fear and the unsettling sensation of someone watching my every move and concentrated on a flashlight. A cool, metal cylinder dropped into my hand, and relief broke through. I flicked on the flashlight and quartered the area. No one was there.

I aimed the light above my head. Inky blackness swallowed the light, leaving no sign of the opening. Fine then, I'd pick a direction and hope for the best. I moved the light in front of me. The alley stretched out in both directions, no signs of an exit on either one. *Forward or back?*

Wolf and Kayden had to be looking for me. Did the connection I shared with Kayden still work? Or would there be a physical representation of it here somewhere since we were already inside my head to begin with? My brain cramped with the paradox, and I forced my mind to blank and not think for a moment. First rule, don't over think things. Too much thinking hurt, so I'd keep it simple.

Step one, check the telepathic line to Kayden.

I dropped into a crouch because my legs were shaking. The answering twinge in my thigh barely made a dent. I flicked off the flashlight so I wouldn't burn through the batteries. It took precious minutes to locate the link to Kayden through the static in my head. Those creepy whispers were still there, heavier, louder, more real. The little spark of gold that I associated with Kayden's presence flickered. I reached out and tugged at it.

No response.

The dull thud of my heart echoed in my stomach like a lead ball. Okay, Wolf said to trust Kayden to be there, that our connection should be able to keep us linked. Maybe instead of tugging, I should call out? I swallowed against my suddenly dry mouth, and sent a hesitant, *"Kayden?"*

A rush of emotions roiled back and found a spot to settle into before Kayden's voice came through, vivid in relief. *"Cyn? Where are you? You were here and then you just winked out."*

"A hole of some kind opened under my feet. I haven't moved, so I should be straight down in front of you."

There was a noticeable pause, then, *"There's nothing here. No hole, no opening, nothing."*

Okay that was not good. *"It's a trap."*

"How do you know?"

"Because I'm staring at mud walls that should only be in Pakistan." Fear bubbled up. *"I can't change my surroundings."*

As connected as we were, I couldn't miss his rising frustration and anger. *"Wolf says he can't sense you, so whatever it is, it's blocking your presence. We need you to find a way out."*

I tamped down my instinctive snap of sarcasm and tried to hold it together. *"It's an alley. Forward or backward. Any suggestions on how to choose the best one?"*

"Flip a coin?" he growled.

"Not helping."

"Sorry, babe." His endearment tugged at me, even as his apology came through loud and clear. *"Wolf suggests you trust your instincts. According to him, chances are good both are going to be a bitch to get through. Can you keep this open as you go?"*

Good question, because my head was already starting to pound under the strain of talking to him telepathically. *"Maybe? It's hard to hold on to you."*

Something switched in our connection, and a mental weight shifted, as if Kayden was now holding the link open between us. *"Better?"*

"Yeah, not sure what you did, but thanks."

Instead of explaining, he said, *"I'm going to just tag along. I'll try to keep quiet, because Wolf and I both think you're going to need everything you've got to get out of there. If you speak out loud, I should hear you. As soon as Wolf picks you up again, he'll be there to help, okay?"*

I nodded. Then realized he couldn't see me and said, *"Got it."*

Getting to my feet, I flicked the light back on and stood. "Okay," I kept my voice low. "Let's see if this works. You reading me?"

"Five by five."

My nerves settled at the military version of 'loud and clear' in Kayden's voice. I ran the beam of light both ways and tried to figure out which one didn't feel off. Since they were both gaping maws of darkness, I snorted.

I walked forward, counting my steps. At three hundred, I stopped. No change in temperature, no change in the clinging darkness. There were some rustling noises, but I couldn't make out what caused them. I retraced my steps back to my original starting point, and then repeated my actions in the opposite direction.

This time, the temperature dropped, the darkness surged, and the rustling noises and the static in my head increased with each step. At two hundred, I stopped and bent over, hands on my knees, sucking in air while sweat dotted my forehead. Okay, this way sucked. It also made my decision easier, even as it scared the crap out of me. "Let's take choice number two."

Kayden's energy spiked with reluctance, but before he could respond, I explained, "This route is scary as hell, but I think that's the point of this. If I take the easier one, I think it draws me deeper away. Remember, whoever's behind this gets off on scaring me. Great way to make sure I don't poke at what he's doing."

"And if you're wrong?"

"Then I come back and try again," I muttered.

"If you can make it back."

"Gee, thanks for the vote of confidence." Hurt and angry, I pulled back.

"Don't! Look, I'm sorry, okay? I just..." he trailed off, his emotions tangling.

It was hard to hold onto my anger when I could feel his emotions. It also showed me something I wasn't sure he wanted me to see. Woven in his frustration and worry were other feelings, ones that stretched deeper than I expected. Ones I wanted to explore with him. Later. If my courage didn't take a hike. Stunned by his unintentional reveal, my hands trembled, and the light shook.

I gave what I could and admitted, "Yeah, me too." I straightened my shoulders and sucked it up. "Let's do this."

Chapter Twenty-Two

As the alley stretched endlessly before me, I wondered at the wisdom of my choice. My teeth were tapping out their own version of Morse Code at the unnatural drop in temperature. Granted, desert temperatures could go from sweltering to freezing, but this was ridiculous. Faint noises echoed around me, not yet making sense but some sixth sense told me when they did, I was going to be in serious shit. Even as I tried to ignore them, they chased me down the narrow confines. Even worse, the undecipherable words circled my brain like hungry vultures just waiting for an opening.

You're not going to make it. You're not strong enough.

You've failed how many times already? What's once more? So stupid. You're doing exactly what he wants.

Keep running, Cyn, I'll be here waiting.

The last one really unnerved me. My connection to Kayden seemed to thin which made it difficult not to pay attention. I tried singing at the top of my lungs. Not an easy feat when you're stumbling through a midnight-drenched alley. It didn't help. The deeper I went, the louder the whispers grew, and the closer those intimidating noises became. Kayden tried to stay with me, but eventually even his voice was swallowed by the dry, rattling accusations. Some of those voices found their mark, drawing blood from past choices and current insecurities, until I was running blind, praying for an end.

I stumbled and fell to my knees, the flashlight flying out of my hand and winking off into darkness. I knelt on the ground, my breath nothing more than ragged sobs. I finally reached a breaking point. "Shut up!"

My strangled scream cut through the rising tide of whispers and haunting din, leaving behind a heavy silence. Then an explosion of light seared my retinas, leaving indelible afterimages. Gunshots, shouted questions, the thud of flesh on flesh, and grunts of pain filled the darkness. Then came the scream that chased the others back.

"Flash!" Blind, I reached out.

A mocking voice filled the tunnel. "Go ahead and fight, Captain, I don't mind."

Horror stripped everything away. *Ellery. That was Ellery's voice.*

No, it couldn't be, he wasn't telepathic. He couldn't be here.

Blue-white flames snapped to life, illuminating Flash's body suspended before me, writing in agony. Every cruel detail was crystal clear. The horror on his face. His eyes pleading for help I couldn't give. His mouth stretched wide in a soundless scream. The flames eating him, inch by inch.

Next to him, Ellery laughed as he brushed his flame-covered hands in a mockery of affection over Flash's head. His eyes were pitch black, his lips twisted into a sadistic grin.

Reality receded and was replaced by this all-too-real nightmare. Driven by a fury honed by time, I launched myself at him, determined this time to make it stop. To save my friend. Yet feet from my goal, my body jerked, and my knees slammed to the ground, held in place by something I couldn't see. No matter how hard I struggled, I couldn't escape. Tears pooled and my desperate, furious scream tore through the nightmare. "No!"

The puppet master laughed. "Poor Cyn, falling apart so soon?" His voice struck like fangs and sank their poison bone deep. "How disappointing. It didn't take as long as I thought it would. You're not a strong as people think, are you? Add a little pressure and you break."

Hatred boiled over. "Fuck you!"

Flash's screams peaked. The mocking laughter and taunts picked up volume as Ellery stalked forward. "Not interested." He covered the distance between us between one blink and the next. He was so close, the warmth of his breath brushed my skin. "However, there's something else I want."

Every instinct protested his nearness, and I scrambled back, barely realizing that the invisible force holding me in place was gone. Even as the fire and screams faded to phantom echoes, Ellery's laughter followed.

The only good thing my frantic movements produced was my flashlight. I grabbed it and swung out, my intention to embed it in Ellery's skull. Instead, there was nothing there. Off balance, I fell forward.

Kayden's voice broke through my panic. *"Take a breath, Cyn. Focus."* It faded in and out. *"He's just playing with you."*

Right, this was not real. It's in the past. Already done. Flash was beyond saving. I got to my feet, my body shuddering as I tried to piece things back together. The dark rippled around me, then disappeared, only to be replaced by a shockingly bright light. The change was too abrupt, and I threw up an arm to shield my eyes.

"Playing with you? Interesting choice of words." The words were casual.

I dropped my arm and blinked frantically, as the world resolved into focus. No more alley, no more darkness, no more dirt walls. Instead, Ellery sat across from me in a nondescript chair in an empty, blank room, watching me with a taunting half-smile.

The worry that he could hear Kayden pinged across my mind, but there was nothing I could do about it. Not yet. Right now, I didn't dare take my attention away from him.

He watched me like a coiled snake. "What do you think you're doing, Cyn?"

I pressed my lips tight, refusing to answer. My mind spun through various scenarios on how to get the hell out of here. This was my mind, right? So, whatever this was, it wasn't really him. It couldn't be him because something about him wasn't right. I just couldn't pinpoint it.

"Are you sure?" His eyes narrowed and he leaned forward, resting his arms on his knees. "How much do you really know about psychic abilities? You spent so much time running away from yours, you're nothing but a babe in the woods. I, on the other hand…" He leaned back with a smile. "I've got quite a few tricks up my sleeve."

Shaken by his apparent ability to read my mind, I tried slamming up my mental walls.

His corresponding laugh left me floundering. "You really think that will work? It was such an epic failure last time. Nothing's changed. I'm in your mind, bitch. Too late to lock the door now." He stood, and behind him, his shadow shuddered and stretched. "You'd be amazed at what the mind can accomplish."

The walls wavered, then steadied.

But he didn't appear to notice. "Every time I acquire a new ability, I play with it, stretch it, then merge it with the ones I already hold. I can break you into little pieces and reform you into exactly what I need." His smile widened and the evil lurking inside began to seep out. "And no one, not you, not that dick Shaw, or even the almighty Delacourt, can stop me."

Maybe he could break me, but there was no telepath in his

list of victims, so he had to be lying. It was a wafer-thin hope to hold on to, but I'd take it. His rising maliciousness sent a tremor through my shoulders, but I lifted my chin, refusing to submit. "You sure about that?"

Something sneaky and sly stared back. "You're going to do what I want you to do."

The insidious whispers returned in a pounding wave. I gritted my teeth and dug deep. "It wasn't you with Tito."

"Sure of that are you?" He stopped inches away, knocking his knuckles against my skull.

I reacted on instinct, my hand moving before my mind could fully comprehend my action. I caught his wrist and twisted it into a wristlock. Utilizing the painful hold, I forced him down and away from me. Just for a second, I thought I had him. Then his image shimmered, just long enough to be a distraction. He struck out, ruthlessly targeting my ribs that were still sore from my previous beating. I lost my grip and stumbled back.

"Who do you think left those bruises all over your pale skin?"

I cradled my damaged ribs and sucked in air. Somehow, I managed to gasp out, "Wasn't you, dickhead." And I believe that because that nagging thing that was bothering me about Ellery finally clicked. Someone else was hiding behind Ellery's face.

What had Wolf said? *My mind, my rules.*

I concentrated on shattering the hold he had on me. On the periphery of my vision the walls undulated, and dark lines, like cracks in a mirror, snaked across the whiteness.

Fake Ellery's head jerked up and his eyes narrowed on the phenomena. He turned back to me with a reptilian movement. "Nice try," he murmured as light flared and the walls re-formed.

Agony burst through my head and dropped me to my

knees. I thought I heard Kayden call out, but the cacophony of wanna-be Ellery's influence shut my awareness of everything else out. I clawed through the pain and found myself staring into his face as he crouched in front of me, watching me with amusement.

"You're not strong enough." The quiet confidence in his statement shook me. "You can't be because I already broke you and you know it.

"Don't touch me," I hissed.

The words echoed between us and resonated in my battered mind, searing through the blankness. The pain was sharp, and I doubled over as a face I didn't recognize replaced Ellery's smirk.

"Don't touch me!" My lips were cracked, hurting. Hands tied behind my back, wrists burning as the plastic cut through skin, I could no longer feel my fingers.

Sitting inches in front of me, the monster smiled. "Then give me what I want."

Dark blond hair, military short, muddy eyes filled with hungry avarice, such an incongruous fit in his All-American face. Who the hell was he?

I shook my head, and it screamed in protest. The movement fuzzed out the edges of my vision.

Water hit my face, and I reared back, gasping for air. Behind me, someone yanked my hair and snapped my head back.

Tito's leering face stared down. "You with us?"

"Let her go." The monster's cold demand got Tito's immediate obedience. He shoved my head forward.

Monster lifted my chin. "Don't pass out on me. We're just getting started, love." He leaned forward, an empty water bottle held between his knees. "Brace yourself, this is going to hurt."

Claws began ripping into my brain, tearing it apart a piece at a time. I locked my jaw, refusing to scream even as I tasted fresh blood that coated my lips.

Rejection of the memory roared through me. In front of me, Ellery's image wavered and reformed into the monster who caused such damage. I wanted to shred the smug smile from his face, but I couldn't.

Deep inside, hidden behind my mental blocks, not his, the truth rang with the crystal clarity of a bell. More memories poured over me. Hours spent tied to a chair, while he tore through every mental block I threw up with ruthless skill. In the end I was left raw and bleeding on so many levels, and open to his suggestions, his will, because mine was curled into a ball in a corner, battered and beaten.

The scream that tore from my throat was hoarse with rage and pain. A wail of denial.

The bastard laughed. "You're mine, Cyn. All mine."

"*You're mine,*" another voice whispered under the horror rolling through me. "*Not his, never his.*"

"*Kayden?*" I was so scared he wasn't real, even my mental whisper sounded weak.

"*You didn't break.*" Faint, but there, he offered me a way out.

Even as the telepath's influence pressed forward, I clutched at Kayden's surety. "*I did.*" At this level of communication, I couldn't hide my shame or the memories.

"*Look around, Cyn.*" Solid and sure, Kayden didn't give me much choice.

I knew on some level that my tormenter was still crouched in front of me, his mouth moving, his voice blending with the others, but I didn't dare listen. Instead, I fiercely concentrated on the fragile link to Kayden.

The walls behind the monster were jagged puzzle pieces.

A fragile hope burst to life. "*That's me?*"

"*That's you.*" Pride and respect colored Kayden's answer.

Did I dare believe him? Wolf's earlier demand echoed through me. '*No matter what, trust Kayden.*'

Behind the telepath, the cracks spread faster. Each gaping

piece reflected a different scene. It was like watching snapshots of my past, decisions I made, trials I endured, and people I loved.

Love, I thought as one particular piece twisted and fell carrying Kayden's image with it. A burst of warmth pushed back my despair and gave me a clear view of what I faced.

A sharp slap jerked my head to the side and the monster's voice burst back in, severing my tentative link to Kayden. "Are you listening to me?"

Looking into his twisted, snarling face, the truth of Kayden's statement settled and became fact. This was me, my world, my head, and no one else could come in unless I let them. My insecurities, my faults, were personified into the one person who scared the shit out of me. This man who tried to break me. Tried, being the operative word. With a confidence I thought forever lost, I said, "No."

The sound of the word acted like a bomb and everything around me silently exploded in a blinding burst. When I blinked my eyes clear, I was back on the couch, lying in Kayden's lap, his fingers tangled with mine, and his face inches away, smiling.

"Welcome back." There was a world of relief behind his simple greeting.

"What happened?"

"You broke the telepath's hold." Wolf sounded tired.

Unable to see him, I started to push up from Kayden's lap. He was there, helping me upright. The change in position caused a moment of light-headedness, but once sitting up, I let Kayden tuck me against his side, my head on his shoulder. Every stiff muscle protested. "So do we know what he was going to have me do?"

Wolf slumped in the chair. "Not yet, but you made it through the blocks."

I wasn't sure that was such a good thing considering those

memories that lurked on the edges of my consciousness. Sleep would be taking a vacation tonight. I sighed. "Well, at least we accomplished one thing."

Wolf pushed up and ran a hand over the back of his neck. His arms dropped to rest on his knees. "Now comes the fun part."

My short-term relief faded under rising nerves. "Fun part?" The last half of my question squeaked.

"We broke his block on your mind. Now we have to figure out how to piece your memory together, so we can see who he is and what he had planned for you to do."

Incredulous, I just stared at him. "I don't think I'm up for another round of psychic cage fighting." The pulsating ache in my head agreed.

Wolf shook his head, then stretched. The dull pops of his joints audible in the quiet room. "If a fight breaks out, you'll only have yourself to blame. With the memory blocks down, we're going to go back through what you remember from Friday through Sunday afternoon. Conversations, places, faces, all of it, until we have everything in your head."

Worry niggled at me. "Why not just have me go back to where it all started, or where they held me, and let me do my Peeping Tom act?"

"A couple of reasons," Kayden answered. "First, taking you back through your memories allows Wolf to see what you're seeing. Once we put a face to our mysterious telepath, we'll put Rabbit on confirming an ID. Linking him to Ellery or Hobbes helps us know who we're facing. Second, after all you've endured, there's no guarantee your ability will actually work right now, and we're running out of time."

Obviously, other things had been coming down the pike while Tito and his buddy were getting up close and way too damn personal with me.

"Whoa, back up," I broke in. "Why couldn't either of you

see him this last time? You were both there. How will this be any different? Who's Rabbit? What do you mean my ability won't work, and did we get confirmation on the exchange?"

Wolf gathered an empty cup and headed for the kitchen, his voice trailing behind him. "You were back behind the blocks; the only reason Kayden could reach you was because of whatever tie you two have going on. Neither of us could see what you were seeing."

"Just hear bits and pieces," Kayden added. "Rabbit is our team's geek. He's been running names from Tito's notebooks through various databases. If we can get him a description, he can add it to his task list."

Right, the other members of Kayden's crew were due in town on Sunday, which was…today. It sounded like they made it in already. "Is your whole team in town?"

"Except for Doc and Tag, yeah. Rabbit's working with Delacourt, Bishop's out with Ricochet tailing Hobbes, and Jinx is running interference with the locals at Tito's shop. You'll meet them tomorrow."

He hadn't meant the last to be a threat, but like the new kid in class, the impending introductions were another thing to add to my worry-later list. Right now, there were other things that took precedence. "And my ability?"

Wolf came back in. "Mental injuries tend to be more lasting than physical ones. Sometimes you don't realize just how bad it is, until you try to use it. It's better to avoid using it too soon. Give yourself time to heal. Psychic abilities are hit and miss."

"They're a damn pain in the ass." But for the first time, I didn't want my ability gone. Not when it finally seemed like it was good for something besides driving me nuts. I fussed with the edge of my T-shirt. The blocks were gone. The whispers, quiet for now. The fact they may come back scared me. "Will we be able to figure out what he triggered me to do?"

"Maybe, maybe not."

I winced at his assessment and blew out a breath. "Fine, what do you need me to do?"

Wolf came over and sat on the floor at my feet, which put his head and shoulders above lap level. He held out his hands, palm up.

I snuck a glance at Kayden, who gave me an encouraging nod. Tentatively, I placed my hands in Wolf's.

"Relax, this won't hurt. Close your eyes. Go back to The Dragon and walk me through what you remember."

"Why not start at the abandoned building?"

His eyebrow arched. "Easier to start at a known point. We were all in contact when you set off after Tito."

"Right," I huffed out. I closed my eyes and went back. "Okay, Friday night crowd, a group of skateboarders tearing down the sidewalk."

"How many?"

"Three, no wait, four."

I slipped into the memory where I captured the one in mid-trick with my camera. "The fourth came up from behind, I stepped out of the way, and something caught my attention a few doors down."

"What was it?" Wolf's question merged into the replay.

"A guy tucked inside the entrance of a store. The store's closed. He's smoking and acting twitchy. Like he's waiting for someone or something."

"What did you do?"

"Used my camera to get a shot of him. It's Tito. I tell Kayden we've got company, then cross the street for a better angle. Finding a good spot, I used my lens to get in close. I think he's watching Hobbes, but he got another text. We know he's working with Ellery, so maybe that's who's texting? Tito looks pissed. Must not like his orders. He types something back and drops his cancer stick. Crap, he's going to move. Have to get rid of my camera without losing sight of him."

"Okay, Cyn, you stash your camera and start to follow Tito." Wolf's soothing voice moves the memory fast-forward. "Where's he going?"

"North and east. Away from the crowds." I can feel my heart picking up speed. "He's taking me downtown. He's jumpy. Not that I blame him, this isn't my first choice for an evening stroll. If he goes too much farther, I could be in trouble. Kayden's still on Hobbes and too far out if things go from sugar to shit. Too many unknowns out here."

A muffled curse sounded from somewhere, but Wolf's voice kept me on track. "Okay, stay with him, Cyn. Where are you two going?"

"He's ducking into a half-burned building. Two stories. It's in bad shape. Only a couple of lights are working. It's dark. My spine's itching, but no one's out there. The weight of my gun in hand helps. Why here? The barbed wire is a bitch and tore my shirt, dammit. Kayden's pissed, but we can't afford to lose Tito. What if he's meeting Ellery? No way in hell I'm letting that monster get away."

"You're in the building." Wolf pulled me back from my anger, giving me space to focus on my surroundings. "What do you see?"

"Not much. Looks like it used to be a club or a restaurant at some point. We're in the back, the floor is a minefield of debris, the ceiling looks like a strong wind will bring it down, and there are so many places someone could hide." I wipe palms damp with nerves against my lap. "Too many shadows, too many hidey holes."

"You're okay, Cyn. What else?"

"Someone's upstairs."

"Tito?"

"Maybe, but it might be two people. I can't tell." Frustration pecks at me. "Need to get closer. Stairs, I need a way up.

Don't want to go up the ones Tito took." Images shimmered in my mind. "There, another set in the front."

"You're going up the stairs."

I nod. "Halfway up, a board creaks under my foot. The voices stop. Shit, I'm stuck. All I can do is crouch here and wait and pray. Stupid, so stupid. Someone opens a door above me, but no one comes down. They're just waiting there. What are they waiting for? I hate this, it's like a game of chicken. What if Tito's coming around to the bottom of the stairs?" Pressure squeezes my chest, making it hard to breathe.

"Is someone coming down?"

"No," a harsh, wheezing denial. "The door closes. I rush back down hoping to get in place before they leave. There's a spot under the back stairs. Not the best, but it'll work. Just in time. Someone's coming down."

"Who?"

The hint of smoke, hairy legs, and a bobbing light. "Tito. And he's using his phone as a flashlight. He's moving off the stairs into the main floor. I wait for anyone else to come down. No one appears. That doesn't make sense. Maybe Tito was talking to someone on the phone? Something falls to the floor above. I'm out of time. If I don't follow him, I'm going to lose him."

"Where is he going?"

"He's searching for me." Contempt rises. "Idiot doesn't even realize I'm behind him." A loud crash, Tito turned, and I wince.

"What?"

"I screwed up, my hip hit some propped-up drywall. He blinds me with the phone." My body tenses. "He's coming at me, and the crap all over the floor is making it a nightmare to get out of the way. Not that he's doing much better."

An echo of pain kissing my ribs is followed by the faint sound of my gun clattering into the dark. "Shit! My gun's gone, my leg just gave out, and Kayden's yelling at me. He needs to shut up. Up, get up, Cyn. No time, he's kicking the ever-lovin' crap out of me. Son of bitch. Need to take his legs out. Get some room to get up."

"You're okay, it's just a memory. Stay with me. You're on your feet now."

"Not for long," I grit out, but my adrenaline eases back, taking panic with it. Tito's enraged face takes on demonic proportions as he barrels toward me. "This is going hurt. Why won't Kayden shut up? Can't deal with him and this jackass at the same damn time. He doesn't recognize me. Wants to know what I want."

"What do you tell him?"

"Just looking for a mutual friend. He doesn't like that." I hiss as the echoes of his hits resonated through me. "Bastard hits mean. We're circling each other and..." my voice trails off as an ominous click sends ice through me.

Warmth enfolds my cold, cold fingers. "We're just watching, Cyn, remember?"

"Yeah. I've got a gun to my head. No chance to get it away yet. Just have to wait it out. They search me and find my knife, then the earpiece." I try to ignore the sickening feel of Tito copping a feel, then the terror of seeing my only link crushed underfoot. "Kayden's going to be so pissed. He needs to be careful. They know I have backup. How did they know?"

"Who's got the gun?"

"Iceman." My wrists tingle with phantom sensation of plastic tightening, cutting into skin.

"Tell me about him." Wolf's command pulls me back from the swirling chaos of panic and nerves.

"Don't know him. Graveyard eyes. They don't fit the rest of the picture."

"Why?"

Memories collide bringing a startling level of detail considering how dim it was in the building. "He's got this generic, American boy-next-door look going on. Military cut on the hair, close to the scalp, dark blond, leaning toward brown. Eyes are muddy brown. No scars, no identifying marks, just those eyes. There's nothing sane behind them." My stomach roils. *Just a memory, girl, it's just a memory.*

"I've got you, Cyn, he can't touch you. What does he want?"

"Ellery." The answer was automatic.

"Why?"

Images crash and tumble, but nothing really makes much sense. The dull thump of a car door. The disorienting sense of being carried. The bittersweet smell of marijuana, and a brief argument overhead.

Everything spins, then settles.

My head feels like an overripe melon, one touch and it'll burst. The evil animal crouched inside my skull is waiting with a cunning patience. Tied to a chair, unable to move, I can only sit there as Iceman stares at me with a cold, cold smile. Behind him, Tito smirks as he leans against a counter.

"Stay with me, Cyn."

I tried to hold onto Wolf's voice, but a deep-seated fear threatens my grip. The claws curled into my brain flex, and I moaned at the pain.

Now Iceman is crouched in front of me, his fingers brushing against the side of my face as he traces Ellery's marks. I flinch from his touch. His smile widens and Wolf slips further out of reach.

The monster in my head rips at me again, and a coppery taste fills my mouth. I spit out the blood and snarl in defiance, even as mocking laughter takes over. There was nowhere to hide. Nowhere the claws couldn't reach. No matter what I try to get him out, he bats me away like a cat with a mouse.

I was losing.

Iceman's hand rose again, and I flinched back. "Don't touch me!"

Desperate to get away, I yanked against the bonds shackling my hands. They won't budge and my fear rockets. Water drips from my face, and Tito's laughter mixes with Iceman's frigid voice. "You're going to do what I want, aren't you, Cyn?"

Pain surpasses levels I didn't know existed. Blackness curls around the edges of my consciousness, luring me with a false escape.

Too much, it was too much.

Something flows around me, dragging me out and away from the pressure and pain. "I've got you, baby. Shh…" It took a moment for Kayden's familiar voice to break through the overwhelming nightmare. "Hold on to me, I got you."

Little by little, the weight of arms holding me tight replace the horror lurking on the edges. As Kayden becomes more and more real, so does the feel of his solid chest under my cheek and his unique spice of sunshine and man. The sensations curl around me and add another anchor. I burrowed into the safety he's offering and mumble against him, "We've got to stop doing this."

Despite my voice being muffled, he heard me. "Can you finish this?"

I didn't want to. No one sane would, but we needed to know what the hell Iceman put in my head. I just didn't want to do it by myself. "You sticking around?"

"Not leaving until you're done."

I nodded. "Where's Wolf."

"Right here."

I lifted my head and found him standing next to us. Concern darkened his face. "You sure you're up for this?"

"Finish it."

The glow around us dimmed, and the nightmare reformed.

This time, with Kayden and Wolf beside me, it was easier to fight the pull. The two men would not let the emotional and physical sensations suck me under.

Iceman had my chin in his hand, and although is voice echoed around us, his mouth didn't move. "You're not going to let your team take Ellery alive. The minute an opportunity presents itself, you will kill him, and anyone who tries to stop you. Do you understand?"

"Why?" My voice was dull.

"He betrayed my employers. Betrayal is not tolerated."

"Your bosses sound like assholes." *Go me.* "I don't work for assholes."

The crack of Iceman's hand on my face registered before his movement did. "No, you work for incompetents. Too bad you chose the wrong team. Your future would be so much different."

The monster in my head tore deeper, but the sensation stayed out of reach, so I was able to ignore it this time. "You know if you had just asked me nicely to kill Ellery, I may have considered it. Now?" With my hands behind my back, my shrug was awkward. "I don't think so."

Even with the emotional distance still holding strong, Iceman's smile curdled my blood. "You'll change your mind."

Again, the monster flexed his talons in my head. The move had fresh blood dripping from my nose. "Nope, don't think so."

The pleasant laugh was disconcerting. It left me unprepared for Iceman's next move. "I'll prove it to you."

The monster tore a chunk from my brain and carved its mark. *Shoot him.*

My hands were free, the weight of my gun familiar. My arms rose, taking aim even as I screamed in furious denial.

Before Tito's grin could disappear, I pulled the trigger.

Chapter Twenty-Three

Wolf left an hour later, leaving my gun with Kayden. I refused to pick it up. Logically I knew it was stupid, but with the memories fresh and vivid, I couldn't touch it. Not yet. Maybe later.

"Wolf's going to work with Rabbit on identifying Iceman." Kayden flipped the locks on the front door. The growl of Wolf's engine rumbling to life filled the quiet. A few moments later, the headlights flashed across the blinds. Kayden settled next to where I was curled up in the corner of the couch, huddled under a blanket. "Talk to me."

I cleared the lump that took up permanent residence in my throat and croaked, "And say what?"

Instead of answering, he rubbed both hands over his face, once, hard, and then blew out a breath. He kept his focus on his hands as he curled and uncurled them on his lap. "This isn't the first time you've pulled the trigger."

My laugh hurt as it came out harsh and brittle. "Not in cold blood. Battle is different, you know that." The insulating numbness started to crack. "I killed an unarmed man."

Saying it out loud made it too real. I threw off my blanket, jumped to my feet, and dashed down the hall to the bathroom. I barely made it in time.

Kayden pulled my hair back and held it as sweat ran hot down my cold face. He didn't say a word. What was there to say?

Although I knew that Iceman's order ultimately controlled my actions, it couldn't erase the fact I wasn't able to stop it. Regret, anger, resentment, horror, all of it washed through me, until only exhaustion remained. The emotional overload had finally blown all my circuits, leaving me curiously grateful at the resulting numbness.

Once my stomach was empty, Kayden handed me a cold washcloth. My hands shook as I put it to good use. Finished, I set it carefully on the side of the nearby tub.

He tugged gently on my hair. "You need sleep."

"I don't think that'll help." If I closed my eyes, it wouldn't be sleep that would find me.

"Fine." He took my hand and pulled me to my feet. He waited as I brushed my teeth. Then he curled an arm around my waist and led me to a bedroom. "Then you're going to at least lay down for a bit. God knows when you slept last."

I rested my head against his shoulder. "There's no fixing this."

His arm tightened. "No, there isn't."

Breath shuddered through me. "What do I do?"

"Right now? Nothing." He flipped on the bedroom light, then led me to the bed. He didn't let go of my hand as he pulled back the covers. "Get in."

Staring at the sheets, I swayed on my feet.

"Cyn?"

I blinked and fought through the numbing haze. "Uh?"

"You need to get in bed."

Right. Bed. I untangled my hand from his and fumbled at my jeans. "Can't sleep in jeans."

Hands brushed mine away and took over. Soon my jeans were puddled at my feet. I crawled into bed and curled into a ball, staring unseeingly at the blinds on the window. My head was empty, but I didn't dare close my eyes. Sounds drifted from behind me, but I couldn't find the energy to investigate. Eventually, Kayden clicked off the light, leaving the hall light to beat back the room's darkness. Panic rose and I called out, "Don't close the door."

"You want me to leave the hall light on?"

"Please."

He didn't answer.

Quiet settled.

The first hot tear escaped, blazing a trail for the others to follow. With my back to the door, I faced the pressing darkness, knowing what waited for me. My eyes burned as I fought the lure of sleep. It was a battle I was destined to lose.

I was so intent on my fight, that when the sheets lifted and a weight settled behind me, it barely registered. It wasn't until strong arms curled around me, tucking me against a hard chest, and hair roughened legs tangled with mine, that I realized Kayden had no intention of letting me fight this one alone. His warm presence slipped into my hollow spaces, crowding out my waiting fears, and silently promised to hold the nightmares at bay. "Sleep, baby. I've got your six."

Taking him at his word, I closed my eyes and surrendered.

━━━━━•◦◉◦•━━━━━

The sun rose at an ungodly hour in summer. Even the blinds had a hard time holding it back. Warm tendrils teased my face, urging me to wake. Not ready to get up just yet, I tucked my face under the edge of the sheet. My movement caused the palm cradling my breast to tighten at the same time as a heavy thigh slid between my legs.

Recognition sparked in my body before my mind caught up. I remembered Kayden slipping into the bed last night, or was it this morning? The fact I managed at least a few hours of sleep was a minor miracle, but I was grateful for the reprieve and didn't want to give it up. Not yet. Too soon, we'd be back in it.

So, I decided to enjoy being wrapped up in Kayden. Considering this was the first time I'd woken up with some-one, it was…nice. Lame word, but it worked. My few prior relationships consisted of scratching an itch, so lingering until morning wasn't my norm. I found courage in the steady, deep rhythm of his breaths. Not wanting to wake him, I carefully feathered my hand over the arm at my waist, keeping my touch light.

His palm rested against my lower stomach, while his other hand continued to cradle my breast, his fingers occasionally flexing. My body found that interesting. I indulge my curiosity and took my time tracing the muscles in his arm, over and over. I enjoyed the freedom to do so. Enjoyed the feel of him.

A soft kiss pressed just below my ear, the silky brush of his goatee sending a parade of shivers over my skin. "Good morn-ing." Against my spine, his chest vibrated.

"Morning." My answer was soft, as I was unwilling to break the strange quiet between us.

He continued to nibble his way down my neck, setting off little fires along my nerve endings.

Wanting more, I arched my neck in silent entreaty, my hand tightening on his arm.

His answer was to nudge the loose neck of my T-shirt aside with his mouth and nip the skin along the top of my shoulder.

His caress caused an unmistakable reaction as my nipples peaked. His hand molded my breast through cotton and lace.

I turned halfway toward him, my spine curving and forcing the aching mound of my breast deeper into his palm. Despite the awkwardness of him being behind me, I sank my free hand into his sleep-tousled hair and tugged to gain his attention.

He lifted his head and his blue eyes, dark and heated, met mine.

"I want to cash in my rain check." My voice was husky, but strong.

"You sure?" He didn't give me a chance to respond, but dipped his head to take my mouth with a stunning intensity that brought every nerve ending to bright, sparkling life. His earlier gentleness disappeared to be replaced by a masculine demand I was all too ready to answer. Our tongues tangled and caressed, each stroke urging the sweet heat of desire higher and higher, until need and want became one.

Only when he drew back did I realize I was now on my back with Kayden rising above me, his chest bare. My T-shirt was twisted and bunched at my waist. Desire darkened his face, turning his gaze heavy-lidded and alluring, and changing the warrior into a dangerously wicked seducer. His deft hands left burning trails along my ribs as they glided over my bare skin. His touch was light, careful of my lingering aches. "You didn't answer my question."

"What do you think?" I undulated under him, my body restless with burgeoning desire.

"I think you're going to have to tell me what you want." He dropped another hot, open-mouth kiss against the base of my throat, using a gentle suction to leave his mark. "Just so we make sure you get your money's worth. I wouldn't want you to leave disappointed." He lifted his head, his smile pure male challenge.

That look brought a previously quiescent temptress to the fore, one who was more than willing to answer his dare. "I want to feel you against me." I let the silk of his hair slip through my fingers and raised my arms above my head, never looking away. "Take it off. Please."

He didn't make me ask twice. His hands drew my T-shirt up and over my head, then threw it off to the side, leaving me only in my green lace bra and panties. "That's much better." He licked his lips, his gaze taking in every exposed inch. He shifted until he was lying next to me, his head resting on his hand, as he used his other to explore. He traced the scalloped edged of lace, his finger dipping inside the silk cups to tease the already aching points.

My body trembled as he continued, going so far as to trace the scar patterns as they dripped over my neck and shoulder. Instinctively, I hunched.

He gave me a hard kiss. "Don't. It's part of you." He took his time kissing over every injury, including the necklace of bruises. By the time he was done, my arms were locked around his shoulders, trying to drag him closer. He pulled my hands away and caught them in one hand, being careful to avoid the lingering marks on my wrists. He pressed them gently against the pillow. "Keep them here."

Curious and aroused, I did, only moving when he made quick work of my bra and left me exposed. With skillful precision he brought my body to a boiling point of mindless need. Fighting through the rushing tide of desire, I raised heavy lids and caught the lust and need warring on his face.

Emboldened by his earlier action, I brought my hands up to cup my breasts, the way I wanted him to, presenting a provocative offering. When his gaze was focused exactly where I wanted it, I drew light, taunting circles around my nipples, sucking in a breath as they tightened to aching peaks.

His gaze sharpened, burned.

"What are you waiting for?" My husky question brought his gaze back to my face.

"I'm enjoying the show." Without taking his eyes from mine, he reached out and followed the path of my touch.

My hands faltered, unable to maintain my teasing as he took over. His hands shaped and caressed, but he continued to watch me, even as I gasped for breath and arched into his touch. He leaned forward until his lips brushed mine. "Tell me what you want." His command stoked the fire between us higher.

"Your mouth on me." It was a struggle to get the words out coherently, but I managed. Barely.

A very satisfied smile curved his lips before he bent his head to take my breast into the heat of his mouth.

I wrapped my hands in his hair and pulled him closer, arching into his touch. Desire roared through me like a wildfire, burning away reality until only Kayden was left. His touch, his taste, just him. The house could burn around us. All that mattered was the feel of his mouth on my breast, the heat of his hands on my skin and the rising, hollow ache between my legs.

I ran my nails down his back, eliciting a sibilant hiss as he raised his head and nipped at my lips. Then he turned his attention to my other breast. As he took over there, I stroked over his chest and down his stomach, my goal was the cotton band of his boxer briefs. I tunneled my hands underneath the material and nipped his shoulder. "Off."

A quick curl of his tongue over my nipple, then he was drawing back, dropping kisses in the valley between my breasts as he went. He raised his head and flashed me a grin as his hips surged into mine, making me lose focus on my current goal. "After you."

I gripped his hips, holding him tight as desperate need left me rubbing against him. His groan echoed mine. His weight settled over me and he cupped my face, taking another breath-stealing kiss. I covered his hands with mine and pulled back, pleased to see his dazed look. "I want to see."

His weight lifted, and then he was standing next to the bed, black boxer briefs barely containing him. I sat up slowly and reached out to touch, only to have him wrap his hand around mine, stopping me before I made contact. He pulled me to my knees. "You first."

Lace and satin sailed past his shoulder to hit the floor. I could feel him looking at me, the heat and weight of it like a caress. Color rushed over my chest and face. I cursed my pale complexion but held still. He crawled onto the bed, and I backed up, falling back as he came over me. He used those strong arms and slowly lowered until his chest brushed mine and he could take my mouth. The man could kiss like no one's business. It didn't take much before I was trying to climb him like ivy. When he let me up for air, I gasped, "Condom?"

He rolled to his back. "Wallet."

I followed, coming up and over, then I trailed kisses down his chest, and over his cloth-covered erection. I laughed as I dodged his grasp and dropped my feet to the floor. I stood and bent over, ignoring the protest of my ribs, to snag his jeans off the floor. A warm hand brushed over my ass, and I grinned. I rifled through his jean's pockets and found my prize. With the condom triumphantly in hand, I rejoined him on the bed. "Don't move. I like you like this."

He grinned and folded his hands behind his head, leaving his honed body open for my enjoyment. He watched through half-closed eyes as I slowly dragged the cotton down and off, unveiled him, unveiling the beauty that was all him. I sank to kneel between his legs as I took him in.

Fully aroused, he was breathtaking. I wrapped my hands around him, reveling in the feel of silk-covered steel. A small drop of precum trembled on his tip. I held his gaze and leaned forward to curl my tongue over him. His taste exploded over my tongue. He groaned, low and long, as his hips surged forward, driving him deeper into my mouth. He curled his hands in my hair, holding my head, and controlling how deep he went.

Wanting to drive him over the edge, I let him. I released him and drew my nails down his hips and around his thighs. He continued to move, in and out, his warm, silk-covered steel dragging over my tongue. My hands found the tight muscles of his hips and held him close. Using every skill I had, I licked and laved, until he was muttering dark promises. He tugged on my hair. "Enough."

His one-word growl left me wet and wanting as my thighs tightened against the swell of need. He changed his hold and brought me up to his chest, taking my mouth with a furious heat. Lost in his kiss, I missed whatever he did, but when I surfaced for air, I was on my back, and we had reversed positions.

There was no way to hide how much I wanted him. It was evident in the moisture coating me. He ran his fingers through it, setting my nerve endings alight. My hips jerked at his touch, wanting more.

He held me open, tracing along my opening and delving into secret creases, all the while driving my need higher and higher. He turned his head, his hair brushing over my over-sensitized skin. He kissed his way up my thigh, coming closer and closer to my heated center.

I watched, unable to move. Like I had done to him before, he held my gaze as his tongue flicked out. A whip of fire traced my folds until it found my most sensitive spot. I keened as my body clamored for more. He didn't make me wait, instead he used his clever mouth until I was a mindless writhing mess, then he brought me to the edge and held me there, dangling.

"Kayden!" His name came out a strangled scream.

He raised his head, his face stamped with dark, possessive pleasure. "Put the condom on me, Cyn."

My hands shook as I fumbled to sheath him. He helped and once it was in place, he rose above me. I widened my legs, giving him room. He took himself in hand and set his tip against my entrance. The ache inside me rose to a screaming pitch and I shifted my hips, trying to draw him in. With an explosive curse, he canted his hips and drove deep.

For an endless moment we lay there, intimately connected. I felt full, almost too full, but pleasantly so, but I couldn't stay still long. The feel of him pushed my desire to higher level. I began to move, the need for that delicious friction driving me. He groaned and set a steady rhythm, sliding in and out with maddening focus. He knelt between my legs, his hands gripping my hips as he guided our dance. He moved with deliberation while I went up in flames.

Unwilling to burn alone, I curled my legs around his hips, and drew him deeper. I grabbed his shoulders and used his body to pull myself into a half-sitting position. The change in position seated him deeper and ripped matching groans from both of us.

"Dammit, Cyn," he hissed.

I continued to wiggle until I was riding him, using his shoulders to maintain my balance. "Dammit, Kayden."

I ran my tongue along his lips as he panted for breath. I rose and fell, altering our pace so he couldn't prepare or counter. My body curling tighter and tighter, but I held back the looming explosion determined to break his control. I wanted him as wild as I felt. I needed it. Needed something to hold onto. I shimmied and arched back as I slammed down.

Finally, he broke. With a harsh curse, he gathered me close, took my mouth with bruising intensity, and then pinned me back down. He leaned over me with one hand gripping the headboard while the other curved over my hip, and then he began to ride me, fast and hard. He found my sweet spot, hitting it over and over, leaving my body helpless to do anything but climb to the inevitable peak.

The world detonated around me. I came, screaming his name, and felt him follow me over, as my name fell from his lips like a curse.

Chapter Twenty-Four

After a shower, where Kayden and I decided to practice our water-conservation skills, he proved he was the man of my dreams. The alluring aroma of freshly brewed coffee drew me down the hall to the kitchen as I finger-combed my wet hair back.

He met me with a kiss and a full cup.

Definitely a keeper.

"Today's breakfast special is yogurt or eggs."

My stomach rumbled as I took a sip of coffee.

He grinned. "Both it is."

He turned back to the kitchen, and I wandered over to the table. A laptop, the screen imitating an etch-a-sketch, sat next to my gun. "Have you heard anything from anyone yet?"

I set my cup down, unable to look away from the Sig. It was stupid to be scared. It was a tool. Like any tool, the handler's hand determined its actions. Tito's lifeless eyes under the neat little hole in his skull mocked me.

"Wolf and Rabbit were on their way about twenty minutes ago."

"Did they find something?" I turned away from the table

and headed to the kitchen where the smell of fried eggs painted the air.

"So they said." Kayden looked up from the stovetop as I stepped in and began opening drawers. "Need something?"

Too many things to mention, but I wasn't ready yet to pick up that conversational gambit. "Yeah, need to clean my gun. Is there a soft cloth around here?"

"Fourth drawer over. Cabinet in the corner has a cleaning rod, bore brush, cleaning solvent, and oil."

A fully stocked kitchen. Sweet. "Thanks."

I gathered what I needed and headed back to the dining room. After lining my supplies on the table, I sat down, ejected the magazine, cleared the chamber, and meticulously field stripped my gun. "They tell you what they found?"

"Nope, unsecured line."

I removed the Sig's slide, pulling it free of the frame before gently removing the recoil spring guide, and then the barrel. Step by step, I reclaimed my gun as I cleaned each part. By the time Kayden brought out a small plate of scrambled eggs and a yogurt, my coffee cup was almost empty. I pulled back the reattached slide until the final click sounded. Satisfied everything was as back to normal as possible, I reinserted the magazine, chambered a round, and de-cocked the gun before setting it aside.

"Happy now?" Kayden pushed the bottle of cleaning solution away to make room for his plate of eggs and took the seat next to me.

Mouth full, I nodded.

"Good."

Neither of us said anything more as we enjoyed our breakfast. Instead of the expected awkwardness of sharing this moment with a man who had seen me in all my naked glory, a comforting sort of peace settled inside me, blunting the ragged edges of yesterday. For a brief, shiny moment, I could almost see what life might be like when this whole nightmare was finished. *If* I wasn't doing twenty-five to life in a ten-by-two cell. "What happens after we stop Ellery?"

He finished his bite before looking at me. "What do you mean?"

"Once your team stops him and retrieves the information, what happens next?" I started in on my yogurt, thinking I might be able to work my way up to asking what I really wanted. "Do I need to get a lawyer, while you all blow out of town?"

He sighed. "Delacourt's not going to leave you hanging in the wind. Tito's death isn't on you, it's on Iceman."

"I know that, but getting the locals to see it that way..." I shrugged. "I think it's going to require some smoke and mirrors."

"This isn't the first magic show my team's handled, baby. Did you forget why we exist in the first place?"

*No, but...*I concentrated on scraping the last bit of yogurt from the cup.

Not fooled in the least, Kayden gave an exasperated huff and ran a hand through his hair. "I thought you were done with running."

Startled, I looked up. "I'm not running anywhere. I'm right here."

He studied me with an unsettling intensity. "Then ask me what you really want to ask, instead of pussyfooting around it."

"Your ability is a massive pain in my ass." My muttered comment got a slow grin, but it didn't soften the serious glint in his eyes. Realizing there was no way to avoid this without pissing him off, I got right to it. "Fine, I want to follow whatever this is between us, but if I join the team, is it going to cause problems?"

"Why would it?"

His nonchalant question raised my eyebrows. "Hmm, I don't know. Maybe because I can't see Delacourt all that keen on fraternization between team members?" The military certainly had some hard and fast rules for such situations, and Delacourt wasn't playing that far outside the Corps.

His grin turned positively wicked. "Are you saying a relationship with me will make you a less effective team member?"

I narrowed my eyes at his humor, and in an attempt to regain a bit of control with him, I licked my spoon clean with provocative intent. His gaze darkened. I smiled sweetly. "Nope, actually I think you having a relationship with me will make *you* a less effective team member." Maybe it wasn't nice to tease him, but he deserved it. "You tend to get a little over-protective, Shaw."

"I'll show you ineffective, Arden," he growled.

Before I could set my spoon down or escape from the table, I was in his lap and his mouth was on mine. Heat and need edged out all my pesky future worries. Here, with him, there was comfort and something I thought I lost a long time ago, a sense of home, of finally finding my place. Granted the last couple of days were far from normal, but if nothing else, they taught me to treasure opportunities like this. Time to grow a pair and grab on.

When he finally drew back, both of us were breathing heavily. Those steel blue eyes took their time inching over my face. His thumb gently brushed my lower lip. "So, you ready to follow this 'thing' between us?" Under his gentle, teasing words, lay a thread of seriousness.

"Yeah." I nipped his thumb. "You ready?"

"*Semper Fidelis*, baby."

Always Faithful. I lopped my arms around his neck and dropped my forehead to his. "*Semper Fidelis*."

When Wolf blew in, he brought not one, but two extra bodies with him. Introductions were quick and dirty. The deceptively slender male with dark hair still in military regulation cut carrying a laptop was Rabbit, the team's techie guru. With them was Jinx, the caramel-haired female with serious brown eyes. Within minutes of their arrival, Rabbit's laptop was up and ready.

"Bishop's on his way in." Wolf stood behind Rabbit's chair. "Ricochet has eyes on Hobbes."

"Do we have a confirmation on the meet, yet?" Kayden pulled up maps on his laptop.

"Hobbes's last meeting today is fifteen hundred at the NSpirit's east valley location," Rabbit answered, the South flowing through his words like thick honey. "According to the flight plan filed this morning, he's flyin' out of Scottsdale Air Park at eighteen hundred."

Kayden frowned. "That leaves us a three-hour window."

I leaned over his shoulder and considered the two pinpointed locations on his screen. The nice thing about Phoenix was most of the streets were laid out in a grid pattern. "A straight route with Monday rush hour would normally take forty to forty-five minutes tops."

"We're monitoring his phone and email," Rabbit drawled. "The most interestin' thing so far is a text from a jeweler that his mistress's necklace is ready for pick up, and his secretary's reminder to pick up the Jimmy Choos his wife ordered. Them women are gonna break that boy's wallet."

Jinx gave a delicate snort. "If his wife finds out about his sidepiece, he'll need more than a pair of Jimmy Choos."

"I don't know, sugar, those fancy la-la types, they play by a whole 'nother set of rules. Maybe the missus is just fine with his little amusements." Rabbit didn't look away from his screen. "'Sides, some men need a little variety, predictable gets boring."

"And God forbid, you get bored, huh, Rabbit?" Jinx's question held a dangerous sweetness.

Rabbit's flying fingers stilled, and his eyes narrowed. Yep, there was no way anyone could miss the dig in Jinx's voice. "Sugar, I'd never mistake you for borin'."

Okay, then. Trying to stay clear of the male-female tension singing between the two as they indulged in a stare down, I kept my head down but caught Kayden's wry gaze. He rolled his eyes and gave me a small grimace, cluing me in that whatever was going on between the two must be par for the course. I shook my head and studied the maps on the screen.

"Here." I pointed to Fashion Square, a large mall in Scottsdale. "Shoes, jewelry, and a camera-free underground parking lot. Perfect spot for an exchange."

Wolf came over. "Best of both worlds, public and private. No one would think twice about this stop. Any other spots?"

Our conversation broke through Jinx and Rabbit's little whatever-it-was, and the techie was back on his keyboard. "Restaurants, coffee shops, a couple of bars, but I'm tendin' to agree, he'll hit the mall. Arden's right, one-stop shopping."

Everyone's heads came up at the sound of a car pulling in. Guns appeared like magic. The blinds were still drawn and even though the only expected company was friendly, none of us were willing to chance it. Jinx moved up to the door, Wolf took the other side, both of them were armed. Rabbit sat like his namesake, his nose twitching, his hands below the table. I held my position behind Kayden, my Sig out but down. I caught the dull gleam of Kayden's piece in his lap.

Wolf peeked between the slats and his fine tension melted away. "It's Bishop."

As fast as they appeared, the guns went back to their hidey-holes. Jinx opened the door and let the larger man in.

"Someone better have some damn coffee somewhere," Bishop grumbled in lieu of a greeting.

The males all looked to Jinx and me. My hands went to my hips. "Really? They always like this?" My last question was aimed at Jinx.

She rolled her eyes.

"You're closer to the kitchen," Wolf said.

"Technically, Rabbit's closer," I pointed out.

"Hell's bells, just set it up in an IV drip," Bishop cut in.

I took in the lines of exhaustion and his nearly feral edge, then heaved an elaborate sigh and headed to the kitchen. "Don't get too used to it."

By the time I returned with a cup in hand, Bishop was sprawled in one of the chairs, his sunglasses on the table beside him. "We didn't get a hit in any of the databases stateside, so Delacourt pulled in a few favors and expanded the search." He plugged away on his tablet.

I came up behind him and held the cup over his shoulder. He took it, but the picture on his screen held me in place. *Hot damn, he found Iceman.* Without asking, I snatched his tablet out of his hands and read the profile. "Reiner Bosch?"

"German national and at one time one of MAD's top agents." Bishop sipped his coffee. "He was reported lost on a mission six years ago."

"What is one of Germany's Military Counterintelligence Service agents doing chasing Ellery?" As I read through the details on Bosch, it hit me I was lucky all he did was screw with my head because according to his stats, he could've done much, much worse. I handed the tablet back to Bishop and took the last chair between Jinx and Kayden. "No way is Germany involved with this."

"I don't think they are either," Bishop answered. "But that doesn't mean that the information on that drive won't create strange bedfellows."

I shifted in my seat and tried to find a comfortable position. The aspirin from this morning was wearing off. "Do we know who he's working for?"

A strange little eye-dance occurred between Kayden, Bishop, and Wolf. Rabbit kept his head down. Next to me, Jinx's fingers picked up a rhythm against the tabletop.

I chose my target and narrowed my gaze on Kayden. "Spill it."

"Shaw." Wolf's low warning didn't take my attention from Kayden.

Kayden held my gaze as a strange tension spun between us. "We're good, Wolf, because Arden's joining the team, aren't you?"

It wasn't hard to miss his underlying challenge, nor did I need our strange emotional connection to understand what was under it. After everything, a part of him was still waiting for me to bolt. For once I wasn't sorry to disappoint. "As long as Delacourt doesn't revoke her invite, yeah, I'm in."

His grin came quick and was filled with satisfaction. It softened the lines of tension on his face. But it didn't last. "Chances are high Bosch is working for Falcon Security."

I waited for more since the name didn't ring any bells.

"Falcon Security is a private firm of mercenaries," Wolf explained.

"Legit to the public eye," Rabbit chimed in. "The mercs are made up of ex-soldiers and ex-operatives from every flavor of the military. Their recruits aren't just homegrown, either. They'll provide top-level security for the right price. Underneath all the spit and polish, we think there's a core group used for shadier deals. One we can't prove exists. Think of them like PSY-IV's evil twin."

I recalled my initial conversation with Delacourt when she was explaining who PSY-IV was and what they did. "So,

Falcon has a group of psycho psychics? Do you think Ellery works for them?"

Bishop shook his head. "We have no hard proof linking Ellery and Falcon, or Falcon to the information, but it makes sense. Falcon tends to broker a lot of dirty deals, and they have people that can get into places others can't. From what I can tell, Falcon may have approached Ellery, but not to recruit. His ability would be considered a liability, no matter who's recruiting. Ellery was just another tool."

"And Bosch?"

"We know he's a telepath based on what he did to you," Wolf said. "If Bosch is one of theirs, it means they're using the same tactics as PSY-IV for recruitment, except they aren't limited to just the U.S. military."

And wasn't that a scary ass thought? Pieces of this mess started to tumble into place. "By taking Ellery into custody, we screwed Falcon's deal, and possibly opened them up to scrutiny. Especially if anyone could link Ellery to them. They won't like that. It could be why they sent that shooter after us. Who, may I point out, we still don't have an ID on."

"Delacourt's still working on that," Bishop said. "More than likely it's another Falcon operative. The sniper probably had two objectives, distract, or disable you and Kayden, and get Tito's journals. There are some pretty heavy names in there, along with contact information. If Falcon's people are in there, we'll be able to tie Tito and Ellery to them. Delacourt's got someone going over them, trying to figure out the links."

Kayden took over. "Ellery thinks the information will give him leverage with Falcon. So long as he has it, they won't touch him. Right now, he believes he's holding all the cards. He's the only one who knows where he stashed the information. He can undercut Falcon's price and sell it to whoever he wants. Which in this case, it appears to be Hobbes who picked the winning number. Making this deal allows Ellery to give

Falcon the finger for hanging him out to dry. Bonus for him, while he's out running free, he can hunt down the ones he blames for putting him in this position in the first place."

I had to agree with their assessment, but Ellery didn't strike me as stupid. "He has to realize both groups are going to be gunning for him. Selling the information to Hobbes won't get Falcon, or us, off his ass."

"No, but it will give him enough money to wipe Reeve Ellery out of existence and bring in someone new," Jinx spoke up. "He's killed, how many psychics that we know about so far? Five? Every time he takes on another ability, his mental stability breaks a little more. At this point, attributing rational decisions to him may not work."

"She's right." My voice sounded as grim as I felt. "Add in his psychopathic tendencies, and he may not be looking to get out of this alive."

That brought up Rabbit's head. "You think he wants to die."

"More like he won't mind dying, if he can take everyone else with him," I corrected. "Something we need to keep in mind as we're laying out this plan. We have to be ready for Ellery to try and take us all with him."

"Delacourt wants him alive," Kayden said.

"I want world peace and a shitload of chocolate," I snapped. "I'm not so sure he'll give us that option. And if that's how he wants to play it, I'm okay with that." Especially if it let me face down Kelsey's memories without choking on my guilt. "Besides, you can't tell me if the choice is him or the info, the order won't be to go for the info." Once the words were out, I tried not to grimace. It was never smart to question your CO in front of the other team members, but right now my emotions weren't the most stable where Ellery was concerned.

Before he could respond, Wolf stepped in. "Cyn." He waited until I looked at him, the eerie color of his eyes reflecting light as if lit from within. A gentle, but steady pressure built in my mind. "You still with us?"

Son of a bitch! "Get out of my head," I gritted out, trembling with the effort not to leap out of my chair and attack him. I threw every bit of strength behind my mental walls and slammed them tight. "What the hell are you doing?"

"Making sure Bosch's commands weren't still active."

His answer sucked the fight right out of me. "I thought we broke his hold."

"Until your latest little rant, so did I," he drawled.

Damn him for making me wonder. I poked and prodded, examining my response, looking for things that didn't fit.

Yes, the need to hurt Ellery for what he did to Kelsey throbbed under my anger and guilt, but it wasn't all-consuming. I ran scenarios in my head, checking my thinking. There were no more whispers, no black-edged thoughts of revenge, nor were there any strange doubts about Delacourt or the team.

"Ellery killed my sister," my voice was low, but level. I held Wolf's gaze with no problem. "I want him to pay for it, but not at the risk of the team or the mission. I know the score, Wolf, personal feelings have no place in the field. Doesn't mean I don't want to wipe him out."

For a moment he didn't say anything, just studied me. Finally, he must have spotted something that reassured him. "Just checking."

"You know," Bishop broke through the moment. "We could use Bosch's orders against him."

"How?" Kayden asked.

"He wants Ellery dead, and anyone else that's around. What if we set Cyn up to give him what he wants? If he thinks he has control of her, he's going to be watching us. Once Ellery is out of the picture, he'll expect her to take out the team."

I was shaking my head before he finished. "No way in hell could I take out an entire team on my own."

"Aww, sugar, don't worry," Rabbit said. "You can't hurt us."

I ignored him and pressed my point. "How could he expect me to survive? One person against five? Six? He's stupid to think it would work."

"He doesn't need to you to survive, just cause enough havoc so he can get the drive." Kayden crossed his arms over his chest. "It might work, Bishop."

"What will work?" The two men's behavior made me nervous. "Hello, care to clue me in?"

"Wolf," Bishop turned to the other man, excitement and caffeine visibly chasing away his earlier exhaustion. "Do you have enough time to work with her?"

Now all three were watching me. It wasn't cool, it was more like being a rabbit at a hawk convention. "What the hell are you guys up to?"

Kayden's grin was all teeth. "Hunting."

Chapter Twenty-Five

Hours later, I was traipsing through Fashion Square with Jinx, just another shopper trolling the racks. *Kill me now.*

Hordes of teenagers who couldn't be bothered to look up from their phones moved en masse like the old centipede arcade games. They clearly expected everyone else to move out of their way or be assimilated. Even in the stores, smaller groups made walking a maze of navigation. Like the two chirping chickees who just stopped without warning in front of us.

"Stop growling," Jinx muttered, as she continued to work her way through a sale's rack. "You'll scare the children."

"They don't even know anyone else exists." Sure enough, the chickees did it again. This time, they almost caused a pileup of strollers. The two young moms glared at them but didn't say anything. They simply readjusted their kid carriers and huffed their way past. "How much longer?"

"I thought women loved to shop." Rabbit, the sexist pig, chimed in.

"Then why aren't you in here?" I tucked my hands into the pockets of my cargos.

Next to me, Jinx smiled. It amazed me how deceptive looks could be. Dressed in jeans and a V-neck, fitted T-shirt in light lavender, Jinx was just another young, good-looking twenty-something, out doing a little shopping. There was nothing to hint at the lethal woman who lurked underneath. I wasn't fooled, she wasn't part of this team because of her sweetness and light.

"Target's en route, ETA fifteen minutes." The new voice held the tinge of an exotic accent, Spanish maybe? It belonged to Ricochet.

"Any shadows?" Kayden asked.

"Negative."

"Party crashers?" I asked Kayden.

Kayden's negative was followed by Wolf's.

I shared a look with Jinx. It worried me that we hadn't gotten eyes on Ellery or Bosch yet. With Hobbes on the way in, where were the other two?

Jinx and I kept our pace casual as we moved downstairs to the lower-level parking garage. I envied Jinx's ability to blend as she dragged me into another store as we stalled for time. Kelsey would've liked her. After spending the last hour and half with Jinx, I discovered a snarky mind lurked behind those big brown eyes. We stopped just before the doors leading to the parking garage and sat on the edge of a brick planter. Just a couple of women taking a break from their power shopping. Bags were clustered at our feet.

"Target's turning into the garage." At Ricochet's warning I tossed my half-finished coffee in a nearby trashcan. Then Jinx and I gathered up our bags and casually strolled out the doors.

The garage was two levels, the street level, and the basement. The basement level was tucked away from the afternoon sun which left it dim, but also trapped the heavy summer heat. Although out of sight, Kayden and Bishop were in position on our level, while Wolf and Rabbit remained on the street level.

"Basement level, east entrance," Ricochet confirmed.

Once Jinx and I cleared the range of the cameras at the door, we ditched the bags and split up, moving between the parked cars as we made our way toward the garage entrance. A subtle growl preceded the glow of lights that belonged to a black executive sedan. The heavily tinted windows kept us blind to the occupants. I dropped to a crouch behind a dusty SUV and watched it prowl through the garage.

Everyone held their position, waiting to see where it would stop.

Somewhere out there, Ellery and Bosch were also watching. Bosch didn't worry me. Not yet. He wanted me here. Whether he brought friends or not, did worry me, as well as what would happen if Ellery saw me before he could meet with Hobbes. Then there was the valid concern of what would happen if innocent bystanders got caught in the crossfire. Fighting threats on urban streets was a nightmare because there were too many variables. No matter how solid the plan, eventually you would be left using your skills and instincts.

The sedan pulled into a handful of empty slots situated near a metal door leading to the back stairs.

"Hold." Kayden's soft order came across the line.

Silence settled over the garage.

I pulled my gun out of my inner pants holster, flicked off the safety, and then settled the weight in my palms. A quick double click in my ear indicated Ricochet was now in position.

Nothing moved around the sedan.

I worked my way closer. The lot wasn't full, but there were enough cars in place to provide cover. It didn't take me long to get an angle with a view of the sedan's back door. Unfortunately, gaining a sight line to the other side that was close to the fire exit would mean risking exposure. I held my position and tapped three times on my earpiece, letting the team know I was in place.

One by one, the rest of the team checked in with soft, reassuring clicks. Rabbit remained above, monitoring the electronic signals, just in case any surprise packages popped up.

My mind was quiet and clear. My pulse remained as steady as did my grip on my gun. It was strange to realize I actually missed this, the action, the adrenaline rush, and even being part of a team.

Bishop's "Head's up" hit moments before the sound of metal scraping concrete echoed through the garage. The fire exit door opened and, backlit by the afternoon sun, there was no way to make out the approaching figure. I tried not to ruin my eyesight and focused on the sedan, tracking the new player from the corner of my eye.

The back door on the driver's side, closest to the exit, opened and Reeve Ellery moved out of the shadows, taking time to scan the garage.

I worked on my mental shielding with Wolf, when he finally announced me passable, I wanted to kill him. Right now, I was grateful for his drill-sergeant mentality. Still, I didn't risk looking directly at Ellery. Sometimes targets could tell when they were being watched. I huddled behind the SUV, watching the action at the sedan and praying my mental shields held. No way did I want to be the reason Ellery got spooked.

I could feel his gaze skate over my hiding spot, once, then twice. Finally, the dull thump of a car door closing came. The breath I didn't realize I was holding escaped. A quick check ensured Ellery was in the car with Hobbes. For the plan to work, we needed Ellery and Hobbes to do the trade before moving in. Long, tense minutes ticked by. It would've been nice if we could've wired the sedan.

The sound of a female voice yanked my attention around. A well-dressed woman stepped out into the garage, a phone plastered to her ear. Her voice was overly loud in the quiet and then came the beep of a car alarm on the other side of me. I moved further into the space between the cars and watched her walk by at a smart clip. She stopped at the Mercedes-whatever-class sitting across from the SUV. It took her three and half minutes to stow her crap and get her ass in gear. The entire time, curses strolled through my head. Each minute that passed gave Ellery a chance to leave. Finally, her taillights slipped out the entrance.

Another minute passed. Then another. Finally, the sedan's back door opened, and Ellery stepped out. He bent down, one arm resting on the edge of the open door to say something to the person inside.

"Go." Kayden's soft command came over the wire.

I rose to my feet, gun up, and closed in on the sedan. "Reeve Ellery," I called out, my voice cold and lethal, keeping his attention on me.

His body stiffened, then he carefully straightened. He faced me over the sedan's roof, his smile just as creepy in real life as it was walking through the memories in the condo. "Hello, Cyn. I've been expecting you."

"Hands where I can see them."

That creepy ass smile just widened. "Nope, don't think so." His gaze slid to my right and spotted Jinx. "Look, you brought friends." He dismissed her. "Where's the rest? Gunderson? Shaw? We have some unfinished business to address."

I ignored him and called out, "Step out of the car, Hobbes."

The back door on the passenger side opened, and an older man stepped out, then moved to the front of the sedan. "What is the meaning of this?"

Ellery took advantage of the momentary distraction and dropped behind the car door. Gunfire sounded, deafening in the garage's confines. My ears rang. Hobbes crumpled to the ground. The sedan's front windshield spider webbed.

"The door," I yelled, hoping someone would cover the fire exit as it was Ellery's only escape route.

I dashed to Hobbes, knelt, and rifled his pockets with one hand. Smooth, hard plastic met my touch. I snagged the flash drive, slipped it into my pocket, and then checked his pulse. "Hobbes' is down, no pulse."

"Got your six," Kayden's muffled voice came through the ringing of my ears.

I worked my way around the sedan, expecting Ellery to pop back up at any minute. Both back doors hung open. Something by the exit door caught my attention at the same time as Jinx's "Cyn!" sounded. Ellery stood next to the fire door, his face twisted into a vicious mask as he kicked against the unyielding metal.

I raised my gun, only to lower it. *Alive, we needed him alive. Dammit.* The earlier gunshots would bring the locals barreling in at any minute.

As I came around the sedan's hood, Ellery turned. Suddenly, the driver's front door swung open on its own, slamming toward me.

I dropped my gun and managed to get my hands up just in time to block it from plowing into my stomach and thighs. Another shot echoed and bits of concrete rained down on Ellery.

"Don't shoot!"

I couldn't tell who yelled that one, as I had my own problems to deal with. Like the stream of fire barreling toward me. I twisted aside and dropped, barely dodging the lethal flame. *Enough of this shit.* I rolled over the concrete and reached out for my gun. Only it skittered out of reach.

"You want it? Crawl for it, bitch," Ellery snarled.

I shoved into crouch and freed the blade tucked along my ankle. "Don't need it that bad, asshole."

This time when I threw, my aim hit true. Ellery toppled over with a howl, my knife sticking out of his thigh.

"You bitch!" He wrapped his hands around his leg as he lay on his side. Fury twisted his face, revealing the monster under his skin. Another lash of flame appeared, but his aim sucked.

"Temper, temper." Hidden behind the sedan, I bent over to pick up my gun. I clicked off the safety as I straightened. Then, as I walked toward him, I raised the barrel and sighted between Ellery's hate-filled eyes. Someone was yelling in my ear, but I there were more important things to worry about.

Ellery lifted a bloody hand, probably to reach for one of his stolen abilities. I kicked out, my boot connecting with his hand. Hard. Then I stomped on the knife still stuck in his thigh, sending the blade deeper. His hoarse scream drowned out the noise in my ear. I sank to a squat and pressed the Sig's barrel into the skin of his forehead. "You should've killed me the first damn time, Ellery."

"Why?" he spat out. "It was much more fun taking you apart piece by piece. You remember how prettily you begged in that alley? I do." He licked his lips. "Must be a family trait, your sister did it too."

Ice-fucking-cold-fury froze everything into crystalline clarity. I rose, gun steady in my hand, and looked down at the twisted piece of shit at my feet. I could feel my mouth stretching into an ugly smile.

I pulled the trigger.

Chapter Twenty-Six

"Cyn! What the hell are you doing?" Kayden ran toward me, his voice harsh and panicked.

Still caught in that horrific blizzard of fury, I turned, gun raised, and felt a one-two punch that knocked me on my ass back behind the sedan. For a moment, I lay there, trying to suck air in without success.

Kayden skidded to his knees next to me. "Ah, hell! Bishop, Wolf, get your asses over here." He tugged my T-shirt up. "Goddammit, I said not to shoot!"

I couldn't hear the reply because the lack of oxygen was starting to have some serious repercussions.

Kayden's gaze met mine and he gave a slight shake of his head. Then the tightness banding my ribs lessened. He put a hand over my mouth, muting my gasp.

Bishop and Wolf dropped down beside us. Bishop spared a glance at Ellery, then turned and gave both Kayden and Wolf a quick nod. Meanwhile, Wolf helped Kayden undo the straps holding my Kevlar vest in place.

"Jinx," Kayden barked. "Hold the perimeter. Rabbit, get me an ambulance, stat."

"Shaw, she's flat lining." Bishop's strained voice was at odds with the amused glint in his eye.

Kayden cursed a blue streak, but his hands were gentle as he massaged my diaphragm so it would stop seizing. I moved my head and got him to release my mouth. Careful to keep my breathing soft, I handed my gun to Bishop, who swapped it with an identical one, except these bullets weren't tranquilizers. With a little help, I tucked it in the small of my back. Wolf was smearing a russet red over my T-shirt that left a gory abstract behind. The three men hovered around me, keeping up the charade. Each one added a little realistic color to their clothes and hands.

Finally, Kayden's leaden voice said, "Call it."

"Sixteen twenty-five." Bishop's response was equally somber.

Kayden squeezed my hand, then rose to his feet, running what appeared to be a blood-stained hand through his hair as he stared around wildly. "Fuck it all. What the hell happened?"

Behind him, Bishop stood and placed a big hand on Kayden's shoulder. "You saw her, Shaw. She shot Ellery at point-blank range. She was going to shoot you."

He shook his head. "I don't believe that."

Wolf gave me a wink. He arranged his face in somber lines before joining the other two. "She broke, Shaw. Sorry, man."

Kayden shrugged off Bishop's hand and snarled at Wolf, then dropped back down beside me.

Above us, Bishop said, "Give him a minute, Wolf."

"We need to call in to Delacourt," Wolf's low tone carried.

"I'll do it," Bishop offered, moving to the front of the sedan.

As he reported my death, I closed my eyes and listened as he filled Delacourt in on the mission details. Finally, he said, "No sir, we haven't searched the car, Hobbes, or Ellery yet. I'm sure the drive's here somewhere." A pause. "Yes, sir." Another pause. "Yes, sir, we'll call for two more buses and have them taken to the hospital and held for transport."

The men on this team deserved Academy Awards.

The faint sound of sirens drifted to us. Within minutes an ambulance pulled up. Kayden stayed at my side. I kept my eyes closed as chaos ensued.

"Sir, you'll need to let us take care of her." Rabbit's voice sounded strange without his drawl.

Wolf dragged Kayden away as Rabbit made quick work of checking my vitals and confirming my TOD. His electronic instruments sang the same monotone theme. No pulse, no heart rate, not one damn beep. The electronics bowed to Rabbit's will, reading only what he wanted them too. Nifty talent.

Then came the hard part. Not freaking out when they zipped me into a body bag.

A metallic hiss sounded as the zip began to close. "Hold up." That was Jinx. "Maybe I should go with her."

Her hand slipped inside the bag and curled over my wrist, a burst of tingling warmth drifted over my chest, then settled like a heavy sweater. I sent a fervent plea that Jinx's illusional ability would hold, otherwise, this would all be for nothing when they unzipped the bag.

"I'm sorry, ma'am, but I can't allow that."

Jinx's hand disappeared and the bag was zipped closed. It was surreal being surrounded by the heavy black material. The hospital was a five-minute ride away, but it took everything I had not to hyperventilate.

As soon as the ambulance doors shut and the siren picked up its eerie wail, Rabbit unzipped the bag over my face. Blinking, I sucked in the cooler air. Above me, Rabbit held a latex covered finger to his lips. A warning to stay quiet. I let my eyes close and kept my breathing shallow, shocked the improbable plan might have actually worked. He tapped my shoulder, and I lifted my lids. He raised an eyebrow in question.

I carefully pulled out the flash drive tucked in my front pocket as he pulled the zipper farther down. We swapped the drives. Just because I was okay playing bait for Bosch didn't mean it was worth risking the actual information. Hopefully, Bosch would have no idea what the actual drive looked like. Once the exchange was complete, Rabbit mouthed, *"Sorry,"* and re-zipped the bag closed.

The ambulance made a sharp turn as it headed into the emergency bay at the hospital. Moments later the ambulance doors opened again. Then I was on a hard surface, wheels rattling across rough concrete, only smoothing out once it hit the interior. Around me, I could hear Rabbit explaining this was one of three incoming DB's. There was some wrangling about the immediate delivery to the morgue for holding, but eventually Rabbit got his way.

A few more rattling minutes passed before I was lifted and laid on a very hard surface. A chill crept over my back. Once more the zipper came down, stopping at the top of my shoulders. Then Rabbit left me alone in a cold, silent room.

Barely lifting my lids, I confirmed I was really alone before I pulled my gun from my back and held it under my hip. No way did I want to face Bosch without some sort of weapon. I checked my mental shields, the way Wolf had shown me, ensuring they were still holding strong. This time, when I found Kayden's subtle glow, it didn't freak me out. Instead, it steadied me. Contrary to appearances, I wasn't alone. Not really.

Then came the hardest part of being bait—waiting.

Five minutes ticked by.

Then ten.

Just as the fifteen-minute mark came around, a soft click in my still functioning communication unit ignited the soft hum of anticipation. I slowed my breathing just as I did when I sighted down a scope and sank into that lethal quiet. The soft swish of the door opening sent a curl of cold air drifting over me. My hand wrapped over the familiar contours of my gun. The nearby air displaced as someone came to stand at my side. I held my breath as the zipper inched downward. When it parted enough to reveal my chest, a soft, excited hiss sounded.

Yep, no way in hell that belonged to a morgue attendant.

The zipper continued its sibilant descent. The heavy material stayed over my arms but stopped just above my knees.

Good enough.

A hand slid over my waist, going for my left pocket. The same one I deliberately slipped the drive into when I was at the garage. I struck out, grabbing the thumb and bending it backward with a brutal jerk. At the same time, I yanked Bosch across my waist, pulling him off balance. His hoarse yell echoed weirdly.

No one expected a dead body to come to life.

I kept ahold of his thumb, and rolled off the far side of the table, dragging him, me, and the bag to the floor. It hurt like a bitch when I hit, but I landed so my shoulder and hip took the brunt of the impact. I let Bosch go as I continued my roll out of the bag and away from the metal table now leaning drunkenly on its side. I came up to my knees and brought the Sig up in a two-handed grip.

Bosch kicked free of the table, sending it screeching across the floor.

"Don't." My warning froze him in mid push-up position.

His body might have stopped, but he had other weapons at his disposal. I flinched as a searing pain smashed against my mind. The distraction gave him the time to push off the floor and slammed into me. We wrestled for control of the gun. He wrapped both hands around mine as he scrambled for control. The entire time, he never let up on the psychic attack.

I was unprepared for a dual level fight. I tried to maintain my mental blocks, but it was difficult when I couldn't evade Bosch's punches. *Where the hell was everyone?* If something didn't give soon, I wouldn't make it until backup arrived.

Cracks appeared in my mental walls, veined with dark intent and insidious persistence. I twisted my hips and rocked Bosch off balance enough for him to lose his grip on one of my hands. I didn't hesitate and sent a short, brutal punch into his kidney. The pressure on my mind stepped back, even as he switched to a two-handed grip to wrench my wrist. Under the brutal pressure, the fragile bones my wrist broke with an audible snap. A searing white swept over my vision, and I lost my gun. I forced the pain back and found Bosch leaning over me with a vicious grin.

I slammed my head into his face, nailing his nose with my forehead. It didn't help the pain in my head, but it sure as hell got him off of me.

He reared back, letting go of my wrist so he could cup the mashed, bloody pulp of his nose. Freed from his weight, I used my heels to get out from under him, then curled both legs and jammed them as hard as I could against his chest. The force of my kick sent him flying back into a tall, metal cabinet where his head left a satisfying dent in the surface.

The pressure in my head was still there, just not as debilitating as before. I sent a mental SOS to Kayden in the brief lull gained by knocking Bosch back. Then I scrambled for my gun in an awkward crawl. As my fingers closed over the matte grip, Bosch's enraged roar filled the room.

I swung around on my knees only to fall back on my ass as I brought my gun up with my left hand as my right was useless. I pulled the trigger, knowing my aim was off. Still, the bullet slammed into his stomach and stopped his forward momentum.

For a moment he stood above me, his hand going to his stomach, as red spilled around his fingers. "You bitch."

"You're the second man to call me a bitch today." My left hand shook, but I steadied it. "I didn't like it the first time, still not liking it now."

Bosch reached out to the nearby counter, using it to help him slide down until he was sitting with his back to the cabinets. He watched me, an unsettling smile curving over his lips. "You think this is finished?"

The pain in my head increased, bringing a tide of soft whispers that seeped through the cracks left vulnerable by the shattering pain of broken bones. I tried to rebuild the walls Wolf had shown me. "Get out of my head."

The whispers grew into a roar, then a mind-shredding shriek, tearing through every block I had. The gun in my hand began to waver. The pressure in my head ramped up, until the urge to claw my own skull open became a viable option. In front of me Bosch began to laugh. "Stupid, weak bitch. You can't win. I broke you."

And that was all it took. "I didn't break." The gun steadied, and I pulled the trigger.

His laughter fell abruptly silent, and the pressure in my head snapped out.

In the ringing silence, a door slammed open. "Cyn!"

"Here." I carefully set the gun down on the floor next to me.

Then Kayden was there, his hands cupping my face. "Are you okay?"

I batted his hands away as Bishop and Jinx came up behind him. "Where the hell were you guys?"

"Someone took out Ellery." Bishop crouched over Bosch and went through his pockets. "He wasn't working alone."

"Did you get him?

"No." Jinx knelt on my other side and lifted my arm.

"Rabbit and Wolf are trying to figure out how the assassin got past them."

I hissed as she gently prodded and poked.

"It's broken."

"Not much of a shocker." The adrenaline began to fade, leaving me shaky. I took advantage of Kayden's presence and dropped my head to his chest. As if that was the signal he had been waiting for, he got his other arm under my legs, and stood. I hooked my good arm around his neck and rested my head on his shoulder. "I'll let you take me to the hospital now."

Then I let go, knowing he had it covered.

Chapter Twenty-Seven

I wound my way closer to my hidden oasis in Sedona as the spice of piñon and juniper mixed with the calming whisper of water dancing through the creek bed. This time, it was all too real, not something I made up to plumb my sub-consciousness. Between the weight of the light backpack and the dark purple cast on my right wrist, I was very much anchored in reality.

I stepped into the clearing and awkwardly clambered to my favorite sitting spot; the large, flat-top rock overlooking the creek. Small pieces of stone shifted under my left palm, leaving me in danger of falling into the water below. A band of steel curled around my waist and kept me from face-planting in a very undignified manner.

"All right?" Kayden asked, holding me steady.

"Yeah, stupid cast," I grumbled.

He helped me over the last few feet until we were both settled cross-legged on the sun-warmed surface, our shoulders brushing. "You've got at least two more weeks with it, so make nice," he teased.

"Don't want to." The lightweight cast wasn't heavy, just

cumbersome. Plus, relearning how to do things with my left frustrated the hell out of me.

He helped me pull off the backpack, and then bumped my shoulder. "You are a sucky patient."

I leaned in and rested my chin against his bicep. When he looked down at me, I batted my eyelashes in an exaggerated show of sweetness. "You're just now figuring that out?"

He dropped a quick kiss on my nose and gave me a relaxed grin. The affectionate move lit off a happy little glow that I was still getting used to. I laid my head against his shoulder and gazed over the hidden canyon, letting Mother Nature soothe me.

The last week had been an emotional roller coaster ride. Between tying up what we could on PSY-IV's case and saying good-bye to Kelsey, I knew that if it hadn't been for Kayden being there every step of the way, I would not be half as steady as I was right now.

After I passed out at the hospital, Kayden had taken me straight to the ER doctor and had my wrist re-set. Then began the repetitious round of Q&As from the locals, who were rather pissed about shots being fired at a mall and hospital under their jurisdiction.

Loopy from the painkillers the doctor had pumped through my veins, I'd been happy to let the rest of the team do the talking. Not that they did much talking. Kayden had stood front and center, legs braced, arms crossed over his chest, and an intimidating scowl darkening his face, as he snapped out terse answers to the blustering police lieutenant. Then Delacourt and feds showed up.

"If I forgot to mention it, Shaw, you sure have some fancy moves on you."

His inquisitive rumble indicated he wasn't following my train of thought, so I clarified. "Your dance with the locals, pretty impressive."

His chest rose and fell with a sigh. "Sometimes it sucks not being able to lay it all out straight."

"True, but who's going to believe the truth?" I deepened my voice, "Look, Lieutenant, staging the gunfight in the garage was our only chance at luring out the sociopathic telepath so he couldn't get his hands on the top-secret flash drive." I let my voice go back to normal and continued in a more serious tone, "You told him what he needed to know without putting the team at risk. We protected the public from the imminent threat Ellery and Bosch presented. That's your job. Yours and the team's. Just because you didn't mention the psychic aspect, doesn't make what you told him any less true. To lure Bosch out, he had to believe I had the drive, killed Ellery, and presented a threat to the team. Otherwise, he would've disappeared back into whatever pit he crawled out of. We did what we had to. Count it as a win."

Kayden tucked me closer to him. "For now. We still don't have a solid tie between Bosch and Falcon Security."

"Chances are we won't, not unless we get someone on the inside, or we get our hands on one of their people."

"They're slippery bastards," he said.

I tilted my head back and studied his worried profile. "Hey." When he looked down at me, I reached out and cupped his jaw. "You and I both know how it works, babe. We take them out one at a time as they come at us. We can't save the world, just bits and pieces at a time. We're not superheroes."

His eyebrow arched. "I don't know, my red cape still fits."

Warmth blossomed in my chest and leaked out of my grin. "Yeah, it looks good on you."

He chuckled.

I resettled against him. "Thanks to Jinx, at least you don't have to visit me in jail." Whatever she did resulted in Tito's death being attributed to Bosch and left me completely uninvolved.

"Yeah, she's good at keeping things smooth."

That was one way to put it. The girl had some serious mojo going on. I'd never even heard of anyone being able to cast illusions so real as to fool most people. It opened a whole realm of possibilities and made her an invaluable asset for a covert team. "Speaking of which, is she still around? I owe her a big thank you."

"She and Rabbit were headed to Vegas this morning. Delacourt wants them to hook up with Tag and Risia before they head back."

After his call to me on Friday, Tag had gone dark and remained out of touch until a couple of days ago. I wasn't sure what happened, but whatever it was must have been huge, because Tag was bringing Risia back to the team's headquarters in California.

Kayden and I were heading out in a couple of days as well, per Delacourt's orders. I promised myself when Tag checked in, I was cornering his ass for worrying me, then I'd pry out every detail of what had gone down.

Kayden and I fell quiet, basking in the peace surrounding us.

It was strange to think that in a couple of days my life would once again change. This time, hopefully, for the better. The heavy chains of resentment and guilt had slowly unraveled as I picked up the pieces of my life without Kelsey. Her absence helped me put things in perspective.

Life was too short to waste worrying about what had been, or what could be.

Kayden helped me box up her personal things from her condo and break the news of her death to her friends and Terrance. Jinx and Rabbit stepped in to help me arrange her memorial.

It was difficult packing her things up at the condo. Memories snuck in without warning. Thankfully, Ellery's presence remained submerged under the happier, more vibrant ones peppered with Kelsey's laughter and joy. It gave me something to hold close when the fear-drenched moments in my cabin's kitchen haunted my dreams.

And that was another thing.

Ellery had left too many marks on my past, including my home. While it had been my family's center, the last horrible week had stained my cabin. Taking it back would take time, but I was determined to stick it out. Years of love and laughter, shared joys and tears, created a deeper impression than Ellery's depravity. So, although I might not be spending much time in Sedona, the cabin would stay mine.

The sun slowly slid behind the red rock walls. Next to me, Kayden shifted. "You ready?"

"Yeah," my answer came out soft, and a little melancholy.

He offered me a hand and helped me to the edge of the rock before returning for the backpack.

I stood there, gazing down at the bubbling creek, flowing fast and furious below me. Kelsey had always loved this spot. When the Ardens took us in, they gave us free rein to explore the area around the cabin. It didn't take us long to find it, considering we spent every free minute climbing up, down, and around every nook and cranny. The desert's wildness had been so different from the urban sprawl both she and I were used to.

Out here, under the wide-open sky, we could be free.

As we got older, this spot became our escape hatch from everyday crap. We took advantage of the summer sun. She'd tan, I'd burn, but we'd be together and that's what counted most, especially as our lives took different paths.

Kayden came up beside me, a silver urn in his big, capable hands. Reverently, he handed it to me. I clutched it to my chest, holding her close to my heart one last time. Tears pressed as echoes of her laughter and teasing mixed with the soft breeze and hushed babble of water. "I love you, Kelsey. Be happy."

I opened the urn and carefully tilted it over the creek at my feet, letting the tumbling breeze take my sister away. Her ashes danced along the water, and then disappeared.

After I replaced the urn's cap, Kayden's arm came around my waist and tucked me into his side. He held me, strong and steady, as quiet tears made their way down my face. It would be a while before her memories would no longer hurt, but there was more to my sister than her death, and that was what I held onto now.

Eventually, Kayden and I ended up on the edge of the rock, our legs dangling over the creek. We had to leave soon, to beat the encroaching night. Yet, I didn't want to be anywhere else, with anyone else.

"Hey, you doing okay?" He broke into my musings.

I cleared my throat. "Yeah, just thinking."

"You having second thoughts?"

"About?"

"Joining the team?"

Yesterday, after talking with Kayden, I had officially accepted Delacourt's offer to join PSY-IV. "Nope." I paused, threading my fingers through the hand on my waist. "How about you? Having second thoughts about having me on your team?"

He nuzzled my neck. "Nah, so long as you remember who's in charge, we'll be fine."

Laughing, I shot back, "That would be me, right, Lieutenant?"

"Think again, oh gunny mine." He wrapped his arms around me and with a mock growl drew me across his lap.

I laughed harder and curled my free hand around his neck to tangle my hand in his hair, while my cast rested across my stomach. "Someone has to keep you on your toes."

He dipped his head and brushed his mouth over mine. "You up for the challenge?"

"Oh, I think so," I whispered, recapturing that teasing mouth with mine.

There was a new depth to the desire that had become my constant companion. During the days and nights we spent together, I found something I thought forever out of reach, a friend, a partner, and a lover.

In between everything else, we made the time to explore each other, inside and out. Each new discovery deepening my initial fascination, and leading to even more profound discoveries, until the emotions I held for him spanned new, unexpected depths.

"Someday you're going to have to take a chance and just jump." The whisper held Kelsey's familiar lilt and brushed over me like a warm wind.

I pulled back slowly and studied Kayden's face, treasuring every line and crease, etching it deep into my heart. A nervous flutter set up shop in my stomach.

His beautiful eyes darkened, and his arms tightened. "What?"

"I love you, Kayden Shaw."

Navy blue flared to brilliant life. "I love you, too, my beautiful, mixed-up idiot."

Kelsey was right, sometimes you got lucky when you jumped.

———————•••••———————

Dive into Tag and Risia's story with TOUCHED BY FATE and find out what happens when a seer's secrets become her only bargaining chip in a high-stakes game of lies & loyalty. Now available at your favorite bookstore.

PSY - IV Teams Books

Welcome to a world where facing danger requires the unique skill set of the men and women of Jami Gray's PSY-IV Teams. As sparks, and bullets fly, love, action, and adventure will target these unique couples as they race through each breath-stealing operation.

Binge the series today at your favorite bookseller!

HUNTED BY THE PAST

Cyn & Kayden

To escape a killer from their past, can a reluctant psychic trust the man who walked away?

TOUCHED BY FATE

Risia & Tag

A seer's secrets become her only bargaining chip in a high-stakes game of lies and loyalty determining her fate.

MARKED BY OBSESSION

Meli & Wolf

A woman in hiding. A telepath who sees deeper than her scars. Can they forge a bond stronger than the obsession stalking them before time runs out?

FRACTURED BY DECEIT

Megan & Bishop

After a brutal attack by a telepath, Megan turns to Bishop for help, but how does he keep her safe when she's threat?

LINKED BY DECEPTION

Jinx & Rabbit

Forced to play intimate criminal partners, will Rabbit & Jinx risk turning illusion to truth as they race to untangle a web of conspiracies and lies?

About the Author

"This story is an emotional roller coaster, from betrayal, anger, fear, love…" —InD'tale Magazine

Jami Gray is the coffee addicted, music junkie, Queen Nerd of her personal Geek Squad, Alpha Mom of the Fur Minxes, who writes to soothe the voices crammed in her head. Her series combine high-stakes urban fantasy and edgy paranormal romantic suspense into books you don't want to put down. Buckle up and get ready for a wild ride through the fascinating worlds of the Arcane, the Kyn, the PSY-IV Teams, and the Collapse.

Come visit Jami's website at **https://www.jamigray.com** and stay up to date on what kind of trouble she's getting into and when you can expect to join in.

amazon.com/author/jamigray

instagram.com/jamigrayauthor

facebook.com/JamiGrayWriter

threads.com/@jamigrayauthor

goodreads.com/JamiGray

bookbub.com/authors/jami-gray

www.ingramcontent.com/pod-product-compliance
Lightning Source LLC
Chambersburg PA
CBHW051007180726
48291CB00006B/2006